DÌLEAS SECURITY AGENCY

MISSING
in action

C.S. Smith

Missing in Action By: C.S. Smith

Published by: Jug End Media, LLC

This book is an original publication of C.S. Smith.

Editor: Liana Brooks

Editor: April Bennett, The Editing Soprano

Cover Design: Deranged Doctor Design

Publisher's Cataloging-in-Publication Data

Names: Smith, C.S. (Cynthia S.), author.

Title: Missing in action / C. S. Smith.

Description: [Charlotte, North Carolina] : Jug End Media, LLC, [2023]. | Series: Dìleas Security Agency ; book 2.

Identifiers: ISBN: 979-8-9858549-2-3 (print) | 979-8-9858549-3-0 (eBook)

Subjects: LCSH: United States. Navy. SEALs--Fiction. | Paris (France)--Fiction. | Washington (D.C.)-- Fiction. | Human trafficking--France--Paris--Fiction. | Criminals--France--Paris--

Prologue

Nathan Long set down his mug and propped his boots on the corner of the desk in his Fairfax Station, Virginia, home office, which he'd affectionately nicknamed the "war room." Burnt-orange blackout drapes covered his polycarbonate bulletproof windows, shutting out any prying eyes and the afternoon sun that had just begun to peek through the clouds.

Leaning back in his chair, he banged away on the game controller in his lap, waiting for his buddy Lachlan to deal with the pretty little redhead who'd sequestered herself in Nathan's hall bathroom. The first time he'd headed to the kitchen for coffee, he got an eyeful of Lachlan and Sophia Russo getting up close and personal in his living room.

Hell, he would have stayed for the show, but he didn't think Sophia was the kind of woman to appreciate voyeurs.

Instead, he'd retreated back to the war room and waited until the sound of the bathroom door slamming served as his cue to grab a cup and beat feet during the temporary lull.

A well-timed virtual grenade toss lit up his monitor.

Damn, I'm good. Another bad guy down.

He'd hang out and kill time and video game enemies until Lachlan let him know it was safe to come out. He never thought he'd see the day Mackay would have his balls twisted in a knot over a woman.

Not after Nadia.

A loud buzz came through his computer speakers.

Visitor at the gate.

Which was a problem.

He dropped his feet to the floor with a thud and tossed the game controller aside. "Hey, Lach, heads up. We've got company."

A few keyboard clicks later, all three of his monitors displayed live camera feeds from around his property.

Lachlan Mackay appeared over his shoulder, green eyes narrowed on the screen.

The center monitor showed his front steel security gate, the cameras giving him a high-def image of the sporty red Lexus convertible parked at the entrance. The persistent buzz came courtesy of a blonde in a khaki trench coat stabbing the intercom button on his brick-clad gate pillar. She scowled at the camera above her head.

Nathan's curiosity spiked along with his libido.

Shoulder-length light blonde hair surrounded a heart-shaped face and pale blue eyes. The woman had a slight cleft in her chin beneath full lips glossed in a peach color. Her nose tilted upward just a touch at the end, giving her a perky quality that kept her overall appearance of sophistication from seeming too snobbish. She cocked a hip and gave the camera a look that told him she didn't plan to go anywhere.

He twisted his head around to look at Lachlan. "Any idea who our guest is? She looks vaguely familiar."

"Yes." Irritation thickened Lachlan's Scottish burr. "Sophia's friend. Get rid of her."

"Ah, the blonde who drove Sophia to work after her run-in with Roshan Haider." Nathan opened the connection on the intercom. "Yes?"

Not his friendliest tone, but he didn't take kindly to uninvited guests. Especially now, with the predicament his former British Special Air Service buddy was in.

"Nathan Long? I need to speak to you. It's urgent."

"Ma'am, do you see all those 'No Trespassing' signs? Whatever you're selling, I'm not buying."

Well, not entirely true. If she'd shown up any other time, he might have let her in. She looked like a classy, intelligent woman who'd turn her cute little nose up at his faded jeans and concert t-shirts.

But if there was one thing he liked, it was a challenge.

"I'm not selling anything, but let me tell you what I know." The woman's gaze somehow found him through the camera even though the video feed wasn't two-way. She inched closer to the intercom and lowered her voice. "I *know* you contacted Sophia Russo with information about Lachlan Mackay. I *know* she met you here this morning, and I *know* she hasn't been seen or heard from since."

He unmuted the intercom. "Sorry, but I *know* I can't help you." He had a sinking feeling it would take more than a verbal brush-off to send Blondie on her way.

"Oh, this is ridiculous," Blondie sputtered. She folded her arms across her chest and glared into the lens. "Sophia was supposed to contact me" —she made a show of raising her arm to check the elegant watch on her wrist— "an hour ago. Which she hasn't." Her baby blues swung back to the camera. "I swear to God, if you don't let me in, I will climb over this gate, march down your driveway, and pound on your door!"

"Her name is Emily. She's a college friend of Sophia's. See if you can find out anything more about her," Lachlan murmured in his ear.

"Easily done." Nathan's fingers flew across his keyboard as he opened up some of his favorite software toys on the left monitor.

"Let's backdoor our way into a few government databases and see what pops up. Running a facial recognition scan—what the fuck?" His gaze narrowed on his center monitor.

The woman was scaling his damn fence.

She dropped down on the other side and began to march up his driveway.

He frantically disabled laser tripwires between the gate and the house. Then he spun out of his chair and palmed his Sig Sauer P226 before waving Lachlan toward one of the monitors. "See if the computer spits out her details. I'll go welcome our guest." The oak floorboards creaked beneath his weight as he hoofed it out of his war room and down the hall to his front door.

Emily rounded the curve of his driveway right as he stepped out onto the porch. He watched her gracefully navigate puddle-filled potholes from the early morning rain shower. As she got closer, she raised her head and came to an abrupt halt at the sight of Sophia's car.

Nathan grimaced. He should have had Sophia park in the garage. *My bad.*

Too late now.

Her gaze traveled past the vehicle to land on his face before dropping to the pistol in his left hand. She stiffened, then squared her shoulders and kept advancing. He let nothing show on his face, even as his body flared to life. This woman had a set of brass ones, he'd give her that.

The security camera hadn't lied. She was a looker. Her eyes had appeared blue in the live feed. They looked greener in person, although it was hard to tell from where he stood.

She stopped at the base of the stairs and peered up at him with a wary expression. "Where is Sophia?"

Emily Dane sucked in a breath for courage and faced the giant with the short, spiky blond hair glaring down at her from a cute front porch with white posts and picket railing fronting a tan brick seventies-style ranch. The door behind him was painted a blue-gray to match the shutters framing the white paned windows.

Her father and brother were both a few inches over six feet. This guy was even taller.

And built.

A lefty. He made no move to conceal the handgun in his giant palm—as if everyone greeted people at their front door in such a manner. Her heart beat triple time. She was pretty sure it wasn't exertion or even fear. Which left...

Damn.

Icy blue eyes regarded her suspiciously over a straight-edged nose. She let her gaze drift over the muscles stretching the fabric of his black graphic t-shirt and noted the tattoos peeking out from under the short sleeves. Faded blue jeans rested low on his hips. His long, muscled legs ended at a pair of tan combat boots that looked almost twice as big as her size nines.

Her hormones shivered in delight. And didn't that just tick her off.

She'd done some digging on Nathan Long. He was a former Navy SEAL, which was both good and bad. Good, in that she knew SEALs, and most of them only killed when they had to, during an op. Bad, in that SEALs possessed deadly skills, and if she was wrong about this particular SEAL, she and her best friend Sophia were in a crapload of danger.

She would have pegged him as an operator even without her research. This guy had the warrior vibe she recognized, having grown up around Team Guys.

The paranoia, too, if his home security was any indication.

"You're big for a SEAL." She almost slapped a hand over her mouth after the words escaped. Where had *that* come from?

Apparently, her ability to intimidate men with her infamous 'take no prisoners' demeanor had taken a vacay and left her stranded on Ditzy Island.

A startled look crossed his face. Then his lips twisted as if he were trying not to laugh.

"It made BUD/S and SQT more challenging," he said in the distinctive Texas drawl she'd picked up through the intercom. "But I got by."

His voice was as deep and rumbly in person as it had been through the speaker at the front gate and reverberated through her body.

His amusement fled as quickly as it arrived. "You know who I am, but I know nothing about you." He didn't stir from his position at the top of the steps, nor did he put his gun away.

"My name is Emily Dane. I already told you. I'm here because my friend Sophia was supposed to meet with you this morning, and I haven't heard from her since."

Judging by how his eyes widened a fraction when she told him her name, he'd put two and two together and come up with Admiral's Daughter.

Her father was highly respected in the SEAL community. Maybe she could leverage that in her favor.

She gestured in the direction of Sophia's car. "Where is she?"

Nathan didn't answer, observing her in silence. Was he going to deny Sophia was in his home when they were both staring at her *freaking* car? And he really needed to come down to her level before she developed a crick in her neck.

She blew out a hard breath. As much as she was enjoying the staring contest—*not*—it was time for a new approach. "Look, I know Sophia came to you looking for answers about Lachlan Mackay. I'm afraid she's in danger."

There. *Danger*. A nice keyword a SEAL could focus on. If she couldn't rouse his sense of propriety, she would appeal to the part of him that had made him want to serve his country. If he was like the rest of his SEAL brethren, he had an alphahole protective streak a mile wide.

"We could use some help." She resisted the urge to do the whole "damsel in distress" thing and bat her eyes.

The blue-gray door behind Nathan flew open.

Sophia stood in the doorway. "Emily."

Nathan Long let out a defeated sigh that seemed to come from the tips of his massive boots.

Emily cocked her brow and gave the big SEAL a victorious smirk. Poor man, he'd actually thought he stood a chance of winning this standoff. He didn't know her.

She'd learned from the best.

CHAPTER ONE

FIFTEEN MONTHS LATER, PARIS, France

Emily steered her rental car, a silver Volkswagen Tiguan, right onto Boulevard de Clichy, and slowed her speed to a crawl, ignoring the impatient honk of the white delivery van behind her. To her left, the boulevard was divided by a pedestrian median filled with trees, walking paths, and park benches. On her right, an eclectic array of storefronts that sold everything from sex and porn to pizza and halal food operated on the ground floors of the nineteenth-century six-story Haussmann buildings that gave Paris its distinct architectural style.

She scanned over and around the parked cars lining the street in front of the storefronts, looking for the two Romanian teenage girls she'd promised to help escape their pimp.

In the meantime, she needed to get her friend and coworker, Bruce Fleming, off the phone.

"This is reckless and dangerous, and as your lawyer—"

"You're not my lawyer, Bruce." She would have never gotten Bruce involved if she hadn't needed his contacts in French law enforcement. As the Department of Justice Attaché at the US Embassy, Bruce worked closely with both senior US and French law enforcement officials to assist in international criminal investigations and prosecutions.

She worked better alone.

"No, but I am an expert on French criminal laws and procedures, and you're putting yourself into a dangerous situation. Let the police handle it. If the ambassador gets wind of this—"

"Jules Mirga doesn't even know who I am, and by the time he does, he'll have bigger things to worry about than me."

Between the information she'd gathered and Catalina and Maya's testimony, the police would have enough evidence to go after the largest sex trafficker in the Ilê de France region.

There.

Past the sex shop with red neon signage, two brunette girls in micro skirts and fishnet stockings darted between pedestrians and parked cars.

"The ambassador never needs to know. Meet me at the police station—gotta go." She hung up with Bruce's protests ringing in her ear.

Before she stopped, she scanned the street for any sign of Daniel Pescariu, the girls' pimp and one of Mirga's minions. Her gaze connected with Catalina, the older girl, who grabbed Maya's hand and jerked her toward Emily's car.

The white van behind her beeped angrily again and swerved into the bus lane on her left to roar past her. Emily lowered the passenger window. "*Allez monte.* Get in."

Catalina yanked open the rear passenger door, pushed Maya into the car, and followed her.

Slowly, don't draw attention. Emily pressed the gas pedal, trying to tamp down the impulse to peel out, tires squealing. She might have done it if she'd had room to maneuver but not on this crowded street.

Behind them, shouts rang out. In her rearview mirror she could see Daniel racing out of one of the storefronts, his curses polluting the air.

The cloying scent of Catalina's perfume—patchouli and roses—saturated Emily's nostrils and triggered an urge to sneeze as

Catalina leaned between the front seats. Her nails dug into Emily's shoulder like claws, her face leached of color. "*Allez vite*. Hurry."

So much for taking it slow.

"Get down." Emily hit the accelerator even as her fingers briefly rested on the lightweight carbonite baton nestled in the side pocket of her driver's door. She'd smeared mud over the Tiguan's license plates in case the pimp was smart enough to record the plate number.

The girls curled into each other on the black leather seat. Emily ran the light at Place Blanche into mid-morning traffic, narrowly missing an oncoming vehicle. The driver swerved to avoid her, honked, and mouthed profanity in her direction as she exited onto Rue Blanche.

The knot in her shoulders loosened. "You can sit up now. Everything will be okay." Hopefully, that was a promise she could keep.

A pair of heads appeared in her rearview mirror. Maya wiped her teary brown eyes with the back of one hand, smearing thick black mascara. Strands of long dark hair clung to cheeks that retained the roundness of youth. "I want to go home. I miss my mama and sisters."

Maya's uncle had sold her into the sex trade a year ago to earn money for the family. Emily's grip tightened on the steering wheel. Even if the young girl made it home, it was possible her family wouldn't take her back, or her uncle would sell her again to another trafficker.

"I'm sure the people at Fondation Espoir will do everything they can to help you."

Madame Légère, the social worker from the organization dedicated to helping victims of human trafficking, had promised Emily she'd meet her at the police station to take custody of the girls.

Her route took her past the upscale department store, Galeries Lafayette, with its iconic glass dome. The ornate window displays reminded her of Saks Fifth Avenue in New York.

Like most major cities in the world, depravity operated in the shadow of luxury.

"Don't be a baby, Maya. What is there for you in Romania?" Catalina's harsh tone drew Emily's gaze back to her rearview mirror. The older girl swept her dark waves up into a loose ponytail. "Daniel will be sorry he mistreated me."

No, he won't. Emily bit back the retort before she could argue and refocused on the Parisian traffic. No matter what Catalina believed, Daniel was *not* her boyfriend. He was her pimp, and belonged in jail, along with his boss. After all, he'd been the one to lure Catalina to Paris at sixteen with the promise of a modeling job.

It was only after she'd arrived with no money and dependent on Daniel for food and shelter that she'd discovered modeling was a cover for forced sex with Mirga's friends and business associates.

Catalina's brashness melted into apprehension like frost in the morning sun. Her voice grew quiet. "Will he go to jail? Jules is the one the police should arrest. He frightens me."

Maya whimpered. The younger girl's fear distracted Catalina and kept Emily from having to answer. Catalina draped her arms around Maya and whispered words Emily didn't understand, but they seemed to soothe the girl.

Patchouli and roses rolled in like a floral wave as Catalina leaned forward again, her hand pressed against Emily's headrest. "Maya may want to go back to Romania, but I don't. Do you think I can go to America? Maybe I could model there. I bet models in America are rich." Catalina was one of the few trafficked girls who had managed to avoid the scourge of drug addiction to cope with the misery of their lives. At eighteen, she still harbored hope that she could be a model and was adamant drugs would ruin her looks.

"I don't know where they'll place you. But you'll be safe." Emily cast another glance in the rearview mirror. "And free."

She'd decided to dig deeper into the sex trade in Paris as part of her work monitoring European human trafficking trends for the State Department. While most political officers were content gathering data and writing reports, she'd ventured to Le Quartier Pigalle, the Bois de Boulogne, and other places in Paris notorious for prostitution, trying to parse out the trafficked women from the independent sex workers.

Eventually, she'd gained Catalina's trust, and the more she learned about Catalina and then Maya, the more determined she became to help them escape Jules Mirga's sex trafficking ring. Which technically was not part of her job at the US Embassy.

But if she didn't help these girls, who would?

The sign for the public parking garage next to the police station was on her left. She pulled into the garage, parked, and grabbed the manila folder on the seat next to her. Taking Maya's hand, she and the two girls exited the garage to the street. Emily cast a worried glance over her shoulder at Catalina when she lagged behind. *Please don't back out now.*

Her friend and fellow State Department employee, Bruce Fleming, waited in front of the station entrance with Françoise Légère. His neatly trimmed brown hair ruffled in the slight breeze, showing off its natural wave. Standing on the Paris sidewalk in his dark gray suit and maroon striped tie, he looked every inch the attractive, urbane American lawyer. A refreshing change from the overprotective alpha male military guys she'd grown up around, thanks to her Navy SEAL father.

The caseworker from Fondation Espoir was a trim woman in her early sixties with a French chic-meets-earth mother vibe. Dressed in an ankle-length black skirt, gray blouse, and ivory and gray patterned silk scarf, she appeared unfazed by the burgeoning humidity of a midsummer day. A wide gray headband held back her shoulder-length white hair.

"Girls, this is Madame Légère, the woman I told you about. She's here to help you." Emily coaxed the teens forward. "You'll be fine. Tell the police everything you told me so they can help the other girls."

Françoise Légère ushered Catalina and Maya into the police station, speaking in the soft, measured tone Emily had found so reassuring when they first met.

"You're supposed to research sex trafficking, not break it up." Bruce's dark brown eyes squinted at her beneath furrowed brows. "This was a terrible idea."

"Yet you helped me anyway." Emily smiled at him as he held open the heavy wood and glass door to the station. "I needed your legal expertise and your connections."

His gaze warmed with something she didn't want to examine too closely. "I'll always help you, but I had to run interference for you at the embassy this time."

She winced. "You did? Sorry."

The small lobby inside the prefecture was quiet and dimly lit. A faint musty odor permeated the walls of the early nineteenth-century building. Emily approached the petite uniformed policewoman on the other side of the counter. The woman responded curtly to Emily's questions.

Oui, the girls and Madame Légère were speaking with an officer.

Non, she could not be present.

Oui, Inspector Pierron from the Judicial Police was on his way.

Emily thanked the woman and headed for one of the chairs in the waiting area and plopped down with a frustrated sigh. Her fingers tightened around the folder—months of research on sex trafficking in

Paris and multiple interviews with both trafficked women and voluntary sex workers who were the eyes and ears of what happened on the streets. They were willing to share what they knew as long as Emily didn't use their names.

Then there was the information Catalina possessed. While she performed various services for the Parisian crime lord and his clients, they talked, content to speak freely in front of someone who, as far as they were concerned, didn't exist but for their pleasure. But Catalina was an astute listener and had an impressive recall of specifics. She'd passed information along to Emily after Emily promised to help her and Maya escape.

Bruce eased onto the seat next to her. "Minister Woodward got wind that you've been harassing a police inspector and is concerned you've overstepped in a French legal matter." His mouth turned down. "She'd have a cow if she knew the extent of it."

"Harassment is a bit strong." Emily's nose wrinkled. "I simply advocated to Inspector Pierron that the police devote more energy to stopping sexual slavery in Paris. And the way to do that is to go after the source."

"You're a political officer—you monitor and report on sex trafficking in France, not go out and try to bust the bad guys."

Her hackles rose at Bruce's chiding expression. "What was I supposed to do? Maya is only thirteen."

The policewoman glared in their direction.

Emily leaned toward Bruce and lowered her voice. "It's taken me a month to gain their confidence and get them to leave Daniel. With what Catalina told me and the information I've gathered, the police should have enough evidence to arrest Mirga."

Jules Mirga was thirty, not much older than her, but the short, black-haired son of Roma immigrants from Poland had managed to claw his way up from the ghettos of Seine-Saint-Denis to become the largest drug and sex trafficker in the Île-de-France region.

"Mirga is a dangerous guy, Emily. You don't want to come to his attention. Let the police handle it. Please." Bruce's cell rang. He looked at the caller ID. "Excuse me. I have to take this." He stood and moved to a secluded corner of the lobby.

Emily studied him through her lashes. Bruce had a bump on the bridge of his nose he'd said resulted from a particularly aggressive, possibly not sober, game of pickup basketball during law school. He still liked a pickup game here and there, as well as tennis and running, and it showed in his lean, athletic build. He'd made it clear his interest in her went beyond friendship. On paper, he was a great catch—stable, on a steady career track as a lawyer with the DOJ. Maybe he was too much of a rule follower at times, but they had similar goals in life and were compatible.

So what was holding her back?

The image of a tall, buff former Navy SEAL with ice-blue eyes popped into her brain.

She shook her head. *Not going there.*

The last thing she needed in her life was another arrogant, overprotective male. Her father, a retired four-star Navy admiral, had spent his career saving the world as a SEAL. He'd taught her how to shoot, get out of restraints, and take down a man who outweighed her by a hundred pounds, yet he still didn't seem to trust her to keep herself safe without intervening in her life.

She reached beneath her blouse to pull out the gold starburst pendant hanging from a delicate rope chain around her neck. A half-carat diamond winked from its center. Her talisman that her Nana had gifted her before she died. Her paternal grandmother, Emily Houghton Dane, had defied the conventions of her age by working with the

OSS, predecessor to the CIA, during World War II before marrying and raising children. Stories of her exploits had fired young Emily's imagination and made her want to be as adventurous and daring.

Emily's fingers closed around the pendant, its sharp points digging into her palm. She could help people, too, in her own way. She'd fought to carve out her own life like her grandmother did, away from her dad's long shadow of influence, and she wasn't about to give up her hard-won independence to another overprotective SEAL.

Even if he was smoking hot and wreaked havoc on her hormones.

The station door opened, letting fresh air and a shaft of sunlight pierce the gloomy interior. Inspector Victor Pierron from the French Judicial Police shuffled through the door, all stooped shoulders and world-weary demeanor. When his watery, pale blue gaze connected with hers, he sighed, his chin dropping to his chest.

"*Bonjour, Mademoiselle.* We meet again." His tie hung in a loose, disheveled knot, and the acrid scent of stale cigarette smoke clung to his suit jacket, reminding her of the many senior enlisted men who had served under her father.

Emily stood and kissed the detective's cheeks in greeting. "*Bonjour* Inspector Pierron." She thrust into his hands the information she'd spent two months compiling, interviewing Catalina and every working girl who'd accept a furtive ten euro note in exchange for a few minutes of conversation away from the watchful eyes of their pimp.

"This information and the testimony of Catalina and Maya should be enough to arrest Jules Mirga. Maya is a minor. You could file felony charges against their pimp, Daniel Pescariu, and use it as leverage to get him to flip."

The inspector looked up from his perusal of the folder's contents. "Mademoiselle Dane, I know you want to help. It is tragic what happens to these girls. But I would request that you let the French police handle it from here."

She didn't miss his emphasis on the word French. She was an American sticking her nose where it didn't belong.

Pierron lifted his hands in a Gallic shrug. "Eh, I have dealt with this ugliness for too long. These traffickers are like cockroaches. You get rid of one, and ten more take his place. I look forward to my retirement." He patted Emily's shoulder before shuffling down the hall where the girls and Françoise Légère waited.

"Will you let me know what happens to Catalina and Maya?" Her raised voice earned her another hostile glance from the woman behind the counter.

The inspector raised his arm but didn't turn around.

Her shoulders slumped on a sigh. Just like that, she was dismissed. Out of the loop. The police were more annoyed by her efforts than appreciative.

Bruce stood behind her, waiting. "You've done what you can. Why don't we grab some lunch?"

"I need to get back to the embassy." Emily pretended not to notice the disappointment blooming in his eyes. "And so do you—I've taken enough of your time."

Her latest report on European trafficking trends was due before leaving town for her best friend's wedding next week. She glanced down the hall where Catalina and Maya had disappeared with Madame Légère. Maybe she had overstepped her bounds, but generating reports didn't save lives—action did.

And you didn't have to be a Navy SEAL to make a difference in this world.

Chapter Two

Nathan Long stepped off the elevator, squared his shoulders, and pulled open the glass doors that led to the suite housing Dìleas Security Agency. Other than the name in gold sans serif letters across the deep blue wall behind the reception desk, it didn't look much like an office that specialized in cyber, facility, and personal security for government and corporate entities. He and Lachlan Mackay, his best friend and president of Dìleas, had wanted a more masculine, military feel to the décor but had been outvoted by Lachlan's pint-sized dynamo of a fiancée, Sophia Russo. She had the former SAS soldier wrapped around her dainty finger and, if Nathan was honest, he wasn't far behind.

Which is why the reception area featured landscape oils and a plant jungle rather than framed poster-sized photos of special forces guys doing their thing.

The space had belonged to a law firm before Dìleas took it over. Sophia lightened the dark gray walls to a pale gray, added a large multi-hued blue area rug over the gray carpet, and hung a couple landscape paintings that featured deep blue water, bright green trees and snow-capped mountains. Then there were the plants. Ficus trees guarded the corners on either side of the seating area made up of a blue couch and two light gray chairs, and a bonsai tree sat on a gray wood-grained coffee table that matched the reception desk.

Penny Turner, Dìleas's official greeter, office manager, and unofficial company mom, sat at the desk, flanked by more potted plants and an orchid the same color as the dark pink blouse she had on. Her diamond stud earrings sparkled and her straight silver hair was tucked neatly below her jawline.

"Mornin', Miss Penny." Nathan exaggerated his central Texas drawl and favored Penny with a smile his mother swore got him into more trouble than it kept him out of.

"Good morning, Nathan. You look nice today." Penny gave him a maternal smile and handed him a manila folder. "For you to sign."

He glanced down at his Lucchese boots, navy chinos, and untucked pale pink button-down. "Thought I'd dress up." It *was* a step up from his typical t-shirt, jeans, and tactical boots. He winked, eliciting another smile from Penny.

Lachlan and Sophia had started the company over a year ago and recruited Nathan and Lachlan's SAS teammate, Ryder Montague, to join them. Lachlan, a Scot, chose the name, Dìleas, a Gaelic word meaning Loyal, a concept important to him after Sophia had helped him put his past behind him and learn to love and trust again.

Ryder currently resided in Paris and headed up the executive protection division for Dìleas. Nathan had no interest in protecting people, just their information. He took it personally when he lost someone, as his time leading a SEAL platoon had proven. He'd been happily going it alone as a white hat hacker before signing on with Dìleas.

But if he was honest, it felt good to be part of a team again.

At least now, his hacker activities came with a fancy title, Director of Corporate Security. The downside was the paperwork and having to dress up and play nice with a bunch of stuffed shirt clients.

On his way to his office, he rapped on Lachlan's door to say hello. "Yo, amigo."

He waited for a response before entering. The last time he busted on in, he'd interrupted Lachlan and Sophia engaged in an activity that had nothing to do with business.

The memory made him grin.

"Come in." Lachlan's voice, tinged with the lilt of Caithness, beckoned from the other side.

Nathan entered, his grin faltering when he spotted the man sitting in one of the burgundy armchairs in front of Lachlan's desk. He came to attention, forcing his right hand to remain at his side and not salute. "Sir."

Old habits died hard.

Retired Admiral Porter Dane stayed seated. His salt and pepper hair and mustache still trimmed to regulation length, the older man radiated as much authority dressed in gray trousers and a neatly pressed white dress shirt as he had in uniform with four stars on his shoulder boards. "At ease, son." He lifted his chin in the direction of the tall, raven-haired man seated opposite him behind the desk. "I was just telling Lachlan that Carla and I would like to host a reception for him and Sophia after they return from their honeymoon to make up for the fact that we are unable to attend the wedding."

His gunmetal blue gaze swept both men. "It will be an opportunity to promote Dìleas with some influential people inside the Beltway."

Nathan's gaze darted to Lachlan before returning to the admiral. "Yessir."

Admiral Dane's connections could give their company a real boost. The admiral's fingerprints showed up everywhere in DC. They were lucky the man considered Sophia a second daughter. His faith in her helped save Lachlan's ass when Lachlan stood accused of trafficking weapons to an Afghan warlord.

The downside? The man was a master chess player and a cagey bastard. One never knew his end game.

Still, he'd been a skilled operator and leader, and when Nathan served under him as a junior officer, he'd respected the hell out of him.

Nathan's thoughts veered to the admiral's daughter, the tall blonde who was Sophia's best friend. Mercurial eyes that were blue or green depending upon what she wore, smart as a whip, and a sassy mouth he found strangely attractive. Emily Dane may have gotten her mother's looks, but she'd inherited her father's fearlessness and tenacity.

He and Emily met last year, and the sexual tension between them sizzled when they were together, although Emily did her best to pretend it didn't exist. Nathan was a former operator, which made him unworthy of her time.

He stared at the man in front of him. *Daddy issues.*

Admiral Dane stood. "I'll leave you two to business. I'm going to say hello to Sophia before I go." His gaze lasered in on Nathan. "I understand you're the best man."

"Yes...sir." Nathan's response dragged over his tongue.

The admiral's hand landed like an anvil on Nathan's shoulder. "Emily's been working too hard on her latest project. Make sure the maid of honor has fun while she's in Scotland." His eyes narrowed. "But not too much fun. That girl finds trouble even when she's not looking for it."

"Yessir." Nathan winced inside. Damned if he didn't sound like a parrot. He reminded himself he was no longer in the Navy and hadn't just received an order from his commanding officer.

The older man left, shutting the door behind him with a decisive click.

Lachlan snorted, his emerald eyes glinting with amusement. "Like you could keep that woman from doing whatever she wants."

"No shit." Nathan laughed. He liked his manhood intact, thank you very much. He dropped into the chair Admiral Dane had just vacated and planted his size fourteens on the corner of Lachlan's burnished oak executive desk, ignoring the pained look his friend sent him.

"You and Sophia packed?"

Lachlan blew out an exasperated breath. "I'm packed and trying to stay out of the way. You're arriving in Thurso on Wednesday?"

"Yep."

Lachlan's hometown was the northernmost seaport city in the Scottish Highlands, more Nordic than Gallic, and slightly more northern in latitude than Juneau, Alaska, which, in Nathan's opinion, made it too damn cold. Thank God Lachlan and Sophia had decided to get married in July.

"Ryder, too." Nathan's lips tilted in a sly grin. "We have your bachelor party all arranged."

Lachlan's gaze narrowed. "Don't do anything stupid."

"Hey, a bunch of British and American operators out having a good time, celebrating your impending marital bliss." Nathan's grin stretched. "What could possibly go wrong?" He chuckled at the alarm widening Lachlan's eyes.

Lachlan stabbed a finger in his direction. "If anything goes wrong, pal, you'll have to answer to Sophia." He shot Nathan an arch look. "And the maid of honor."

Nathan held up the folder in his hand like a shield. "I'd rather fast-rope into a hot zone." Sophia was a tiny thing, but she could be fierce when it came to her love for Lachlan. His buddy was a lucky man, and he deserved it. He'd been through hell.

Nathan had to admit, there were moments when he was a bit envious of the relationship they had.

As for the maid of honor, he secretly enjoyed how her eyes flashed and her chin jutted when he did something to irritate her. Like, breathe. Or stare at her like he planned to strip her naked and nibble his way from her pert little nose down her long legs to her polished toes, not to mention tasting everything in between.

Down boy. He was looking forward to crossing swords with Sophia's feisty best friend again. It had been months since he'd last seen her. Their time spent together as best man and maid of honor would be interesting, if not entertaining.

He refocused on the groom-to-be. "Relax, it's all good. The wedding week festivities will go off without a hitch. And Ryder and I will make sure the company doesn't implode while you and Sophia are making like bunnies on your honeymoon."

Standing, he gave Lachlan a mock salute. "I relieve you."

Lachlan gave a faint smile and returned the salute. "I stand relieved."

CHAPTER THREE

THE BLACK CURSOR SCOLDED Emily as she stared at the words on her computer screen, her fingers drumming an impatient tattoo on the light oak veneer of her government-issue desk while her coffee sat cooling beside her. A tedious compilation of faceless numbers for the State Department's *Trafficking in Persons Report* didn't show the flesh and blood people—predominantly women and children—who made up those depressing statistics.

She wheeled around in her chair to glance out at the beautiful summer day from the tall, six-paned window pouring natural sunlight into her utilitarian office. Cubicle, actually. Her walls, if they could be called that, consisted of her coworker's two six-foot metal filing cabinets in front of her desk, the backs covered in gray acoustic panels that doubled as her bulletin board.

On her left, two shorter, four-foot-tall cabinets formed the half wall that shielded her workstation from passersby and afforded her the illusion of privacy. Stacks of reports littered the small side table to her right. Her own set of tall filing cabinets separated her space from the coworker behind her.

A frustrated sigh made its way from her chest to her throat as she resumed her staring contest with the cursor. It had been three days since she'd convinced Catalina and Maya to go to the police. At least Madame Légère had called to let her know the girls were safe.

She hadn't heard from Inspector Pierron.

Bruce's top half, dressed in a navy suit and teal pin-striped tie, appeared on the other side of her half-wall. He rapped his knuckles on the metal cabinet. "Knock knock. Did you see the society section in today's paper?" He stepped into her space and dropped his copy of *Le Monde* in front of her.

"Good morning to you, too." Emily reached for the newspaper and flipped to the section in question. She scanned the article on sex trafficking, her shoulders tightening. "This is investigative journalism? The reporter offers general statistics, interviews a couple of prostitutes, and alludes to recent arrests but doesn't mention Mirga."

She looked at Bruce. "I don't understand. He's head of the biggest sex trafficking ring in Paris. How do you write an article about sexual slavery and not mention him?"

"Who knows?" Bruce shrugged. "Maybe the police need to gather more evidence before they arrest Mirga and are keeping details out of the press." His voice sharpened. "Emily, it isn't your job to take down Jules Mirga."

A dull ache tap-danced on her temples as she let out a harsh breath. "He preys on women and children, plying them with drugs, abusing them, using their bodies to make money. Money they never see. If I can—"

"You're going to step on toes," Bruce interrupted her tirade, "and it *will* affect your position here at the embassy. You're supposed to be working with French officials to support *their* efforts, not go off half-cocked on your own to see justice done like you're Jack Reacher."

She cringed inside at his admonishment, as if she was someone who needed to be talked off a ledge.

His tone softened. "I admire your passion and understand your desire to save those girls. When I got my nephew into rehab, I felt the same way—I wanted to make sure his dealer never sold drugs to anyone else. But it would be best if you backed away. You helped Maya and Catalina. Let that be enough."

Emily squeezed her eyes shut.

Her father's voice echoed in Bruce's words. *Everyone has a role to play,* he'd say. *Do yours.* Of course, to the admiral, her role was to have her nice, safe career, marry a nice, safe guy—a guy like Bruce—settle down, and eventually give her parents grandchildren.

Ugh.

"Earth to Emily."

She lifted her lashes to see Bruce's hand waving in front of her face. He straightened and rolled his shoulders. Her stomach sank. She had a feeling she knew the direction his thoughts had shifted.

"Are you free tonight? I thought we might go to the Raphael Terrace, have some wine, and admire the Eiffel Tower from a safe distance."

Yep. She'd guessed correctly.

He really was a nice guy. Maybe she should take him up on his offer and see if it led to anything more. Stable and steady was good, right?

Say yes. Give him a chance.

"That sounds like fun," she gave him a wide smile to show him she meant it, "but I'm snowed under with work. I'm taking a few days off next week for my best friend's wedding in Scotland. I'm the maid of honor." Her gaze strayed back to the newspaper, and she sighed. "It'll be nice to focus on something happy for a change."

Lately, her life had become an endless crusade for justice, leaving her personal life non-existent.

After what Sophia and her fiancé, Lachlan, had gone through last year, this wedding had to be perfect, which meant Emily needed to step it up with her maid of honor duties. She was looking forward to a weekend of fun and celebration. Maybe she'd meet a hot guy and have a fling.

Unbidden, an image of Lachlan's best man flashed behind her eyes, and a whisper of heat warmed her insides.

"Not you."

Bruce drew back with a frown. "Why not me?"

Emily blinked. "What? No, it's not you. I was thinking about something else." *Someone else.* "Work's been crazy—that's what I meant to say." Her cheeks heated. She gave Bruce another bright smile. "Maybe when I get back from Scotland?"

"Sure. I've, uh, got to get back to work." Bruce stepped outside her cubicle, then stopped, resting his forearms on her half-wall of cabinets. He glanced around before meeting her eyes, his brown gaze steady. "Emily, you're in Paris, the City of Lights. Make sure you don't spend so much time focusing on your job that you miss everything else. You know, life, fun, friends," he paused, "romance."

She winced. Message received. "I'll take that under advisement, counselor. See you later."

Jules Mirga lay on a rectangular table, a sheet folded at his waist, in a small, nondescript room in the private offices of one of his sex clubs. A slight girl with large dark eyes and curly black hair spread oil on her hands and pressed her fingers into the tight muscles of his shoulders. Lavender and sandalwood soaked into his skin.

"Harder."

The fingers on his back flinched at his sharp command, lifting briefly before pressing deeper. The phone he'd placed next to his head vibrated. He opened his eyes, looked at the number, and stabbed at the connect button on the screen.

"I've been waiting to hear from you. Why didn't you warn me?" Red seeped into his vision and pounded at his temple as he listened. "I don't care for your excuses, *putain*. The police are all over my organization. You're supposed to make sure that doesn't happen."

The hands massaging him stilled.

He cranked his head around. "Did I tell you to stop?"

The girl trembled and shook her head. Warm oil drizzled down his spine.

"How did this happen?" He listened some more. "An American? Who is she?"

The voice on the other end rose in pitch.

Pathetic fool. "I don't care what you think," Jules cut through the arguments. "She put her nose where it did not belong. Send me her information." His voice lowered. "Remember, *mon ami*, what I have done for you—what I still do for you."

He disconnected the call, and a moment later, his phone vibrated with an incoming text containing a photo of an attractive blonde. Her hair fell in gentle waves to just below her shoulders. Her eyes were large, and her lips full and pink. His body stirred.

He would enjoy teaching this Emily Dane not to interfere in his business.

Chapter Four

The rhythmic clacking of the ScotRail train lulled Emily's eyes to half-mast as she rested her head against the cool glass of her window seat. At six pm, the sun still cast an intense western glow over the stark browns and greens of the Highlands. In mid-July, the sun technically set at ten, but the land remained bathed in a twilight that persisted until sunrise, around four thirty. There would be no true night for at least another month.

Scotland was beautiful, stark, and wild, like its legendary Highlanders. She pictured Lachlan Mackay with his high cheekbones and emerald eyes. Even with his neatly trimmed short black hair, he resembled the Highlander leading his men into battle in the oil painting that hung over the gas fireplace in Sophia's condo.

Her and Lachlan's home now.

In the glass, Emily's eye roll reflected back at her. Her best friend had her hands full with the former SAS captain.

From out of nowhere, a jaw-cracking yawn seized her. It'd been a long day of travel from Paris to Thurso, Lachlan's hometown and where Sophia and Lachlan had chosen to marry. Straightening in her seat, she pulled out a slip of notebook paper from her brown Coach travel tote, unfolded it, and scanned her handwritten checklist.

1. Check on floral arrangements and cake delivery times.

2. Make sure wedding gown is steamed.

3. Telephone restaurant to confirm arrangements for bridal shower.

4. Don't talk about work. This is Sophia's weekend!

5. Don't sleep with the best man.

Emily withdrew a pen from her bag and underscored the last item on the list in sharp, black ink.

Nathan Long had shown up in too many of her nighttime fantasies—not that she'd admit it to anyone, not even Sophia. She made a point of never asking about him when they spoke, even as she soaked up every morsel of information Sophia offered about her fiancé's best friend.

The first time she met Nathan, fifteen months ago, she'd climbed over his security gate and marched down his long gravel driveway, looking for Sophia. Around the bend, a six-foot-six giant with short, spiky blond hair waited in front of a tan brick ranch, holding a gun.

She'd gone to his home because she'd thought Sophia's life was in danger. She hadn't expected her heart to beat wildly and every nerve ending in her body to light up when she laid eyes on Lachlan's best friend.

Nathan Long threw off her equilibrium. He was beyond sexy with all those delicious muscles and tats. He behaved like a lone wolf, barricaded behind a security gate and No Trespassing signs, but he'd charged straight into danger without hesitation alongside Lachlan to rescue Sophia.

Typical Team Guy.

She'd known plenty, was related to two, refused to date any.

So why couldn't she toss this one in a mental drawer and move on?

She was her own woman; independent and career-focused. There was no place in her life for another overprotective man who would try to fence in her ambitions in the name of safety when she was perfectly capable of taking care of herself.

Her lips firmed. She and Nathan would do their parts as maid of honor and best man this weekend, then she would return to her life in Paris, and he'd return to his life in DC.

The train slowed with a jolt. A male voice with a musical lilt came through the speaker system to announce their impending arrival into Thurso Station, or *Thursho* as he pronounced it. She shoved her pen and list into her handbag and turned her attention to the scenery outside her window.

Up ahead, she spied a large gray shed with a rectangular white sign that read, *Welcome to Thurso* in bold black letters. The tracks ended inside the shed, making this seaport town the literal end of the Far North Line.

A smattering of people waited along the outdoor concrete platform to greet disembarking passengers.

Was that? Her shoulders tightened. *Yes, it was.*

Nathan towered over the sparse crowd, arms folded and stance wide in faded jeans and black t-shirt.

The train's pneumatic brakes hissed as it slowed into the station. Nathan scanned windows. On the platform, a raven-haired girl with a nose ring hovered nearby, trying to catch his eye. Usually, he'd smile back, flirt a bit, but not today.

The only woman he wanted to see was inside one of those cars.

A flash of pale blonde caught his eye. He followed the shoulder-length hair up and locked gazes with Emily. Blood rushed straight to his groin.

She looked down, freeing him—and his unruly dick—from the hold of her baby blues. Or were they green today? Either way, he was looking forward to seeing them again, even if they were staring at him in annoyance, which was likely.

Shortly after the train came to a complete standstill, her tall slim form appeared at the stairs of the carriage to his left in a light green blouse, black slacks and matching boots.

He strode over and commandeered her navy suitcase while offering her his other hand. It hung outstretched in the air, waiting.

"What, darlin', no kiss hello?" He piled on his Texas accent and flashed a grin.

Pink bloomed across her cheeks, and his smile widened. Her eyes were a seafoam green today, matching her blouse.

A spark of defiance lit her face, and her lips thinned. She ignored his chivalry, taking the four steps down onto the platform unassisted.

Still feisty, his Emily.

His amusement vanished. She wasn't his, he scolded himself. She didn't want to be his. He'd have fun riling her up, watching her eyes flash as she verbally flayed six inches off his height.

He must be a masochist because he looked forward to their sparring.

She adjusted the straps of the tote bag on her shoulder and tilted her head back to meet his eyes. "Hello, Nathan. I see you drew the short straw. Thank you for picking me up." Those prim and proper words came out all breathless and husky, like she'd run a mile before she uttered them.

He yanked his gaze from her mouth before he embarrassed himself. "I offered."

They followed the crowd exiting the platform through the tiny station and out to the parking area.

His fingers brushed her lower back. She tensed, and he shoved his hand into the pocket of his jeans to keep from touching her again while he racked his brain for a safe topic of conversation.

"Lachlan and Sophia are the guests of honor at a dinner hosted by his parents so the rest of the extended Mackay clan can meet the bride before the wedding."

"Oh geez. Poor Sophia."

Nathan grunted. "Yeah, I get the feeling she's not used to large family gatherings."

He and Emily neared the white tin can rental, a Kia mini something or other that he'd gotten stuck with because all the larger vehicles had been unavailable. He should have corralled Ryder and asked to borrow his larger rental sedan.

What he wouldn't give for his Ford F-150 right now. God Bless America.

He tossed her suitcase into the trunk and eased himself into the driver's seat, his head and shoulders almost landing in Emily's lap as he leaned over to fold in his legs and close the door.

Her body went rigid. Her scent—vanilla with a hint of spice—filled his nose. Sweet and spicy, like her.

He straightened as much as possible, his hair brushing the fabric of the interior roof.

Emily snickered.

"What?" He glanced her way before starting the car.

"You make this look like a clown car."

"It *is* a clown car."

He threw the car in reverse and twisted to look over his shoulder before backing out. He headed toward the inn that served as lodging for the guests and as the wedding reception venue. At least it was only a few minutes away.

The air between them grew thick in the silence.

Emily cleared her throat. "So, how is the job with Dìleas Security Agency coming along?"

"Good. Lots of work." His hand brushed her leg when he shifted gears on the manual transmission, and she jumped like a scalded cat.

He pretended not to notice. "But Lachlan and Sophia take care of most of the administrative bullsh—ah stuff, so I can do what I do best."

"Which is what, exactly?"

"Back door my way into government or corporate security setups and show them what they need to fix before some bad guy, or bad government, gets in and steals information they don't want stolen."

He caught her smile out of the corner of his eye. "So, you're a hacker."

"Yes, ma'am. A damn fine one if I do say so."

"And you do."

He grinned in response and turned onto the two-lane road leading to the inn.

Low stone walls lined both sides of the street. A field of mowed grass lay opposite the hotel, and beyond that, the rocky beaches of Scrabster Harbor and the Pentland Firth. Behind the hotel, sheep grazed contentedly in another field.

Their lodging and the reception venue was a copper-roofed, beige stucco two-story building, larger than it appeared, but still small enough that Lachlan had reserved every room for the wedding. Modern sunroom extensions jutted out from the structure's main floor, expanding the hotel's restaurant and meeting spaces and giving them an open, airy feel.

Nathan brought the car to a stop in front of the steps leading up to a set of double doors that served as the hotel's main entrance.

Emily's hand gripped his thigh when he moved to unlatch his seat belt. Her slim fingers and pink-tipped nails branded him through his jeans, locking him in place. Apparently she didn't mind them touching as long as she was the one initiating it.

She withdrew her hand back to her lap, and he could breathe again. "I don't know how to say this diplomatically, so I'm just going to say it."

This should be interesting. He lifted his brows at her and waited.

"Sophia is my best friend. Lachlan is yours. It would be awkward if anything were to happen between us, so let's make sure it doesn't."

Emily dropped her little declaration like a bomb, then dug into her purse and pulled out a circular tube of glossy pink stuff, staring into the flip-down mirror on her sunshade as she swiped some over her lips.

He zeroed in on her shimmery, pink lower lip.

He wouldn't mind biting that.

"Nathan, did you hear what I said?" Her gaze focused on him now, narrowed with irritation.

"What?" *There was more?*

"I grew up around Team Guys. I'm not interested in a fling with one." She wouldn't look at him as she returned her lipstick to her bag.

Fling? That stung. He wasn't sure what their relationship would be if they ever got together, but he knew in his gut it wouldn't be a Wham Bam Thank You Ma'am roll in the hay.

Not if he could help it. Emily had been on his mind and in his dreams since she'd stormed onto his property last year.

The few times they'd been in the same room, she did her best to ignore him unless he did something to raise her hackles. Then her eyes would get all fiery, her full pink lips would purse rather than narrow, and she'd let fly with some comment meant to cut his balls off but which secretly amused him. When she got riled up, it wasn't only anger he saw in her pretty eyes.

Miss Emily got turned on by their sparring.

He leaned into her space. "Former Team Guy." Her and her damn daddy issues. "I've been told I'm rather good. You might regret not taking me for a test drive," he paused a beat, "*Princess.*"

Her head whipped around, bringing her lips close enough that puffs of minty air caressed his lips when she spoke. She speared him with a withering look, her eyes darkening to moss.

"That's exactly the arrogance I expect from a SEAL," she huffed before she scrambled out of the car and marched up the stairs minus her luggage.

"Whatever you say, darlin'," he called after her, grinning when her back stiffened.

She marched through the hotel doors like she owned the place.

Nathan sobered. As much as he enjoyed poking the bear, she was right to set boundaries. And if he were smart, he'd stay within them.

Their best friends were about to marry each other. After everything they'd been through, Lachlan and Sophia didn't need any drama surrounding their wedding festivities.

He unfurled his stiff body from the Euro car with a groan.

Look, but don't touch.

Not his forte, but he could resist temptation for one weekend.

Then he'd head home and find a warm, willing woman to take his mind off the one who wouldn't give him the time of day.

CHAPTER FIVE

THE CHURCH LACHLAN AND Sophia had chosen to be married in was an impressive display of gothic architecture, its tall, square tower topped by four pointed turrets dominating Thurso's town center. Across the street, the bright green lawn and ornamental gardens of Sir John's Square was a postage stamp of bright colors amidst the blocks of tan and gray brick and stone buildings. Mother Nature had decided to grant Emily's friends a boon on their wedding day, gifting them with sun and temperatures in the low sixties Fahrenheit, which Emily had discovered was about as warm as it got in this northernmost Scottish coastal burgh. A mild breeze carried in the smell of the sea from the nearby Pentland Firth.

Emily stood in the vestibule and peered into the sanctuary, down the long red carpet dividing rows of varnished wooden pews to where the organist had begun to play the first notes of Pachelbel's *Canon in D* on the imposing two-story pipe organ. Floral arrangements of white roses, hydrangea, and freesia surrounded by eucalyptus, ivy, and ferns perched on white pedestals around the altar. Two similar arrangements in floor urns graced each side of the altar steps, where Lachlan and his groomsmen stood waiting.

Fiona, Lachlan's sister, was the first bridesmaid up. She began her slow march down the aisle in her navy tea-length off-the-shoulder dress, her long black hair put up in a twist.

Emily turned to face the woman who'd become her best friend their freshman year of college. "Are you ready?"

Sophia Russo nodded, her hazel eyes shimmering. Her auburn hair was swept into a soft updo, her delicate features framed by loose tendrils. The petite redhead clutched her bridal bouquet of peach and white roses, blue thistles, and delicate sprigs of white heather. "I'm more than ready."

Janie, one of Emily and Sophia's college roommates, began her trek down the aisle. Emily lowered the tulle veil over Sophia's face and fluffed her chapel-length train one last time before squeezing the bride's hands. Her Jasmine Brandt floral lace A-line wedding dress boasted a sweetheart bodice with off shoulder swag sleeves. Embroidered floral appliques covered the bodice and sleeves and cascaded gracefully down the tulle skirt.

It was a breathtakingly romantic dress and fit Sophia perfectly.

"You look beautiful. I'll see you up there."

The wedding director, a rather prim, no-nonsense Scottish woman in a conservative black dress, waved Emily forward.

She proceeded down the aisle in slow, measured steps, clutching her maid of honor bouquet—peach-colored roses bundled with blue thistles and sprigs of baby's breath and tied in a navy ribbon that matched her dress.

Ignoring the guests seated in the wooden pews, she focused on the men gathered at the steps leading up to the altar. Lachlan looked every bit the stunning Highlander in a black argyle kilt jacket and matching waistcoat atop the navy blue, dark green, and black tartan of Clan Mackay. His eyes warmed as he gave her a brief nod.

An invisible magnetic pull drew her attention to the man at Lachlan's side. Nathan wore a tailored black tuxedo and crisp white shirt, highlighting his broad shoulders and dangerous sex appeal. He had shaved his usual scruff and tamed his hair with product.

His gaze swept her, and one side of his mouth lifted in a close-lipped smile before he winked.

A wild fluttering erupted in her chest.

Her toe stubbed the carpet, and she stifled a curse. Nathan would not make her fall on her face and ruin Sophia's grand entrance.

She yanked her gaze away to focus on something safe—the middle-aged priest in his white cassock—and took her place beside the other bridesmaids.

The organist began to play *Trumpet Voluntary*. Sophia and her father appeared at the back of the church and on cue the congregation stood.

An audible inhale drew Emily's attention to Lachlan, and her eyes misted at the look on his face as he stared at his bride.

Shoot. She couldn't get all sappy now. She needed to keep it together for her friend.

Sophia and her father began their slow march down the aisle, the bride's gaze locked onto her husband-to-be, her smile beaming through the wisp of veil.

A sudden pang of loss tweaked Emily, followed by a stab of guilt. Her best friend was marrying the man of her dreams. She wasn't losing her friend, but their relationship *had* changed and would continue to evolve with Sophia's marriage and her work with Lachlan running his new security firm.

Sophia didn't seem to mind putting aside her own career goals for Lachlan. And she had, going from lobbying Congress for international development funding to aid war-torn countries like Afghanistan to promoting Dìleas's security services to government entities and corporations. She'd fallen in love, and suddenly, nothing else mattered.

The same thing had happened to Emily's mother. After college, she'd had a promising career in her father's financial services firm, and she'd given it up to marry Emily's father, a Navy lieutenant junior grade who'd just earned his SEAL trident, and follow him around the country as he rose through the ranks of his naval career.

Emily stole a peek at Nathan. Despite her efforts to keep him at arm's length, she couldn't deny her attraction. Not just to him physically, although she'd spent many a night fantasizing about what it would be like to have sex with him. His loyalty to his friends and his easy-going, laid-back sense of humor had wormed their way beneath her skin. He'd be easy to fall into a relationship with. The problem was, he was an alpha male, like his buddy Lachlan, and it wouldn't be long before he'd expect her to change her life to accommodate him.

She had her own career path mapped out, and she wasn't giving it up to support anyone else's goals.

Her musings ceased when Sophia handed her the bridal bouquet before twining her fingers with Lachlan's. The priest raised his hands in blessing. "Let us pray."

Nathan took his seat at the head table inside the reception room at the hotel. Most of the guests had arrived well ahead of the wedding party, already found drinks at the bar, and made their way to the white-covered round tables ringing the parquet dance floor.

This damn tuxedo shirt and bowtie cut off his circulation and reminded him of his Navy dress whites. The look might be dashing, but it wasn't comfortable. He should be more sympathetic when the ladies in his life complained about their heels.

A black-clad server poured champagne in the flute at his setting, then gave him a friendly smile. Nathan stared as the bubbles rose to the top to burst with a kinetic fizz.

He had to admit, he'd gotten the feels as Lachlan and Sophia said their vows. Sophia's face radiated her love for Lachlan, her vows spoken softly but without hesitation. Nathan hadn't seen Lachlan's face, but his friend's voice cracked for a brief moment, his emotions evident to the congregation.

This wedding reminded Nathan he wasn't getting any younger himself. He'd been off the Teams for almost three years—*Jesus*—had it been that long? He had a steady job now and a good paycheck.

The casual relationships he indulged in were getting old. He wanted a wife, kids, a marriage like his parents had. Forty years and still going strong.

He wanted a love like Lachlan and Sophia had.

His gaze slanted to Emily, seated only three chairs away as she tried to pretend he didn't exist. They'd done their part as best man and maid of honor, maintaining a friendly façade, but it hadn't stopped him from letting his gaze linger on her when she wasn't looking. The navy dress she wore exposed the delicate lines of her neck and shoulders and made him want to run his lips and tongue over all that pale skin. The A-line skirt covered her knees but gave him a tantalizing view of her toned calves atop a pair of high-heeled navy pumps. Already five-ten in bare feet, she towered over half the men in the room in her heels. And she didn't care.

However you described it, Emily looked elegant. Classy. A look that was as natural on her as breathing.

He signaled one of the roving wait staff. "Can you grab me a beer? The local amber ale."

He needed something besides champagne to quench his thirst and his libido. He could handle keeping things polite and platonic between them this week, but the effort was starting to tick him off.

He was getting damn tired of Emily doing her level best to ignore the sexual tension between them.

"Ladies and gentlemen, may I have your attention, please," the DJ announced, drawing the focus of everyone in the room to the main doors where the bagpiper who'd played at the church as guests arrived stood at the ready. "Introducing, for the very first time, Mr. and Mrs. Mackay."

Nathan stood and applauded as Lachlan and Sophia swept into the room to the cheerful tune of "Mairi's Wedding" on the pipes, greeting guests on their way to the head table.

"How you holding up?" Nathan asked as Lachlan took the seat next to him. The Scot was as relaxed as Nathan had ever seen him, the shadows that used to lurk behind his eyes vanquished.

Lachlan leaned over to murmur in his ear. "Let's get this bloody party started so I can take my bride and begin our honeymoon."

"Have you told her where you're going yet?"

"No, but I did tell her what kind of clothes to pack, so she knows it's someplace warm." Lachlan gave Nathan a knowing grin and added in a low voice, "Not that she'll be wearing clothes most of the time."

Nathan chuckled. "Well, as your best man, allow me to get the ball rolling."

He rose from his seat and tapped his fork against the flute in front of his plate. More guests followed his lead, the sound gathering momentum in a symphony of stainless steel against crystal.

Conversation ebbed.

Nathan cleared his throat and looked around the room. "Lachlan and I met in Afghanistan. It was love at first sight. On his part, of course. He was in awe of my superior warfighter skills as a Navy SEAL."

The chuckles turned to good-natured boos from the current and former soldiers of the British Army.

He grinned and raised his glass to the crowd before turning to Lachlan. "Seriously, we had some good times, and then we got snake-bit pretty hard." Their friendship, begun in combat, was forged in the crucible of betrayal and death. He and Lachlan shared a look full of memories.

The room got quiet.

Sophia's hand crept over Lachlan's.

Nathan's gaze shifted to the woman who saved his best friend's life in more ways than one.

"Then my boy here met this pretty little lady, and before I knew it, she had him lassoed and hog-tied. He didn't know if he was coming or going. For those of you who speak the Queen's English or the Gaelic that Lachlan uses when he's cussing me out, Lachlan fell in looooove."

The room erupted in laughter. Nathan grinned.

He turned to Lachlan. "Sophia is extraordinary. You deserve her, amigo. 'Course, I don't know what she did to deserve you…"

Lachlan laughed, something he didn't often do but did more of since Sophia became part of his life.

Nathan raised his flute. "I will always have your back, my brother, and Sophia's. To my best friend and business partner, and his beautiful wife. To Lachlan and Sophia Mackay."

"To Lachlan and Sophia!"

Emily took another long sip of champagne. It seemed someone toasted the bride and groom every five minutes after Nathan's best man speech and throughout the meal. And now all the dancing was making her thirsty. The explosion of bubbles tickled her nose and left a crisp floral taste on her tongue. Was this her third or fourth glass?

The music shifted to a slow, romantic number. She stood on the edge of the parquet floor and cradled her flute as individuals drifted off and couples pressed together, shuffling in small circular patterns. The newly married couple swayed at the center, oblivious to their surroundings.

A broad palm touched her lower back as the masculine scent of citrus and sea breezes embraced her. A deep, masculine voice caressed her ear. "Care to dance?"

Nathan.

She kept her focus on the dancing couples. "I'm not sure that's a good idea." Her voice came out husky, and she took another sip to moisten her suddenly dry throat.

Heat from Nathan's palm passed through the silk of her dress and arrowed straight to her lady parts, making her thighs clench.

"Are you afraid, Princess?"

The challenge in his voice yanked her gaze to his icy blue eyes. She glared at him over the rim of her flute and drained the rest of her champagne in one long pull. How juvenile.

She should ignore him.

Shoulda, woulda, coulda. Like she'd ever ignored a dare.

Depositing the empty glass on the table behind her, she grabbed Nathan's hand and marched out to the dance floor, ignoring his chuckle.

He wrapped his arm around her waist and tugged her into an embrace more appropriate for lovers than polite acquaintances. She molded to his body, from her breasts to her thighs.

Her hands flew to his chest, intending to push him away so she could take a breath.

Instead, her traitorous body melted. He was warm and rock-solid, his muscular thighs brushing against her as they moved in sync. They danced well together, and she couldn't help but think of other things they could do in rhythm.

A shiver rippled through her.

Nathan's body stiffened. His step faltered before regaining its smooth glide on the dance floor. A hardness that hadn't been there a moment before brushed against her stomach.

She kept her gaze on the black tuxedo studs on his broad chest.

Until he nuzzled her hair, and her eyes drifted shut.

Each strand Nathan touched transmitted his heat directly to her center, where a desperate need pooled. She couldn't take a deep enough breath and had to resort to small, rapid ones. Beneath her palms, his heartbeat quickened. Hers rose to match it.

In the warm shelter of his arms, she let herself imagine what it would be like to give in to this crazy chemistry she had with him. To let go and run her hands and mouth over his rugged ridges and planes, trace his colorful tattoos with her tongue. She pictured his big hands on her skin, torturing her with need. His sheer size made her feel petite and feminine, as did the way he carried himself.

A man in complete control of his environment. *A warrior.*

Everything she didn't want. She needed to remember that.

She pushed against his chest. He let her go and stepped back.

Remember your list.

"What list?" Nathan's brows furrowed as he peered at her.

Oh hell. You could probably fry an egg on her cheeks right now.

"What did I tell you the other day? This *thing*," her finger wagged back and forth between them, "cannot happen."

His gaze searched hers, probing for answers she had no intention of giving. Then he leaned down until his mouth was a hairsbreadth from hers.

Beer-laced air caressed her lips. She wanted a taste.

"It was only a dance, sweetheart."

He left her staring at his back as he sauntered over to join one of the groomsmen, Ryder Montague, holding up the corner wall by the doors leading out of the room. Another tall and well-built hottie, a Henry Cavill look-alike with electric blue eyes. And former SAS. He'd recently moved to Paris, but this was the first time she'd met him.

Probably an alphahole, too. Like Nathan, the big jerk.

She needed something stronger than champagne.

Emily stomped her way to the bar.

"Give me some scotch, neat." The bartender's eyes widened. "And make it a double."

"What?" Nathan missed whatever it was Ryder had just said to him as they nursed beers in the corner of the reception room.

Emily threw back a tumbler of whisky over by the bar. He visually traced the graceful arch of her neck as she drained the glass.

"I said, when will you and Emily stop pretending you're not attracted to each other?"

Nathan turned away before Emily caught him staring at her like a horny teenager and took a swig of his beer.

"She's made it clear Navy SEALs are not on her 'to do' list."

He stared into the brown longneck bottle he held. "Besides, she's Sophia's best friend and Admiral Dane's daughter. I hurt her, and it'll be a race to see who cuts off my 'nads first."

"I don't know, mate." Ryder's bright blue gaze met Nathan's before it followed Emily to the dance floor. "Emily doesn't seem like the type to fall apart if it didn't work out between the two of you."

Nathan shrugged. "It doesn't matter. She keeps telling me she's not interested. I need to listen to what's coming out of her mouth, not what her body language is saying."

"What if she changes her mind?"

Nathan glanced at his friend before zeroing in on the blonde in navy silk gyrating to the beat. He gulped more of his amber ale before answering.

"She wouldn't have to ask me twice."

CHAPTER SIX

ONE LAST GLASS OF wine, and then she'd turn in. Emily sank with a tired groan into the brown leather booth tucked into the corner of the dimly lit hotel bar. Her feet ached, but if she took her pumps off now, she'd never get them back on. She yawned and slumped further into her seat. A tired-looking waitress with salt and pepper hair dropped off the glass of white wine she'd ordered at the bar from the goth-looking bartender.

Sophia and Lachlan's wedding and reception had gone off without a hitch. Now the pair were on their way to honeymoon somewhere warm, the destination known only to the groom. That would so not work for her. However, Sophia hadn't seemed to mind being kept in the dark.

Emily sipped and let her gaze drift. A TV mounted in the corner showed highlights from the day's soccer matches around the UK. A young couple shared a late meal in another booth. A silver-haired man in a tweed sports coat nursed a beer at the varnished oak bar.

Movement at the pub's entrance caught her eye. Nathan stood at the threshold, his gaze roving like he was conducting a threat assessment.

Emily ducked beneath the table and pretended to root for a dropped napkin. Maybe when she came back up, he'd be gone.

All she wanted was to enjoy her last glass of wine in peace. Tomorrow, she'd start her journey back to Paris. It would be months before she crossed paths with Nathan again, and by then, she'd find a way to get over this irrational surge of hormones that only seemed to occur around him.

When she summoned the courage to sit up, he'd taken a seat at the bar. He'd changed out of his tuxedo, and the long-sleeved maroon shirt he wore defined the muscles in his back and arms and magnified the width of his shoulders.

Her palms tingled at the memory of their slow dance, his hard chest, the way his arousal had caressed her stomach as they moved together. She gulped her wine to drench the slow burn kindling between her thighs. The crisp, pale liquid slid down quickly, and her half-empty glass taunted her.

How much had she had to drink today?

Too much if she couldn't corral her thoughts of Nathan back into neutral, non-sexual territory.

The bartender poured Nathan his beer, shamelessly flirting as her kohl-rimmed eyes devoured him like he was a giant piece of chocolate.

Emily's lips thinned when his teeth flashed in the long mirror behind the bar. Did he find Morticia attractive? More wine slid down her throat.

How long had it been since she'd had sex?

Too long. She'd been too busy gathering information on the streets of Paris about Jules Mirga and his criminal empire to make time to date.

Her hips moved with a restless longing. She bit her lip as indecision warred with desire.

Nathan wanted her. She could have him.

One night. Just one.

Sophia and Lachlan would never know. They could scratch their mutual itch and move o—

Her glass halted midway to her mouth. What was she thinking? She'd spent the entire weekend trying to convince herself not to succumb to her urges where Nathan was concerned.

The bartender brought him another beer. Her fingers brushed his as she handed him the mug. Even from a distance, Emily could see that the woman's expression conveyed an unmistakable invitation.

Oh, hell no. Emily's resolve to keep away from Nathan drained away with the rest of her wine. If anyone were getting some of that hot body tonight, it wouldn't be Morticia. She rose from the booth and strutted to where Nathan sat before the sensible part of her brain could stop her. Her fingers curled over his broad shoulder in a blatant, feminine display of possession.

Go troll somewhere else, sister. She gave the bartender a tight-lipped smile. "I'd like another glass of Sauvignon Blanc."

"Put her wine on my tab." Nathan tilted his head to the side, amusement dancing in his eyes. "Did you locate whatever you were looking for beneath the table?"

She should have known he'd notice. He'd been trained to notice everything.

"No." Ignoring the heat in her cheeks, she lowered her voice to a seductive whisper. "What I'm looking for isn't under that table."

He stilled, his gaze boring into hers, pupils dilating. "Change your mind?"

She didn't have to guess what he meant by the question. Her fingers tightened on his shoulder.

One night.

She would get him out of her system and move on. Accept Bruce's dinner invitation the next time he asked and see where that led.

"Yes."

The bar stool he'd been sitting on went flying and would have hit the ground if she hadn't grabbed onto it. Reaching into his back pocket, Nathan extracted his wallet, tossed several British pounds on the bar, then turned and held out his hand.

His broad palm and long fingers made hers look delicate and small. She laced their fingers.

He pulled her down the dimly lit corridor toward the guest rooms. No doubt, everyone in the pub knew precisely what their hasty departure signified. She should be horrified.

Instead, all she could think about was how the hand wrapped around hers would feel on the rest of her body.

He came to a sudden stop and she plowed into him. "What are—"

Nathan's tongue invaded her mouth, cutting off her words in a scorching kiss that curled her toes and sent a damp heat to soak her panties. He tasted of beer, a trace of mint, and testosterone. As quickly as his lips and tongue had taken her, they were gone.

"Your room or—"

"Whichever is closer." Her voice came out a breathless pant. If he didn't hurry, they would do something wildly inappropriate in the corridor.

"Mine." Nathan's answering growl was deep and hungry. He pulled her halfway down the hall, stopping in front of one of the doors. The lock retracted with a click at the touch of his keycard.

As soon as they were inside, Nathan shut the door with a kick of his boot. "Dare I ask what brought this on?"

Now that they were doing this, she made no attempt to mask her appreciation of his physique, dragging her gaze over his broad shoulders and chest to the conspicuous bulge in his jeans. "I'm horny."

"Yeah, me too." Nathan reached for her. Their mouths met in a clash of desire, tongues dueling as they explored each other.

Her back met the wall, every inch of her pinned in place by his hard body. Another rush of heat pooled between her thighs. She kissed him until she couldn't breathe, then yanked her mouth from his to draw in a lungful of air before dragging his lips back to hers.

The man could kiss.

She couldn't wait to see what else he could do with that skillful tongue.

Long fingers cradled her breast, then slipped beneath her bra to stroke her nipple to a hard point, sending an electric shock straight to her core. She jerked her hips against his erection. Nathan's other hand found her zipper. Cool air met her back in slow increments, sending ripples of desire down newly exposed skin with every graze of his fingers. The material slid down in a silken caress to pool at her feet.

How had she thought his eyes were icy? They burned with a crystal blue fire, scorching her flesh everywhere his gaze touched. His skin stretched tight over high cheekbones, and the appreciation on his face heightened her sense of feminine power.

She stepped out of her dress; adorned only in her grandmother's starburst pendant necklace, barely-there lacy navy bra and thong, and navy pumps. She gave him a saucy smile. "You're overdressed, cowboy."

Emily yanked his shirt out of his jeans and pushed the material up until he took charge and lifted it over his head. The shirt sailed further into the room to land on the floor.

"So are you." His voice was little more than a guttural growl.

The sound of it heightened her need. She arched a brow, running her palms in a slow glide over the lacy cups of her bra.

"I'm only wearing a bra and panties."

His eyes blazed. "Like I said. Overdressed."

If she didn't touch him right now, she would die. Her nails scraped smooth, warm skin near the waistband of his jeans, and he flinched, sucking in a hard breath. They wandered over six-pack abs that flexed beneath her fingers to his broad chest with its dusting of light brown hair and flat, pink nipples.

Silk over steel.

If she were a cat, she'd be purring right now.

She traced the Navy SEAL's trident insignia tattooed over his heart. Raising on tiptoes, she kissed, then nipped the skin beneath.

Nathan threw back his head with a grunt. The world tilted as he swept her into his arms and strode to the bed.

She landed on the mattress with a bounce. He followed her down, trapping her beneath him. The rough fabric of his jeans rubbed against her panties and thighs and did little to hide his desire.

With a flick of his wrist, the front clasp of her bra gave way. Her nipples were hard points, already hypersensitive to his touch.

He latched onto one and nipped, then laved it with his tongue. Her back arched, and before she had the chance to recover, he moved to the other breast and did the same before sucking her tip into his mouth. She felt every tug in her womb.

"Nathan..." she panted his name. Her legs churned beneath him in restless need.

He needed to be inside her. *Now.*

Her palms caressed a path to his jeans to tug at the button.

His hand trapped her fingers, stilling them, the laugh rumbling from him low and cocky. "Not yet, darlin'. I'm still working on the appetizer."

"Jerk." She gave a frustrated moan.

He chuckled again. His tongue dipped into the hollow of her navel, making her squirm, before he continued south.

Her head hit the mattress, hips arching helplessly against his sensual onslaught. Anticipation fired her nerve endings, making her skin pebble as Nathan's warm, moist breath hovered over the juncture between her legs.

He curled his fingers around the edges of her flimsy lace thong and slid it down over the pumps she still wore before throwing it over his shoulder. His broad palm drifted down her calf to lift her foot.

"Nice shoes." He kissed one ankle, then the other, before draping her legs over his shoulders and settling between them.

The breath rushed from her lungs in a soft cry when his mouth claimed her. His wicked tongue stabbed in and out, stroking, teasing, sucking, drawing more wetness from her that he eagerly lapped up. He hummed his pleasure, the vibration teasing her already hyper-sensitive clit. His soft hair caressed her inner thighs even as a hint of five o'clock shadow scraped the tender skin.

Emily's entire body jacked tight as a bowstring as her world narrowed to Nathan's mouth. Her pelvic muscles tightened, sensation rushing to one focal point. She slammed her eyes shut in anticipation of the fall.

Cool air replaced his lips.

What the hell?

Her eyes flew open. She propped on her elbows and glared at Nathan.

The bastard had an evil grin on his face. "Not yet."

Bossy, domineering male.

Her breath sailed out on an irritated huff. *Fine.* She would come on her own then. Her hand glided over her breasts, down her torso toward her sweet spot.

Long fingers trapped hers. "So impatient."

"Don't be a tea—"

Her response shattered under Nathan's renewed assault. His tongue and fingers drove her hard this time and kept going as she plummeted over the edge. A breathless scream erupted from her as her body seized in wave after wave of raw pleasure.

She wanted it to end.

She wanted it to go on forever.

He kept at it until she collapsed, boneless. The room could catch fire, and she wouldn't have been able to move. After that orgasm, she half expected to see flames licking the window drapes.

Nathan stood and extracted a foil wrapper from his wallet. He kicked off his shoes and shoved down his jeans.

Commando? Her brows rose as she took a good long look at his impressive size and length.

Once he'd sheathed himself, he prowled over her, a big cat hunting his prey. He manacled her wrists with one hand and lifted them over her head, pinning her in place.

The dominant position should have irritated her, but it didn't. It turned her on even more.

"You ready?"

She would burn to death from the fire in his eyes if he didn't hurry. "God, yes. Fuck me already."

His gaze narrowed on a promise. "I'm gonna make you come so many times, you won't remember your name."

An answering lust squeezed her thighs against his hips. "Big words. Let's see if you can back them up." Her reply ended in a gasp as he filled her in one savage stroke.

He gave her no gentle introduction to lovemaking. The headboard made a rhythmic thud against the wall with each powerful thrust of his hips.

Her nails scored the back of the hand holding her a willing captive. It didn't take long for her internal muscles to tighten once again.

Nathan released her and withdrew. Before she could protest, he flipped her onto her stomach, yanked up her hips, and drove into her from behind.

Her second orgasm hit like a freight train, ripping his name from her in a breathless moan. "Nathan!"

He didn't stop, his thrusts fierce yet controlled. He felt even bigger at this angle, if that was possible.

Emily couldn't think—she could only feel. Her hands clutched the duvet, the side of her face pressed into its downy softness.

"So good." Nathan's voice was strained as he pistoned in and out, big hands gripping her hips, fingers digging into her flesh. "So fucking good."

The pressure built again at his relentless pace. He slid one hand from her hips to squeeze and caress her breasts, then moved to her center, his fingers stroking her to an impossible third orgasm.

Lights winked behind her eyelids. Her knees gave out, and she collapsed face down on the bed, a boneless rag doll.

Nathan groaned as her inner walls pulsed around him.

Only he wasn't done. He pulled out, flipped her over, and plunged into her again, pushing through swollen, sensitive tissue, sending aftershocks of pleasure through her veins. His thrusts quickened and became erratic until he threw his head back, the tendons bracketing his throat in sharp relief as he came with a shout.

He collapsed onto her, his cheek pressed into the duvet, his breath coming in harsh gasps.

Emily's chest tightened. She slammed her eyes shut as an unfamiliar rush of emotion overwhelmed her. Her hands caressed the damp skin of his back until his breathing slowed.

Finally, he propped himself on his forearms, and her chest expanded in relief. The weight of his stare pressed against her closed lids. She didn't dare open them with her emotions so near to the surface. He might misinterpret her feelings.

It was just fantastic sex.

Nothing more.

There couldn't be more because he wasn't the kind of man she wanted.

His lips, cool to the touch, whispered across hers before he rolled off the bed and padded to the bathroom.

A chill ghosted across her skin at the absence of his body heat.

This was it. One and done. She should leave.

She would leave.

Soon.

She summoned her last reserve of energy to kick off her shoes and crawled under the covers to escape the chill. Her tired brain barely registered the dip in the bed behind her and the muscular arm that pulled her back against a warm wall of flesh.

She'd be gone before he woke.

Nathan wrapped himself around Emily and pressed a gentle kiss to her neck, breathing in her spicy vanilla scent now mingled with the smell of sex. The slow rise and fall of her shoulder and her sleepy mumble brought a satisfied smile to his lips. After the long day they'd had and then playtime, she'd crashed hard.

His hand smoothed over her body. *Damn*, he couldn't stop touching all that soft skin.

Sex with Emily had been everything he thought it would be and more. It would be a long time before he got her taste out of his mouth. Or the vision of her eyes darkening to a blue topaz when she came. And the sounds she made.

His dick began to harden again.

They were combustible together in a perfect way.

Tonight had to have changed her mind about not dating him.

They might live in different countries, but his expertise in cybersecurity meant he could work from anywhere. It wouldn't take much persuading to convince him to spend a couple weeks in Paris after Lachlan and Sophia returned from their honeymoon. Hell, he could stay with Ryder. The Englishman came from serious money and, at the moment, was running the executive protection division from one of his family's homes in the tony St. Germain neighborhood while he and Lachlan sorted out the location of Dìleas's permanent European office.

His head sank into the pillow, lethargy slowing his thoughts. Now that he'd had a taste of Emily, he had no intention of walking away.

Heat and a sensation that made her insides clench and liquify pulled Emily from a deep, dreamless slumber. A sleepy hum vibrated the inside of her cheeks. She kept her eyes shut and let her other senses process her surroundings. Warm steel at her back. A heavy arm draped over her hip, the hand attached to it burrowed beneath the sheet and playing with her clit. Her hips began to move of their own accord.

Leisurely kisses caressed her neck. A rod of hard flesh pressed against her bottom. The body behind her moved in the same ancient rhythm as hers.

Emily's eyes flew open to an unfamiliar room darkened by blackout curtains as her brain came back online.

She was still in Nathan's bed.

She must have dropped off to sleep, exhausted from a long day and mind-blowing sex.

His hand glided from her sex over her hip and stomach to toy with her nipple. His breath bathed her ear, sending shivers down her spine.

She sighed and pressed herself back into his body. She'd keep reality at bay for a while longer, warm and protected and surrounded by Nathan. It'd be easy to get used to this feeling.

A twinge of unease slithered into her brain.

This was about sex, nothing more.

She turned, pushed Nathan onto his back, and straddled him, rubbing her mound against his erection.

He groaned, hips arching.

"My turn to play." Her turn to be in control.

"Consider me your playground, darlin'." She felt his arm move and the bedside lamp switched on, it's dim light bringing Nathan into focus when before, he'd been in shadows. For a moment she wanted to demand he turn off the lamp so she could feel her way around his body without him seeing his effect on her.

Nathan's hungry gaze devoured her, setting her skin aflame.

Maybe the lamp could stay on.

He raised his arms and locked his hands behind his head.

*Hmmm...*Where to begin with so much territory to explore? She'd start at the top and work her way down.

Her tongue traced the outer shell of Nathan's ear. He stiffened, and a smile creased her cheeks. She moved down the side of his neck, kissing her way to his collarbone.

In her mind, she traced his eyebrows with her fingers, slid them down the bridge of his nose and over his lush, masculine lips. Kissed his strong jaw and brushed the side of her face against the shadow of stubble...

...but only in her mind.

Touching him like that for real seemed too intimate. Instead, she moved to his chest and tasted the salty skin beneath his trident tattoo.

Farther south, she dipped her tongue into every ridge of his abdomen. His cock strained toward her, seeking her attention. She wrapped her fingers around his width and pumped as she nuzzled him and blew softly on sensitive skin. Sliding her cheek along his length, she licked the crown and tasted salt.

Nathan groaned, his erection swelling in her grip. "Babe, I don't think I can hold out much longer."

She gave an evil laugh. "Poor baby. Condom?"

He reached over to the nightstand and fumbled with his wallet. A foil wrapper sailed in her direction.

She tore it open with her teeth, sheathed him, then positioned herself. They groaned in unison as she sank onto him. Fully seated, she could swear he touched her womb.

Their eyes met and stayed locked just long enough for the feeling of unease to resurface in her brain. She slammed her lids shut to break the connection and began to move.

They found a rhythm, moving faster and faster until her grandmother's pendant bounced wildly between her breasts, her inner muscles tightened, and that heady sensation of diving into freefall overwhelmed her. She cried out as she came, digging her nails into Nathan's pecs.

"Every tight inch of you is squeezing me until I go blind." Nathan's words were savage, filled with lust. "You feel so fucking good."

He came with a hoarse shout, pushing up into her, locking them together with a firm grip on her hips.

Emily dropped onto his chest, her breath coming in shallow pants. His heart galloped in her ear. Their mingled sweat coated her skin. Up and down his chest rose, fast, then slower, as her eyes drifted shut.

It was just sex.

Chapter Seven

The distant sound of rushing water woke Emily. Rays of early morning light streamed through a gap in heavy forest green drapes. Her body ached, but in pleasant ways. Arching, she pressed her nose into the pillow and inhaled citrus, ocean breezes, and sex.

The space next to her was empty, the sheets pushed back, the pillow dented from the head that had slept on it all night. She placed her hand on the mattress and absorbed the residual heat from Nathan's body into her palm. Her nipples tightened.

She groaned. *Emily, you idiot.*

She'd had sex with Nathan.

Twice.

The one thing she'd sworn not to do, and it had been every bit as amazing as she'd feared.

Panic had her bolting from the bed faster than any cattle prod could. Why was she still in his bed instead of back in her own room as she'd planned? That's not the way flings worked. You had sex, and once you came down off the high, you gave the other person a peck on the lips, told them you had a great time and got the heck out of Dodge before they asked whether they'd be seeing you again.

She needed to get out of here before Nathan finished his shower.

Her bra and thong lay amidst the wreckage of clothing scattered across the floor. She tugged on her underwear with desperate haste, then yanked up her dress and got it zipped.

Mostly.

Phone. Where was her damn phone?

Right, she'd purposely left it in her room yesterday so she'd focus on the wedding and not be tempted to look at her emails and messages.

Pumps and room key in hand, she slipped from Nathan's room to hustle down the hall on bare feet. *Please don't let me run into anyone I know.*

A tall figure in navy running shorts and an olive t-shirt rounded the corner to witness her walk of shame.

Luck wasn't with her this morning.

Ryder Montague stopped, his gaze flickering over her partial state of undress. Other than a hint of amusement in his electric blue eyes, the Englishman's expression gave away none of the thoughts that must have run rampant through his mind.

"Good morning, Emily."

I need to get out of here.

Back to her real life. Back to work that mattered. She needed to find out what the French police were doing to break up Jules Mirga's sex trafficking ring. There'd been nothing on the Parisian digital news sites and social media. If she had to march into Inspector Pierron's office and demand answers, she would.

She latched onto Ryder's arm, holding him to her when he started to walk past. "Is there any chance you can drive me to the train station? Like, in ten minutes?"

Ryder glanced down the hall in the direction of Nathan's room before clearing his throat. "Yes, of course, if that's what you want."

She gave him a quick hug. He wasn't quite as tall and broad as Nathan, but the man was hot. Why hadn't she contemplated a fling with him?

You know why, her inner voice mocked her. Ryder didn't make her heart race and her lungs fight for air the way Nathan did.

"Thank you. Meet me in the lobby. I won't be long."

He lifted a hand in acknowledgment as she scurried down the corridor before she encountered anyone else.

Once she reached her room, she threw on black slacks, added a long-sleeved deep purple blouse, and gathered her hair into a messy ponytail. She stuffed her clothes and toiletries in her suitcase in a haphazard manner that she knew she'd regret later.

Her phone trilled from deep inside her tote bag.

She froze at the sound, her stomach doing a nervous flip. What if it was Nathan? What would she say?

When the ringing stopped, she pawed through the bag to see who'd tried to reach her. Relief loosened her shoulders when she saw the missed call was from Victor Pierron, not Nathan. There were also three missed calls yesterday from Catalina.

No messages.

Emily frowned. She'd told Catalina to ditch her phone so Daniel wouldn't have a way to trace her. She hit redial, ready to lecture the girl over her carelessness. Madame Légère needed to know as well. Her call went unanswered.

Emily glanced at the time. She did not want to chance running into Nathan. Her emotions were too raw, too scattered to handle seeing him and pretend last night hadn't shaken her to her core. She'd call Catalina again once she was on the train.

Her phone rang again before she could stow it back in her bag. *Victor Pierron*. She tucked it between her ear and shoulder and zipped her suitcase. "Good morning, Inspector."

"Mademoiselle Dane. Where are you?" Inspector Pierron's voice held an undercurrent of urgency that lifted the hairs on Emily's neck.

"I'm in Scotland. Why? Do I need to come in? I'll be back tomorrow if you need to take my formal statement." She took one last look around the room before letting it close behind her, then wheeled her luggage down the hall to the lobby with brisk strides. Ryder stood waiting by the front doors.

"Stay there if you can. I've received information that Jules Mirga has discovered your identity and may be planning to retaliate against you."

Icy fingers clutched her spine. "How? And why would he bother with me? Shouldn't he be more worried about the police? Why hasn't he been arrested yet?"

Pierron ignored her rapid-fire questions. "He is a bad-tempered man with a long reach. Perhaps now would be a good time for a vacation, *non*? Give him time to forget about you."

Seriously? Would the inspector have given her that advice if she was a man? She wasn't going into hiding because Jules Mirga was throwing a hissy fit. She had a job to do. "What about Catalina and Maya? Are they safe? Catalina tried to contact me yesterday. She didn't leave a message."

"The girls are safe with Fondation Espoir. It's you I'm concerned about."

"I've just been on vacation. I have to get back to work." Her muscles twitched with nervous energy. Nathan could make an appearance at any minute. She needed to be on her way. "Inspector, Jules Mirga may be vindictive, but he's not stupid. He has too much to lose by threatening a political officer with the US Embassy. I doubt he wants to attract the attention of my government."

She was close enough to Ryder for him to overhear her end of the conversation, and, judging by the way his brows furrowed, he didn't like what he'd heard.

Great. Another overprotective male to deal with.

"I have to go," she told the French detective, "Let's plan to meet after I get back to Paris tomorrow morning. My train arrives from London at eleven."

Hanging up, she dropped her phone in her bag. Right now, the only thing that mattered was getting out of here.

"Everything all right?" Ryder asked.

"Fine." She gave him a breezy smile, trying not to fidget under his careful scrutiny. "A work matter. I have it under control."

He didn't look convinced but didn't say anything further as he took her suitcase from her. She followed him outside to his vehicle. The hotel grew smaller in the sedan's side mirror as he drove her to Thurso train station.

Emily sagged into her seat, her head resting on the window. She toyed with her grandmother's pendant and avoided her eyes in the glass. This was no tactical withdrawal. It was a coward's retreat.

Hopefully, the next time she saw Nathan, which likely wouldn't be until she went back to the States for the Christmas holiday, this attraction would be a distant memory, left in the Highlands of Scotland where it belonged.

Ryder parked at the station. Despite her protests that it was unnecessary, he wheeled her luggage into the station to a wooden bench mounted below one of the station's palladium windows. Her train wasn't due for another hour and a half, and the station resembled a ghost town.

"Would you like me to wait with you?" Ryder scanned the empty room.

"No, I'll be fine here." The look she gave him was polite but firm. "I can take care of myself." She didn't need Lachlan and Nathan's friend hovering to protect her from—she looked around—well, nobody, while she collected her scattered wits.

He hesitated, then gave a brief nod. "Goodbye, Emily. I'm sure we'll see each other again."

She gave him a cordial smile in return. "We do live in the same city after all, and now that we've met, we should do lunch or something. Thanks for the lift." It was the polite thing to say. Ryder seemed like a nice guy, but she didn't need to be spending time with Nathan's colleague.

The door closed after Ryder with an overly loud thud in the empty, cavernous space. Emily rested her head against the wall with a weary sigh.

Whatever had possessed her to take the train so she could experience the Scottish countryside? It was thirteen hours to London, where she'd spend the night, then hop on the Eurostar tomorrow morning for the two-and-a-half-hour trip to Paris. She would have been back in Paris by nightfall if she'd flown. Another rash decision she was coming to regret.

At least one of them she could put behind her here and now.

She pulled her phone back out and texted Bruce. *I'll be back at work tomorrow morning.* Her fingers hesitated over the screen, then tapped out, *I'm ready to take you up on that offer of dinner at Raphael Terrace.*

Nathan rubbed his hair briskly with a towel before he swiped it over the rest of his body and tossed it into the tub in his hotel bathroom. He brushed his teeth and pulled on jeans and a black AC/DC t-shirt. Images of Emily and their night together ran through his brain in an X-rated slide show that threatened to wreak havoc on his self-control. He put down his toothbrush and ran his hands through his hair, creating tousled spikes.

What was he going to say to the beautiful blonde in his bed? *Hey, when can we do this again?* She'd spent the night. That had to be a sign she wasn't ready to write him off just yet.

Emily had to be hungry by now. They'd go to breakfast and figure out how to move forward.

Easing open the bathroom door, he stepped into the bedroom and stopped short when he spied the empty bed with rumpled sheets. Emily was gone, the only remaining trace of her the lingering scent of her perfume.

"Not even a kiss goodbye. How rude."

Talk about the shoe being on the other foot. He was usually the one making a hasty exit. He grabbed his wallet and room key and stalked out of his room down the corridor, his movements jerky as if all his neurons were firing in opposite directions.

She didn't get to pretend last night never happened.

He knocked on her room door. "Emily? You want to grab some breakfast?"

Silence. He rapped on the dark wood again. "Emily, you in there?"

Still no answer. He paced away, then turned back, fist poised to rattle the door off its hinges. He stopped himself before it made contact.
Why was he going all neanderthal? Maybe she was in the shower or
had already gone to breakfast.

The morning buffet was set up in the hotel dining room. A brief
scan of the sparse crowd confirmed Emily wasn't there. He was supposed to take her to the train station in an hour. She wouldn't be able
to avoid him then.

Hell. He'd go for a quick run and work off this edgy, unsettled
feeling.

Back in his room, he threw on running clothes, laced up his sneakers, and headed toward the rocky shoreline of Scrabster Bay. Morning
fog obscured the nearby Orkney Islands.

The rhythmic pounding of his sneakers helped him gather his
thoughts. He hadn't been this distracted by a woman in a long time.
Emily had made it clear she had no interest in him beyond a fleeting
sexual attraction. And at first, that was all he'd thought he wanted, too.

Some casual fun between the sheets.

They didn't even live in the same country.

He jogged down the short set of stairs to the sandy beach. Lachlan
and Sophia's wedding had him thinking all kinds of crazy thoughts
about finding someone special and settling down. Maybe he'd let his
physical attraction to Emily develop into something more, something
it wasn't meant to be. She was a complication he didn't need, and not
just because she was Sophia's best friend. Even he knew better than to
cross Admiral Dane.

He ran another ten minutes before turning around. Emily might
be wondering where he was by now. The ride to the station should
be enough time for them to discuss how to behave moving forward.

Back at the hotel, he took another quick shower, then went to Emily's room.

Like earlier, his knock went unanswered.

Where the hell is she? Hands on hips, he resisted the primitive urge to kick in the door and headed to the reception desk in the lobby instead.

"Excuse me, ma'am."

The young redhead behind the counter looked up, her eyes widening as pink flooded her cheeks.

"I'm looking for Ms. Dane. Has she checked out yet?"

The woman's fingers tapped across her computer keyboard. Her brows furrowed. When she looked at Nathan, her smile was guarded. "Yes, sir, she checked out forty-five minutes ago."

Nathan forced his lips into a stiff smile. "Thank you." So, she'd caught a ride to the station to avoid him.

At that moment, Ryder stepped into the lobby, duffel bag in one hand, the other holding a garment bag slung over his shoulder.

Nathan lifted his chin in greeting. "Checking out, amigo?"

Ryder nodded. "Lachlan did leave us in charge whilst he and Sophia are away. I've got a meeting in Paris tomorrow with a potential client."

"Have a good trip." Nathan clapped him on the shoulder. "We'll touch base when I get back to DC." He paused. "You didn't happen to see Emily this morning, did you? I was supposed to take her to the train station." He had his answer when his friend's expression turned studiously neutral.

"I ran into her after my workout, and she requested a ride," Ryder told him. "She seemed rather eager to leave."

An unexpected pang of disappointment stabbed Nathan in the chest. He said goodbye to Ryder and returned to his room to pack.

Emily's message was crystal clear. Last night was a mistake. One he wouldn't make again.

He'd been a warfighter. A part of him always would be. And Emily had decided that someone like him didn't fit into her refined, cosmopolitan world of diplomacy and privilege.

Chapter Eight

The following morning, Emily stepped off the Eurostar train from London onto the platform, made her way through Passport Control and into the noise and bustle of Gare du Nord in Paris. She followed the crowd down the escalators to the main hall. The cavernous station had been built with an abundance of glass windows and skylights and was full of natural light from the sunny summer morning. People schooled around her like fish, chattering away predominantly in French and English. Her curious ear picked up a smattering of other languages that she instinctively tried to identify.

She'd spent the night in London at the hotel adjacent to St. Pancras station after the thirteen-hour rail journey from Thurso, so at least she'd gotten a few hours of sleep in a proper bed, a shower, and changed into tailored navy trousers and matching suit jacket over an ivory silk shell. Now that she was back in Paris, she slipped effortlessly into work mode, checking her phone.

Eleven fifteen. She might make it to work shortly after noon if she went straight to the embassy.

The conversation with Victor Pierron hovered in the back of her mind. She'd had over twenty-four hours to process his warning, and the more she thought about it, the less convinced she was that she was in any real danger. Mirga was probably huddling with his lawyers somewhere, trying to weasel his way out of prosecution.

Even so, once she got to the embassy, she'd reach out to the inspector to see if he had any more news. The last thing she wanted was for word to get back to her boss that she might be in the crosshairs of a Parisian crime lord. The woman would be on the phone with Emily's father before her office door closed behind her, and—Emily shuddered—all hell would break loose.

She also needed to get in touch with Madame Légère about Catalina and Maya to ensure they were safe. Catalina hadn't answered the phone or called Emily back after repeated attempts to reach her. Maybe that was a good sign, and it meant she'd done as Emily instructed and gotten rid of the phone.

Strolling amidst the sea of travelers, she clutched her purse, mindful of ever-present pickpockets. Tantalizing aromas of fresh bread and coffee reached her nose, and her stomach growled, a visceral reminder that she hadn't eaten this morning. She stopped at one of the shops lining the concourse and purchased a baguette and coffee.

A sudden blow to her side made her stumble, sloshing hot coffee onto her hand.

Ow! That burned. Someone gripped her elbow. She looked up to see a man in a navy pin-striped business suit with slicked black hair and dark eyes.

He let go and stepped back. "*Excusez-moi, Madamoiselle. Je suis vraiment désolé.* I'm so sorry."

She blew on her reddened skin as best she could with a coffee in one hand and a paper bag with her baguette in the other. A glance down confirmed her purse was intact, her suitcase unmolested.

Something about the man seemed vaguely familiar, but she couldn't place him.

She gave him a polite smile. "*C'est bon. Ne vous inquietez pas.* Don't worry about it."

Behind the businessman, a younger dark-haired man in casual street clothes hovered nearby. His flat black gaze sent a prickle of unease across the back of her neck.

"*Excusez-moi.*" She went to sidestep the businessman, and he moved with her, blocking her path.

"Emily!"

She whirled toward the sound of her name. "Bruce?"

Bruce weaved through the crowd toward her in a dark gray suit and purple pin-striped tie, waving his hand.

She glanced over her shoulder at the businessman. Both he and the dark-haired guy with the creepy stare had disappeared. Her body sagged from the release of tension. Clearly, Inspector Pierron's warning had her on edge.

Bruce reached her side.

"What are you doing here?" she asked. Talk about great timing.

"I thought I'd surprise you, so you don't have to drag your luggage onto the Metro or fight off all the taxi scammers." He took hold of her suitcase. "We'll Uber. My treat."

She took another glance behind her. "Did you see that guy standing next to me when you called my name? The one in the suit?"

"No, why? Was it someone you recognized?"

"No, he bumped into me."

"Did you check your purse?"

"He didn't steal anything." She tried to shrug off lingering unease. Her appetite gone, she took one bite from her baguette and tossed it and the rest of her coffee into the nearest trash bin.

Bruce ushered her out the exit, his hand resting on the small of her back. They were immediately bombarded by men trying to get them to take one of the many illegal taxis that scammed tourists with little knowledge of French and even less knowledge of how to get around

Paris. Bruce's arm moved to circle Emily's shoulder as he fended off the hustlers with a firm no and led Emily down the street a block away from the station where their Uber would pick them up.

Once they were away from the crowd, he removed his arm. "I may have had an ulterior motive."

She gave him a puzzled look. "Oh? What's that?"

"Discussing dinner plans."

That's right, she'd texted him while waiting for the train out of Thurso. "Not tonight. I'm whipped." As if to prove her point, a yawn snuck up on her and she lifted her palm to cover her mouth before shooting Bruce an apologetic glance.

Though if she was serious about putting Nathan behind her, she had to give Bruce a chance. "Sometime this week?"

"Just let me know the day." He pointed to a black Peugeot pulling up to the curb. "That's our ride."

Nathan unfolded his big frame from his main cabin airplane seat as best he could, taking care not to slam his head into the ceiling. At least he'd gotten the aisle. An hour before he was supposed to board his flight in London back to DC, Ryder called and asked if he could make a quick side trip to Paris to meet with the head of the Diplomatic Security Service at the US Embassy there. Ryder couldn't tell him much over the phone beyond that.

So instead of boarding his business class flight to Dulles, he found himself on a cheap-ass budget airline to Charles De Gaulle.

And instead of putting Emily Dane in his rearview mirror, he was showing up for a meeting at her workplace.

Ironic after Emily took off from his bed without so much as a *see you later*.

His mood soured. They needed to come to some agreement before Lachlan and Sophia returned from their honeymoon. Like it or not, they'd be seeing each other again, given that Emily and Sophia were best friends, so they might as well put their night of hot sex behind them and at least try to be friendly.

He grabbed his carry-on from the overhead bin and shuffled down the aisle, breathing a sigh of relief when he exited the plane and could stretch his back and shoulders. He texted Ryder that he'd arrived and headed toward Customs.

His meeting at the embassy wasn't until tomorrow. Today was as good a time as any to meet up with Emily. Of course, she might blow him off if he gave her advance warning.

A smirk twisted his lips. Imagine the look on her face if he simply appeared on her doorstep.

After grabbing a quick lunch from the embassy cafeteria, Emily waded through emails and sat through a mind-numbing afternoon staff meeting.

Inspector Pierron hadn't reached out to her again, and when she called him back, she got his voicemail. "Inspector, I'm back in Paris. Let me know if there's any new information on Jules Mirga."

She wanted to ask why the man was still free, but it wouldn't do to antagonize her one decent contact at the French Judicial Police. She left a message for Madame Légère at Fondation Espoir as well.

By five pm, she was ready to drag herself and her luggage home and get a decent night's sleep.

Bruce appeared at her cubicle. "Ready to call it a day?"

She gave him a weary smile. "I think I'll take a cab rather than lug all of my stuff on the Metro."

"Good call." He grabbed the handle of her navy suitcase.

They'd made it down the steps of the embassy's main entrance when Emily's neck tingled with a primitive awareness. She looked around, her gaze landing on the giant man with tousled dirty-blond hair, dressed in faded blue jeans and a black retro Iron Maiden t-shirt, who lounged inside the black wrought iron security gates. He ignored the curious glances from the embassy employees streaming past him, his icy blue stare locked on Emily.

Nathan. Her heart took off at a gallop even as her feet ground to a halt. What was he doing here? He hadn't shaved since the wedding, and the light brown scruff only made him look sexier, more dangerous.

Her body leaped to attention, her traitorous brain reliving the sensory details of his hands on her, the feel of him driving so deep inside she didn't know where he began and she ended.

"Do you know that guy?" Bruce's question jolted her from her staring contest and reminded her she wasn't alone. His gaze bounced from Nathan to her and back to Nathan.

Her lips thinned. "Excuse me a moment."

Nathan kept his gaze locked on Emily as she exited the embassy with some brown-haired guy in a gray suit and purple tie, her suitcase in his grip. She wore a dark blue pantsuit that was both professional and classy. He glanced down at his jeans and t-shirt. Another reminder that she was out of his league.

She looked over to where he stood waiting and stopped in her tracks, forcing suit guy to do a quick pivot so he didn't crash into her.

He took his attention off Emily long enough to glance at her lackey. The guy was giving him the once over as well, his expression and body language all "who the fuck are you."

A corporate suit—lawyer—if Nathan had to guess.

And he had the hots for Emily.

Emily's eyes narrowed, her lips pressing into a thin line. She marched toward him, leaving suit guy to follow in her wake, dragging the luggage.

"What are you doing here?" She glared at him, her light blue eyes darkening to blue topaz.

Like they did when she was turned on.

Fuck. He needed to forget that last part, as it was doubtful there'd be a repeat performance.

"Last minute business meeting in Paris." He made sure to keep his tone neutral and not let his thoughts invade.

"Emily?" Suit guy had caught up and was hovering over her shoulder.

She started like she'd forgotten he was there. "Bruce, this is Nathan Long," she paused, "the, ah, best man from my friend's wedding. Nathan, this is Bruce Fleming, an attorney with the embassy."

Nathan gave the guy a nod. Fleming looked in decent shape, but Nathan could beat the crap out of him drunk, with a broken leg and both hands tied behind his back.

The direction of his thoughts must have shown on his face because the lawyer went pasty and took a step back.

Nathan couldn't help the smug grin. He glanced down at Emily. The grin died with a shrug at her narrowed gaze and pursed lips.

"I thought we could grab some dinner." Maybe discuss why she'd fled the scene rather than deal with the fact they'd slept together.

"I can't." Emily's gaze flew to Fleming. "Bruce and I already have plans."

Nathan had a feeling that was news to the lawyer, but to his credit, he took the ball and ran with it.

"Raphael Terrace, right? Seven o'clock?" Fleming shot Nathan a triumphant look that made Nathan's fingers curl into his palms.

Emily patted the lawyer's arm. "Why don't you go on. I need to speak to Nathan. I'll catch a cab home and be ready at seven."

Fleming gave Nathan a wary look. "Are you sure?"

"She's perfectly safe with me." Nathan hadn't meant for his voice to come out as a low growl, but this guy needed to shove off before he forgot his manners.

"I'll be fine," Emily assured her, what, boyfriend? "Nathan is a...friend."

A friend who's seen her naked and screaming her pleasure. For some reason Emily's vague description of their relationship stung. As for Fleming, he wasn't her boyfriend, although Nathan was pretty sure the guy would be happy to audition for the part. Emily wouldn't have had sex with him if she were in a relationship.

"If you're sure." Judging from the look on Bruce's face, he wasn't happy at being sent away. "I'll see you at seven." He shot another glare at Nathan before heading out the gates.

"Bye, Brucie," Nathan couldn't resist calling after him.

Emily elbowed him.

"Ow," Nathan rubbed his bruised ribs, "what'd you do that for?"

"You know why—you were barely civil. Bruce is a friend."

"Bruce wants to fuck you."

"Nathan!" Emily's eyes rounded.

"What? It's true. The question is, do you want to fuck him?" He wasn't sure what made him ask, and in such a crude manner.

He wasn't sure he wanted the answer.

Her eyes narrowed on him again. "Don't be crass. And who I have sex with is none of your business."

"So you've made clear."

Anger, and, if he wasn't mistaken, a touch of guilt flashed in her eyes.

Shit. This conversation was going south fast. He sucked in a lungful of air to breathe calm into his body. "Why did you run?"

Emily wouldn't meet his eyes.

Then she squared her shoulders and lifted her chin. "Look, our night together never should have happened. But it did, and we need to move on, find a way to be friends for Sophia and Lachlan's sake."

His stomach sank at the resolve in her voice. "I agree."

It's what he'd come here for, right? To try and find a way to be friends with Emily. Because she'd never allow herself to see him as anything more. "Friends?" He stuck out his hand and slapped a smile on his face he didn't feel.

Her soft palm slid into his, and he tried not to remember how it had felt wrapped around his cock. "Friends," she replied.

"And, as your friend, may I call you a cab?" He took the handle of the suitcase Fleming had been carrying and fell in beside Emily. They exited through the embassy gates onto Avenue Gabriel.

Nathan spotted a lit green taxi sign atop a black Renault coming toward them on the street and threw up his arm. The car pulled over to the curb. He opened the back passenger door for Emily, then lifted her suitcase into the car's trunk.

"Maybe I'll see you tomorrow." He could see the no forming on her face and clarified. "My meeting is here, at the embassy."

"Oh." She bit her lip, her attention shifting to her lap.

He couldn't bring himself to tell her to have fun on her date tonight—he wasn't that much of a masochist.

He crouched to her level. "If we're going to be friends, Em, we've got to learn to be around each other without it being weird. Might as well start practicing." Was it his imagination, or did her lips tremble?

"You're right. Come find me after your meeting, and we'll...have a cup of coffee or something."

"Good deal." He shut the car door and stared at the back of her blonde head as the cab pulled back into traffic.

Emily had placed him firmly into the friend zone, and there wasn't a damn thing he could do about it.

CHAPTER NINE

An HOUR AND A half later, Emily stood in her one-bedroom apartment in the Marais district of Paris, examining her thin-strapped black satin minidress in the full-length mirror on her closet door. She'd paired it with a hot pink silk wrap and a pair of mid-heel black sandals.

Her gaze drifted to the four-inch Manolo Blahnik crystal-encrusted stilettos she'd purchased in a weak moment and was still looking for an occasion to wear. Given she was five-ten, they'd been a silly purchase. She'd tower over most men with them on, including Bruce.

I wouldn't tower over Nathan.

"Dammit." She slammed the door on her wardrobe.

Nathan had been a weak moment and one she wouldn't repeat. His sudden appearance at the embassy today shattered what little equilibrium she'd managed to regain after leaving Scotland yesterday morning.

But she'd handled it.

And Nathan had agreed just to be friends.

So why was she feeling so melancholy, as if she'd lost something precious she might never get back?

"Suck it up, buttercup." She stepped into her bathroom to apply her lipstick and glared at her reflection. "Best sex you ever had doesn't mean you won't find better." Tonight was about Bruce and seeing if their friendship could lead to anything more. She'd train her body not to melt into a puddle of goo whenever she was around Nathan.

Her apartment intercom buzzed, letting her know Bruce was downstairs. She dropped the lipstick, her phone, and mini wallet into a black clutch and hurried to press the button to let him into the building.

Five minutes later, he knocked on her door. His gaze swept her dress with obvious approval. "You look beautiful." He'd changed out of his suit and wore a pair of gray slacks and a navy blazer with an untucked white button-down open at the collar.

"Thank you." A sudden attack of guilt dropped her gaze to her shoes. "I'm sorry to spring our date on you like that."

"I'll take spending time with you any way I can get it." Bruce's quick smile faded to a guarded curiosity. "What's up with that guy, Nathan? He looks a bit rough around the edges."

"SEAL," she replied. "Well, former SEAL."

"Ah, like your dad and brother." Understanding lit Bruce's gaze. "For a minute, I thought something might be going on with the two of you."

"Nope." Her smile was a touch too bright. "Just friends. We were best man and maid of honor together at our best friends' wedding." She ignored the skeptical look on Bruce's face. "He handles cyberse-curity for Dìleas Security Agency, the company my friend Sophia and her new husband Lachlan started."

An awkward silence followed, broken when Bruce cleared his throat. "Well, shall we go? I managed to get us a private table on the rooftop."

During the twenty-minute cab ride, she told Bruce about Sophia and Lachlan's wedding, leaving out any reference to Nathan. They checked in on the ground floor and took the elevator to the rooftop terrace. It was still daylight, and the temperature had cooled slightly to the mid-seventies with a light breeze. Large concrete planters with ornamental trees and neatly trimmed bushes covered the terrace giving it a garden-like atmosphere. They were seated at a small square table next to the decorative black wrought iron fence border with a view of the Eiffel Tower.

It was a nice view, even for someone who lived in Paris and saw the famous landmark daily. Emily didn't want to consider how much it had cost Bruce to secure it. Her stomach gave a nervous flip. *You opened the door to this date. Give him a chance.*

She unfolded her napkin and placed it in her lap. "Have you heard anything from your legal contacts about the police investigation into Jules Mirga? I can't believe they haven't arrested him yet. I left a message for Madame Légère at Fondation Espoir to check on Catalina and Maya, the two girls I brought to the police—"

"Emily." Bruce's hand had crept across the table while she spoke. He gave her fingers a gentle squeeze. "For once, leave work at the office."

Emily stiffened at the gentle rebuke.

His gaze softened. "Let's get to know each other, really know each other."

"Sorry." She gave him an apologetic smile. It shouldn't be that hard to find something else to discuss besides work.

The waiter approached with their bottle of wine. Emily took an obligatory sniff of the cork and a sip before pronouncing the wine acceptable, and after the waiter poured, they ordered their meals.

"I talked your ear off in the cab about my friend's wedding. It's your turn."

She listened politely as Bruce talked about the embassy basketball league he played in and his favorite pastry shop near his apartment that made fantastic chocolate croissants. His hands waved in the air while he spoke. She'd never noticed how pale and smooth they were, free of scars and calluses. His nails looked so neatly filed and buffed she had to wonder if he visited a salon.

So different from the rougher, tanned skin of Nathan's hands.

"Emily."

She gave a guilty start. "Hmmm?"

"I asked if you have a favorite hole-in-the-wall type restaurant in your neighborhood that's your go-to for weeknight dinners."

She pursed her lips and gave it some thought. "There's a really good crêpe place that most tourists pass by because it's not fancy. And one street over from my apartment building, there's a restaurant that I swear makes the best falafel in all of Paris." Honestly, it was a good thing she did so much walking because the food was amazing.

The waiter arrived with their dinner, and they fell into an easy conversation about their favorite foods and then moved on to favorite museums. The lights of the Eiffel Tower twinkled in the distance, and a cool breeze kept the humidity down.

It was lovely. Nice and normal.

Emily yawned.

She slapped a hand over her mouth and gave Bruce a wide-eyed look. "Sorry. I'm just tired from my trip."

Before Bruce could respond, Emily's clutch began to ring. She fished her phone out and glanced at the screen. *Madame Légère.*

"Don't answer." A strained smile accompanied Bruce's request.

"I'm sorry." She bit her lip. "I need to take this."

"*Bonsoir* Madame Légère."

"Emily, I'm glad I reached you. Have you heard from Catalina?"

The concern threading the social worker's voice had Emily sitting straight in her chair. "She tried calling me over the weekend, but I was out of town. I've left her several messages." Her stomach cramped. "What happened?"

"She left the house in Orleans, where we had placed her and Maya. I believe she may have been in touch with Daniel."

Emily mouthed a silent curse. "I told her to get rid of her phone so he couldn't track her down. I can look for her. I know where Daniel pimps out his girls." She ignored Bruce's heavy sigh across the table.

"I have people searching, but no luck so far," Madame Légère said. "You realize if she's gone back to the streets, we cannot force her to leave."

"I refuse to believe she returned voluntarily. She wanted out too badly." Emily fidgeted, her muscles bunching with the need to act. "Please call me if you find out anything." She hung up.

"You're not going to leave this alone, are you."

Her shoulders drooped at the disappointment in Bruce's voice. She let him read the answer in her eyes.

He gave a defeated sigh. "Dessert?"

When she shook her head, he summoned the waiter for the check.

In the cab on the way back to her apartment he reached for her hand, and she let him. His grip was warm and comfortable, but it didn't make her heart race.

She waited until they were in the lobby of her building to let him know their evening together was at an end. "Thank you for dinner. I had a nice time, and I'm sorry about the phone call."

Guilt stabbed her at the disappointment on his face.

He stepped into her, his arm snaking about her waist. Emily watched his lips descend, then closed her eyes as their mouths joined. The kiss was pleasant, but it didn't set her body on fire like Nathan's kisses.

Pulling away, she gave Bruce an apologetic smile. "My trip is catching up to me. I'm exhausted."

"Get some sleep. I'll see you tomorrow." His lips touched hers again in a brief kiss. He waited until she'd unlocked the main doors with her fob and stepped inside before leaving.

Emily took the elevator to the fourth floor. She *was* exhausted but couldn't sleep until she'd spent some time looking for Catalina. She changed into jeans and a plain navy v-neck t-shirt and covered her hair with a blue patterned scarf. Even though the sun had set, she couldn't run the risk of Daniel or any of Jules Mirga's goons recognizing her.

Donning a lightweight black blazer, she slipped into a pair of black flats, transferred her folding baton, phone, and wallet to a cross-body purse, and headed for the Metro.

She started in the Quartier Pigalle, strolling along Boulevard de Clichy, where she'd picked up Catalina and Maya. She approached some working girls as unobtrusively as possible and showed them Catalina's picture on her phone. No one had seen the girl.

After two hours, exhausted and dispirited, she decided to call it a night. She'd start again tomorrow after work. If Catalina were back, someone had to have seen her.

The overhead lights inside the concrete tunnels of Pigalle Metro station cast a fluorescent glare over the sparse late night crowd of mostly tourists as Emily trudged to the number twelve line toward Madeleine. When the train doors slid open, she took a seat, casting furtive peeks at her travel companions. There were no signs of anyone skulking around, paying her more than a passing glance.

A girl in her late teens scurried onto the car as the doors closed. Dressed in slim black jeans and a red tank, her long black hair cascaded below her shoulders. Kohl and several coats of mascara rimmed her large brown eyes.

Her gaze landed on Emily, and she smiled shyly before taking the seat next to her.

Emily smiled back and resisted the urge to move. There were plenty of open seats. Why had the girl sat right beside her?

Maybe she felt safer being near someone.

Or she was a pickpocket.

Emily pressed her purse closer to her side with her elbow.

"Mademoiselle Dane, you are Emily Dane, *non*?" The girl's heavily accented French reminded her of Catalina.

Emily stiffened and took a closer look at the girl. "How do you know my name?"

The girl shifted closer. Her voice dropped to a low whisper. "I know what happened to Catalina."

Emily's breath caught. "Tell me."

"Daniel contacted Catalina. He told her he loved her and begged her to return to Paris." The teen licked her lips and briefly scanned the other passengers before returning her gaze to Emily. "He went to pick her up."

Shadows filled the girl's eyes. "She should have stayed away."

The train entered Saint-Georges station and slowed to a stop. The girl stood.

"Don't go." Emily grabbed her arm. "Where is she? Where is Catalina?"

The girl shook off Emily's grip and bolted through the opening doors.

"Wait." Emily lurched to her feet and ran after the girl. A flash of red caught her eye. She followed it, breaking into a jog, dodging exiting passengers as she tried to close the gap between her and the girl up the stairs and onto the street.

The girl halted next to a black BMW SUV parked down the street from a crowded outdoor restaurant.

Emily slowed to a walk, her hands outstretched. "I just want to ask you some questions, that's all."

The girl sent her a look of regret that made tiny hairs on the back of Emily's neck stand on end.

Too late. Hard metal pushed into her back. She froze.

Something pricked her neck before a firm hand gripped her shoulder, hot breath bathing her ear. "Jules wants you alive, but if you make a scene, I'll make you wish you were dead."

The driver's door opened on the BMW. A giant, muscled man as big as Nathan with shoulder-length black hair, a beard, and dark eyes rounded the front. He handed the girl some cash. "*Allez*, get lost."

The teen disappeared back into the bowels of the Metro station.

Emily breathed in calm. She was on a street full of people, and she had her baton. The idiot holding a gun to her side was unlikely to shoot her in front of everyone. He was probably counting on her being too scared to resist.

He didn't know her.

Her knees buckled as the street tilted sideways. The world spun.

The man behind her caught her. "*Chère*, do you not feel well?"

Emily's head felt unmoored from her neck. Goosebumps broke out on her skin. "I tha somtng won, wat you do?" Her tongue was too thick to form words.

The big man chuckled. "Eh, she's drunk. I told you we shouldn't have ordered that second bottle of wine. Let's get her home." He moved to her other side and grabbed her arm, lifting her to her feet.

Emily tried to twist out of their grasp, finger-jab them in the eyes. Something, anything, but her arms wouldn't work. Adrenaline surged, battling the drug trying to shut down her body.

Her flats scraped the sidewalk as the men sandwiched her between them and walked her to the SUV. The big man lifted her into the back seat, where she collapsed in a boneless heap.

Help! Her brain screamed, but nothing came from her mouth. Face pressed against the black leather, she felt the vehicle sway as it surged forward.

Then, nothing.

Nathan took a seat next to Ryder and glanced around the office of Special Agent Richard Goodwin, the Bureau of Diplomatic Security's Regional Security Officer assigned to the US Embassy in Paris. The office wasn't large, but it was private. Morning sun streamed through the six-paned window that overlooked the embassy's interior court-yard gardens. The wall on Goodwin's right held the obligatory framed photos of the President and the Secretary of State. The guy had a nice desk, solid wood—mahogany from the looks of it—with matching dark wood bookcases lining one of the interior walls.

"How can Dìleas be of service, Agent Goodwin?" Ryder asked.

Nathan tugged on the light blue and navy patterned tie Ryder had insisted he wear. It was a good thing he'd packed some nice gray trousers and a navy blazer for Lachlan and Sophia's rehearsal dinner. The sooner he got out of them and back into jeans and a t-shirt, the better. "We were surprised to get your call."

Goodwin was in his late-forties, with tight black curls trimmed close to his head, intelligent dark brown eyes, and a demeanor that advertised him as former military. He raked both Nathan and Ryder with a steely-eyed look. Nathan knew the man had assessed them and made a judgment call on their worthiness. "I have reason to believe a criminal organization in Paris is falsifying US passports to shuttle trafficked women and girls between the United States and Europe."

Nathan exchanged a puzzled glance with Ryder before turning back to Goodwin. "You have security specialists here at the embassy that can investigate the source of the forgeries."

Goodwin nodded. "I do." He leaned forward, arms on his desk. "Given the quality, we think someone inside the embassy is involved. Unfortunately, my people haven't been able to identify the culprit."

"You think you can't trace the source because someone on the inside is working against you?" Ryder said.

"I'm conducting my own investigation of both US and local embassy personnel." Goodwin's chair creaked as he leaned back and steepled his fingers, his face set in grim lines of determination. "This goes beyond human trafficking. We believe the women are used as mules to transport drugs and cash. It's a very lucrative operation, and, given the potential for bribery, I want someone from the outside to see if they can identify the forger."

"How did you hear about us?" Nathan knew from Ryder that Goodwin had gotten Ryder's phone number after contacting Dìleas's Virginia office and speaking to Penny.

Goodwin gave Nathan a faint smile. "I served under Admiral Dane."

"You were a SEAL." Nathan's brows rose. That explained a lot.

"Team Three. The admiral said you also served under him and had the technological savvy to do the job. Plus, you already have the necessary security clearances through your company, so we won't waste time I don't have." Goodwin pushed a folder across the desk to Nathan.

"You'll report directly to me. For obvious reasons, no one can know what you're doing. I don't want our forger getting spooked."

Nathan took the folder. "Our president and senior vice-president are on their honeymoon, but I'll ask Penny, our office manager in DC, to forward a contract listing the scope of work and our fees."

The agent stood, bringing Nathan and Ryder to their feet. "I've got another meeting to get to, gentlemen, if you'll excuse me."

Nathan shook hands with Goodwin. "We'll get you some answers."

"I'm sure you will." The agent walked them to the door. "One other thing; the man we believe is behind this operation is named Jules Mirga. The French police have dragged their feet investigating him. I suspect he has friends in the right places. Check with the political officer assigned to monitor sex trafficking in the region. I believe she's compiled a dossier on the man. It should save you some time." Goodwin glanced at Nathan. "If you worked under the admiral, you may have met her. She's the admiral's daughter, Emily Dane."

Nathan choked.

Ryder slapped him on the back. "You all right, mate? Tie too tight?" Amusement brightened Ryder's eyes.

Nathan sent his friend a dirty look before returning his attention to Goodwin. "Yessir. We're acquainted. I'll check in with her."

He and Ryder said goodbye to Goodwin and headed down the corridor toward the staircase that would take them to the main atrium lobby.

Nathan waited until they were out of earshot. "God hates me."

Ryder's lips twitched. "Or, God has a sense of humor." He glanced at his watch. "As much as I'd love to see this reunion, I have a video conference at eleven with a contact in London."

"Coward," Nathan muttered. "I'll see you back at your place later."

Ryder gave him a brief salute and took the stairs.

Nathan kept going down the hall until he found a young female embassy staffer. A wave of his guest badge, along with the infamous Long smile and an extra helping of his Texas accent, and Nathan had the location of Emily's office on the fourth floor.

He took the elevator up two floors and strolled past cubicles, searching for a familiar blonde head.

"Can I help you?" A pretty brunette wearing a short brown skirt and cream top stepped into his path and batted her big blue eyes at him.

Nathan pegged her as a perky summer college intern from some ivy league school. He waited while her gaze slow-walked up his body to his face. When she reached his eyes, he gave her a polite smile. "Yes, ma'am, I'm looking for Emily Dane."

The young woman's face fell. She pointed to a cubicle down the row of cubicles against the exterior wall. "Her desk is over there. But I haven't seen her come in yet. I know she missed our section meeting." Her voice lowered to a conspiratorial whisper. "The minister was not pleased."

Nathan frowned at the unexpected news. "If you don't mind, I'm going to leave a note on her desk."

"Sure, go ahead." The intern returned to a table in the center of the room with stacks of papers arranged in neat piles.

Nathan stepped into Emily's office space, scanning for any information on her desk or pinned to the blue wall panel behind it that would provide an answer as to her whereabouts. A nagging sense of unease tightened his shoulders. There was probably a perfectly reasonable explanation for why she wasn't at work and missed a meeting. Maybe she didn't feel well and had called in sick or had a meeting out of the office she'd forgotten to tell her boss about.

"What are you doing here?" Emily's lawyer friend glared at him from the other side of a short set of cabinets.

"I had a business meeting in the embassy." Nathan straightened. "Where's Emily?"

Fleming's jaw tightened. "I don't know. I haven't seen her since dinner last night." The lawyer didn't look too smug, so maybe the date hadn't gone as well as he had hoped.

The thought almost made Nathan smile.

He looked around at the other embassy employees seated at their desks. "How does no one know where she is?"

"Emily has a bad habit of going off and doing her own thing." Bruce let out a weary sigh. "She mentioned something last night about going out to look for one of the girls she rescued who may have gone back to her pimp."

Nathan whipped out his phone and pressed Emily's number.

"Visitors aren't supposed to bring electronics into the building."

He ignored Fleming's public service announcement. Emily's number rang and eventually went to voicemail. He hung up and typed out a text. *Call me. It's urgent.*

"If she went to look for this girl, I need your best guesses, Fleming, as to where she might be."

The lawyer paled. "Check the Quartier Pigalle. The Bois de Boulogne is another area. It's on the western edge of Paris. A lot of sex workers set up shop there." He paused. "Emily picked the girls up from Boulevard de Clichy. You might want to start there."

"Jesus," Nathan swore, "are you telling me she's been to all these places on her own?" Emily was taking a considerable risk approaching trafficked women alone with no one watching her six. Rushing off to save the day on her own could get her killed.

Like it had Joe.

Don't go there. The memory waited in the wings ready to take center stage and remind him of his failures.

Fleming nodded. "She was determined to collect enough evidence to get the French police to arrest Jules Mirga, the head of the criminal organization responsible for most of the sex trafficking in the Paris region."

"Jules Mirga." Nathan's blood chilled. Emily was chasing the same man Special Agent Goodwin believed was running a drug and money laundering operation between Europe and the US using trafficked women.

"Son of a bitch." Did she even know what kind of man she was up against? Mirga had money and connections and wouldn't hesitate to eliminate any obstacle in his path, including a US Embassy employee sticking her nose into his business.

The lawyer shot Nathan an anxious glance. "She wouldn't let it go. Do you think she's in trouble?"

Emily was in more danger than she realized. Nathan needed to find her. Now.

Sweat coated his forehead and his pulse took off on a fifty-yard dash. He rattled off his cell phone number to Fleming. "Let me know if you hear from her."

He barely made it outside the embassy gates before he called Ryder. "We have a situation. I need your help."

Unlike Emily, he knew the consequences of acting alone.

CHAPTER TEN

FEAR JOLTED EMILY AWAKE, her heart racing.

Everything ached. Her throat, her head, her shoulders.

She coughed, her throat dry and scratchy. Was she getting sick?

Shades of red and black swirled into her consciousness. A girl in a red top. On the Metro. She'd seen Catalina.

Catalina!

Emily tried to surge to her feet. Metal dug into her wrists—cold and unforgiving.

Like the black gun that had been shoved into her back. The two men who'd grabbed her. Done something to her so she couldn't fight back. Shoved her into a black SUV.

The rest of her memories filtered in. The girl had led her into a trap. She'd been drugged and had woken up here in the middle of the night.

Wherever here was.

Night had given way to daylight. Now that she could see, she surveyed her surroundings. She lay on a bed, her arms stretched over her head and handcuffed to a black metal headboard. Her gaze traveled down her fully clothed body to the leather ankle cuffs that bound her to the footboard.

Relief made her lightheaded. If she could trust her eyes and how she felt, she'd been kidnapped and drugged but not raped.

Yet.

The white plaster wall in front of her was bare. Sunlight bathed the room from a tall casement window to her left. The sounds of city traffic seeped through the glass. The faint smell of roasting meat made her stomach gurgle. She was in a house in a populated area.

But where?

The creak of a chair shot Emily's pulse to the ceiling.

She turned her head toward the sound. A young black-haired male in jeans and a navy and red Paris Saint-Germain football jersey sat in a chair propped against the door to her prison, staring at his phone. His head bobbed to a melody only he could hear through his earbuds.

"Hey." Her shout came out as a hoarse croak. "Who are you?" she demanded in French. "Where am I?" She worked to keep her voice steady. Let them think she wasn't afraid.

The young man looked up, and she couldn't help her gasp. *The train station.* She'd seen him at Gare du Nord, watching her when the guy in the suit knocked into her, spilling her coffee.

Without a word, he stood and moved the chair away from the door so he could leave the room. She heard the scrape of a key in the old mortise lock from outside.

He'd locked her in.

Don't panic, think.

Her grandmother's pendant still hung around her neck, a comforting weight in the hollow of her throat. Her kidnappers would regret that oversight. One summer, when she was thirteen, her father had decided to teach her and her brother how to get out of handcuffs, flexicuffs, duct tape, and rope.

Lifting her knees, she dug her heels into the mattress and pulled against the ankle bindings as she scooted toward her hands. She needed to get the necklace within reach of her fingers.

The key scraped, and the doorknob to her prison turned.

Emily dropped her legs back to the mattress. Better her captors think her helpless until she could figure out where she was and how to escape. Getting herself out of her restraints would be only half the battle.

The younger guy had returned and brought with him the businessman from the train station, now dressed in slacks and a button-down gray shirt.

His gaze raked her with a sneer.

Emily shivered, her skin turning clammy. Now she remembered why he'd seemed familiar to her. She'd seen him in photographs next to Jules Mirga when she'd been researching social media and online news sources for any information on the crime lord. If she remembered correctly, he was Mirga's cousin and right-hand man, Constantin.

"Emily Dane." The mattress shifted beneath Constantin's weight. He trailed the backs of his fingers down her cheek.

She yanked her head to the side, her stomach curdling at his vile touch. "Get your hands off me."

He held her chin in a bruising grip as he forced her to look in his direction. His dark eyes burned with the knowledge that he had all the power and she had none. "You've cost my cousin a lot of money."

Money? If the police kept up the pressure on Jules Mirga, he and this jerk cousin of his and all their dirty minions would lose a lot more than money. "You and your cousin have ruined too many people's lives, especially women and girls. You should all rot in jail."

He let go of her chin and flashed a cruel smile before his fingers curled around the v-neckline of her t-shirt and yanked. The fabric tore with a loud ripping sound. He kept it up until the shirt hung open from her shoulders to the bottom hem, exposing her black lace bra and bare stomach.

His finger traced a lazy pattern over the swell of her breasts. "Jules and I planned personally to teach you the consequences of your actions. But plans change. *Quel dommage.*"

Bile rose to burn the back of Emily's throat.

"Such pretty flesh. I'm sure you will command a high price." He leaned in, his breath reeking of garlic and misogyny. "We have a client in Syria who collects women. He has a special interest in blondes."

Fear clawed its way into Emily's chest as the magnitude of his statement sunk in. "Do you think no one will notice if I disappear?" She willed the tremor from her voice. "That my government won't look for me? Your cousin is the first one they'll suspect."

Her bravado was only skin deep. What if no one realized she was missing until it was too late?

Constantin's fingers curled around her throat. "Where you're going, *chère*, they will never find you. Once our client is tired of you, he'll send you somewhere no one will think to look—if you are still alive." His fingers tightened until her lungs screamed for air and she fought panic.

With a brush of his lips over hers, Constantin released his hold and strode from the room.

Emily sucked precious oxygen through bruised tissue in harsh, desperate wheezes.

The bedroom door slammed, the sound a coffin lid on her future. She'd researched sex trafficking and understood the threat. She could disappear into a hell from which she might never return—beaten, raped, drugged, and sold multiple times until her trail was impossible to follow and she was an imprisoned sex slave.

She had to get away.

Before she disappeared forever.

CHAPTER ELEVEN

NATHAN SETTLED ONTO THE rooftop of a five-story residential building in the Paris suburb of Seine-Saint-Denis and tapped his mic. "I'm in position."

He peered through the scope of the MK 12 sniper rifle. Thank God Ryder ran executive protection for Dìleas and had the weapons and gear they needed because they'd had no time to waste. Adjusting the scope, he trained his sights on a similar structure across the narrow city street.

Residual heat from the day clung to the dark gray slate roof tiles beneath him, warming his thighs through the polyester and cotton rip-stop of the black convertible pants he'd picked up at a sporting goods store, along with a pair of black hiking boots that had good traction but pinched his toes because they weren't quite his size. The knit ski mask bunched above his forehead at the moment was courtesy of Ryder. Buying a face covering in the middle of summer to go with black clothing might have earned him scrutiny he didn't need or have time for.

If he'd known he was going from a wedding straight into a mission, he would have packed accordingly.

Emily's phone had last pinged from a tower near the Saint-Georges Metro station around midnight but hadn't pinged in the twenty-two hours since. With Ryder's help in the translation department, Nathan had jumped onto his computer and discovered everything there was to know about Jules Mirga.

Mirga owned several properties around Paris and its suburbs, mostly nightclubs, a couple of sex shops, and a catering company. Plenty of places to run his criminal enterprise behind a thin veneer of respectability. His home was a luxury apartment in Montmartre.

It was unlikely he'd taken Emily there.

Nathan had dug deeper and expanded his search to Mirga's family. They'd stayed in Seine-Saint-Denis, where they all grew up. It was a rough-and-tumble suburb of Paris with a high immigrant population, poverty, and crime. He found a building registered to Mirga's cousin and one in the name of a woman who turned out to be Mirga's sister.

The building across the street belonged to the cousin, Constantin Mirga, Jules's number two guy. From what Nathan could tell, he didn't rent any of the apartments out to strangers.

Which made it a likely place for Mirga to take Emily—if he still had her. If she hadn't already been smuggled across the border. If she was still alive.

He shut down the what-ifs.

He'd lie here all night if he had to. Hell, he'd stay here all week. Only Emily didn't have a week. They needed to have guessed right about this building.

Unbidden, chaos erupted behind his eyes. A mountain in Afghanistan. *"Cover and move!"* Bullets raining down. Joe Logan running. Missiles flying. Bodies vaporizing. The death spiral of an Apache helicopter and its crew. Joe's battered remains.

It had been Nathan's job to protect his guys and get them back alive. He'd failed Joe, and he'd failed the Apache crew. He'd failed the families they never went home to. He'd failed himself.

He wouldn't fail Emily.

Emily peered through her lashes at the youngest of her captors. Constantin had called him Sami. She suspected he also was a member of the Mirga family, although he'd ignored her attempts to try and engage him in conversation.

"I need to use the toilet." She'd been shackled to this damn bed since they'd abducted her late last night, other than the two times they'd allowed her to use the bathroom. They'd given her no food, and the only water she'd gotten was when she'd cupped her hands and drunk from the bathroom faucet.

Sami looked up from the movie he was watching on his phone. He stood and exited the room. She listened to his footsteps tread down the stairs, filing away all the details she could. She was on the top floor of a multistory house, judging from the slanted ceiling. How many stories she wasn't sure, but the brief glimpse she'd gotten out of the window showed her the roofline of the building across the street. Four, maybe five stories would be her guess.

The small bathroom was just past the stairs on the hall and contained only a toilet and sink. The first time she'd been allowed up, early in the morning, she'd heard the murmur of male voices downstairs, and the second time, later in the afternoon, a feminine voice was mixed in.

Emily's stomach rumbled with the remembered smell of roasted meat, butter, and garlic from the midday meal.

Sami returned with the big man with shoulder-length black hair, who Emily had secretly nicknamed Hulk. He produced the key to unlock her handcuffs and unbuckled her ankle straps.

"*Allez, vite.* Hurry up." He stepped back only enough to allow her to swing her feet over the edge of the bed.

She was tempted to lift her knee high enough to nail him in the balls, but her chances of escape were slim to none without a weapon and Sami blocking the door.

Now that her limbs could move freely, her circulation returned in what felt like hordes of angry fire ants rushing down to bite her fingers and toes. She rubbed her skin to lessen the pain and stood, examining the barren room. The only other furniture besides the bed was the chair Sami perched on and a large eighteenth-century walnut armoire.

By now, she could draw the intricate scrollwork on the armoire with her eyes closed. It was better than thinking about what lay in store for her once they decided to move her.

Her blazer, head scarf, and purse were nowhere in sight. Come to think of it, neither were her shoes.

Hulk grabbed her arm, leering at her exposed bra.

The realization of how vulnerable she was fluttered madly in her stomach and shortened her breath. She grasped the tattered pieces of her shirt together with one hand to try and cover herself as he man-handled her out of the room to the toilet. The door banged behind her. He'd be waiting on the other side. He had been the last two times.

She hurriedly did her business in case he got impatient and opened the door. Then she sat on the closed lid and allowed tears to form. The embassy had to know she was missing by now. Bruce would be concerned, and the police and the diplomatic security service would have initiated a search.

And what about Nathan? She'd told him to find her after his meeting. Would he assume she was avoiding him and had blown him off?

What if no one found her in time?

The door shuddered beneath Hulk's fist. Her time was up.

She opened the door and winced beneath his bruising grip as he frog-marched her back down the hall to the bedroom.

"You don't need to tie me up. It's not like I can go anywhere."

Hulk was unmoved. He grabbed her wrists and handcuffed them to the headboard.

"Can I at least have something to eat?" How long were they planning to keep her chained to this bed with no food?

He buckled her feet into the ankle straps.

"Is Jules ever going to show his face, or will he let his cousin Constantin do the dirty work for him?"

As if she'd conjured him, Sami stepped aside to allow Constantin to enter the room.

He pocketed the phone held to his ear. "You might wish to learn patience, Mademoiselle, and the art of keeping your mouth shut and obeying. Your new master may not be as tolerant as we have been."

Her mind searched desperately for a bargaining chip. "Contact my father. He'll pay a ransom for my safe release." Or at least he'd pretend to. He'd more likely personally assemble an off-the-books team of SEALs who would rescue her and eliminate Mirga and his goons all hush-hush so as not to tick off the French government.

Maybe Nathan would be on that team.

She bit her lip to the point of pain to hold back more tears. If she wasn't rescued in time, at least she had the memory of a fantastic night of sex with him to disappear into her mind when other men took her autonomy over her body away from her.

"Your father?" Constantin sneered, "Jules has no interest in setting you free. He wishes to make an example of you." His gaze raked her exposed skin. "Get some sleep. You have a long journey ahead of you tomorrow morning."

Emily's breath caught and held, refusing to leave her lungs. Terror danced in black spots across her vision. They were moving her in the morning.

She'd rather die trying to escape than let them.

"Tell Jules that if I disappear, he's a dead man," she called after Constantin as he walked to the door, "and so are you. My government won't stop looking for me, nor will my family and friends." She let her lips tilt in a knowing smile when Constantin turned around. "They won't play by the rules when they come after you."

Constantin huffed a laugh and didn't even bother to respond, clearly not intimidated by her threat. He exited the bedroom, taking Hulk with him while Sami resumed his position by the door.

Emily's thoughts ping-ponged around her head before settling on a course of action. Sami occasionally left the room for a few minutes to use the toilet or eat. The next time he did, she'd have to make a break for it. It was her only shot.

She waited for what felt like an eternity, then tried to mimic the slower, shallow breaths that signaled sleep. Eventually, her ears picked up the creak of floorboards as Sami rose from his chair. The door opened and closed. The key scraped in the lock.

Her eyes flew open.

Finally. It was now or never.

She dug her heels into the mattress and pushed her body toward her cuffed hands as far as her bound ankles permitted. Her fingers latched onto the chain around her neck, holding her grandmother's brooch, and she yanked, a shimmer of regret sweeping her as two of the gold links gave way.

Time to put her dad's lessons to work.

Brooch in hand, she thumbed open the clasp and grasped the pin. In a matter of seconds, her hands were free. Struggling to sit, she ripped the leather cuffs from her ankles. Escaping through the door was out. She tiptoed to the window, each step painstaking to avoid floor creaks, and peered out into the night, then down.

One, two, three, four. Five stories.

Sweat dampened her palms. She wasn't a fan of heights. She scanned the room for another option, finding none.

Heavy footsteps echoed on the stairs outside the door.

She was out of time. Her fingers scrabbled at the center latch, thick and clumsy. "*Come on.*"

Behind her, the key rattled in the lock.

She gave up finessing the latch and yanked, nails shredding, pulse thundering.

The door at her back opened, then hit the wall with a thud.

"*Putain!*"

She glanced over her shoulder at the man who'd cursed her.

Constantin.

Nathan banished the past back to where it belonged and scanned windows through his night vision scope. Families milled about the first three floors. The top two, however, he'd seen only men, about six different ones, their silhouettes tempting his trigger finger. He mentally cataloged every person on the street, any movement in the adjacent buildings, the angles of the shadows cast by the streetlamps, and from the sliver of moon overhead.

Movement in front of one of the top-floor windows drew his attention. He peered through his scope. A blonde, her form silhouetted by an interior lamp, tugged at the latches of the casement window.

Emily. Bingo.

A cold calm settled over him. "I've got eyes on target, window B five."

Fifth floor, second window from the left. Now he and Ryder needed to figure out the best way to get in and get her out with only the two of them, no backup, and no green light from a higher authority to take out hostiles.

Piece of cake.

A hand wrapped around Emily's neck and yanked her back from the window.

Fuck.

So much for a planned tactical entry. He radioed Ryder. "We're out of time. I'm going rooftop."

There was no time to break down his rifle. Nathan yanked down his face covering and slid his long gun between the straps of his knapsack, then rappelled down the side of the building, careful to avoid any noise that would alert the occupants to his presence.

Ryder took out the nearby streetlamp with a suppressed round.

Nathan clung to the shadows, darting across the street and into the alley behind Mirga's building. He boosted himself onto the back-courtyard wall and free-climbed up the edifice, using window ledges for purchase.

"Cover me," he whispered into his headset. If someone caught him in the middle of his Spider-Man routine, he'd have to rely on Ryder to have his six.

He hoisted onto the roof, placed his rifle and knapsack against one of the chimneys, then fashioned a web sling to anchor his rappel line before lowering to the window where he'd seen Emily. Perched on the narrow concrete ledge, his nine mil holstered on his thigh, he peered in.

A black-haired bad guy lay on top of Emily, pinning her to the bed. She struggled beneath him, her hands secured to the headboard.

Nathan's temper ignited, his mission calm eroding. He'd seen a lot of things that didn't sit well with him when he'd deployed with the Teams, but he'd never lost his cool. Canvas the room. Calculate the odds. Drive on. Adjust as circumstances required. The mission always came first.

But this was Emily. No one hurt Emily.

The man cursed at her in French as he pulled back his arm, then delivered a swift blow to her stomach.

Her pained cry colored Nathan's vision red. He grasped the side of the window frame and, with an angry snarl, slammed his boot into the center stile of the casement. Shattered glass and wood flew inward. He launched himself into the room, a predator locked onto his prey.

Dark eyes widened in surprise and dawning fear.

Nathan grabbed his enemy in a bear hug and held the man's gaze long enough for him to see his death before he wrenched his head with a violent torque. Vertebrae snapped, his enemy's face frozen in a mask of fear and disbelief before going slack. His limbs, lacking any direction, collapsed.

With a grim sense of satisfaction, Nathan dropped the body to the floor.

CHAPTER TWELVE

EMILY SHRIEKED AS CONSTANTIN flew backward into the grip of an enormous, hooded figure dressed in black. A snapping sound, like knuckles cracking, and her captor crumpled to the floor, a limp ragdoll.

She curled her knees to her chest and tugged frantically on the handcuffs chaining her to the bed.

Out. She needed out. Or she was going to die.

The intruder moved to the bedroom door, then back to Constantin, rifling through his pockets. He returned to the door, locked it, and tossed the key with a careless gesture. It hit the floor with a plink and slid along the varnished surface to disappear beneath the bed. The man's back and arm muscles bulged as he half carried, half dragged the antique armoire to barricade the entrance.

Emily tried to calm her frantic breaths and marshal her thoughts. She was chained to a bed, trapped in a room with a killer who could crush her between his giant, gloved paws with minimal effort.

Constantin lay on the floor, and judging by the faint odor reaching her nose, he'd lost control of bodily functions.

She clenched her teeth to hold back a whimper.

The doorknob rattled. "Constantin, *qu'est-ce que ci ce pass*?" Sami yelled. "What's going on?"

The killer yanked off his hood. Short, dirty-blond hair stood at attention, freed from the confines of the knit mask.

Emily's vision swam, relief so intense it made her lightheaded.

Nathan.

He pulled a knife from a pocket on his pants and pried open the handcuffs.

She breathed the familiar scent of ocean breezes mingled with testosterone-laden sweat as he leaned over her. "You okay, darlin'?"

Her own freaking superhero. She wanted to kiss him right now. "Good timing. But ten minutes earlier would have been really great."

Nathan's answering grin turned her brain to mush. He'd had the same look after giving her the first of many orgasms in his hotel room in Scotland only days ago.

Her ankle throbbed, her stomach cramped, men who wanted her dead were about to burst through the door, and she was thinking about sex.

Maybe she'd taken a blow to the head as well.

The pounding on the door intensified. "Constantin!"

"We gotta go." Nathan lifted her off the bed and set her on the floor.

Fiery shards lanced her ankle. She let out a gasp as it gave way.

Nathan grabbed her around the waist, keeping her upright.

"His attempt to make sure I couldn't escape." Her gaze darted to Constantin's body before fleeing to the safety of Nathan's broad chest.

A thud rattled the door, then another. The angry, desperate shouts grew in number. Hulk had joined Sami outside the door and brought friends. Another blow and the door gave way, slamming into the barrier of the armoire.

Nathan stepped through the splintered remnants of the window onto the narrow concrete ledge below it. "We're going out the way I came in, Spidey-style." His voice was a steady ship in a sea of turbulence. "I'm going to lift you. Put your arms around my neck, your legs around my waist, and don't let go."

"Nathan." He was insane. She couldn't breathe.

The armoire shuddered.

"Trust me, babe."

Nathan balanced on the ledge, one gloved hand gripping his rappel rope. He wrapped an arm around her waist and lifted her through the shattered window frame.

Her skin turned clammy. She squeezed her thighs on his waist, hugged his neck, and slammed her lids shut so she wouldn't see the five-story drop.

They were out of time.

Emily clung to Nathan like a sexy, long-limbed monkey. Feet braced against the side of the building, he used his rope to pull them the short distance to the roof and sat Emily on the edge.

"Scoot back."

When she complied, he hauled himself up and retrieved the rope just as the first head appeared in the window. The man shouted back into the room, then disappeared.

They might not make it down before the bad guys made it outside to greet them.

He balanced on the roof tiles and hoisted Emily to a standing position. Her face was pale and creased with lines of pain, her breath coming in shallow bursts.

"You're not going to quit on me now, are you, Princess? I didn't think your daddy raised a quitter." He needed her to stay focused, and if pushing this particular button did the trick, he'd do it.

Emily's chin tilted, her eyes narrowing. "Are we going to stand on this roof all night, or do you actually have a plan to get us out of here alive?"

There was his spitfire.

"Hooyah." He picked up his bag and long gun, slung them over his shoulder, and helped her hobble over the slanted roof to the backside of the building, his grip firm on her upper arm.

"Sit." He fashioned another web sling anchor on a back chimney and secured the rope before picking her up. "I need you to hang on tight."

Her arms circled his neck, squeezed like a python, cutting off his air supply.

"Not that tight," he wheezed.

They loosened a fraction.

"Don't fall." Pain and fear laced her whisper.

He fed the rope down the side of the building facing the alley.

Ryder's voice came through his earpiece. "I've got activity, C-1, over."

Shit. Hostiles coming out the front of the building, as expected.

Nathan touched his mic. "I need a distraction."

"Roger that."

Seconds later, a flash of light crested the rooftop as an explosion echoed from the front street. Chaos ensued—shouts of alarm, doors slamming, footsteps slapping the pavement in a frenzy of activity.

Nathan began his descent.

Emily's dark blue shirt was in tatters, her breasts, barely concealed in a black lacy bra, pressed against his chest. Her face burrowed into his neck, warming his skin with moist puffs of air.

He concentrated on fast-roping before he got distracted by the feel of her, missed a grip, and dropped them on their asses into the courtyard below. The second his boots hit the ground, he ditched the rope and began to run, his arms wrapped around her as he put as much distance between them and Mirga's men as possible. He set her down in a secluded, shadowed doorway a block away and radioed Ryder their location. "Hurry, amigo."

Two minutes felt like two hours before Ryder's black Range Rover, lights off, rolled to a stop in the street. Nathan put Emily in the back, tossed his gear in the cargo hold, and hopped in. He looked at his watch. Barely twenty minutes had passed since he'd first spotted her in the window.

In the back seat, passing streetlamps illuminated Emily's face in intermittent waves. Her hair was messy, her makeup smeared, and she looked exhausted.

He'd noticed the red smudges on her throat. Some fucker had choked her. His vibrant, feisty Emily looked defeated, vulnerable.

Anger, cold and deadly, iced his veins. He'd kill everyone in that house who'd laid a hand on her.

Had they...? His lungs constricted.

No. He wouldn't go there. Not now, at least. She was alive, and he'd make sure she stayed safe.

"Are you all right, Emily?" Ryder glanced in his rearview mirror, then at Nathan before his focus shifted back to the road. He turned up the heat in the car.

Emily managed a weak smile. "I will be now. Thank you, Ryder." She turned her gaze to Nathan. "Thank you both." The sheen in her eyes made his chest ache.

He gave her a reassuring smile.

"How did you find me? How did you even know I was missing?"

"I stopped by your desk after my meeting," he replied. "One of your colleagues said you hadn't come in yet, and you'd missed a meeting. Fleming showed up, and he had no idea where you were either. No one could reach you on your phone, and you weren't at your apartment."

"So the embassy knows I'm missing." Her body slackened in relief. "Did they contact the police?"

Nathan shrugged. "I have no idea what your bosses know. I gave Fleming my number, and he texted later that he was in contact with Inspector Pierron. That's all I know."

Her brows furrowed. "You weren't working with the police or the Diplomatic Security Service?"

"Nope." He shook his head. "The police and the DSS would have tied our hands, Em. I wasn't going to wait for them to get off their asses to investigate. As it was, I may have violated a few French laws to obtain the information that led Ryder and me to you."

She gave him a wan smile. "You did your hacking thing."

"Maybe." He allowed himself a brief smile before sobering. "I wasn't going to be tied down by operating within the law if it meant not getting to you in time. I read up on Mirga and know what he's capable of."

Emily shuddered, a shadow passing over her face that made his stomach knot.

"You don't know the half of it. You got to me in the nick of time. They were planning to move me in the morning. I think..." Her lips trembled. Tears glistened in her eyes, and he watched her battle to keep them from falling. So determined to be tough. "I think they were planning to smuggle me into Syria."

Fucking hell. Nathan's heart stopped before starting up again and trying to break out of his chest. He'd come too close to losing her.

She shifted in her seat and winced, reminding him that she had at least two injuries he knew about, her ribs from where that asshole had punched her and her ankle.

"We need to get you to a hospital."

"No." She shook her head. Her tousled hair batted her cheeks.

"Yes." He wasn't backing down on this one. "You need to be evaluated, and the police will want to collect…"

His throat closed up. He couldn't get out the words.

Understanding lit her face. "I wasn't raped, Nathan." Emily's words were soft but delivered without hesitation.

His lids slammed shut on a wave of relief that nearly left him boneless.

"But if I go to the hospital, it will trigger an investigation for which we can't control the narrative."

His eyes flew open.

She held out a hand, and he turned in the front seat so he could reach back and wrap her fingers in his.

"I'm pretty sure Constantin is dead. The French police aren't going to focus on the fact that you killed to save me. They'll go after you because you operated outside the law to do it." Wrinkles appeared on her forehead that he wanted to brush away with his lips. "We must get our stories straight before I go to the police."

"She's right," Ryder said, "We need to get the police to go after Mirga for Emily's kidnapping without ending up in jail ourselves. I know a private physician. We could have him come to my residence to check Emily over. He'll be discreet."

Nathan's spine let him know it didn't appreciate the game of twister he was playing holding Emily's hand, but he wouldn't let go until she did. "Mirga isn't going to tell the police he lost a man tonight because he'd have to explain how, and I doubt he's going to admit he was holding you hostage. Let Ryder's doctor examine you."

Emily bit her lip. "Okay." She released his hand. "Then we need to get our stories straight before I call the embassy to tell them I'm safe."

Ryder turned off the A3 and headed west on Boulevard Périphérique toward his family's vacation home in the Seventh Arrondissement of central Paris. He pressed a button on his visor to open the electronic gate guarding the entrance to the private courtyard and parked the Rover next to his "toy," a metallic blue Porsche 911. The SUV's xenon headlights bathed the sports car and the stone edifice of the mansion in a cold white light.

Emily's eyes were closed. She didn't stir when Ryder shut off the motor.

Nathan opened the rear passenger door and lifted her gently into his arms. She mumbled something he couldn't make out.

"It's okay, babe. You're safe. I've got you." He was rewarded when her body relaxed further into him.

Ryder led the way through the enclosed garden area to the home's ground-floor entrance. "I'll call Dr. Giroud."

Nathan tightened his grip on Emily and climbed the stairs to the second floor guest bedroom where he was staying. Emily didn't wake when he placed her on his bed. He watched her chest rise and fall. Listened to the soft sound her breath made in and out of her nose. Told the adrenaline still coursing through his veins to stand down.

Emily was safe, and she needed tending. He took the stairs to the kitchen.

Ryder sat at the small bistro table near the bay window. "Dr. Giroud will be here in twenty minutes."

Nathan nodded. "Where's your first aid kit?"

Ryder pointed to a bottom cabinet. Nathan pulled out an ace bandage, a cold pack, and the French equivalent of ibuprofen. He poured water into a glass and headed back upstairs to Emily. She looked fragile, curled up on his bed in her tattered shirt and jeans, her feet bare.

He sat on the edge of the bed and gave her a gentle shake. "Emily, wake up, darlin'."

Her eyes opened, cloudy with fatigue. "Nathan?"

"Sit up and take some pain meds." He checked her pupils for signs of a concussion, found none, and held the glass to her lips. "You can go back to sleep until the doctor arrives."

"Where are we?" Her words slurred.

For a moment, he pretended they were back in Scotland, and her condition resulted from too many glasses of wine rather than whatever hell she'd been through in the past twenty-four hours so he wouldn't punch a hole in the wall. She didn't need any more violence.

"We're at Ryder's. You're safe."

Once she'd swallowed the pills, he pulled back the duvet and sheet, helped her remove what was left of her blouse and trousers, and then gently took hold of her foot. Despite the swelling, her ankle seemed slender in his big hands as he secured the cold pack with the bandage.

He tried to be discreet as his gaze roamed her exposed skin, looking for telltale signs of abuse beyond the blows to her midsection and ankle and the bruising on her throat. He couldn't find any, and his chest expanded in relief.

She mumbled a sleepy thanks before fatigue pulled her under again. The bedcovers rose and fell in subtle waves in time with her breaths.

For the first time in hours, Nathan exhaled.

CHAPTER THIRTEEN

JULES MIRGA CLIMBED THE five flights of stairs in his cousin's apartment building, every step sending shards of grief into his chest to pierce his lungs.

He dreaded what he would see when he reached the top.

Constantin was dead. His beloved cousin, best friend, and trusted lieutenant in the business. How had this happened? In one of his properties, no less.

His older sister's boy, Sami, waited at the top of the stairs, his eyes wet.

Jules reached the landing and pulled the boy into a hug, gripping the back of his head. "Tell me," he hissed.

The boy tensed but didn't try to pull away. He knew better. "I'm sorry, *Oncle*. I left the woman for only a few moments to go downstairs for a cigarette break. She was handcuffed to the bed. Constantin went upstairs, and I heard him shout at her." Sami paused.

Jules squeezed the back of his neck. "And did you go to see why he yelled?"

"Not at first. I heard a thud on the floor, and then the bedsprings squeaked, so I thought..." Sami sucked in a breath. "I thought Constantin would prefer I not enter."

"You thought he was fucking her even though I forbade it." Jules loosened his grip. Constantin had been his second in command. Even though they were all family, Sami wouldn't dare go against Constantin's wishes unless Jules himself ordered him to.

"We heard a loud crash. Me, Hugo, and Pierre ran up the stairs. The door was locked. We called out for Constantin, but he did not answer. The armoire blocked the door. By the time we pushed it out of the way, the woman was gone, and Constantin lay on the floor." Sami's voice wobbled. "Dead."

Jules's shoulders tightened. He would not enjoy telling his Syrian contact that he'd lost his prize. The man had been most excited about the idea of possessing the beautiful daughter of a high-ranking American military official. He'd been willing to pay an extraordinary sum.

"Show me Constantin."

Sami opened the door to the attic bedroom.

Jules eased into the room, his nose wrinkling at the smell of death already taking hold.

Constantin lay on the bed, covered in a sheet. Jules grasped the edge of the linen, his stomach in knots. He prayed to the *Vierge Marie* for his cousin's soul, held his breath, and pulled back the material just enough to expose Constantin's face.

His cousin's skin was pale, almost gray, his black hair and lashes standing out against the lack of color. His head hung at an angle, detached from the spine.

Jules touched Constantin's cheek and recoiled at the lack of warmth. He pulled the sheet down further to expose more of Constantin's body. Besides his skin color and the rigidity evident in his limbs, his cousin could have been asleep.

Rage swept through him, a violent windstorm that nearly choked him. "Did you see the man who did this?" It had to have been a man. The American woman would not have had the strength to sever Constantin's spine in such a brutally efficient way.

"It was a big man, a blond. He carried the woman up to the roof and down again before we could reach the streets."

A soldier. One with deadly skills.

How had he found Emily so soon?

Jules drew the sheet back over his cousin's face. "Tell Hugo to bring around Constantin's car. We need to make his death appear to be an accident. And clean up this room. The police will no doubt be arriving soon, and there can be no evidence for them to find."

His informant knew better than to betray him. He had too much to lose. But Jules would use him to find this man, this soldier who'd stolen his prize and killed his cousin.

He would avenge Constantin.

CHAPTER FOURTEEN

EMILY'S EYES FLEW OPEN to an unfamiliar setting.

The girl in red. Cold metal bruising her wrists. Constantin's dark eyes and hot breath as he pinned her to the bed.

Her heart jackhammered in her chest, adrenaline shooting through her veins.

Diffused early morning light beamed through gauzy sheers covering a set of French doors that led to a small balcony. Elegant sage silk drapes flanked each side of the doors, stretching from the high ceiling to the white oak floor. The walls were off-white, in contrast to the white tray ceiling and the white bedding she lay wrapped in. Bedding that smelled like Nathan.

Her brain filled in the blanks of her memory, and she sagged onto the mattress with a shaky sigh. She was in Ryder's home. Nathan had rescued her from Constantin Mirga and his thugs.

She shivered, remembering how fast Nathan had moved. The brutally efficient way he had ended the threat against her. His strength as he carried her while rappelling their route to freedom. She knew what SEALs trained to do, but she'd never seen one in action.

That was late last night.

The last thing she remembered was Nathan waking her up, an older, gray-haired man next to him who introduced himself as Dr. Giroud. He'd kicked Nathan out of the bedroom and asked her questions before performing a brief physical exam. Other than some bruised, but not cracked, ribs and a sprained ankle, she'd come through her ordeal relatively unscathed.

Physically, at least.

She shifted on the bed and winced. Her ankle ached and was heavy beneath the covers. Sitting up, she threw back the duvet and sheet. She was dressed only in her bra, panties, and an ace bandage that wrapped her ankle, securing a cold pack.

Nathan. He'd helped her remove her destroyed shirt and her jeans. Her memory was cloudy, but she was pretty sure he'd also wrapped her ankle.

His touch lingered on her skin.

A warm, fuzzy sensation squeezed her heart. She squashed it with a mental high-heeled boot. Nathan had gone all big bad Navy SEAL and rescued her, which she appreciated, but she refused to play the damsel in distress.

Jules Mirga had messed with the wrong woman. He needed to go to jail, and she would help put him there.

Unwinding the bandage, she placed the now-warm cold pack on the bedside table. Her ankle was swollen but not too severely. Blood pooled in a dark purple swath beneath the bone, and higher, where Constantin's boot had landed. She stood, carefully shifting weight to her injured leg.

Sore but walkable.

Coffee first. Then she had to call into work and let them know she was okay and would be in later in the morning. She hobbled to the black marble fireplace in the room and braced herself before meeting her eyes in the gilt-framed mirror over the mantle.

Bird's nest for hair, raccoon eyes.

Her hand flew to her bare neck. *Nana's necklace.* Her most precious possession.

She bit her lip hard, blinking away a sudden surge of weepiness. Now that she was standing, her priorities shifted. Bathroom first, then coffee.

The bedroom door opened to a narrow hall. Emily found the bathroom, used the toilet, then washed her hands at the sink. She washed her face and finger-combed her hair into some semblance of order.

Nathan and Ryder were somewhere in this house, and she needed to have on more than underwear before encountering them. Although what she'd wear was a big question mark. Her jeans had to be nearby, and maybe she'd find a shirt in the chest of drawers or the closet.

She hobbled back to the bedroom and came to an abrupt stop. A short-sleeved fuchsia shirt and clean, black jeans lay on the end of the bed, along with a pair of panties and matching bra.

Her face heated, and a flash of annoyance tightened her shoulders.

Hers, if she wasn't mistaken, from her apartment. Of course, it wouldn't be a problem for a couple of former operators to gain entry to her home. Her sneakers sat on the floor next to the bed, complete with a pair of black ankle socks.

She glanced down at her swollen appendage. Even with the laces loosened, those might be a tight fit.

On the night table lay a golden pool of chain. Emily's eyes flew wide.

Nana's pendant.

Her spirit lightened as she ran a finger over the gold metal. Nathan must have grabbed it when he rescued her. The fact that he would even think to do that in the middle of chaos made the warm fuzzies rush back. She lifted the necklace and examined the chain. Someone had bent the links back into place so she could wear it.

Fastening the pendant around her neck, she dressed, leaving her feet bare, and limped down the central staircase to the first floor, the smell of coffee guiding her to the kitchen.

She took a moment to appreciate the elegance of the colonial blue cabinets, brushed marble countertops, and full-sized appliances, all finished in stainless steel with copper accents. She'd been too out of it to pay much attention to Ryder's home late last night, but this place had to be in the multimillion-dollar range. How did a former British Army soldier afford such opulent digs?

Clearly there was more to Ryder Montague than met the eye.

Nathan sat at a bistro table near a bay window, his long fingers flying over a laptop keyboard. He looked up at her approach and shoved back his chair.

She waved him away. "I'm fine."

He stood anyway and moved to a stainless-steel carafe on the kitchen counter. "Coffee?"

"God, yes, thank you. Cream and one teaspoon of sugar."

She settled into one of the chairs at the table. "What time is it?"

"Eight o'clock." He placed a mug in front of her.

She inhaled, her eyes drifting shut at the smoky, burnt chocolate smell of dark roast. "Mmmm." Her lashes lifted, and heat arrowed to her center at the carnal gleam in Nathan's eyes.

"I take it the coffee's good." His voice was a deep, sexy rumble.

She crossed her legs and squeezed. "Where's Ryder?" She wouldn't do anything stupid as long as Ryder was in the house.

Nathan's brows arched with a knowing look. "Gone. He had to run some errands." A roguish grin creased his cheeks. "You're perfectly safe with me."

Safe with Nathan? Hardly.

If only he didn't look so hot towering over her with that ever-present five o'clock shadow, black t-shirt stretched tight, and worn jeans that clung to his muscled thighs, and—

She averted her eyes.

"I need to call Minister Woodward and explain my disappearance." She sighed. "I don't suppose anyone found my phone and wallet?"

Nathan shook his head. "Your phone last pinged at Saint Georges Metro station the other night. I'm assuming that's where Mirga's men abducted you?"

She nodded. His direct stare had her chin lifting. "Say what you want to say."

"You shouldn't have been out there on your own looking for the girl, Emily. You put yourself in danger needlessly."

"I can handle myself."

His only response was a raised eyebrow, which irritated her because she knew he was right.

Not that she'd ever admit it.

Girl. Catalina. Her eyes flew wide.

"Oh, God, Catalina! I need to call Madame Légère and see if anyone from Fondation Espoir has been able to locate her."

Nathan threw up a hand. "First things first. You need some food in you. Then you need to call the embassy, and we have to work out our story for the police."

"That's three things first." Emily took another sip of her coffee and marshaled her thoughts. "Okay. How's this? Jules Mirga's men kidnapped me. You and Ryder were able to track me down."

She gave him a pointed look over the rim of her cup. "I'll leave it to you to decide what to tell them about how you procured the information on my location. Then you snuck in through the roof and spirited me away before Mirga's men knew you were there." She needed to protect Nathan and Ryder from any repercussions resulting from her rescue. "We can't tell them about Constantin."

"He hit you." Nathan's voice was a deadly whip of anger that made her cringe, his eyes cold as frost. "I don't regret what I did, and if I have to answer to the French authorities over it, I will."

He was the epitome of a protective alpha male looming over her, stance wide, arms crossed, an unyielding expression tightening his jaw. His attitude should piss her off because it reminded her of how her dad, and even her brother, behaved whenever she did something they considered risky.

But her abduction had shaken her, leaving her unmoored, and Nathan was close enough that she could smell his unique blend of sea and citrus. He radiated heat like a fire she could use to keep fear at bay, his body a solid fortress within which she could be safe for just a little while.

Frustration and desire dueled for supremacy, squeezing her lungs. Her hand crept to her grandmother's pendant.

She refused to be afraid.

Emily stood. Nathan didn't back up to give her room, so they were toe to toe. Against her will, her palms found their way to his broad chest. "Thank you."

For her nana's necklace. For killing a man to save her. For caring enough to put all his efforts into hunting her down and finding her before she disappeared into slavery and certain death.

Nathan's pupils dilated, his muscles tensing beneath her hands. "Em."

She knew he intended to kiss her before he lowered his head. Her eyes fluttered shut.

His tongue touched her lips, slid along the seam, seeking entrance.

She gave him permission and opened. He tasted like coffee and safety.

Their tongues dueled gently, not with the fierceness they had the night of Lachlan and Sophia's wedding.

He felt safe.

But never boring.

He pulled back, breaking the kiss before she was ready.

Regret shadowed his eyes. "You need food, darlin', and to touch base with your boss and the police. If we keep this up, you'll end up back in bed, and I'll be in there with you."

"I could use a bite."

Of food, Emily. Food.

He nodded. "I'll rustle up some grub." He went to the refrigerator and bent over to peer in, giving her a perfect view of his backside.

Emily's mouth went dry.

Ryder needed to return. Soon.

Three hours later, Emily was seated inside a conference room down the hall from Minister Woodward's office at the embassy, along with the minister, Special Agent Goodwin from DSS, and Inspector Pierron.

Ryder and Nathan had taken her home to change into work clothes and get her credentials before they headed to the embassy. The two men waited downstairs in the atrium lobby for Agent Goodwin and Inspector Pierron to interview them when they finished with her.

Minister Jaqueline Woodward sat at the head of the table, dressed in a tan blazer over a black shell, her frosted blonde hair styled straight and tucked behind her ears to hang just short of her shoulders. She listened, hands folded on the table, while Agent Goodwin and Inspector Pierron quizzed Emily on her abduction.

"Did you ever see Jules Mirga while you were being held?" Inspector Pierron asked.

"No," Emily replied, "but his cousin, Constantin, was there. I recognized him from photographs taken with Jules."

"Can you identify the location?"

Emily hesitated. "Not really. I'd recognize the room they kept me in. Nathan Long and Ryder Montague know the location."

Agent Goodwin scribbled notes on a yellow notepad. "And how did Mr. Long and Mr. Montague find you so quickly?" He pinned Emily with a curious stare. "We weren't notified you were missing until late yesterday afternoon."

"You'll have to ask Nathan and Ryder, but I'm grateful they did. Jules Mirga was planning to send me to Syria. This morning." A shudder wracked her body. She bit her lip to still the tremble.

Minister Woodward's finger beat a slow rhythm on the wood, a movement that had Emily's shoulders tightening because the minister only did it when she was irritated. She gave three final sharp taps and sat back. Her stare lasered in on Emily, her lips a thin line of disapproval.

Emily licked her lips and braced for the lecture.

"You've made a habit lately of disappearing from the office without letting anyone know where you'll be, which is why it took until late afternoon for your coworkers to grow concerned enough about your whereabouts to inform me."

"Monsieur Fleming contacted me," Victor Pierron added. "He thought your disappearance might have something to do with the telephone call you received last night from Madame Légère."

Emily's palms flattened on the table as she leaned in and locked gazes with the detective. "Catalina is missing. Did Madame Légère tell you? You need to look for her. She's in danger if she's back with Daniel. If Jules Mirga was bold enough to go after me, God knows what he'll do to her." Her fingers curled inward at the sigh forming on Pierron's weary face. "Did you even read the information I gave you? Catalina has been at parties where Mirga entertained high-end clients. She memorized names, faces, and details of the conversations between the crime lord and his associates. It's why I asked Fondation Espoir to move her and Maya out of Paris to a safe house. Why is Mirga still free?"

"Mademoiselle Dane," Pierron's tone reflected his impatience, "as we've discussed before, it is not so simple. There are many layers of individuals between Jules Mirga and the trafficked girls, the money, the drugs. Even with your kidnapping. You say you never saw him at any time. We would need to prove he directly ordered your abduction."

Emily opened her mouth to argue. "But I—"

"Emily," Minister Woodward cut her off. "Enough. You overstepped your authority with this project to free trafficked girls and gather information against Jules Mirga, and endangered your personal safety."

A primal scream of frustration roared through Emily's head, although she was smart enough not to release it into the world. She'd been trying to do something good, and she was having her hands slapped like a naughty preschooler. Everyone was so damn focused on rules and procedures rather than action.

The minister waved her hand in dismissal. "I think we've gathered enough information from you for the moment. Please wait outside while I speak with Special Agent Goodwin and Inspector Pierron."

"Yes, ma'am." Emily exited the room and closed the door behind her before leaning against the corridor wall, her stomach doing summersaults.

Everything she'd worked so hard to achieve hung in the balance. And Catalina was in danger, only no one but her seemed desperate to locate her.

The minutes ticked by, feeling like hours. Her anger and frustration morphed into a dread that tightened her muscles and poured acid into her stomach.

Finally, the door opened. Agent Goodwin stood at the threshold. "Come in, Ms. Dane."

She crept inside and resumed her seat at the table. A cold sweat dampened the small of her back.

Jacqueline Woodward's expression was no nonsense. "Agent Goodwin, the inspector, and I all agree that your safety in Paris cannot be guaranteed right now. I'm placing you on a paid leave of absence, effective immediately, until the French police determine it's safe for you to return."

Emily's throat constricted. "But Minister—"

"That's all, Ms. Dane." The minister's irritation was evident in the piercing blue gaze she leveled at Emily. "I strongly urge you to use your time back in the States to review the parameters of your job and your responsibilities as a foreign service officer representing the interests of the United States so when you return to your position here in Paris, you better understand your boundaries."

Emily's face flamed at the reprimand. "Yes, ma'am."

"Bring the gentlemen from Dìleas Security Agency upstairs, then make the necessary arrangements to turn your work over to your colleagues and book a flight back to the US for tomorrow."

Emily slipped from the room, her vision blurring. A paid leave of absence was better than an official reprimand on her record, but Minister Woodward's criticism weighed heavily on her shoulders.

She stepped gingerly down the grand staircase to the atrium foyer, mindful of her ankle. Her boss was sending her back to the States like a naughty child who'd broken the rules and colored outside the lines. All because she wanted to make a difference in the lives of some desperate girls and see a predator punished. It was ridiculous that her job required her to collect information on sex trafficking, but she wasn't allowed to actually do anything to stop it.

Nathan and Ryder stood at the base of the stairs admiring the Gilbert Stuart oil painting of George Washington. Nathan looked up and caught her eye. Whatever he saw in her face had him at her side before she reached the last step.

"What's wrong?" His crystal blue gaze narrowed on her, his jaw a hard line.

Ryder stood two steps below them, a flicker of concern darkening his eyes.

Her chin wobbled before she could suck it up and regain control. "Minister Woodward has ordered me to take a leave of absence and return to the States until further notice."

"Good. At least you'll be safe there." Nathan went to put his arm around her.

She shook him off with a glare. "How am I supposed to leave, not knowing if anyone will find Catalina? If she's even alive?"

Nathan didn't understand. He only cared about wrapping her up and keeping her safe. Just like her dad would do.

Oh, God.

Her parents. She closed her eyes as her stomach went into freefall. Wait until her parents found out.

"The minister, Agent Goodwin, and Inspector Pierron are waiting for you," she told the two men. "Remember, you never saw Constantin."

She turned, her spine a steel rod, and led them up the stairs and down the hall to the conference room. "Right in here."

"Emily." Nathan's fingers cupped her chin, forcing her to meet his gaze. "Don't leave the embassy grounds until we're done here and can escort you back to your apartment."

"I don't need a bodyguard." Right about now, she wanted to be left alone to lick her wounds.

If it was possible, the line of Nathan's jaw got even harder. "Too bad. You're getting one until you get to DC. Then you can do whatever the hell you want. Promise me you'll wait."

"Fine," she snapped. *Alphahole.*

She shut her eyes, inhaling through her nose to calm the tide of frustration threatening to drown her. It wasn't Nathan's fault she was in this position.

Of course, now he thought that gave him the right to dictate her every move. Her eyes snapped open with a glare in his direction.

He lifted an arrogant brow in response.

Gritting her teeth, she forced herself to rein in her temper and remember he and Ryder had put themselves in a precarious situation to save her. They needed to stick to the story they'd come up with. "Good luck."

They both nodded in acknowledgement, then stepped into the room.

CHAPTER FIFTEEN

"As I TOLD YOU," Nathan said, "once we narrowed down the property owned by Jules Mirga's cousin, we set up surveillance. After approximately two hours, I spotted Ms. Dane through a top-floor window and scaled the building, entering through the window to retrieve her, leaving out the way I came in to avoid detection and hostile action." He forced his body to remain relaxed as he recited the story he, Emily, and Ryder had all agreed upon.

He took a sip of the water Minister Woodward offered them when they came in. Even the conference room they were sitting in was ornate, with plush carpet and artwork framed in gold-leaf on the walls. The table was a rich dark wood, maybe walnut or mahogany, with matching chairs. It wasn't until you got above the public reception areas and the office spaces of high-ranking officials that the embassy took on a more barren government look.

"So you're telling me that you managed to scale a building, sneak in through a fifth-story window, free Ms. Dane, and carry her over the rooftop and back down the building, spiriting her away, all without her abductors' knowledge?" Agent Goodwin voiced the question in a neutral tone, but his eyes held a wealth of skepticism.

Nathan looked the former SEAL square in the eye and lied his ass off. "Yessir. We got lucky." He didn't think the agent believed him, but maybe he'd keep his opinion to himself. After all, Nathan had done what was needed to save Admiral Dane's daughter.

"How did you find the information on Jules Mirga and his operation so quickly?" the French detective asked. "Emily was barely missing for twenty-four hours."

Ryder fielded the question. "Dìleas Security Agency operates in both the United States and Europe with the appropriate licensing. As a security company, our methods and practices are, of necessity, confidential but comply with the laws and regulations of each country we operate in."

Nathan hid his smile. That was Ryder's polite, British way of saying *none of your damn business.*

It appeared to work because no one challenged him, not even the inspector, who Nathan would have thought would be up in their faces about taking the law into their own hands.

He took a good long look at the Frenchman. The man's shoulders sloped downward, he smelled of cigarettes, and he looked like a guy beaten down by life. He'd asked surprisingly few questions of Nathan and Ryder, letting Agent Goodwin take the lead.

This was the guy Emily had been working with to bring down Mirga? Nathan didn't want to judge but the guy didn't seem all that interested in the fact that an American and a Brit performed an unauthorized hostage rescue in his jurisdiction from the home of a guy that should be under investigation, if not already in jail.

"Well, gentlemen, unless you have any other questions for Mr. Long and Mr. Montague, I think we're done here." Minister Woodward looked at Goodwin, who nodded, and Inspector Pierron, who responded with a typical French shrug.

She turned her attention to Nathan and Ryder. "We appreciate your assistance in rescuing one of our employees from a tough situation. Special Agent Goodwin will be in touch if he or Inspector Pierron require anything further." She stood, bringing the men in the room to their feet.

"Ma'am." Nathan shook the minister's hand before she left.

The back of his neck tingled with the knowledge that he was under scrutiny. He turned to find the inspector giving him a speculative look.

"It's fortunate for the men who abducted Emily that they did not come across you, *non*?"

Nathan held the older man's stare. "Lucky for everyone," he drawled, trying to keep the sarcasm forming in the back of his throat in check. "We're happy to leave their apprehension to you guys."

He'd have been happy to kill every single one of them and save the police the time and effort.

Pierron nodded his agreement. "Perhaps you could convince Mademoiselle Dane to do the same." He lifted his hand in a tired farewell before trudging through the door.

Nathan stared after him with a frown. Pierron's parting comment had held an undercurrent of urgency to it that tightened the back of Nathan's neck.

Agent Goodwin picked up his notepad and pen. He speared Nathan with a knowing look. "The police aren't going to discover any dead bodies when they raid this house in Seine-Saint-Denis, are they?"

"I don't know, sir." Nathan kept a straight face. "Criminals like that lead dangerous lives. You never know what the police might find."

Goodwin snorted. "It might be time for you to head back to DC. You can work on your side project for me from your computer in the States as easily as here. Maybe if the police can wrap up Mirga and put a dent in his operation, it will spook whoever's forging passports for him. Ryder can handle any local follow-up."

"Yessir. I was planning to leave anyway and escort Emily back home."

"Good. Make sure she gets there in one piece." Goodwin's head shook back and forth as he walked from the room. "The admiral will have a cow when he finds out about this."

Nathan winced. *True that.*

He didn't want to be around to witness that particular family re-union. He'd escort Emily on the plane ride home, and if no one met her at the airport, he'd offer to drive her to wherever she was staying, then skedaddle so he didn't get hit by shrapnel when her daddy showed up. The admiral was intimidating as hell, but Nathan had a feeling his daughter could more than hold her own against the old man.

He turned to face Ryder. "I might ask you later to bring my stuff to Emily's."

Ryder's brow quirked. "You're staying with Emily?"

"You've seen the kind of trouble that woman gets herself in. Once we leave this building, I'm not letting her out of my sight until we get off the plane at Dulles."

A ghost of a smile hovered over Ryder's mouth. "I have an athletic cup you can borrow if you need it."

"Thanks." Nathan snorted. "I probably will."

Emily stared blankly at the acoustic panel behind her desk, her emo-tions drained, leaving her an empty shell. Since her dismissal from her meeting with Minister Woodward, Agent Godwin, and Inspector Pierron, she'd managed to book a seat on the one o'clock flight to

Dulles leaving the next day and sort through her research folders, leaving notes for Bryan, the colleague who'd be taking over her assignment while she was gone.

She'd lost valuable contact information with her phone. Some of it she could retrieve from the cloud once she got a new cell, but the rest would require her to piece together information from the notes she'd taken while interviewing Catalina, Maya, and some other girls on the streets.

On impulse, she slipped the folder containing her notes into her tote bag. She might be officially off the job, but unofficially, she planned to continue her investigation into Jules Mirga and his criminal enterprise.

"There you are." Bruce cruised around her cabinets and grabbed her in a bone-crushing hug. "I was so worried. Where have you been? No one could get ahold of you."

For a moment, all she could do was stare. Had it only been two days since she'd been sitting with him on the Raphael Terrace admiring the view of the Eiffel Tower? "I lost my phone."

"You lost your phone?" Bruce frowned. "Why didn't you come to work or at least call in? I even stopped by your apartment building at lunchtime, but you didn't answer. Then I called Inspector Pierron and notified DSS." His face puckered. "Nathan Long stopped by your desk. He was worried, too."

"He found me."

Bruce stilled, then crouched a bit to peer into her eyes. "Are you okay? Where did Long find you?"

She sighed. "In an apartment building in Seine-Saint-Denis where Jules Mirga's cousin and his thugs were holding me hostage."

The color leached from Bruce's face. "You went looking for that girl, didn't you."

Sparks kindled in her blood that began to burn away the numbness surrounding her. "Her name is Catalina. And she's still missing."

"Emily. You ready to go?"

Bruce stiffened at the sound of Nathan's voice behind him. "Where are you going?" He left off *with this guy,* but Emily saw it written on his face.

Her shoulders slumped. "Minister Woodward is making me return to the States until this mess blows over."

"And I'm making sure she gets there safely," Nathan growled.

Bruce's eyes flashed with irritation before he let out a dispirited sigh. "Maybe it's for the best." He sidestepped so that he was directly between her and Nathan. "I'll miss you."

Emily caught Nathan's eye roll over Bruce's shoulder and sent him a warning glare.

The longing in Bruce's eyes made her want to bolt, and the fact she wanted to run made her angry with herself. Bruce was a great guy and a friend, but he considered her fight for justice a sign of a rebellious streak rather than a passion to do the right thing.

And he didn't make her insides melt like—her gaze darted back to Nathan, who watched her with those crystal blue eyes.

One corner of his mouth lifted as if he could read her thoughts.

Her face caught fire. She threw herself at Bruce in a hug that was a touch too enthusiastic. "I'll see you when I get back." His startled look of pleasure made her feel two inches tall.

"I'm looking forward to it."

Nathan's jaw hardened but he stayed silent as Bruce brushed past him.

He reached around her and lifted her tote. "We'll get you a new phone, then grab a late lunch to bring to your apartment. I want to limit the time you spend in the open."

"Whatever." For once, she was too tired to argue.

She took one last look around her workspace, then followed Nathan through the maze of cubicles, saying goodbye to the other political officers and interns on her floor. Her throat swelled, making it hard to sound like she wasn't on the verge of falling apart.

Her colleagues' curious stares burned a hole in her back. She held back threatening tears and lifted her chin, her back ramrod straight. She'd be damned if she let them see her cry.

They could gossip about her fall from grace after she walked out the door.

Chapter Sixteen

Nathan inspected Emily's apartment on the fourth floor of an eighteenth-century building in the Marais district. Ryder had been the one to get into her apartment last night and retrieve some clean clothes while Nathan stayed with her, so he hadn't known what to expect.

It was quaint—if by quaint, one meant tiny. At least the high tray ceilings and tall French doors in the living room let in the sun and gave it a more spacious feel.

He eyeballed the room's only pieces of furniture—a dusky pink velvet couch, a small, oval marble-topped coffee table, and a floral accent chair in pastel pinks and greens wedged into the corner next to a non-working marble fireplace. An ornate mirror stretched to the ceiling over the fireplace mantle. In it, he could see that the lowest-hanging teardrops on the fancy crystal chandelier almost skimmed his head.

Add some drawers and hanging rods, and it could be his mother's fancy walk-in closet back home in Texas.

He lowered himself gently onto the couch and stretched his arms along the back. His fingers dangled over both ends. As a place to sleep, it wouldn't accommodate someone his size, no matter how hard he tried to make like a pretzel.

Really, the only place he could comfortably sleep would be Emily's bed.

And that was going to be a problem. This would test his ability to keep his hands off her.

He stood, taking three long strides to what would be considered a galley kitchen in the US. The space between the counters barely accommodated two people at the same time, especially when one was his size. White cabinets on top, a half-size stainless-steel fridge at the end, a sink and faucet, a four-burner glass stovetop, and a mini washer and dryer beneath the white marble counters.

He frowned. Who the hell did their laundry in the kitchen?

Emily had set a bistro table and two chairs between the kitchen and the living room, the tall, high-back chairs cushioned in pastel green. The only other rooms in the apartment were a bedroom and, presumably, a bathroom. She'd disappeared in that direction shortly after they arrived from picking up their lunch at the falafel place after a visit to the phone store.

Her brand-new phone lay on the counter.

Nathan glanced toward the bedroom door before picking it up and entering the password he'd watched her put in at the store before she set up her biometrics. A few taps later, he'd downloaded an inconspicuous app so he'd be able to track her more quickly in the future without having to hack into her account.

He cast another furtive look toward the bedroom as he set down the phone. It wasn't the first time he'd downloaded spyware on her cell. He'd done it to her and Sophia's phones a year and a half ago.

Emily had been less than pleased.

Tough.

He was going to keep her safe no matter what it took.

"Emily?" He strolled through the open bedroom door. Inside was a queen-size bed flanked on one side by a small square table and lamp. Two black framed canvases with color splashed all over them like a preschooler's art project hung over the bed. There were more tall casement windows with long, lilac-colored drapes for privacy. The wall opposite the bed had a built-in wardrobe and a set of drawers. There was no room for any additional furniture.

"In here."

He followed the sound of her voice to a narrow door on the other side of the closet. The door opened, and Emily stuck her head out. "What's the matter?"

"Just wondering where you were." He gazed over her head into the bathroom. Like everything else in the apartment, it was compact. A toilet, a single sink with a cabinet beneath it, a narrow linen closet, and a standing shower.

Emily's spicy vanilla scent wafted toward him. His body reacted instinctively, tightening.

A faint tinge of pink appeared on her cheeks. "It's only me, and housing is expensive in Paris."

He held up his palms. "Not judging. Just trying to get the lay of the land, such as it is." He backed away and returned to the living room.

Emily followed and went to the kitchen. She still had a noticeable limp but could walk on her injured ankle, which was a good sign. She took down two plates from a cabinet and grabbed some silverware, setting it on the table next to their takeout. "Wine? Water? I don't have beer."

"Water's good." He sat on one of the high-backed chairs and wedged his knees beneath the table. "You book your flight yet?"

She nodded, setting their places before returning to the kitchen and taking an open bottle of white wine from the fridge. "The one o'clock tomorrow afternoon to Dulles," she called over her shoulder.

"I'll book the same flight. I've got to get back to the office. Penny's been on her own for over a week now." He glanced over at the tiny pink sofa. "We need to rustle up something for me to sleep on tonight."

Emily returned from the kitchen with a glass of wine and a frown. "There's no way you can stay here. I mean, where would I put you?"

The bed was big enough for two, but he didn't think she'd appreciate that helpful suggestion, and if he had to keep his hands—and everything else he owned—to himself while lying in bed next to her, he damn sure wouldn't be getting any rest.

She eased onto the other high-backed chair. Their knees brushed. Emily jerked back, moving her legs to the side to avoid touching him.

He suppressed a sigh.

The bed definitely was not an option.

"I can sleep on the floor—I've had worse accommodations."

Hell, this was luxury five-star lodging compared to some of the places he'd hunkered down in when he was on the Teams.

He pulled the containers from the restaurant out of the paper sack and opened them, waiting until Emily had served herself the falafel pita she'd ordered before he pulled out the one with a mixture of falafel and lamb shawarma.

"That's ridiculous." Sparks danced in her blue-green eyes. "Go spend the night at Ryder's, where there's plenty of room."

Nathan said nothing, letting his stare deliver his message.

The sparks dimmed. She stared down at her meal. "I promise not to leave my apartment without you."

Yeah, she didn't like having her wings clipped. He knew that about her. She was damned independent. He supposed he should count it a victory that she'd agreed to stay put in her apartment until the flight out tomorrow.

But he wasn't budging on leaving her unprotected.

"If someone is watching you, all they have to do is wait for me to leave. Use your head." He didn't need to see her eyes narrow on him and her cute little nose wrinkle to know he should have left off that last part.

Nathan ran his fingers through his hair resisting the urge to tug on it. It was getting long enough to brush the tops of his ears. He needed to get it cut or suck it up and tolerate the annoying tickle until it grew long enough to tuck behind them. "Look, Em. I understand you don't want me here. Once Mirga's been neutralized, you can have your life back." He caught the tremble in her lips before she raised her glass for another sip.

"I can't believe the minister is sending me back to the States."

Was it his imagination, or were her eyes shiny?

"It's only temporary." He had no doubt that once Mirga was contained and Emily out of danger, she'd hightail it back to her life here in Paris, and he'd be lucky to catch a glimpse of her whenever she visited Sophia.

The thought dampened his mood. *Hell.* He needed to stop mooning over her. They weren't meant to be.

She turned down his offer to clear the plates and wash the dishes when they finished. He set up his laptop on the table, then texted Ryder.

We fly out a 1300 tomorrow. I'll be staying here until then.

Emily stepped from the kitchen, still avoiding his eyes. "You can sleep on the living room floor if the couch is too small. I'll see what I have to pad the floor with."

"Thanks."

She'd conceded. At least for the moment. He'd take what he could get.

"I've got several phone calls to make now that I have a phone again, and I need to pack," she said. "I'll be in the bedroom so you can work here in peace." She grabbed the tote she'd carried home from her office and disappeared into the bedroom.

"Put some ice on that ankle while you're on the phone," he called after her and was rewarded with a gusty sigh.

Emily re-emerged and hobbled to the kitchen, filling a plastic bag with some ice cubes from the freezer and cold water. "There, Mr. Bossy-Pants," she held up the bag, "satisfied?" She returned to her bedroom and yanked the door shut with more force than was needed.

"Not even close," he muttered. He unwedged his legs from beneath the table, walked into the living room, and stepped through the French doors onto the miniature balcony, peering down at the streetscape below. Emily was hurting but instead of turning to him for comfort and support, she saw him as part of the problem.

He stared down at the couples strolling along the sidewalk, enjoying each other's company. A week ago, he'd stood in as Lachlan's best man, envious that his buddy had found the love of his life and was settling down. Now, here he was in the city synonymous with love, in a tiny apartment with a woman he wanted so badly his teeth ached, and he'd never felt more alone.

Her shiny new phone lay on the bed next to her, daring Emily to stop procrastinating and dial up her parents' number. She had her pillows bunched behind her back for support and her legs out in front of her.

Her ice pack was now a tepid bag of water. She took it off her ankle and placed it on the bedside table.

Might as well get it over with. "Here goes nothing," she muttered.

Her mom answered. "Emily, sweetheart. How nice to hear from you."

"Hi, Mom." Emily teared up. After the trauma of the past two days, she hadn't realized just how badly she'd needed to hear her mother's voice.

Carla Dane's voice sharpened. "What's wrong."

How did her mom do that? All she'd done was say hello, and her mom knew.

"I'm okay, but I got into a bit of a situation." She glossed over the details to keep her mom from freaking out and simply said she'd been trying to help some girls escape their trafficker, who took exception to her interference and held her against her will, but it was all good because she'd been rescued and was unharmed.

"And now, Minister Woodward wants me to return to the US for a little while until the French police arrest the trafficker and get him off the street."

"Thank God you're okay." Her mother's relief was audible. "When are you coming back?"

"Tomorrow afternoon. My flight leaves for Dulles at one."

"Dulles? Why aren't you flying into Hartford?"

Before she could explain to her mom that she wasn't traveling to her parent's house in Connecticut but staying in DC instead, she heard her father's voice rumble in the background. Emily tensed as she listened to her mother relay the story she'd given her before her mom came back on the phone.

"Hold on. Your dad wants to speak to you."

"How does a political officer whose job it is to analyze information and prepare reports wind up in the crosshairs of a sex trafficker?"

"Hi to you too, Dad."

There was no need to tell her father the complete story. As soon as he got off the phone with her, he'd be on the phone with her boss and probably the DSS Regional Officer—another former SEAL—and have every sordid detail.

"I met some of the trafficked girls while doing research. One of the girls I helped get free went back to her pimp. I was out looking for her."

"Alone, Emily Rose?"

She hated when he used her middle name in that tone of voice. It signaled his disappointment and frustration that yet again, she'd done something he considered foolhardy, or impetuous.

"Dad, remember all those skills you had me learn? Self-defense, target practice, how to get out of handcuffs—that worked, by the way. I can take care of myself."

"Except in this situation, you couldn't," he said. "I worked in the special operations community for thirty years surrounded by men with extraordinary skill sets, and none worked alone. There's a reason why teamwork is the most critical component of a successful mission. I guarantee the police who located and rescued you quickly did it through teamwork."

Emily's eyes rolled to peer up at her ceiling. Oh, it killed her, but she was about to make her father's day. "The police didn't rescue me. Nathan Long did."

The Paris Catacombs at midnight wouldn't be as quiet as the silence that descended over the telephone line.

"That boy was a damn good SEAL. I hated that he got out."

The pride in her father's voice sparked her temper. "The former SEAL can go all Rambo, and he's your golden boy. You're so proud of him. I try to help out some desperate girls and bring down an evil man, and I'm foolish?"

"Did Nathan act alone?"

She pictured the man currently taking up way too much space in her apartment crashing through that fifth-floor window, taking out Constantin, then scooping her up and climbing with her over a rooftop like Spider-Man.

"Kind of," she mumbled.

"Kind of? Either he had help, or he didn't."

Crap. "Ryder Montague was with him."

"So," the gotcha in her dad's voice was enough to make her crave another glass of wine. Maybe even the whole bottle, "the former Navy SEAL tracked you down and worked with a former SAS soldier to put a rescue plan in place, which they then executed successfully. Teamwork."

"Yes, Dad, teamwork makes the dream work. Now I need to pack. I'll call you tomorrow afternoon when I get to DC."

And figured out where she was going to stay. Sophia and Lachlan were still on their honeymoon. She could crash at their condo while they were gone, but they'd be back in a week, and nothing put a damper on newlywed life like an uninvited houseguest.

"You won't need to call us. We'll fly down from Connecticut in the morning and meet you at Dulles."

"That's not necessary." A throbbing knot of tension took up residence behind her eyes.

"Your mother and I want to see you. Who's staying with you? Please tell me you're not alone. You need protection."

Wine, she needed wine.

"Nathan's here. I've got to go. Bye, Dad, love you and Mom." She hung up, tossed her cell on the bed, then dropped onto her mattress, eyes closed, arms and legs splayed. A vision slammed into her brain of her on the bed in Constantin's fifth-floor room, handcuffed, ankles bound. His groping fingers assaulted her all over again.

She bolted upright, stomach churning.

The memories had been hazy at first, but they came back now in sharp relief. Constantin trapping her beneath his body, his hot breath bathing her face, the pain and nausea from his boot slamming her ankle and his fist in her stomach.

She'd felt afraid. Violated.

Emily hopped off the bed, her cozy refuge suddenly a stranger to her senses. Constantin was dead. He couldn't hurt her anymore.

And though she was grateful, a part of her still reeled from the brutally efficient way Nathan had ended the Frenchman's life. Her father had always refused to discuss the things he'd done as an active-duty SEAL. War was indifferent and death was personal, he'd say. She needed to focus on the good in the world, not the bad.

She'd chafed at his attempts to shield her. Now, she understood what he'd meant, at least a little.

Shaking her head to banish the memories, she limped to the kitchen. Nothing good would come from replaying yesterday's events.

Nathan still perched at her table. He ignored her and continued to tap away at his keyboard. What could he possibly be doing that kept him so busy?

On the kitchen wall, the old-fashioned clock she'd picked up at a flea market read close enough to five o'clock for her to declare it cocktail hour.

She opened the refrigerator and stared at an unopened bottle of Pouilly-Fuissé. *Why not?* She needed the distraction. She was stuck in a tiny apartment, unable to escape a man she wanted to flip off one minute and climb all over the next. She rooted through her kitchen drawer for the corkscrew and went to work on the wine.

Glass in hand, she took a generous swig and stepped out of the kitchen to glare at the source of her frustration. "What are you doing, writing a book?"

His eyes slanted in her direction. "Making my flight reservations. And working. Ryder and I are running Dìleas while Lachlan and Sophia are on their honeymoon."

His reply took the wind out of her sails. Here she was, restless and out of sorts because her life was a mess, and Nathan was just trying to do his job.

She took another gulp of her wine. The memory of her abduction hovered like an unwanted mirage in her head.

Nathan's tattoos shimmered over flexing biceps as his fingers flew over the keyboard, his chiseled face a mask of concentration.

Those fingers had smoothed over every inch of her skin as she lay trapped between his muscular thighs. His broad chest had brushed her nipples with every thrust until she thought she'd come from that alone. His breath had been hot in her ear. And other places.

She hadn't been afraid then.

A languid heat loosened her muscles. Moisture glistened along her hairline. She took another gulp of wine and resisted the urge to fan herself as a dangerous idea took hold.

Maybe she could chase away the bad memories with good ones.

Nathan looked up at that moment and caught her staring.

Emily couldn't look away.

His expression froze, eyes narrowing. She'd been eyeballing him a second ago like he was an hors d'oeuvres to go with her wine. Now, the tables had turned.

Never releasing her from his stare, he closed his laptop and sat back. A long moment passed between them. His eyes asked a question and her body answered, nipples a rigid outline against her shirt.

Her lungs constricted, shortening her breath.

"If you're gonna look at me like that, babe, you'd better be damn sure you're ready for my response." He stood, rounding the table to pluck the wineglass from her nerveless fingers. "You sure?"

Replace the bad memories with good ones.

She licked her lips. "I'm sure."

His head lowered. He took her mouth with a passion she met in kind. Her fingers gripped his hair as their lips crashed, their tongues battled, tasting, demanding more. His unique masculine scent invaded her senses.

She plastered herself against his hard body as if she were trying to meld them together into one and was rewarded when he growled into her mouth, the evidence of his desire pressing into her stomach.

Cool air flowed down her front where his warm heat had been. She blinked. "What's the matter?"

He'd put distance between them.

Nathan plowed shaking fingers through his short hair and stared at her with a pained expression. "Dammit. You've been through the wringer. Maybe this isn't a good idea?"

The question in his voice made her lips twitch. The knowledge that he'd step away if she asked dissolved any lingering jitters about having a man touch her so soon after her ordeal.

Not any man.

Nathan.

In her head, she ran through reasons she should take the out he was giving her. Having sex again would make it more difficult to face him down the road. Their best friends had just married, and it would be awkward. She didn't need another protector in her life. The list went on.

And none of it seemed to matter right now.

She smiled. "I just realized something."

"What's that?"

"White wine gets me into trouble around you."

His laugh was a low rumble. "Maybe you should switch to red."

"Maybe." She searched his eyes and nodded, coming to a decision. "I need you to fuck me senseless."

So much for her inner voice. To prove her point, she stepped into him and ground her hips against his crotch.

He threw his head back with a grunt and pulled her in tighter. "Such a potty-mouth."

His reaction rippled through her, ramping her desire. She dug her nails into his nape and locked him to her before pulling his head down to meet hers.

Nathan was her anchor. Her safe place.

She wasn't going to think too hard about the fact that she'd never wanted those things from a man.

His big hands cupped her bottom. He hauled her up to straddle his waist, knocking her foot against his thigh.

She gasped into his mouth as pain lanced her ankle.

Nathan froze. "You okay?"

"Mmm hmm," she mumbled against his lips.

He stumbled to her bedroom, never breaking their kiss as they greedily drank in each other. His shoulder hit the door frame with a thud. "Shit."

She giggled.

Placing her carefully on the bed, he glanced at her foot.

"It's fine." The throb was already receding. She pushed onto her elbows and gave him a saucy grin. "Take your clothes off."

"Pushy little thing." He yanked his shirt over his shoulders and dropped it to the floor. "What the lady wants, the lady gets."

He reached down to unlace his boots and toed off his jeans.

Again, with the no underwear.

"You forget to do laundry?"

Her gaze traveled the vast expanse of muscled, tattooed skin in front of her. She lingered on the part jutting arrogantly forward, ready to rock her world.

"Didn't have time. Too busy trying to save your pretty ass."

Emily gave him a wicked smile and patted the bed. "Down, on your back, sailor." When he hesitated, she wagged her finger. "Uh uh, what the lady wants, the lady gets, remember?"

"I'll lay on the bed if you get naked."

She pretended to think about it until he lunged at her. Laughing, she warded him off with a raised palm. "Okay, I'll get naked, but you're on the bottom."

Grumbling, he positioned himself and stretched out. He barely fit, his heels dangling over the end of the bed.

Emily devoured him with her eyes while she shed her clothes. He was a beautifully proportioned man, worthy of a Renaissance sculptor, and all hers to play with.

She climbed between his legs and wrapped her hand around his cock, remembering the feel of him inside her, filling her. Leaning over, she licked the slit of the mushroom-shaped head, tasting salt and sex.

Nathan's back arched as air rushed from his lungs with a moan.

Moisture pooled between her thighs. Her tongue traced him, smooth, velvet over steel, before taking him into her mouth.

He groaned, his pleasure making her even wetter. She sucked him in, hollowing out her cheeks. His hands lifted to her hair, and she batted them away.

"No touching." She was the queen, and he was her subject to command.

"Fuck." His cock swelled even more in her grip.

The sound of his voice, husky with need, shot right to her womb. She'd thought she'd have some fun and torture Nathan. Now she had to wonder which one of them she was torturing.

He laced his fingers behind his head, and she rewarded him by taking him as far into her mouth as possible while her hand pumped in a steady rhythm. Up, down.

His body heaved.

Her own body tightened, needy for release. One of her hands left Nathan to trail down to her sex.

Nathan's hands flew from behind his head to lift her mouth off him. He grabbed her hips, lifted her, and joined their bodies with an untamed thrust. Their simultaneous moans filled the room.

"We do this together."

She blinked at the fierceness in his voice, the lust burning in his eyes. His cock flexed inside her. Her head dropped back on her shoulders as her inner muscles clenched.

She braced her hands on his chest and began to move.

His hips surged, lifting her off the bed, driving him deeper into her. The boundary between pleasure and pain blurred. His fingers moved to her sex, toyed with her clit.

"Nathan." His name tore from her as she came in hard, pulsing waves. No one had ever made her feel this good.

"So tight." Beads of sweat glistened on Nathan's skin as his thrusts increased and became erratic.

His eyes widened in alarm before rolling back. "Oh, fuck. I can't—you feel so fucking good."

She frowned. "Can't what?" *Come?*

Oh, she'd beg to differ.

His gaze was wild, unfocused when it met hers. "I'm not wearing a condom. I've never not suited up before."

Oops. How had she not noticed that? "You don't have any with you?"

"Trust me, if I thought there was even a chance of us doing this again, I'd have gotten some more."

For one crazy moment, she didn't care. Possession roared through her with a frightening fierceness. She had a claim to him no other woman had.

Could she take the chance?

No. She was on the pill but missed taking it yesterday when she'd been held prisoner. Even though he hadn't orgasmed inside her, they'd already taken a big enough risk.

Nathan must have read her decision on her face. He lifted her off him and threw an arm over his eyes, his breath a series of harsh, heaving gasps as he struggled for control. His fully erect penis, glistening from her juices, beckoned.

He'd given her an orgasm. It was only fair she return the favor.

Emily placed her lips to his ear. "I've got your six, Lieutenant."

A shiver rippled through him.

She grinned, trailing her hand over the ridges of his abdomen.

Nathan let out an agonized groan as her fingers curled around him, her mouth taking him in.

She tasted herself, mingled with his unique salty essence. A surge of heat threatened to melt her into a puddle all over again. She took him in as far as she could, sucking, licking, pumping him with one hand while the other fondled his sac.

Beneath her, Nathan tensed, then lifted off the bed as he came with a shout. After his hips stilled and he sagged into the mattress, she gave him a final lick, practically purring with contentment.

Funny, she'd never really enjoyed going down on a man like that before, but seeing such a big, powerful, dangerous man come apart beneath her had been a major turn-on.

He rolled over, chest heaving, and wrapped her in his arms. "You can have my six anytime."

Emily played with his hair, passing the damp strands through her fingers while his breathing slowed. His heart beat in a steady, thumping rhythm. She shouldn't feel this content, lying here with a man so wrong for her.

Her chest tightened. Nathan was under her skin.

Because he was incredible in bed—she told herself—not because he was funny, loyal, treated her respectfully, and had rescued her from Mirga and his thugs. And certainly not because he made her realize that the other men she'd been with had been safe, predictable.

Men who'd never made her feel out of control.

Her dad would be so pleased. She gagged as she scrambled off the bed like it was on fire, hobbling into the bathroom.

Nathan bolted upright. "What's the matter?"

"I'm sorry, this was a mistake. We can't keep doing this." She pulled a towel from the linen shelf and wrapped it around her body.

He appeared in the doorway, anger flaring in his icy eyes. "Why the hell not?"

"Why not?" She clutched the towel to her breasts. "Because this will never go anywhere. It can't. I have a job and a *life* that I love. I don't have time for a relationship, especially with a bossy, controlling alpha male."

Nathan folded his arms over his chest, a glint of anger sparking in his eyes. He invaded her space, naked and too close. "Is that why you tucked tail and ran in Scotland?"

It was getting hard to breathe. "I didn't want you to get the wrong idea. We had sex. That was it."

And they had just done it again.

Nathan's jaw tightened. He bent, bringing their faces level. "It was more than sex. If you're too much of a coward to admit that, fine, run away. Again." He straightened. "I'm not your daddy, Princess."

Oh, that was a low blow. Her palm itched with the need to slap him.

"No, you're the man my dad would love. You're a SEAL. You belong to a Team. You run off to do big things and change the world and no one blinks an eye. In fact, you get applauded for it. I try to do the same thing and I get in trouble."

They glared at each other until the sound of a phone ringing broke their impasse.

"You can have the shower first," Nathan growled. He walked away, still naked. As angry as she was, she still couldn't help but admire the taut muscles of his magnificent ass.

Emily sagged, welcoming the discomfort of the bathroom sink digging into her back. Nathan's deep voice rumbled in the background.

He reappeared, phone at his ear. "It's Ryder. He's brought my things. I'm going downstairs to meet him." He grabbed his clothes and boots from the floor before stalking out of her bedroom.

She latched the bathroom door with unsteady hands.

The look in his eyes. They'd flattened like he'd shut away his emotions or had given up trying to care.

A strange ache took up residence in her chest. As soon as they got back to DC, she and Nathan would part ways, and she'd work on returning to Paris, her career, and her life.

She had to.

Before she lost a part of herself to him that she might never get back.

CHAPTER SEVENTEEN

EMILY FOUND HERSELF GLARING at the back of Nathan's head the next morning as Ryder pulled his Rover up to the departures level of Terminal 2E at Charles De Gaulle International Airport.

They'd barely spoken two words to each other last night. Emily had taken the bottle of Pouilly-Fuissé with a plate of ham, bread, and cheese and retreated to her bedroom. She'd numbed her brain with wine and Netflix until she was too tired to ruminate on her mess of a life.

Nathan had returned to his computer and was still sitting there when she went to bed. She had no idea where he slept or if he even had, but by the time she emerged in the morning to give him access to the bathroom, he was packed and ready to go.

The uncomfortable silence stretched her last nerve and made her queasy.

She compared the two men seated in front of her. *Tall, broad-shouldered, extremely fit. Good looking. Dangerous.* Sophia's husband, Lachlan, was as well.

Her lips twitched despite the tension in the vehicle. Did hot men flock together like pretty girls did?

Ryder was classically handsome, the guy next door, tall with broad shoulders, a chiseled face, striking blue eyes, and wavy brown hair.

On the other hand, Nathan did not look like the guy next door unless you lived next to a motorcycle gang. She'd seen firsthand what he was capable of when he snapped Constantin's neck.

But when he smiled and those icy eyes warmed, he made her insides melt. When his stare said he wanted to rip off her clothes, back her against a wall, and plunge deep inside her?

She squirmed in her seat. Her panties got wet just thinking about it.

Nathan chose that moment to lock eyes with her in the mirror. His pupils dilated, and the look she'd just pictured came over his face.

Emily dropped her gaze to her lap and tried to slow her breathing.

This was why she needed to get away from him. He was dangerous.

She went to open her door.

"Wait." Nathan threw up his right hand, his voice a whip of authority. "Stay in the car with Ryder until I get our bags."

Her hand stilled on the door handle. She doubted Mirga had sent his goons to the airport after her. But then again, if Constantin was dead—and she was pretty sure he was—Jules Mirga might be looking for revenge.

A chill chased up her spine to the back of her neck. Once she got to DC, she'd call Inspector Pierron and plead with him to keep Nathan's and Ryder's names out of any public reports regarding her abduction.

When Nathan opened her door, his expression, and body language were all business. "Ready?" The stone-cold warfighter looking back at her wasn't the man whose touch had made her forget herself. "Let's check our luggage and get through security as quickly as possible."

She leaned over the front seat to give Ryder a peck on the cheek. "Goodbye and thank you."

A slight tilt of Ryder's lips passed as a smile. "Be safe, Emily."

Nathan's body shielded her as she slid from the back seat, his scent enveloping her in an olfactory caress. He passed her the handle of her rolling suitcase, his hand moving to the small of her back. His gaze roved the crowd of travelers as they approached the airline counter to check their bags.

His alert posture only served to jack up her own tension. She looked around, half expecting to see Sami or Hulk hovering nearby, and leaned closer to Nathan.

The woman at the check-in counter reviewed their boarding passes and passports. She gave them a bright smile. "Would you like to see if I can find you two seats next to each other?"

Emily pasted on a polite smile. "No, thank you. That's okay."

It wasn't until after they'd passed through security, had purchased some snacks, and were at their boarding gate that Emily relaxed. Surely she was safe now.

Nathan opened his laptop. "Don't go anywhere without me." Then he proceeded to ignore her.

She sat and stewed in miserable silence. The distance between them was her fault. One she didn't know how to fix because she couldn't admit she was wrong and make herself vulnerable.

They didn't speak until their boarding group was called. When they stepped onto the plane, Nathan turned left.

"Business class, huh?" she said. "Must be nice."

He spared her a glance devoid of emotion. It made her stomach cramp. "I'm six-six. Seven or eight hours seated in coach with my knees under my chin and my elbows plastered to my side isn't my idea of a good time." He gave a brief lift of his chin. "Have a good flight."

The person behind her in line huffed an impatient breath. Emily continued to row twenty and stowed her carry-on in the overhead bin, keeping her phone and earbuds out before taking her seat.

Fatigue took her over with the speed of a freight train, weakening her defenses, and making her melancholy. She hadn't slept well last night, knowing Nathan lay in the other room, angry and hurt by her behavior. Lewis Capaldi sang in her ear about losing love, and she had to screw her eyes shut before she started bawling. She stayed that way while the rest of the plane boarded, and the flight attendants went through their safety briefing.

The plane taxied to the runway and took off. Only then did Emily open her eyes to stare out the window as they ascended.

The Eiffel Tower winked in the distance, the urban mass giving way to suburbs, then patches of woods and farmland before being obscured by clouds. Slipping away, like the life she'd made for herself, the career she was building, the women and girls she was determined to help.

Was Catalina okay? What about the other women and girls still trapped in Mirga's organization?

She'd be back. Soon.

That was a promise to herself she intended to keep.

When the pilot announced they were twenty minutes from landing, Emily made a quick visit to the plane's bathroom to touch up her makeup and brush her hair. Knowing her parents, they'd be waiting for her at Dulles, and she intended to face her father in her version of full battle rattle—perfectly applied makeup, not a hair out of place, and fashionably tailored clothing that projected sophistication and authority. Her limp was sure to make him demand an explanation. The man missed nothing.

Fifteen minutes after she'd returned to her seat, the plane jolted as it touched down on the runway with a roar of reverse thrusters.

Welcome back to the United States.

She spotted Nathan in the passport line. He was hard to miss. She took advantage of their distance to stare at his drool-worthy physique. His faded jeans cupped his firm butt as lovingly as his black t-shirt showed off his muscular back and arms.

As if he sensed her scrutiny, he turned, his gaze immediately finding her.

The shock of his crystal blue gaze connecting with hers felt like it had the first time they'd laid eyes on each other, sucking the air from her lungs.

He gave a barely perceptible nod and faced forward again.

"That man is so fine, isn't he?"

Emily tore her gaze from Nathan to see the three twenty-something women in front of her had noticed her ogling.

Her face heated. "Yes, he is."

The girl with the long brunette hair gave her a conspiratorial smile. "I wonder if he's married or has a girlfriend. I'd so like some of that."

A pang hit Emily square in the chest, harder than she'd expected. Her throat tightened. She shrugged, not trusting her voice. The catty part of her wanted to tell the three women that she had gotten "some of that," as the one girl had put it, and it was, indeed, fine.

But that might lead to them asking why she wasn't up there with him, why he'd barely acknowledged her presence.

Nathan kept his distance at the baggage carousel until the light went on and the loud buzzer went off. When she looked up from watching the suitcases slide down the ramp onto the moving carousel, he was next to her.

Damn, he moved like a big cat.

"How was business class?"

He shrugged. "Good. And coach?"

She made a face. "It's coach. At least I got some sleep."

He grabbed his black duffel off the carousel and set it at his feet. She waited for him to leave, but he stayed, scanning the luggage as they passed. Finally, her big navy suitcase appeared. Before she could reach for it, Nathan grabbed it and set it down in front of her.

"Thank you." As if she didn't feel bad enough. Even angry with her, he had manners.

They walked together through the final passport control and out of the restricted area into the public arrivals section of the terminal.

"You need a ride home?" he asked.

"No, my parents insisted on flying from Connecticut to meet my flight."

She spotted her dad just then, dressed in tan slacks and a light blue golf shirt. Her mom stood next to him, ever the fashionista in her Lily Pulitzer sundress with strappy pink heels, her blonde hair arranged in a French twist.

"And...there they are." She put her hand up to her mouth and muttered. "Run for it while you can."

Nathan laughed.

A tall blond sauntered up to her parents, holding coffee. *Alex.* Her brother was here, too?

Emily's mom spotted her first. Her dad and brother followed the direction of Carla Dane's gaze.

A huge lump knotted Emily's throat at the relief on their faces. She blinked back tears and hurried toward them, trying not to limp.

"Emily, thank God." Her mother enfolded her in a warm embrace. Her father and brother joined in, forming a protective cocoon. She bit her lip hard to keep a sob from tearing free. She was a little girl again, wrapped in the safety and security of her family's love.

For a moment, she never wanted to leave.

But their security was a crutch. And, at times, a burden. She was an adult and needed to act like one. "I'm okay, really." She stepped outside of her family circle.

Her mom brushed her hand along Emily's hair, her gaze searching for truth in Emily's words.

"Baby sis." Alex hugged her, lifting her feet off the ground.

She gave him a tight squeeze. Only three years her senior, he could be an overprotective pain in the butt like their dad, but she missed him. With her being in Paris and him an active-duty SEAL, it was rare they got to see each other anymore.

Alex lifted his chin at someone over her shoulder. "Hey, man."

Not someone. Nathan.

Emily's shoulders tightened as Alex let her go to bump fists with Nathan.

She should have known they would know each other. The SEAL community was a relatively small, tight-knit group. Her brother was an officer, having graduated from the Naval Academy, and Nathan had been an officer as well.

Admiral Dane shook Nathan's hand. "Son, I can't thank you enough for what you did." Her dad's voice cracked, his façade shifting from commanding officer to a father who'd nearly lost his child.

Emily teared up all over again.

Before Nathan could reply, Emily's mom had him wrapped up in a hug. "Thank you for saving my daughter." She took Nathan's face in her hands, and he obligingly bent at the knees so she could kiss his cheek, his face reddening.

"Yes, ma'am." The look he shot Emily was one of a man in dire need of rescue himself. "I was in the right place at the right time."

Emily waited until her family finished fawning over her knight in shining armor to make her stand. "I'm happy to see you guys, but you didn't need to fly down from Connecticut to meet my flight." She turned to her brother. "And you didn't have to drive three and a half hours from Little Creek."

Her mother squeezed her arm. "We had to see for ourselves you were okay."

"You should request a transfer back to the States. It's not safe for you in Europe right now," her father said in his commanding officer voice.

And so it begins.

They hadn't even made it out of the airport.

"I'll make my own career decisions, Dad." Her spine was so stiff it threatened to snap. "My job is in Paris, and I intend to return to it."

The admiral scowled. "You're a grown woman who put her nose where it didn't belong and got kidnapped and nearly killed. God knows what might have happened to you if it wasn't for Nathan and Ryder."

"Those girls needed my help, and my *job* is to monitor sex trafficking in Europe." Her voice rose. "Jules Mirga is one of the largest traffickers in France. I can help send him to prison. You would have done the same thing."

"Rosebud, you're a foreign service officer, not an operator. It's not your job to rescue anyone." Porter Dane crossed his arms and glared down his nose at his daughter. "You have a bad habit of going off half-cocked on your own whenever you perceive an injustice."

Emily's eyes widened in indignation. "That's not fair. When have I ever done that?"

"High school, when you ran down that purse snatcher armed with a knife," Alex said.

She glared at her brother. "I didn't know he had a knife, and I perfectly executed an X block, then disarmed him."

"The time in college you waded into a group of drunk marines in a seedy bar to rescue some girl instead of calling the police," her mother added.

"There wasn't time to call the police. She looked scared to death. And the marines backed off."

"Lucky for you," her father growled. "How about when you thought the Colombian Ambassador's son was dealing drugs and tried to set up a sting? I had to do some damage control over that one."

Her face pinched. "Yeah, okay. That one was a mistake—when I was fourteen. But geez, way to keep score, people."

She didn't need her family trotting out the dirty laundry with Nathan listening. Maybe a sinkhole would open beneath her feet and swallow her up.

Her father speared her with a determined look. "You're coming home with your mother and me to Connecticut. We can keep you safe until this Mirga criminal is arrested and put in jail."

The admiral took her suitcase and started for the exit.

"No." The word flew out of her like a bullet, halting his stride.

"Emily Rose." Emily barely felt her mother's hand on her shoulder. She resisted the urge to shrug it off.

"Now isn't the time. Let him calm down first," her mother whispered.

"No," Emily repeated, forcing her voice to remain level. "I'm not coming to Connecticut with you. Sophia won't mind if I use the condo while she and Lachlan are on their honeymoon. I'm only staying until the French police have news on my case, and I can convince Minister Woodward to let me return to Paris."

"Dad spoke with Agent Goodwin," Alex whispered in her ear. "He knows Mirga threatened to send you to Syria."

Crap.

Still, her father couldn't win this one. It was too important. Her independence was at stake. She stayed locked in a visual tug-of-war with him. Many a Navy SEAL had shrunk an inch or two under that glare. She wouldn't be the one to break.

The admiral's eyes narrowed. "Fine," he snapped.

Her dad didn't give in that easily, not even to his *Rosebud*—his nickname for her for as long as she could remember.

Emily waited for the other shoe to drop.

"But you need protection." Admiral Dane thrust out a finger toward Nathan. "Lieutenant Long lives here. I'll make arrangements with Dìleas for his services."

The look of panic on Nathan's face would have been comical if it wasn't so insulting.

"Why do I need a bodyguard?" Emily demanded. "It's not like Mirga will come after me in the States. He doesn't have that kind of reach."

Alex leaned in again. "If the guy in Syria is with ISIS, who's to say he wouldn't tap some of those connections to get his hands on the daughter of the former commander of US Special Operations Command?"

She elbowed her brother in the ribs. "You're not helping," she hissed. Why did her dad and brother always gang up on her?

This is why she couldn't be with Nathan. She needed another alpha male in her life like she needed a hole in the head.

"Sir, I'm running Dìleas while Lachlan and Sophia are on their honeymoon. Ryder Montague is in charge of our executive protection division. I'm sure he can arrange for someone to stay with Emily."

Emily looked away, her face heating. This was a first, a guy trying to pass her off to avoid spending time with her. Nathan didn't want to be her bodyguard.

She didn't want to spend more time with him, either. *Really.*

"Porter." Carla Dane's voice held a note of warning. She fixed her husband with a steely look. "Emily is a grown woman. She gets to make her own decisions."

Emily's brows lifted. She'd rarely heard her mother openly contradict her father.

The admiral's lips thinned, but he stayed silent.

"Hoo boy." Alex fought a grin behind the rim of his coffee cup.

Her mother slipped an arm around her and hugged her tight. "I know what you're thinking, sweetheart," she whispered in Emily's ear, "but he's your father, and he loves you. Try to remember that when you chafe at his overprotectiveness."

"How do you put up with him?" Emily whispered back.

Her mom's smile grew wider. "I learned a long time ago how to handle your father." She gave Emily a pointed look. "And I know someone just like him."

Emily gasped. "I am not like Dad. Alex is like him."

Carla Dane laughed. "You both are."

"I'm going to stay at Lachlan and Sophia's condo, at least until they come home." Emily glanced at her father's grim expression, then at Nathan's wary one. "Then, I'll decide what to do."

Her mom nodded before speaking to the group. "Emily's had a long day. Let's get her settled into the condo and have an early dinner so Alex can return to base." She leveled a stare at her husband. "You and I will check into a hotel tonight and catch a flight back home tomorrow morning."

"We need to stop by the storage place in Chantilly so I can get my car," Emily added.

The admiral's posture radiated his displeasure. He grabbed Emily's suitcase without another word and strode through the exit doors.

"We'd better catch up to Dad before the parking shuttle arrives and he leaves us here." Alex threw up a hand at Nathan. "Nice seeing you, man. You dodged a bullet getting stuck with my sister."

"Alex!" Emily and her mother's voices rang out simultaneously.

Alex laughed. "Kidding, kidding." He peered over his shoulder at Nathan and mouthed, *Not kidding.*

Emily stuck her tongue out at her brother before pivoting to face Nathan, suddenly unsure what to say. "Well, that was fun. I guess I'll see you around."

"You be careful, darlin'." Nathan's knuckles whitened around the handles of his duffel. "If you need anything, call me. Promise?"

That melancholy feeling she'd had on the plane returned. "I promise." She watched him saunter away from her toward the exit.

"I thought you swore you'd never date a SEAL."

She whirled at the sound of her brother's voice to find him eyeing her with a speculative look.

"I'm not." Her hand fluttered in the direction Nathan had disappeared. "We're not."

"Uh-huh."

"Shut up, Alex."

CHAPTER EIGHTEEN

NATHAN STEPPED THROUGH THE glass doors of Dìleas Security Agency the following day, ready to get back to some semblance of normal. "Mornin' Miss Penny. Did you keep the place together while everyone was gone?" He glanced around the reception area at the plant jungle. "Looks like you kept Sophia's nursery alive."

"Good morning, Nathan." Dìleas's office manager greeted him with a smile. She wore a bright green blouse today with matching emerald stud earrings. "Thank you for sending photos of the wedding. Sophia looked beautiful in her wedding dress, and Lachlan, so handsome in that kilt."

The wedding felt like years ago to Nathan, considering what went down after.

"They'll be back in a few days. Meanwhile, I've got a lot of work to catch up on. Did you receive a contract from a Special Agent Goodwin of the Diplomatic Security Service in Paris?"

Penny nodded. "I've printed it out and it's on your desk." A cautious look entered her eyes. "Admiral Dane is waiting for you in your office."

Shit. Nathan's shoulders jacked tight. "Did he say what he wanted?"

The old man hadn't gotten his way yesterday. That had to have been a first.

"No. He only said it was urgent he see you this morning. He said he had a late morning flight to catch."

Nathan sucked in a lungful of air before letting it out in a noisy sigh. "Wish me luck."

He headed to his office, his hand hesitating on the doorknob before he took a deep breath and entered.

Admiral Dane stood with his back to the door, staring out Nathan's window. "Lieutenant."

"Sir." Nathan dropped his laptop and briefcase on his desk but remained standing. He couldn't make himself sit unless the admiral did.

"I spoke with Rich Goodwin. I think we both could read between the lines of that story you and Emily told. Only someone with your training could have pulled that off."

Nathan smiled. "Never out of the fight, sir."

The admiral turned from the window to meet Nathan's eyes. "Do you miss the Teams?"

"Every day," Nathan replied without hesitation. "But I made my decision, and I'll stand by it. And," he added deliberately, "I'm part of a new team here at Dìleas."

"You'll always be part of the SEAL community, son. Which is why I'm counting on you to continue to keep Emily safe."

Nathan blinked, his neck prickling in warning. "Sir? Emily made it quite clear yesterday afternoon that she didn't need or want a body-guard."

Especially not him.

"I reached out to Lachlan. I'm employing Dìleas Security Agency for personal protection services for my daughter. Jules Mirga is a dangerous man. I don't trust him to leave Emily alone, even if he's arrested.

He has a long reach and connections with dangerous people in the Middle East."

Nathan's jaw set as irritation jacked his muscles even tighter. "You contacted Lachlan while he was on his honeymoon?"

"I consider this an emergency. Lachlan agreed." The admiral didn't even have the grace to look embarrassed.

"Does Emily know you're hiring her a bodyguard?"

The admiral gave him a cagey look. "Not a bodyguard. Someone who can keep an eye on her and monitor any potential threats to her safety. You know her and have mutual friends. Find a reason to spend time with her."

For one brief moment, Nathan contemplated telling the admiral the truth: *No can do, Admiral. I've had sex with your daughter. Twice. And as much as I'd like to do it again, she wants nothing to do with me. You'll have to find someone else.*

Hell no. He wanted to live to see tomorrow.

"Why me? Ryder can assign someone to shadow Emily. Someone she doesn't know."

Admiral Dane stepped into Nathan, invading his space. "You can set your own schedule, you're a paranoid son of a bitch, and I know you have a top-notch security perimeter around your house. Emily will be safe with you if another threat arises." The admiral lowered his voice. "Don't forget I've seen you in action, son. I know your skill set. I'm asking you to keep my daughter safe."

Nathan let out a defeated sigh. Why the hell was he even bothering to resist? The admiral had spoken to Lachlan. If he refused, Lachlan would want to know why, and he'd have to go into more of an explanation than he was comfortable with. "Yessir."

The admiral nodded and clapped Nathan on the shoulder. "Good. I'll ask Penny to email me a contract to sign. Keep me posted."

After the admiral left, Nathan sunk into his chair and dropped his head into his hands. "Son of a bitch." How was he supposed to get over Emily when fate kept throwing them together?

How was he supposed to get her to agree to spend time with him?

By offering her a carrot.

She was skittish around him, but what did she want more than anything?

To bring down Jules Mirga.

He glanced at the contract on his desk from Agent Goodwin, awaiting his signature.

There was his leverage. He needed Emily's research and insights into Mirga's operation to unearth the forger and tie Mirga to the drugs and money crossing international borders using trafficked women and girls.

He knew just how to bait the trap.

Emily stumbled out of bed late in her home away from home—Sophia's condo in Old Town Alexandria.

Well, it had been her home away from home. Since Lachlan moved in several months ago, she'd felt more like a visitor than a roomie.

Her bedroom walls were decorated similarly to her apartment in Paris, with paintings and other framed pieces of local art she'd picked up on the streets or in flea markets during her travels. The styles were diverse, some modern, others more traditional, but they all reflected in some way the culture of the artist and their region or country.

She padded down the hall to the kitchen and started the coffee. While it brewed, she let her gaze wander the condo. It looked pretty much the same as it had before Lachlan moved in, with one significant difference—the oil painting mounted over the gas fireplace with the black-haired Highland warrior Sophia said reminded her of Lachlan.

The coffeemaker noisily spit out the last drops of brew into the carafe. Emily poured herself a mug and took a cautious sniff of the half-and-half in the fridge.

Eh, borderline, but desperate times and all that. She added some of it to her coffee with a teaspoon of sugar.

Her parents should be on their way back to Connecticut by now, and her brother had returned to his naval base last night. Much to her surprise, her father hadn't mentioned her need for a bodyguard after their confrontation at the airport, and she'd actually had an enjoyable dinner with her family.

Poor Nathan. He'd almost gotten roped into spending more time with her, which was probably the last thing he wanted to do.

Taking a seat at the dining room table, she opened her laptop and said a prayer that Minister Woodward hadn't notified someone in IT to put a temporary block on her log-in credentials for remote access. She gave a fist pump when her work screen popped up with her email and document folders.

First things first. She emailed Madame Légère to ask about Catalina. Then she emailed all her contacts in Paris with the news that she'd been sent to DC on assignment but would be returning soon. She left out that her assignment was to sit on her bum and twiddle her thumbs while she contemplated her transgressions and waited for the police to arrest Jules Mirga.

It was already noon by the time she finished with her emails. She armed herself with another cup of coffee and scrambled up the three

eggs left in the egg carton. A grocery run was definitely in order if
she planned to stay here. If the police didn't arrest Mirga soon she'd
have to find another place to live. A hollow ache took up residence in
the region of her heart. Three was definitely a crowd when two were
newlyweds.

After her meal, she showered, dressed, and ran to the grocery store
for a few essentials before spending most of the afternoon combing
the Internet for any new information about Mirga.

Her cell phone dinged with an incoming text. *Nathan.* Her pulse
fluttered.

I need your research on Jules Mirga's operation.

She frowned and texted him back. *What for?*

*Remember my meeting at the embassy? Got an assignment from
Special Agent Goodwin.*

That made no sense. Nathan's meeting had been arranged before
her kidnapping.

Which meant whatever interest Agent Goodwin had in Jules Mirga, it wasn't related to her. Why hadn't Nathan told her about it
sooner?

Unfortunately, she knew the answer. *Maybe because you were too
busy pushing him away.*

She had most of her research stored in electronic files. She could
email them to Nathan. That way, they wouldn't have to meet
face-to-face and be all awkward with each other.

Although not all of her research was on her computer. She'd taken
the folder containing her handwritten interviews with several trafficked girls she'd met.

Her body hummed with a frisson of excitement. Maybe she didn't
have to sit here sidelined after all. If DSS was interested in Mirga, it
wasn't just a French matter anymore. Her research—combined with

Nathan's hacking prowess—might be the key to finally unearthing enough evidence to dismantle Mirga's trafficking ring and put him in jail for a very long time, especially if his activities had triggered an investigation by US authorities.

If she were going to get back in the game, she'd need Nathan's cooperation.

And to do that, she had to make her case in person.

She sucked in her lips. Nathan was going to help her bring down Jules Mirga.

Even if she had to eat humble pie.

Nathan pulled out one of the rib eyes he'd bought earlier in the day and set it on the counter before heading out to his deck to start the grill.

Emily hadn't replied to his request earlier for her research on Jules Mirga.

Hell. She wasn't going to make anything easy on him.

He lit the grill, set it to high heat, and headed back to the kitchen to start the sides.

A loud buzzing came from the war room. Someone was at his front gate.

He threw a bag of red potatoes into the microwave before heading to his office to see who was disrupting his dinner.

"I'll be damned." His center monitor displayed the video from his front gate, and none other than Miss Emily Rose Dane pressed his intercom buzzer like she was in a game show trying to beat the other contestants to the answer.

Just like the first time he'd ever laid eyes on her.

His strategy had worked, after all.

This time she was dressed in a green silk tank top and black shorts that exposed legs that went on forever. He zoomed out to check out her footwear—strappy black sandals with a heel.

Maybe she'd scale his fence again.

He pressed the intercom, failing to keep the amusement from his voice. "Yes?"

She glared at the camera positioned over her head. "I know you can see me, Nathan. Let me in."

He grinned. "Ma'am, do you see all those 'No Trespassing' signs? Whatever you're selling, I'm not buying." He swore he could see her eyes—more green than blue today—flash over the video feed. His body stirred in response.

Her hands went to her hips. "Oh, for God's sake. Must we play this game? Do you want the information on Jules Mirga or not?" Her painted toes in their strappy black confines tapped an impatient rhythm on the gravel.

He thought about making her work a little harder to get her way, but she probably *would* climb his fence. He opened the gate and watched as she got back into her sporty red Lexus and barreled down his driveway.

Just like last time, he met her outside his front door, although this time, without his Sig Sauer.

Climbing out of her car, she gave him a quick once over. "What, no gun?" She sauntered toward him, all sassy mouth and killer bod.

The impact hit him in the chest like a lightning bolt and traveled straight to his groin. If only she'd give him a chance to show her how good they could be together. "I'm making dinner. Care to join me?"

She bit her lip, suddenly looking unsure. It was a look he wasn't used to seeing on her.

"Are you sure?"

"I'm sure."

"Then yes. That would be nice. Thank you."

He held the door open and breathed her in as she slid past him into the house. He could snort her scent and get high off it like a drug.

Brushing past her into the kitchen, he took out the second rib eye, then pulled the potatoes out of the microwave and popped in the green bean casserole.

"Make yourself at home while I cook the steaks."

Emily looked around. The hallway she stood in led to an open kitchen and spacious living room. These rooms were familiar. They were as far as she had made it into Nathan's house last year when she'd come searching for Sophia.

The kitchen was dated, with light oak cabinets and white marbled laminate counters. The breakfast nook, which looked to be Nathan's only dining area, had an oval table and four ladderback chairs. A brown leather couch and two overstuffed armchairs flanked a rustic coffee table in the sunken living room. Over the mantle of the beige brick fireplace hung a painting of a cowboy riding herd beneath a vibrant sunset. It was a striking painting and spoke of Nathan's Texas roots.

She watched him at the grill on the back deck. Smoke drifted upward, and flames leaped to grab the meat he held between a pair of tongs. Her mouth watered. She could picture the fat from the lovely, marbled rib eyes dripping onto an open flame, igniting a flare-up to lick at the meat and create a nice crusty outer coating. Her stomach gurgled in response.

In the kitchen, the microwave dinged. Emily went to investigate and removed the dish inside. She lifted the lid.

Green bean casserole? She stirred the mixture with the spoon lying on the counter and tested the temperature before returning the dish to cook for two more minutes. A microwavable bag of small red potatoes cooled on the wooden cutting board.

Instead of standing around doing nothing, she should try to be helpful. She rummaged around the cabinets until she found two placemats, some dishes, silverware, and—she wanted to clap—a bottle of Zinfandel.

Nathan stepped inside with the platter of steaks.

"I didn't know how you liked your meat, so I made it medium."

"Perfect." Emily gave him a polite smile. "Thank you for cooking."

His only response was a grunt.

Yeah, he probably wasn't that thrilled to see her.

He placed the platter on the table. In the kitchen, he removed the casserole from the microwave, dumped the potatoes into a bowl, set both dishes on the table next to the steaks, and poured the wine.

"Have a seat." He gestured Emily to one of the chairs.

Emily sat and carefully cut one of the steaks in two, putting half on her plate, followed by a generous dollop of casserole and a few potatoes. She took a sip of wine, savoring the vibrant, fruit-forward red. "It's perfect, thank you."

Nathan took the other steak, a mountain of casserole, and almost all the remaining potatoes. Huge forkfuls of food disappeared at a blistering pace.

Her brows lifted. "Hungry?" At least he chewed with his mouth closed.

"Umm-hmm," he mumbled through a mouthful, never slowing.

She'd been thinking about her situation and how to make the best of it. Nathan was an accomplished hacker. Ryder had connections all over Europe. She could enlist their help to track down Catalina and dig for more evidence against Mirga.

Maybe Nathan would be in a cooperative frame of mind with a full stomach.

Or not, given how they'd parted ways.

Only one way to find out.

"I need to find a way to bring down Jules Mirga, and I'd like your help." Her pulse banged against her throat. After all the times she'd pushed him away, he would probably laugh in her face. She took another sip of wine and braced for his reaction.

He set his fork down long enough to pick up his glass of wine. Her gaze lingered on the play of muscles in his throat as he took a swallow before answering. "I'm already working on it."

"So it would seem." It would have been a nice detail to know about before they left Paris. "How is Jules Mirga part of your job for Agent Goodwin?"

Nathan wiped his mouth with his napkin and pushed aside his plate. "Goodwin believes someone inside the embassy is helping Mirga forge passports so he can send trafficked girls and women between the

US and Europe, not only to service clients but also to ferry drugs and money."

Emily's eyes widened. "Money laundering, drug and sex trafficking across international borders?"

Nathan nodded. "Goodwin is using Dìleas as an outside consultant because no one on the inside can identify the forger. He's keeping it quiet, so the guilty person or persons won't know he's closing in on them until it's too late."

Excitement gave Emily a renewed burst of energy. "If we can prove Mirga is behind the forgeries, we can tie him to the entire operation, and then the US Government has a case against him, regardless of what the French police do."

"Bingo."

Her forearms hit the table as she leaned in, her attention completely focused on Nathan. "What have you found so far?"

One corner of his mouth lifted. "I'll show you mine if you show me yours."

His comment fell into a sudden awkward silence.

Emily fidgeted in her chair, eyeballing her plate as if it held the secrets to the universe. They'd already done plenty of showing each other what they had. What they needed was a reset.

"Look, Nathan." She ignored the subtle tensing of his muscles. "We're in an awkward place, and it's my fault."

His brow arched.

She grimaced. "I'm used to relying only on myself. It's easier that way." Her eyes met his. "I *like* it that way. But if we work together using the information I've already gathered and your hacking skills, we can unearth Jules's dirty secrets and expose his operation."

And she could get back to Paris that much sooner. Resume her life.

"Deal?" She stuck out her hand.

Nathan let it hang out there for a long moment before his fingers enveloped hers. The heat from his palm warmed her insides with a rush of awareness. Maybe touching him hadn't been such a good idea. Those hands had caressed her intimately, something her brain was all too happy to remind her.

"Deal." He held her hand hostage. "To be clear going forward, what are we, Emily? Work partners? Friends?" His crystal gaze narrowed on her. "Something more?"

She bit her lip and gently tugged free from his grasp.

Something more that can't continue.

"I think it would be best if we were work partners and friends. Just...friends."

Although friends with benefits was incredibly tempting.

But something told her she wouldn't be able to keep her emotions out of it enough to say goodbye when she returned to Paris.

She mustered up a smile. "Thank you. I'll make this partnership as easy as possible on you."

Nathan choked on his wine. He tipped his chair back and raked her with a heated look that melted her insides. "If there is one thing I know, darlin', it's that there is nothing easy about you."

Emily's cheeks flamed. She bit her upper lip to keep a sarcastic response from slipping out, proving Nathan's point.

Standing, she gathered up the dishes and carried them to the kitchen, scraping them clean before she added them to the dishwasher.

"So, where do we go from here?"

Nathan figured there were a couple of different ways he could an-swer that question. Unfortunately, Emily's focus was solely on them working together. There was no "where do we go from here" beyond bringing down Mirga for her.

He had two objectives—finding Mirga's lackey in the US embassy and keeping Emily safe without her knowing she was now a job, courtesy of her daddy and his behind-the-scenes maneuvering.

Now came the tricky part.

"Why don't we work from here? If Minister Woodward has sent you home on an enforced leave of absence, I doubt you'll be very welcome at the State Department."

Her grimace and reluctant nod told him he'd gotten that one right.

He pressed his advantage. "I've got plenty of space for us to spread out, so we aren't on top of each other. My connections are secure—we can do some behind-the-curtains snooping into online servers when needed, and I have a fully stocked kitchen."

Indecision was as plain on her face as a billboard. "I need to find a place to stay before we start."

"Stay here." He was a damn masochist. He really was. But it was the perfect solution to his problem. To keep her safe, he needed to get her into a secure environment.

Emily gnawed on her lip like it was chewing gum. "I can't."

Hell, he'd tossed it out there, he might as well try and run it into the end zone. "Why not? I have two spare bedrooms. And if you want my help, it means we work on my time, which often means late into the night." He quirked a brow and threw her a look of challenge. "As you've said. We're partners and friends. Nothing more."

Her fingers drummed a nervous tattoo on the table.

He went for the touchdown. "Worried you won't be able to keep your hands off me?"

Emily's eyes narrowed to slits. It was all he could do to keep a straight face. Sometimes, she made it too easy.

"Please," she drawled, "I think I can manage."

The haughty disdain on her face made him glad he was sitting down so she couldn't see the sudden bulge in his jeans. The woman could shrink a man's balls with that look, but it had the opposite effect on him.

She rose from the table and pushed in her chair, seeming to have decided. "Okay." She gave a sharp nod. "I accept your offer. When can we start?"

He wanted to let out a "hooyah" at the top of his lungs. Instead, he said, "First thing tomorrow morning. You can bring your stuff over. I'll make breakfast."

Emily left after she promised him she'd be back first thing in the morning.

Nathan headed to his war room. He opened the tracker app he'd installed on Emily's phone and monitored her progress until her phone's location told him she was safely back at the Mackays' condo.

Lachlan had texted him earlier and confirmed Admiral Dane's arrangement. Other than sending a thumbs-up emoji, Nathan hadn't replied.

Settling back in his chair, he plopped his boots on the desk and sent Lachlan a text.

The package is secure. Thanks for turning me into a bodyguard.

L: *The admiral insisted. I don't like keeping this from Sophia.*

N: *I don't like keeping it from Emily, but she wasn't receptive to the idea, and I agree with the admiral. She needs protection.*

L: *We're both going to catch hell for this when they find out, pal.*

N: *Wouldn't be the first time. How's the honeymoon? Keeping your bride entertained, or is she already bored and in the market for a real man?*

L: *Fuck you.*

N: *You're not my type.*

L: *Be back soon. Keep me posted.*

N: *Gotchu.*

L: *One more thing.*

N: *Amigo?*

L: *Fuck you again.*

Nathan chuckled. Lachlan had no sense of humor when it came to his wife. He scanned his monitors. Other than a possum scurrying across the gravel driveway, the scene was quiet. Satisfied nothing warranted more scrutiny, he strolled down the hall to his master suite.

Tomorrow, Emily would move into his home to become his official partner and he, her unofficial protector.

He needed to show her that being with him, being his teammate, wouldn't smother her independence. Maybe if she believed that, she'd stop kicking him to the curb every time they got close and acknowledge that they had a connection that went beyond sex.

A connection that made them stronger together than either one of them were alone.

Chapter Nineteen

When Emily arrived the next morning, Nathan was already at the stove whipping up a batch of scrambled eggs. After opening the gate, he moved his motorcycle to the back of the second bay in his garage and had her park there, then unloaded her suitcase.

She had on a powder blue V-neck t-shirt this morning and slim black yoga pants that hugged her slender curves. Her hair was caught in a high ponytail and she wore minimal makeup. The girl-next-door had taken the place of the sophisticated style maven, and damn if this version of Emily Dane wasn't as attractive as the other.

He led her down the hall where the two spare bedrooms were located and opened the door to the last bedroom on the end. His sister had helped him decorate this room. It wasn't as elaborate as what she'd done in his master suite, but he rarely had guests. A Native American quilted bedspread in shades of blue, orange, and deep red draped the queen-size lacquered pine bed. Matching nightstands and a chest of drawers rounded out the furniture.

"Is that where you're from?" Emily had moved to get a closer look at the two framed landscape prints of Texas Hill Country mounted on the wall behind the bed.

"I'm from Waco, but we had a vacation home on Buchanan Dam." He'd grown up fishing and hunting in Hill Country with his family, and it still held a special place in his heart.

"The closet." He pointed to the white bifold doors. "The bathroom's the middle door on the hall." He placed her suitcase on the bed. "Breakfast is ready. You can unpack after you eat."

She gave him a hesitant smile. "The smell of coffee and bacon is a siren's song I can't resist." She followed him back to the kitchen and poured herself a cup of coffee, adding cream and sugar while he dished the eggs onto a plate.

Her lashes fluttered as she took a sip. "Mmmm."

Dammit, the way this woman drank her coffee made his dick stir every time. He thrust the plate at her. "Here."

The word came out harsher than he'd intended. She gave him a pointed look, and Nathan tensed. If she made some smart-ass comment about his manners, he might seal his lips over hers to shut her up. He motioned to the kitchen table, where he'd already set out the bacon and toast, then grabbed his plate.

This living arrangement was going to kill him.

Someone got hangry in a hurry. Emily took her plate to the table and watched through her lashes as Nathan slammed scrambled eggs onto his dish like he was giving them a beatdown in a wrestling ring. He'd gone from congenial to snarly in a heartbeat.

Surely they could have a nice, normal conversation as friends. They needed to if they were going to survive living in the same house without killing each other or falling into bed together.

She'd start. "How did you end up becoming a white hat hacker? That's what you did, right? Before joining Dìleas."

Nathan took a seat and swallowed a forkful of food before he answered. "I was a computer science major in college. Hacking has always been a hobby."

"Always?" She tilted her head and gave him a speculative look. "Have you ever illegally breached a government network?"

His studiously blank expression had her shoving a piece of bacon in her mouth so she wouldn't laugh.

"Why did you go into the foreign service?" he asked.

She spread butter on a slice of toast while she contemplated her answer. "My family has a long history of service—both my grandfathers, my dad's mother, my dad, and now, my brother." Her shoulders lifted and fell as she met Nathan's curious gaze. "I wanted to serve, too, and I've always been interested in government and international relations."

"Maybe you should have picked the FBI or CIA instead."

"Why?"

"Because you seem to thrive on danger."

His dry tone raised her hackles. She stabbed the air with her second piece of bacon. "That's not true. Just because I think Jules Mirga needs to go down doesn't mean I was looking for trouble."

"Oh?" His brows lifted. "What were you looking for?"

"For the police to do their job! I was only trying to help." She shoved the bacon in her mouth and chewed furiously, then used her fork to stab the air in place of the bacon. "Catalina helped me gather evidence against Mirga, and I wasn't going to pay her back by walking away. And Maya's a young girl whose childhood was ripped away from her." She waited for the inevitable lecture about overstepping her authority and needlessly putting herself in danger.

Instead, Nathan drained the coffee in his mug, then stood. "Then let's do what the police haven't done, find the evidence we need to bring Mirga down."

He started clearing the dishes from the table while she sat back and tried to keep her mouth from hanging open. She'd half expected his offer of a partnership to be nothing more than an attempt to keep her busy and out of trouble, probably at her father's urging.

Those annoying warm, fuzzy feelings were back. Her gaze fell to the tabletop while she fought for control.

"We'll need to install an OpenVPN protocol on your laptop if you don't already have it. I have secure Wi-Fi as well." Nathan scraped the plates and loaded them into the dishwasher before he poured himself more coffee and returned to his seat at the table. He shot her a look beneath lowered brows. "It'd be a good idea if you kept off social media and didn't advertise your location to anyone you may get in contact with."

She gave him her best Kardashian pout. "Awww, no TikTok videos?"

His left eye twitched. "You think I'm overreacting when it comes to your safety."

"Jules Mirga isn't going to come after me here, in the States."

"And last year Lachlan assumed what happened in Afghanistan would stay in Afghanistan. But it didn't, and Sophia became a target. Remember?" A muscle in his jaw joined the eye twitch. "So, humor me. Let's not make it easy for Mirga."

She wanted to point out that the circumstances weren't exactly the same, but she was afraid his entire face would seize. The easiest thing to do was to pretend to acquiesce so he didn't go into full on overprotective alpha male mode. She nodded.

"Let's get to work." Nathan stood and strode down the hall to his office, leaving her to trail in his wake.

The war room, as he called it, had originally been a small, formal dining room that Nathan had closed off and renovated into his workspace. He'd angled his desk so that he could look out the window but not be directly in front of it, and he could look out his door but not be directly in front of that either. The walls behind his desk were a blank canvas. The walls on the opposite side were empty as well. In fact, it was surprisingly sterile, given what she knew about the man.

"I think you've taken the minimalist look a bit too far in here."

He took a seat at his desk and glanced around. "I work in here. Don't need any distractions. Also, when I video conference, I don't want photos of me and my friends, many of whom are still on active duty, to end up being viewed by the wrong set of eyeballs."

"Would it kill you to get a plant?"

His lips quirked into an amused smile. "Now you sound like Sophia."

She pulled a chair up to his desk and opened her laptop. After she got connected to his secure network, she accessed her State Department account and logged in. "Mirga uses several of the girls in his nightclubs to service more exclusive clients. He also sends girls out to work the streets under the control of pimps, like Daniel Pescariu, and some of the younger girls, like Maya, are advertised on dark web social media sites that promote sex with minors."

Nathan made a sound of disgust. "How does he get these girls?"

Emily sighed. "Many, like Catalina, are lured to Paris under what's known as the Lover Boy scheme. A trafficker woos them online with promises of romance and a better life. Others, like Maya, are sold by members of their own families in exchange for money. Some arrive looking for work, but lack of skills, language barriers, and desperation makes them easy prey. Once they get to Paris, Mirga's pimps confiscate their passports. They're often beaten and given drugs, then forced into sex work."

She pulled from her laptop bag the folder of handwritten notes she'd taken while interviewing several girls and opened it. "Catalina often worked in Mirga's high-end clubs, servicing some of his special clients."

Nathan scanned the top page. "What kind of special clients?"

"Heads of other criminal organizations he does business with, government officials, foreign dignitaries."

"Anyone he wanted to reward or have something to hold over them," Nathan added. "I need names of all his associates, business partners, anyone you've identified as having a link to Mirga, to look for a connection to the consular affairs employees who have access to passport documentation."

She gave him a slow smile and handed over her notes. "I've circled the ones you might want to investigate first."

While Nathan did his thing, Emily took her laptop into the living room and made herself at home in one of his oversized leather chairs. Her temple ached in a low-level throb. She still hadn't gotten an email reply from Madame Légère about whether anyone from Fondation Espoir had made contact with Catalina. She checked the time. It was almost five pm in Paris. If she called now, she might be able to catch the social worker on the phone.

As luck would have it, Madame Légère was still at work. "*Bonsoir*, Emily. I wondered if you would call. It is so sad, *non*?"

Emily straightened in her chair as dread slithered its way up her spine. "What's so sad?"

Silence greeted her for agonizing seconds. "I'm sorry, *chère*. I thought you would have known by now. Catalina was found dead in an alley in the Quartier Pigalle. Inspector Pierron said she died of a drug overdose."

"No." Emily closed her eyes, her heart a lead weight in her chest. "That's not possible. Catalina wasn't an addict." The girl had been adamant that drugs would destroy her looks and pointed to so many of the other girls as proof.

Emily's lips felt numb as she thanked the social worker for letting her know. Madame Légère assured her Maya remained at the safe house in Orleans.

She hung up, guilt clawing her insides. If she hadn't been in the US, she might have been able to track Catalina down and persuade her to return to Fondation Espoir. If that hadn't worked, she would have paid for a plane ticket with her own money for the girl to leave the country.

Now it was too late.

She stabbed out the number for the French Judicial Police. "Inspector Pierron, *s'il vous plaît*. It's Emily Dane from the US Embassy calling."

A few moments later, Pierron came on the line. "*Bonsoir*, Mademoiselle. I did not know you had returned to Paris."

"I haven't. I just heard about Catalina." Emily struggled to maintain her composure. She wasn't supposed to get emotionally invested, but she'd been the one to persuade Catalina to leave. Had convinced her that the police and Fondation Espoir would keep her and Maya safe. "Tell me what happened. Madame Légère said it was a drug overdose. Surely you don't believe that?"

Victor's heavy sigh buffeted her ear. "Mademoiselle Dane, I believe in what the facts tell me, *non*? The girl had toxic levels of opioids, mainly heroin, in her system. You tried your best to get her off the street. It is not your fault she went back—you know it happens all the time."

Emily's back teeth clenched. "She didn't use drugs. Jules Mirga had her killed." The police were going to write Catalina off. Just another prostitute who had lived in the shadows and died there.

"There is nothing you can do now for her. I'm sorry. *Au revoir*." The inspector hung up, not giving her a chance to say more.

Dammit! She leaped to her feet and paced Nathan's living room. Victor Pierron wasn't going to give her any information, and she couldn't push him any harder in case it got back to Minister Woodward that she was overstepping her authority again. Her job would be finished, possibly her career in the foreign service, if she disobeyed her boss's order.

She hated not being in Paris.

Bruce. He could make some inquiries for her without letting the minister know. She quickly dialed his cell.

"Hey Emily, how's life in the States? I hope you're taking advantage of your time off."

She gritted her teeth in irritation at his cheerful tone. "It wasn't my choice to be here. I need your help. Catalina, one of the girls you helped me get off the streets, was murdered."

Bruce went silent for a moment. She could hear the sounds of street traffic in the background. "I'm sorry. I heard. The police said she overdosed."

"She didn't overdose, Bruce, come on." Her words came out louder than intended, and she glanced down the hall toward Nathan's office before lowering her voice to a harsh whisper. "You know as well as I do, Mirga murdered her. I need you to help me get a copy of the official report."

"Minister Woodward told you to stay out of it. Don't risk your career over this, Emily. Mirga's gone underground, and the French police haven't found him. Stay in the US, and don't make waves until the minister lets you come back."

Emily stifled the frustrated scream that wanted to escape her throat. "You won't help me."

"Don't be angry. I care about what happens to you." His voice dropped to a husky whisper. "I miss you. I'd like to be able to take you out again when you get back. Someplace nice—you name it."

"I've got to go." She hung up, fighting back tears. What did she do now?

Her gaze again wandered down the hall.

Nathan.

Nathan had just finished sending Admiral Dane a report on Emily's status as his houseguest when there were two soft knocks on his door. "Come in." He closed out his email so Emily wouldn't get a peek at his correspondence. He didn't like deceiving her, but her father was right—she needed protection.

To say she'd be furious when she found out would be a polite understatement.

The door opened and Emily stepped in, head bent, shoulders slumped.

"What's wrong?" He stood, jacking to attention at her posture.

Her face crumpled. "Ca-Catalina is dead."

His guts tied in a knot at her tears. He rounded his desk and pulled her into his arms.

Her slender fingers gripped the back of his t-shirt. She pressed her face into his chest with a stifled sob. "No one cares that she's dead. No one cares that bastard Mirga is still running around France somewhere, free. The French police don't care, Bruce won't help me, and if I push people for answers, I could lose my job."

He rocked her gently, letting her cry it out. "I care. Don't think for one minute Mirga won't pay for what he did to you. What he did to Catalina. What do you need, babe?"

She raised her tear-stained gaze to his. "I want to see the police report. They said Catalina died of a drug overdose. But I know Jules Mirga murdered her."

"If you tell me where to look and help me with the French, I'll get into the system and unearth that report. If it's online, I can get to it."

"That's so illegal," she breathed before gifting him with a faint smile.

What was a little not-so-legal hacking? He'd done it before, plenty of times. Hell, he'd risk jail if she kept looking at him like that. As long as he didn't get caught, Lachlan wouldn't have to know, and Dìleas's reputation would stay clean.

He cupped her head between his hands and wiped away tears with his thumbs.

Her breath hitched at his touch, her eyes darkening.

His body flared to life. He fixed his gaze on her pink lips and lowered his head. Just a little taste. Nothing more.

Emily's eyes drifted shut and she softened, melting into him.

A loud electronic buzzing sounded from his computer. His head snapped up.

Fuck.

Emily's eyes popped open. "What's that?"

"Someone's at my front gate."

CHAPTER TWENTY

A GRAY RAM PICKUP sat at the top of Nathan's driveway. He zoomed the camera in on the short, wiry driver with thinning light brown hair who stood in front of the intercom on his gate pillar, then panned to the truck where two more men sat inside.

The driver waved, then saluted with his middle finger.

Nathan's lips tilted upward, then compressed in a line. Shitty timing for an impromptu visit.

He turned to Emily, who peered at his monitor with open curiosity. "Why don't you go grab another cup of coffee while I deal with my visitors."

She narrowed her eyes but did as he asked and left the war room.

Nathan's finger stabbed at the intercom. "You assholes ever heard of calling ahead?"

The voice on the other end barked out a husky laugh. "L-T, open up. We thought we'd pay you a visit on our way back to Dam Neck. We brought beer."

"It's too early for beer, Senior Chief."

What was he going to do? He never turned away his former teammates when they were in the area. How was he going to explain Emily's presence in his home? The minute they heard her last name, they'd know who she was, and then, he'd never hear the end of it.

He certainly couldn't tell them the admiral had made him Emily's undercover bodyguard.

"Are you gonna let us in or what?"

The guys knew he was home; it'd raise more suspicions if he didn't let them in. A quick cup of coffee, and then he'd come up with a reason to send them on their way.

"Yeah, hold on." Nathan hit the button to open the steel security gate and strode back to the kitchen.

Emily sat at the table, sipping from her mug.

"I think you should go to the guest room and stay there until I tell you to come out."

The mug halted halfway to her lips. "Why, what's going on?"

"Some of my guys decided to drop in. Do you want the fact that you're staying in my home to be conversational fodder for the East Coast SEAL community? It won't take long for your brother and father to find out."

His buddies would be at his front door any minute. Nathan scanned the room for evidence of her presence before dropping the words he knew would get her moving. "Of course, your dad will assume you caved about needing protection. He'll be thrilled when he hears you're staying with me."

Her eyes narrowed as she stood.

Gravel crunched under the tires of Chief Patterson's truck.

"You might want to hurry."

Emily's head made a quick pivot toward the driveway and back, but she did as he asked. Her bedroom door snicked shut right as a knock rattled his front door.

Nathan took one last look around. The only evidence of her presence in his kitchen and living room was her spicy vanilla scent. If his guys picked up on it, he'd tell them it was an air freshener or some shit. Thank God he'd had her park in the garage.

He yanked open the door and clapped palms with Jake Patterson, one of the best operators he'd had the privilege of working with. "Senior Chief."

"L-T, good to see you."

Standing behind the chief were Petty Officers First Class Mayhew and Dixon. Danny Mayhew's tousled blond hair and beard reflected the more relaxed grooming standards afforded to SOF members. He grinned and threw up his right hand in a mock salute. Tavari Dixon, nicknamed "Slap Jack" for his resemblance to the *2 Fast 2 Furious* actor, gave Nathan a close-mouthed smile and a nod.

Nathan stood to the side, letting his friends file into the kitchen. "Coffee?"

At their nods, he handed each of his friends a mug before joining them at the table. "On your way to base?"

"Yeah. We don't have to report until Monday, so we figured we had time to check on you." Senior Chief Patterson's gaze narrowed on Nathan. "I heard you formed some company with that SAS guy, Captain Mackay."

Nathan nodded. "Now I have a legitimate reason to hack into people's computer networks. And a steady paycheck."

"You should have never left the Teams, man." Danny shook his head. "The Lieutenant we have now is a temp—not as tight with the guys as you were."

Nathan's shoulders tightened. He shifted his gaze to his back deck, where a squirrel tried unsuccessfully to pillage the birdfeeder. "It's been almost three years. You guys have done all right without me. Besides, by now, I'd be on instructor rotation somewhere."

He wasn't going to rehash why he left. What happened in Afghanistan happened. Nothing was going to bring Joe Logan or the others back.

His teammates filled him in on the everyday squabbles and life in the spec ops community. He missed this—bonding with the guys, the adrenaline rush of the life. He brushed aside a pang of regret. It wasn't until he'd joined Dìleas that he realized how much his solitary life as a white hat hacker had isolated him from being part of a community, of having people he could rely on.

And seeing Lachlan with Sophia, he'd also realized he wasn't content anymore with casual female companionship. He wanted a woman who would challenge him and have his six, who'd be a lover and a friend. Who he could grow old and gray with.

The central air kicked in, blowing cool air through the supply vent in the floor, carrying with it the faint scent of vanilla and spice.

Nathan's gaze crept down the hall toward the guest room.

Emily cracked open her door as stealthily as she could and held her ear to the narrow opening. She might need to stay hidden, but that didn't mean she couldn't satisfy her curiosity about Nathan's relationship with his former teammates.

The relaxed banter made it clear they liked and respected him. It would be so much easier to keep her relationship with Nathan a professional one if he had some obvious flaw she could use against him. Well, other than the fact that he was a former SEAL and someone her father would approve of.

But he also was funny, warm, and, let's face it, hot as hell. She had an estrogen flash just from the memory of Nathan's wicked tongue and how he liked to use it.

"You should have never left the Teams, man," one of the men said.

She slipped through the door, edging farther out into the hall.

Why *had* Nathan left the Navy? His teammate's tone made it sound like it hadn't been voluntary. But he was intelligent and highly capable—she'd seen proof of that firsthand.

A chair creaked.

Crap. Nathan couldn't catch her eavesdropping.

She took a quick step backward, her empty coffee mug in her grip. It slammed into the door frame, slipped from her fingers, and shattered on the floor.

The last piece of ceramic hadn't stopped quivering before Nathan appeared. He glanced at the mess on the floor, then to her, his lips compressed in a thin line.

Fire bloomed across her cheeks. "Sorry." She'd screwed that up royally. She opened her mouth to say more when a shaggy blond head appeared over Nathan's shoulder.

"Well, hello there." The bearded surfer dude grinned. "Is Poppa Bear keeping Goldilocks a prisoner in his cottage?"

Nathan's chin hit his chest.

Emily grimaced, then threw back her shoulders. She had outed herself—might as well go all the way. "Looks like I need more coffee." Head high, she stepped gingerly over the remains of her old mug and shouldered past Nathan.

Three men stood behind him in the hall—the blond, a short wiry brunette, and a guy only a couple of inches shorter than Nathan with light brown skin and cropped black hair styled in a fade. They parted like the Red Sea to let her pass.

She sailed into the kitchen, doing her best to look like she belonged, and poured herself another cup—not that she needed any more caffeine. Her nerves were strung tight enough to hit a high C.

Nathan's sigh was so deep it sounded like it started in his toes. "Gentleman. Meet Emily Dane." He introduced each of the men in turn.

"Emily Dane? You wouldn't be related to Admiral Dane, would you?" Chief Patterson's gaze swiveled between her and Nathan. The questions in his eyes were so obvious she was surprised they didn't hover over his head in neon thought bubbles.

"I'm his daughter."

She waited for the reaction, which never changed. You'd think she had farted in church. As a unit, Nathan's friends froze, then swiveled their heads to stare at him like he was missing brain cells.

SEALs. They were arrogant and cocky and feared nothing. But her dad was a legend in the community, and no one was going to make the mistake of messing with his only daughter. If she weren't so annoyed, she would have laughed at the looks of sympathy the three active-duty operators threw Nathan's way.

Fortunately, she knew SEALs and how to deflect the heat.

She took a seat at the kitchen table. The three visitors joined her, and Nathan leaned against the kitchen counter, ankles crossed. She cradled her chin in her hands and gave them all a mischievous smile. "Tell me everything you know about Nathan and make it as embarrassing as possible."

Nathan groaned and buried his face in his hands. His friends hooted.

"Me and Nathan were in the same BUD/S class." Danny, the attractive blond with the tousled hair and beard, rubbed his hands together as he leaned forward in his chair, his eyes twinkling. "Remember, L-T, when we were doing that night evolution in the zodiacs, and you'd snuck your phone in your dry bag?"

Emily listened raptly as Danny settled into his narration.

"So, we're out there for-frigging-ever, no sleep, practically halluci-nating, and we get near that bridge, you know the one?"

The senior chief and Tavari both nodded.

"Nathan takes out his phone and orders pizza."

The senior chief snorted and shook his head. Tavari smiled, show-ing a set of beautiful, straight white teeth.

Emily snuck a glance at Nathan, his arms folded across his chest. The corners of his mouth tilted in amusement.

Danny threw up a hand. "It gets better. He slips out of the boat and starts swimming for shore. We're thinking he's out of his mind—he's gonna drown. But he's the strongest swimmer in the boat, ya know? He makes it to shore, and we lose him in the dark. Now we're worried he's gonna get kicked out of the program because he's disappeared."

The SEAL leaned forward, blue eyes sparkling, elbows on the table, and stared straight at Emily. "Twenty minutes later, this square box wrapped in a black plastic garbage bag rises out of the water next to our boat, and it's Nathan with the pizza."

Emily almost snorted coffee through her nose. She stared at Nathan wide-eyed.

He shrugged his big shoulders and gave her a lopsided grin that made her heart flutter as the other men laughed.

A strange warmth flooded her chest. She forced her attention back to the others before it spread to the rest of her body.

Senior Chief Patterson took over story time from Danny and launched into his own "remember when." The picture that emerged of Nathan only strengthened Emily's impression of him as a decent man, a good leader, an officer who watched out for his men, and a skilled operator.

Still, she ended up with more questions than answers. Curiosity may have killed the cat and—according to her father—might kill her if she wasn't more careful, but she had to know more. "Why did you leave active duty?"

Nathan's expression blanked except for the muscle that ticked along his jaw. He shrugged. "It was time."

The other men had grown unnaturally still.

"L-T is a good guy. It wasn't anything he did." The tall one, Tavari, hadn't spoken more than two words since she'd come out of hiding. The fact that he said something now spoke volumes. His stunning gray eyes were steady as he met her gaze.

Nathan stared at his boots. If his posture and granite expression were anything to go by, he'd barricaded his emotions behind an invisible wall.

Senior Chief Patterson coughed into his fist. "I think it's about time we got going." He gestured at the two petty officers. They all stood and nodded at Emily. "Ma'am."

Each one clapped Nathan on the shoulder as they filed past. Nathan followed them out to the truck.

Emily cleared the mugs from the table and began to hand wash them to keep busy as she waited for his return. Her thoughts swirled together in a messy, chaotic stew. Something had happened to push Nathan out of military service against his team's wishes.

When the front door opened, she placed the mug she'd just washed on the drying rack and dried her hands.

"You don't take orders very well." Nathan's deep voice rumbled behind her.

"Good thing I'm not a sailor." Right now, her curiosity about Nathan took up all her brain space. She turned to face him. "Being on the Teams was important to you. What happened to make you leave the Navy?"

"Ask your father."

Her chin lifted. "I don't want to ask my father. I'm asking you."

"You know I can't talk about missions." He sounded resigned, not the easygoing, wisecracking Nathan who drove her nuts.

She forced herself to stay where she was and not wrap her arms around him—a gesture that might be unwelcome given the stiff way he held himself. Nathan lived behind the walls of his gated home, but she knew instinctively he wasn't a solitary person. He enjoyed being part of a team.

"So, it was because of a mission?" She needed to know what happened more than she needed to breathe.

He shrugged. "A mission went FUBAR. People died. Decision makers above my pay grade needed to blame someone, and Lachlan and I were the obvious choices."

Shock stiffened her spine. *The hostage rescue mission.* She didn't know all the details, but she knew people had died. That mission was the reason Lachlan Mackay's past had come back to try and destroy him and take her friend Sophia with him.

Indignation replaced shock. "How dare they hang you guys out to dry."

A wry smile curved Nathan's lips. "Lucas Caldwell, the FBI Assistant Director your dad knows, was a colonel on the JSOC command staff at the time. He went to bat for us." He paused. "So did your dad. The final after-action report called it an intelligence failure, and we weren't officially reprimanded, but Lachlan and I knew our careers were over. As soon as my tour was up, I got out."

"You were a good officer. Your men respect you." She crossed the short distance between them and laid her palms on his chest. He was warm and solid beneath her skin. "It's not right. They were your family."

Nathan covered her hand with his larger one, trapping it to his body. "They're still my family, and I have a new team at Dìleas—they're family, too." His icy eyes warmed as he gazed down at her. "It was my decision to leave, Em."

Slowly, the warmth changed to something more intense. His nostrils flared. The skin over his cheekbones tightened, as did his fingers on hers.

The need to comfort him like he had her earlier shifted as flames licked her insides. Surely desire this hot would burn itself out quickly and leave them both cold in the aftermath. This wasn't a forever kind of feeling.

Was it?

Whatever it was, she was helpless to fight against it now. She grabbed the back of his neck with her free hand, stood on her tiptoes, and pressed her lips to his.

Nathan pulled her into him and took control.

Emily let her eyes drift shut and focused on every place their bodies met—his muscular chest against her full, heavy breasts, his strong sheltering arms, the hard ridge between his thighs that made her ache to be filled by him. Her tongue clashed with his for supremacy. She was no shrinking violet—she'd give as good as she got.

She let go of her death grip on his neck and wedged her hand between them. Cupping him through his jeans, she gave a light squeeze.

His deep rumbling groan, and the knowledge of the power she had over him, made her even wetter than she already was. She fumbled with the button on his jeans, desperate to wrap her fingers around his length.

In the space of a heartbeat, he stiffened. His hand covered hers, stilling her attempt to get into his pants.

Her eyes flew open as he stepped back, putting space between them.

Frustration creased Nathan's face. "We can't do this. Not until you decide what you want, Emily. I want more than to be relegated to the friend zone, and whenever we get together, you freak out because I'm not the kind of man you want to be with." He brushed past her to his office, slamming the door loud enough to wake the dead.

Heart racing like it was running the Kentucky Derby, she staggered backwards. She and Nathan had a mutual attraction that burned with the intensity of a bunker-buster bomb, but she couldn't afford to have it burrow deep enough to penetrate her heart. Her body still humming with need, she retreated to one of the chairs in the living room, taking in her temporary quarters with a scowl.

What had made her think moving in with Nathan and working together was a good idea?

Chapter
Twenty-One

Nathan cloistered himself inside his war room and dove into his project for Special Agent Goodwin before he changed his mind and went in search of Emily to finish what they'd started.

One of the best ways he'd found to unearth information was to employ the six degrees of separation model of social networks. Put simply, people figured out intuitively the shortest path to deliver something to an unknown person by sending it to the person they knew with the most connections and asking them to do the same—the old "friend of a friend" technique.

In the modern world of social media, six degrees of separation was now closer to two or three.

Using a few different algorithms, Nathan could search the Internet and find out what connections existed between the list of names Agent Goodwin had given him from the US Embassy in Paris and Emily's list of Jules Mirga's clients, collected from her interviews with the trafficked women and girls. It was like assembling a jigsaw puzzle, complete with a basketful of dirty laundry. He identified three people on Goodwin's lists with ties to Mirga or his clients and found six more using those connections.

Mirga used twenty-something girls as his mules. Goodwin said the passports were clean in that they hadn't been altered, which meant they used stolen or forged identifications to apply for new passports.

Plenty of American girls had driver's licenses and school IDs but didn't have a passport. Or if they did, they only used it infrequently. If their information was stolen, say from the government database by a State Department employee, someone at the embassy could process a replacement using a blank passport book, and voilà, a trafficked girl with a similar appearance suddenly becomes Vivian Delgado from Queens, New York.

A couple of hours in, Nathan narrowed down his list of suspects to two of the local embassy employees and two Americans. One of the Americans, Theresa Mead, aged twenty-eight, currently worked as a passport specialist in DC but had been posted at the embassy in Paris. A backdoor peek into her personnel file revealed she left the job in France after having an affair with a married high-level staffer in the Ministry of Europe and Foreign Affairs, which made her or her French lover vulnerable to blackmail if the information got into the wrong hands.

The other guy, Jerome Whitley, forty-five, was a career civil servant. From what Nathan could tell, he held a mid-level managerial position in the Bureau of Consular Affairs and had a debt problem stemming from a divorce. He was also a frequent visitor at one of Mirga's clubs.

Nathan emailed the information to Goodwin to follow up on, sat back in his chair, and rubbed tired eyes. As much as he'd like to finish for the day, he'd promised Emily that police report on Catalina, and he intended to keep his promise.

He found her in the living room, sitting cross-legged in one of the chairs, so dialed into whatever she was reading on her laptop, he had to call her name twice to get her to look up.

"Emily."

"Hmmm?"

"How about we look for that police report?"

Her face lit up, and she practically flew from the chair. "You'll do it?"

He frowned at her surprise. "I said I would."

She came at him like she intended to hug him, and he tensed, waiting for the feel of her soft curves against him, her vanilla-spice scent to fill his nose.

Her arms dropped. Instead, she gave an awkward pat. "Thank you."

He needed a beer.

He grabbed one from the fridge while Emily poured herself a glass of water before they headed back to his war room.

"Mirga's gone into hiding, but I'm convinced he's still in control of his business." Emily took a sip of water, her lips thinning. "He needs to pay for what he did to Catalina."

Nathan set his bottle on the coaster he kept at his desk because even though he didn't live with his mother anymore, certain rules stuck with him, like no water rings on the furniture. "Let's see if we can get you that report. You're going to need to point me in the right direction."

"Okay." She moved her chair closer to peer at the monitor. "The DRPJ—the Judicial Police—fall under the Police Prefecture of Paris. They would be responsible for investigating Catalina's death. I can show you their public website, but I don't know how you'll access their internal files."

He breathed her in and willed his body not to react and gave her his trademark cocky grin. "Write down all the names in French and be ready to translate." His fingers flew over the keyboard. "Leave the rest to me."

It took some creative know-how but eventually, with Emily's help, he found his way into the DRPJ internal servers. Using the information she provided, he found the report filed on Catalina Giurescu and downloaded it before he slipped out of the server, leaving no digital fingerprints behind.

Emily leaned into him, her breath bathing his shoulder as she read the report. He might not be able to read it, but he could read Emily's face as her features pinched and a sudden sheen of tears appeared in her eyes.

"You okay, darlin'?"

She shook her head. "It says the police found Catalina's body in an area known for prostitution, but she likely died elsewhere and was dumped in the alley." Her voice wavered. "Like garbage."

Nathan reached out and squeezed her hand. Pain radiated off her. A pain he'd do anything to take away.

"Scroll down."

He complied until she told him to stop.

She summarized for him. "Fresh needle marks on Catalina's skin indicated drug use, likely heroin. Bruising on her face and abdomen, abrasions on her knees and elbows."

"She was beaten." Anger turned Nathan's voice into a guttural growl. He still didn't understand men who used their superior strength to abuse women rather than protect them.

Emily's hand flew to her mouth, her face leaching of color.

"What?" Nathan had a sick feeling he knew what. The people who'd abused Catalina hadn't been afraid to drug and beat her. It wasn't a stretch to imagine what else they hadn't been afraid to do.

The sheen in Emily's eyes gathered volume. A tear leaked down her cheek. "She was raped."

"I'm sorry." He reached out a finger and gathered up the moisture.

"Final toxicology results are pending, but the preliminary cause of death is"—She shot from her chair, her body vibrating with rage—"fatal heroin intoxication? You've got to be kidding me. The report clearly states Catalina was abducted, beaten, and raped, and what do they list as her cause of death? Drug overdose. Case closed. Another sad story of a lost girl on the streets."

His brave, strong Emily crumpled, her hands flying up to cover her face. "This is my fault—I convinced her to do it. I promised nothing would happen to her, and Mirga had her killed for leaving and giving information to the police."

The sob that tore from her ripped out his heart. He stood and wrapped his arms around her, half-expecting her to reject his attempt to comfort her. Instead, she sagged against him and cried while he envisioned all the ways he could torture Jules Mirga before ending the miserable bastard's life. His hold on Emily tightened. Mirga wasn't going to get the chance to get anywhere near her again, no matter how much she wanted to bring the crime lord down.

He wouldn't allow it.

Shit. His eyes rolled up to peer at the ceiling.

He'd officially become the overprotective asshole Emily was so afraid would try to rein her in.

Eventually, her sniffles dried up. She stepped out of Nathan's arms and gave him a sheepish smile as he handed her a tissue.

"Wow, I snotted all over you twice in one day. Sorry about that."

"You're entitled." He considered the fact that she allowed herself to be vulnerable in his arms a victory of sorts.

She dabbed her eyes, then wiped her nose. "I'm going to make that bastard pay."

Nathan's mind raced. If he went with his instincts and informed her there was no way in hell she was getting anywhere near Mirga, he could pretty much give up any hope that she'd ever see him as anything more than the guy she regretted having sex with.

If he gave her the reins and let her lead the effort to bring down Mirga and his sex-trafficking empire, he was letting her risk her own safety, but maybe she'd realize he wasn't trying to curb her independence or make her weak.

He wanted her just the way she was—stubborn and independent, full of passion.

Someone who kept him on his toes. Who reminded him that life was full of risks but offered great rewards. He needed to protect her more than he needed to breathe, but, dammit, he wanted her to protect him as well. To watch his six. Be part of the team he'd formed with his friends at Dìleas when he didn't think he'd ever be part of a team again after he left the SEALs.

He wanted her to need him.

But to do that, he had to let her take point instead of forcing her to follow behind him.

"How are we going to do that?" He forced the words out before he changed his mind.

She started to reply, then stopped when his words penetrated.

"We?" She eyed him warily.

He sighed, rubbing his hand over his hair. "If we do this, Emily, we do it my way. I'm not willing to take unnecessary risks with your life."

"You'll let me be part of it, though, right? I won't let you shunt me off to the side."

"Let's see if we can track down Mirga's whereabouts. Then we'll come up with a plan." He locked eyes with her. "Together."

"Thank you." She gripped his hand and squeezed. Her skin was warm and soft, and the smile she gave him reached her eyes.

Maybe there was hope for them after all.

Chapter
Twenty-Two

Jules Mirga stabbed out his third cigarette in the past hour, dropped it into an empty bottle of Château La Conseillante, and resumed his pacing. He was going crazy, cooped up like an animal in a cage. He'd been clever to procure this tiny cottage on the outskirts of Noisy-le-Grand and keep it hidden from everyone but his cousin.

Constantin, his best friend since they were boys. Dead. At the hands of some American soldier, who'd taken Emily Dane from him. He grabbed his makeshift ashtray and hurled it into a wall. Glass shattered, spilling ashes and cigarette butts on the floor to mingle with bottle shards.

Sami ran into the room, gun drawn.

Jules flung his hand toward the mess. "Clean that up."

The American woman would pay for the trouble she had brought to him.

His phone rang. He snatched it off the table. *His informant.* "What?"

"Emily Dane has been sent to the US."

"*Fils de pute!* Have you found out the name of the *salaud* who killed Constantin?"

"Jules, I beg you. Leave her alone. It will only make things worse for you. Stay away from Paris for a while and let this blow over."

Rage boiled in Jules's blood. "How is the boy, *mon ami*? Is he staying clean? Does he enjoy his new life?" His voice rose to a shout. "My cousin is dead. That meddling bitch and her rescuer owe me a blood debt, and I intend to collect."

The voice on the other end remained silent for several seconds before speaking. "If I give you the name of the man who killed Constantin, will you leave Emily alone?"

Jules let the man sweat out his answer for a full minute.

"I might." He needed this *imbécile*'s cooperation to set his plan in motion. He intended to turn the meddlesome blonde over to his client in Syria as promised, but if saying otherwise made the man cooperate, so be it.

"The man who rescued her is a former Navy SEAL. He escorted her back to the States. I believe he is serving as her bodyguard."

"What is his name?" A renewed burst of energy shot through Jules. He'd kill this SEAL and hand the Dane woman over to his client. His informant would need to die as well. He knew too much and seemed to have developed a conscience where the woman was concerned. Unfortunately, it would take time to cultivate another source as helpful as this one.

The man hadn't answered him. Jules tightened his grip on the phone. "I asked you a question. Do you have the name of the man who killed Constantin?"

"His name is Nathan Long."

"Excellent work." A visceral satisfaction filled Jules. "You will be rewarded."

"I don't want any more bloodshed. It was unnecessary to kill the Giurescu girl."

Really? This *crétin* was worried about the death of a whore?

"Please, *mon ami*, I cannot be held responsible for her actions once she chose to return to Paris." Jules hung up and turned his attention to his immediate problem. How to get Emily Dane to return to Paris and bring her bodyguard with her.

Sami was on his hands and knees, cleaning up the glass and ash from the bottle Jules had thrown.

Jules smiled. "Leave it, Sami. I have an assignment for you and Hugo."

Catalina was dead. But the other girl was still alive and well.

CHAPTER
TWENTY-THREE

EMILY SCURRIED FROM NATHAN'S office to the kitchen before she did something stupid, like kiss him. Every day in his presence weakened her resolve to keep her attraction to him under control so she could put him behind her when it was time to leave.

She scanned the refrigerator contents. Hamburger, chicken breasts. *Hmmm*. She wasn't in the mood for chicken but could use the ground beef to whip up an easy meat sauce. A quick look through Nathan's cabinets produced spaghetti and pasta sauce, which she could jazz up with the meat, garlic, and spices. Thirty minutes later the pasta boiled, the sauce simmered, and another bottle of red wine breathed.

And she missed Nathan's presence even though he was just down the hall.

"Dinner's ready," she called out. She set the table, then drained the pasta, and threw together a salad with what she found in the fridge.

Awareness danced across her neck. She glanced up.

Nathan stood at the entrance to the hallway, hands in his back pockets. The stance stretched the fabric of his t-shirt even tighter across his muscled chest. He watched her with a predatory intensity that made every part of her come alive.

How long had he been lurking there silently, like a big cat?

"I'll pour the wine." The words were benign but the way he uttered them, his voice low and rumbly, reminded her of sex and vibrated through her body, making her skin hypersensitive.

She concentrated on not burning the sauce as he reached over her to lift wine glasses out of the upper cabinet. The space seemed to shrink, becoming claustrophobic. Nathan's chest grazed her hair, and she froze.

"Thank you for making dinner." Puffs of air tickled her ear, making her shiver.

"You're welcome." Her reply came out breathless. He stepped away and she could breathe again. She added the sauce to the spaghetti and set the food on the table.

Nathan took a seat and gestured for her to fill her plate first.

As she reached for the salad tongs, her phone dinged with an incoming text. The tongs halted mid-air between the bowl and her plate.

Don't do it. It would be rude to get up in the middle of dinner and see who it was. But what if it was news from France? Maybe the police had finally arrested Mirga.

"Go ahead." Nathan's lips tilted in an amused smile. "You know you want to."

"Sorry." She sent him an apologetic glance before jumping up to grab her cell off the kitchen counter.

The text was from her brother and contained a laughing face emoji and a thumbs up emoji. *So, you're shacking up with Nathan Long? Glad to hear you took Dad's advice.*

Oh, good grief. That hadn't taken long. Who said men weren't horrible gossips?

"You roll your eyes any harder, they'll get stuck that way," Nathan observed from his chair.

"The SEAL grapevine has been busy. My brother knows I'm staying with you." She glanced around at the domestic tableau and her stomach flip-flopped at the realization she felt comfortable here, even with the sexual tension that flared between her and Nathan whenever they got too close. "It's only a matter of time before my father finds out."

Nathan's gaze searched hers. "Would it be so bad for him to know? You're both getting what you want. You want my help to bring down Mirga, and he wants you safe."

"I don't need you to be my bodyguard." The words snapped out of her without thought.

Nathan's expression closed down.

She wanted to kick herself. Taking on Mirga was dangerous—she wasn't stupid. Having Nathan by her side made her breathe easier, and the fact that he wasn't trying to keep her from participating made her heart do funny things.

And she liked him. A lot.

Too much.

He wasn't just a guy with a hot body who was great in bed.

Not bothering to respond to her brother, she dropped her phone back on the counter and returned to the table. After that brief exchange, the only sounds in the room came from the clink of silverware against ceramic and the tap of wine glasses on the table.

Nathan shoveled forkfuls of pasta and salad into his mouth. How he inhaled food so rapidly without appearing vulgar was a mystery. He lifted his head, and her attention snagged on the movement of his throat as he drained his glass of wine.

A pulse of need tightened her throat, making it hard to swallow. The safest thing to do would be to remove herself from his presence for the rest of the evening. "I think I'll take my glass of wine and have a bath before turning in."

"Use the tub in my bathroom if you'd prefer—it's nicer," Nathan offered. "Take a look at it while I clean up dinner." He stood to clear the table.

Common sense said she should politely refuse. It seemed a bit too intimate.

Meh. Why not at least look? She wouldn't mind a peek into his personal space, see if it told her anything more about him than what she already knew.

After a wine refill, she wandered past Nathan's office to his bedroom, nudged open the door, and stepped inside, coming to an abrupt halt. Not what she'd expected. Pale gray walls. A weathered, charcoal gray headboard lorded over a California king mattress covered with a lush, navy comforter.

Nathan's bed was massive, like the man.

She ran her finger over one of the pillowcases—silky and cool to the touch. He had a sensual side, but she'd already known that from the time he'd devoted to running his fingertips and tongue over every inch of her when they'd gotten together. Her brain thoughtfully provided a visual, hardening her nipples and sending a burst of liquid heat to dampen her panties.

Muttering a curse under her breath, she put her back to the bed and examined the rest of the room. Nightstands matched the oversized bed. A chest of drawers of the same dark wood took up space on the opposite wall. Elegant, navy silk draped each side of the double windows.

Her lips tightened. A woman had decorated this room.

None of your business. They couldn't have the kind of relationship where it mattered. Because if they did, everything in her life would change. Every goal she set for herself would be framed through the lens of how it impacted her *and* Nathan.

She wandered to the dresser and picked up the framed five-by-seven of a younger Nathan and his family at his graduation from SEAL qualification training, where he received his trident.

Nathan's father was almost as tall as his son, with dark hair but the same crystal blue eyes. His mom was also tall, and blonde, her eyes a darker shade of blue. His sister was a carbon copy of their mom. His two brothers, like Nathan, were a mix of their parents.

Her heart did a strange little flip at the pride and love written across the faces of the Long family. She placed the frame back on the dresser.

The master bath connected directly to the bedroom. Emily stepped into it and resisted the urge to squeal. Now this was her kind of bathroom. Contemporary gray tiles overlaid the floor and walls of a spacious walk-in shower. As if that wasn't impressive enough, a spa-sized garden tub sat next to the shower. She peered over the edge.

Jets.

She definitely was taking a bath here.

Her gaze wandered to the granite countertop with double sinks and weathered charcoal cabinets that matched Nathan's bedroom furniture. The rest of his home might scream outdated bachelor pad, but his bedroom and master bath were straight out of the final reveal in an HGTV show.

Still, she couldn't shake the feeling she was enjoying another woman's design.

She twisted on the tub's double faucets and held her fingers beneath the stream of water until the temperature was right, refusing to ruin her opportunity to lounge in luxury by obsessing over who was responsible for it. Hustling to the guestroom, she gathered her nightgown, robe, and body wash.

When she passed by on her return trip, Nathan was still cleaning up the kitchen. "I'm using your tub—thanks." *Don't say it, don't say it*—"Your bedroom and bathroom are certainly a step up décor-wise."

Damn, you said it.

Something that felt uncomfortably like jealousy had taken control of her tongue.

The corner of his mouth lifted. "My sister's final project for her interior design degree. She's bugging me to redo the kitchen and living room next."

Sister.

The giddy feeling in her chest was so inappropriate. Snagging the rest of the wine from dinner, she hurried down the hall and closed the bathroom door. After checking the water level, she added her body wash—vanilla chai. It might not make bubbles, but it was better than nothing.

As she lifted her t-shirt, her gaze caught on the speaker mounted in the corner of the ceiling. She froze, the shirt dangling from her fingers.

Nathan had this place wired to the hilt with security. Was there a camera, too? Did he have a voyeuristic kink?

Her body flushed. She squeezed her knees together, her breaths quickening. Maybe she'd put on a show he'd never forget just to torment him.

"No, Emily, bad idea." Tugging her shirt back on, she walked to the hall and called out, "There are no cameras in this bathroom, are there?"

A short bark of laughter came from the kitchen. "No, darlin', but thanks for the suggestion. If you'd like, I can put one in tomorrow."

"It wasn't a suggestion, you perv." Okay, she was the pot calling the kettle black. The thought of him watching had turned her on a little. "What about the speaker? Can it play music?"

Nathan appeared in the hall. "What kind of music?"

"Something soothing. Light classical or soft jazz?"

He nodded. "Let me see what I can do. Take your bath. I can turn it on from the war room."

She didn't have to be told twice. Paradise awaited.

Back in the bathroom, she disrobed and sank into the water to her chin. Closing her eyes, she leaned her head on the edge of the tub and reached for her wine. Strains of Vivaldi floated overhead. The tension she'd felt all day slowly evaporated with the water's heat. She wasn't going to worry about Jules Mirga, her career, or the sexy man skulking in another part of the house.

Her mind wandered as she relaxed. Despite her best efforts, it drifted to Nathan. His body. The expression on his face when he went down on her the night of Sophia and Lachlan's wedding and again in her apartment the day after he rescued her. She shifted in the water, restless, remembering how he looked as he climaxed, his head thrown back as he thrust into her, the cords in his neck standing out in stark relief.

Ugh. Now she was horny, and it was Nathan's fault.

The only way she would relax was to take matters into her own hands. Eyes closed, she pictured him as her free hand dipped beneath the surface and brushed her breast, thumbing her nipple. The sensation made her legs churn, creating ripples in the water. Her hand continued over her stomach down to her sex. She bit her lip as her fingers rubbed her clit. She moved them faster, pushing one finger inside as her pace became frantic. Water splashed onto the ledge.

Almost there. Her body tightened. She came with a moan, only stopping when her clit became too sensitive to touch. She breathed in deeply through her nose until her pulse returned to normal.

Now she could enjoy her bath.

A very male grunt had her shooting upright in the tub, eyes wide.

Nathan stood at the doorway, hands gripping the frame over his head. His gaze burned her skin as it traveled over her breasts, stopping at the hand she'd just used to pleasure herself. A look molten enough to reheat the cooling water crossed his face and ensnared her.

Her body tightened as the afterglow of her orgasm disappeared.

"If you wanted to come, all you had to do was ask." Nathan's body was jacked so tight he wasn't sure he could take a step without coming in his jeans.

Emily had been in his tub so long he'd gotten concerned, especially when she didn't respond to his polite rap on the door. When he opened it and saw what she was doing, he stood there like a peeping Tom instead of doing the polite thing and easing the door closed again.

Holy hell, this woman did things to him no other woman had. Had she been thinking of him while she pleasured herself?

"Why are you in here?" Her voice was breathless. Must have been a good orgasm.

He could do her one better.

"You were quiet for so long I thought you might have drowned." Every intention he'd had about keeping Emily in the friend zone where she seemed to want him flew out the window. He stepped into the bathroom, his eyes on the breasts she still hadn't covered.

"Baths are for relaxing. It's not a shower." Her comeback might be snappy, but her gaze raked him hungrily.

He could work with that.

"I knocked. You didn't answer." Another step, then another. He dropped to his knees next to the tub. His finger traced the plump flesh of her bottom lip, then lowered to her collarbone before moving over the swell of her breast, circling her nipple without touching it.

Her pupils flared, darkening her eyes to topaz. "Join me." Her husky invitation dripped with desire and was all the invitation he needed.

He shot to his feet, ripped off his shirt, yanked off his shoes and socks, and sent everything sailing over his shoulder in a careless gesture. Wheeling toward his bathroom vanity, he tore open the drawer where he kept a box of condoms and pulled out one of the foil packets.

He shucked off his jeans. Her eager gaze had him hard as a tent pole and he breathed a sigh of relief when his erection sprang free from its confines.

"Do you even own underwear?" Her brow quirked as she gave him a sassy look.

Any response he might have given was short-circuited when her hand wrapped around him. The move stopped him in his tracks better than a Taser.

She rose to her knees and licked his crown. The feel of her tongue on him sent a lightning bolt to his groin and tightened his balls. A deep groan ripped from his chest.

His fingers threaded into her hair as she wrapped her lips around him and sucked, one hand on his thigh and her other massaging his sac. His hips jerked. It was everything he could do not to come. Emotion swelled his chest as he stared down at her blonde head while she worked him. He could barely breathe from it.

"Emily, look at me."

She peered up at him, her blue eyes burning with a pleasure that threatened to drop him to the tile floor if the building orgasm didn't take him down first.

"You are so fucking beautiful—you don't even realize your power over me." He'd never felt this way before. Somehow, the one woman determined to keep her emotional distance from him had burrowed her way into his heart.

She dropped her lids, shielding her reaction to his words.

Disappointment knifed through him, then scattered as Emily's nails dug into his thigh and she took him deeper. His body reacted with an instinctive thrust, his thoughts disintegrating under a wave of hot, consuming lust.

Fuck. He couldn't hold out much longer. He wanted inside her before he exploded.

Shifting his hands from her hair to her shoulders, he held her in place as he pulled away. The protest forming on her lips died when he grabbed the foil packet off the counter, ripped it open with his teeth, and suited up. He lifted her and stepped into the tub, then lowered them into the water, draping her over his hips. His hands tight around her waist, he thrust until he was balls-deep inside her tight, hot sheath.

Water sloshed in waves over the tub onto the bathmat and floor. Her head fell back on a moan, jutting her breasts forward like a decadent offering.

He sucked one rosy tip into his mouth before turning his attention to her other breast. Waves of tepid tub water crested over them as his hips thrust in a gentle rhythm.

Emily's eyes were screwed tight.

No. She wasn't going to get off while shutting him out. He wouldn't let her. "Open your eyes, Emily."

She gave a slight shake of her head.

His fingers dug into her hips. "Look at me, Em. Don't be a coward."

Her eyes flew open and locked with his, defiance and a hint of fear in their depths.

Yeah, he knew that would get her attention. "Don't look away, babe."

"Shut up and get me off." She met his thrusts, urging him to move faster as the heat between them built to a roaring inferno.

His fingers danced across her clit as his pace accelerated. Her inner walls tightened around him. Close, so close.

Emily lowered her gaze.

"Look at me." The harsh command flew from his lips. She was not going to hide from him. His fingers moved faster, harder. "Come for me."

"Nathan." His name left her lips with a wail, her fingers digging into his shoulders, her eyes dilating with pleasure as her body fisted him in wave after pulsing wave.

He held her stare as his own body seized, letting her see into his soul without flinching. Everything he felt for her, everything he thought they could be together, was there.

Her eyes slammed shut, breaking their connection.

Nathan swallowed his frustration as she collapsed against his chest. She might be willing to share her body with him, but she still was afraid that sharing her heart would make her weak. Diminish her independence.

He held her in his arms until the cooling water pebbled their flesh. There was no point challenging her fears right now. "That was fun."

She gave a tired laugh. "You get to clean up the floor. That's where most of the water is." Hands braced on his chest, she stood, keeping her gaze averted.

He admired her breasts and the rounded curves of her ass as she stepped out of the tub and wrapped herself in one of his oversized bath towels. Her body language made it clear what she planned to do—run away to the safety of his guest room and pretend this never happened and that it wouldn't happen again.

The hell it wouldn't.

He wasn't ready to let her go just yet. He stepped out of the tub, water dripping everywhere as he padded to where she stood and dropped a soft kiss on her ear, satisfaction filling him when she shivered.

"Stay with me tonight." He pointed over her shoulder to his bed. His breath caught and held, waiting to see if she would stay or flee this thing between them that was so much more than sex.

Not that a locked door would stop him. The only way she was sleeping alone tonight was if she looked him dead in the eye and told him she didn't want to share his bed.

She had her luscious lower lip gripped between her teeth, indecision warring on her pretty face.

He turned her to face him and pressed his lips to hers in a gentle caress. Her body melted into him. She kissed him back, hands gripping his biceps.

Hope surged through him. "Stay. Please."

Releasing her, he grabbed a towel and tossed it on the floor to mop up the water. If she did go, he didn't want to watch.

"Just for a little while," she whispered.

"We've got movers coming from the east." Danny Mayhew's voice pierced Nathan's ear, his tone urgent.

God dammit. Nathan grimaced. He turned to the Air Force controller embedded with his team. "Call in close air support. Can you get a laser lock on the coordinates of the incoming hostiles?"

"Working on it," came the terse response.

Pffftt. Something skimmed Nathan's cheek and kicked up dirt a yard in front of him.

"Hostiles above us!" Joe Logan yelled.

Nathan dove for cover as another round hit the dirt next to him. "Where the hell did they come from?"

His question disappeared into the rat-a-tat-tat of multiple automatic weapons fire. He swiped at the wetness on his cheek and came away with a bloody glove.

"Cover and move!"

Their air support, an Apache attack helicopter, hummed in the distance.

Before the Apache launched its weapons, they needed to get the hell off this ridgeline.

Nathan pressed his mic. "Charlie, CAS on station, fall back." He turned to his air controller. "Make sure the pilot knows the coordinates are danger close."

"RPG!"

Nathan whipped his head around to see Joe Logan charge up the slope, his rifle spitting out a steady stream of bullets. He peered through *his NVGs and caught sight of three enemy fighters, each shouldering a rocket-propelled grenade launcher.*

"Call off the Apache."

The words were still leaving his mouth when the Hellfire missile fired from the helicopter and the RPGs launched by the insurgents passed each other, each hitting their marks. The ground where the enemy fighters had been standing exploded in a fountain of flames, dirt, and flesh.

Two rocket-propelled grenades missed the helicopter, but the third one found its mark with a direct hit on the Apache's tail rotor. The aircraft fell from the sky in a clumsy spiral, hitting the mountainside, shredding trees, and exploding in a fireball.

"Charlie One to base, we have a helo down, repeat, we have a helo down." Nathan charged up the ridge. Where was Joe?

"Charlie Three, respond."

"Nathan." A soothing, feminine voice sounded in his earpiece amidst the chaos.

Emily?

He whipped his head around, searching desperately for her. It was too dangerous for her to be here.

"Nathan, wake up. You're safe."

He followed the sound of her voice. The stark mountainside in Afghanistan faded in the dim light of the table lamp by his bed.

It had been a while since he'd had that dream.

"Are you okay?" Emily was sitting up, the top sheet gathered to her breasts in a white-knuckled grip, eyes wide. He'd half-expected her to sneak back to the guest room in the middle of the night.

"Yeah, shit. Sorry. Did I hurt you?"

She shook her head.

He swiped his hand down his face, then focused on her full lips, the pert tilt of her nose, the tousled blonde hair curling over bare shoulders. The need to protect her overwhelmed him. He couldn't fail Emily.

"I won't let anyone hurt you."

Her eyes widened further at the savagery even he could hear in his vow.

"Are you sure you're okay?" Her death grip on the sheet loosened. She brushed her fingers along his cheek.

He breathed in calm before forcing a cocky grin to his lips. The need to touch her, feel her warm and alive beneath him, drove him hard. "I can think of something that will make me very okay." He yanked on the sheet and pulled her naked body over his.

Her lips tilted to one side even as her eyes searched his. "You are such a perv." She lowered her mouth to his.

Nathan left his fears in the past and drank Emily in like an answered prayer.

CHAPTER
TWENTY-FOUR

SUNRISE PUSHED TENDRILS OF light through the trees, flooding the gap in the navy drapes. Emily eased back the covers and slid from Nathan's bed, half-expecting a hand to halt her escape. Nathan lay on his back, covers bunched around his waist. His bare, sculpted chest rose and fell in a slow, deep rhythm. His forearm rested over his eyes.

He was asleep. *She* should be, too. They hadn't exactly nodded off after she joined him in bed last night. The man had serious stamina. Then after his nightmare, the look in his eyes when he'd sworn to keep her safe had cracked open her heart.

She grabbed her clothing and crept to the guest room.

Last night hadn't been simply about physical release. There'd been emotion embedded in their caresses. She refused to name what she'd seen in his eyes, but she'd never felt as vulnerable.

Nor as safe.

Which scared the hell out of her.

Gathering fresh clothes, she locked herself in the hall bath. Without waiting for the water to warm, she stepped into the shower. Icy spray shocked her skin, gave her goosebumps, and jolted her out of her morning fog. She poured a generous amount of shampoo into her hands and lathered her hair.

Remember your career. Her life plan didn't include falling in love with a SEAL.

Her hands stilled.

Love?

White suds ran in rivulets down her body. Pangs squeezed her chest—she couldn't draw in air. Her breaths became desperate gasps.

She shut off the water and sat on the tub's edge, head between her knees, water dripping onto the floor.

What had become of her life?

She'd achieved every goal she'd set—attending a prestigious university, passing the Foreign Service Officer Test, and landing a plum posting in the embassy in Paris.

Then she'd set out to rescue Catalina and Maya and help put away an evil sex trafficker because collecting data on the problem wasn't enough for a Dane. Danes took action.

Keep her attraction to Nathan under control? A piece of cake turned into humble pie.

She'd become a spectacular failure, personally and professionally. Catalina was dead because of her. She'd put her career on shaky ground by interfering in internal French matters. She'd been sent back to the States as punishment, at least until the police located and arrested Jules Mirga.

And she had allowed herself to fall in love with a Navy SEAL.

Nathan was precisely the wrong man for her. Another protective alpha male.

And yet, he was funny, and cared about her. He hadn't tried to smother her. He'd promised to help her bring down Mirga, and he hadn't tried to move her to the sidelines.

Don't be a coward, Em.

Nathan's voice spoke in her head as clearly as if he was in the bathroom with her, whispering in her ear.

She wrapped a towel around her hair, then grabbed another and briskly dried off her body before slipping into her underwear, a flouncy navy skirt and pastel pink short-sleeved top. Her grandmother's pendent lay heavy against her skin.

Her reflection in the steam-fogged mirror seemed to mock her.

"What's it going to be?" she asked it.

Was she going to keep denying her feelings for Nathan or see if this relationship could become something more?

For the first time, she let herself flirt with the idea that she could have everything she wanted—her career, her independence.

And Nathan.

Makeup on, hair dried, and dressed, she headed to the kitchen to start breakfast, her mind whirling with what, exactly she'd say to him.

She'd fled from his bed. That's how he'd see it, at least. And it was the truth.

But she'd decided to stop running from her feelings.

Water rushed through pipes in the living room wall adjacent to his bathroom. He was in his massive, tiled shower. She pictured his body, water caressing all that skin and muscle.

Every delicious inch.

Her breasts tingled, desire heating her blood. She glanced down at her clothes. She could dry her hair again.

The sheets on his bed were still mussed from their lovemaking. Stripping, Emily tossed her clothes on the bed and padded to the bathroom. The clear glass door of the shower gave her a full view of what she'd come for. A naked Nathan, eyes closed, head tilted beneath the spray as he rinsed his hair, waters streaming over parts of him she intended to lick.

She yanked open the door and slipped inside.

Nathan's lids flew open to spear her with those blue eyes, heated from within by an icy fire. "I thought maybe you'd run away again." His big hands wrapped her waist, pulling her into his hard body. He shifted so the spray wouldn't hit her in the face.

"I thought about it." Her fingers slid over the tattoos decorating his arms.

He dropped his head to her shoulder and nibbled on the delicate juncture of her neck, sending shivers coursing through her. "What made you change your mind?"

I love you.

She wasn't ready to say that out loud, so she stood on tiptoe, bringing her face closer to his. Sliding her fingers over the bridge of his nose and across his lips, she brushed her cheek against the stubble shadowing his jaw. "You said we'd bring down Jules Mirga together. We're a team."

She nipped at his lower lip, then sent one hand down his broad back to squeeze those perfect glutes. "And teammates watch each other's six."

A low rumble of laughter vibrated from his chest to hers. "Is that what this is, darlin'? You watching my six?" His hands lowered to her bottom and lifted, bringing them flush. He turned and pressed her into the tile wall.

She gasped as cold stone met her back and wrapped her legs around his hips, his erection pressing into her belly. "Well, you do have a rather nice six."

"Mmmm." His lips trailed their way from her shoulder to her breast. He stopped to plant a kiss on her grandmother's pendant. "I'm glad you approve."

She barely had time to take a breath before he positioned himself and thrust, driving deep into her. They both moaned.

"Jesus, Emily, you feel so damn good." Nathan's whisper was hot on her wet skin. He shuddered in her arms.

He thrust again, sending shockwaves of pleasure through her. Water sprayed off his shoulders, coating her face in a mist. Their lips met in a wild kiss.

She was drowning in a tidal wave of sensation wrapped in his arms, her grandmother's pendant trapped between them as he drove into her again and again. It was all she could do to cling to his wet shoulders and hold on for dear life. He stole her reason and her heart with every thrust, every caress.

"You are so fucking beautiful. So hot you set me on fire. And I still want to come back for more."

"Nathan." His name slipped from her lips with a moan. Tears pricked her eyes at his words. Everything she was feeling gathered in her throat. An overwhelming sense of vulnerability kept the words from escaping. She took his mouth and poured her emotions, the things she couldn't say, into him.

His chest heaved against her breasts. He stroked her clit and her orgasm rushed up to take her over with such force she screamed into his mouth, her nails digging into his skin.

"Fuck." His hips churned, then he stilled and threw his head back with a shout, pouring himself inside her.

When he was finished, his forehead hit the tile next to her face with a thunk. "I'm dead," he gasped. "It was a good death, mind you, but I'm still dead."

She giggled. "You're not dead, but you may be concussed." Her legs slid down to regain purchase on the floor. The water pelting Nathan's back had turned cold. "You may want to shut off the water before we become icicles."

He reached behind him and twisted the faucet. When he lifted his head, his gaze was pensive. "I didn't use a condom."

She'd loved the feel of his bare flesh inside of her. "I'm on my birth control. And I'm clean."

"Yeah, me too." One side of his mouth tilted in a grin. "Put your makeup on this morning already, didn't you."

Her eyes rounded. "Oh my God, tell me I don't look like a raccoon."

"An adorable raccoon."

She shoved against his shoulders with a shriek and scrambled from the shower, wrapping herself in one of his giant bath towels before she gathered up the nerve to peer at the mirror over the closest sink. Sure enough, her mascara now resided in black smudges beneath her eyes.

Nathan appeared behind her, still naked. He wrapped his arms around her towel-clad body and kissed the top of her head.

She stared at their reflection as the evidence he'd come inside her leaked down her thighs.

They looked right together. They fit.

Her fingers lifted, surrounded the starburst pendant lying below her damp collarbone. Birth control or not, she'd never before let any man get away with not using a condom.

"I can see all those thoughts competing for supremacy in your head," Nathan murmured in her ear.

Her gaze flew to meet his in the mirror.

"We make a great team, Emily, in more ways than one. Just let yourself feel it, don't overthink it." He dropped his arms and stepped back, giving her a light pat on the butt. "I'll make breakfast."

She could only nod and hurry from the bathroom. By the time she emerged from her room, dressed, her hair and makeup redone, Nathan had whipped up a batch of pancakes and sausage.

He handed her a cup of coffee. "Cream and sugar's already in it."

She took a sip. *Perfect*. "You're quite handy in the kitchen. I'm going to get fat if I stay here much longer."

He set the platter of pancakes and sausage on the table and slanted her a look that stole her breath. "We'll find a way to burn the calories."

Her body shivered in response.

Focus. They couldn't spend all day having sex, no matter how much she loved that idea. They needed to find a way to end Jules Mirga and his criminal empire. It was the least she could do for Catalina now.

Her appetite disappeared at the thought of what she'd read in the police report. She had to force bites of Nathan's fluffy buttermilk pancakes down. As soon as she returned to France, she intended to have words with Victor Pierron, even if it got her in trouble with Minister Woodward. How could the police classify Catalina's death as a drug overdose when it was obvious she'd been held against her will, beaten, and abused? Mirga had to have a friend in the department, someone in a position of power.

"What's our next move?" she asked.

Nathan speared more pancakes from the platter to add to his plate. "I've asked Ryder to set up some visual surveillance at Mirga's properties to see if we can catch him coming and going from any of them. So far, he's managed to elude the authorities."

"What about your investigation for Special Agent Goodwin?"

"I've narrowed down a couple of people in the embassy, and at the State Department, for Goodwin to look into."

"How does that help us flush out Mirga?"

"Disrupt his transatlantic operation and he may make a mistake, reach out to people we're watching, or even expose himself." Nathan's gaze was steady as he met her eyes. "We'll find him."

Emily stabbed at the sausage on her plate. "And when we do? Will the police do anything?" She wished she had the power to declare

Mirga an enemy combatant so he could get taken out rather than go through the criminal justice system all lawyered up.

"As much as I'd like to kill him for what he did to you and Catalina, this isn't a military operation." Nathan must have read her mind. "We need to let the authorities handle Mirga. All we can do is dump enough evidence in their lap that they have no excuse not to lock him up."

"I need to go back to France. I'm useless here in the States. If I was in Paris, I could be out, interviewing some of the girls on the streets, following his pimps," her hand fisted, "do something other than sleuthing on the Internet."

"Don't discount what you can discover online," Nathan replied. "Your boss sent you packing for a reason. You'll put your job in jeopardy if you defy her."

"She made me take a leave of absence from my job, but she can't dictate where I am while I'm on leave."

Nathan sighed, running a hand over his hair, creating more tousled spikes. "Let's work the problem from here a couple more days and see what we come up with. If we run out of leads, we'll return to Paris and start snooping around."

Her heart did a funny flip in her chest. Hope surged, warm and tingly. "You'd come with me?"

Nathan snorted, his eyes narrowing on her. "Do you honestly think I'm going to let you prowl the streets of Paris asking uncomfortable questions of dangerous people without me? I said I had your six. I meant it."

Okaay. A bit alphahole of him, but she'd accept it. She was bound to attract unwanted attention like she had last time.

Her stomach cramped at the memory. Yeah, it wouldn't hurt to have a badass six-foot-six former SEAL next to her this time around.

"Deal. We give it a couple more days, and if we can't find Mirga, we go to Paris."

Nathan sat back in his chair, his eyes twinkling. "Look at you, all rational and clearheaded."

"Shut up before I change my mind," she snapped.

He had the nerve to chuckle. "I cooked, you clean."

Alphahole.

CHAPTER
TWENTY-FIVE

EMILY SPENT THE REST of the morning reading work emails. Once she'd caught up, she called her parents to let them know she was no longer staying at the Mackays' condo.

Her father could barely contain his glee at her living arrangements. "I'm glad you came to your senses. Nathan can keep you safe."

Next time she'd call rather than video chat so she could roll her eyes or stick out her tongue rather than be an adult. "He's not my bodyguard. I needed a place to stay so I wouldn't be a third wheel at the condo when Sophia and Lachlan return from their honeymoon, and Nathan has a couple of spare bedrooms. Plus, we're working on a project together." She was tempted to let her snark fly and make some flippant remark about enjoying the sex, too, but she wouldn't do that to Nathan.

Her father's smug expression sent off warning flares in her head. "Whatever you call him, or don't call him, keep him with you until Jules Mirga has been dealt with."

"Yes, Dad. Gotta go. Love you." She hung up and flopped back on her back with a sigh. Her phone, still in her hand, rang. *Inspector Pierron.*

"Mademoiselle Dane?"

"Yes, Inspector. Do you have any news on Jules Mirga?" *Or Catalina*, she added silently. The police report was a farce, and he'd signed off on it.

His sigh, usually weary, had an edge to it that had her sitting up. "The DCPJ has decided to take more definitive action to locate Mirga, thanks to pressure from your government. I'm afraid I do not approve of the plan, but I agreed to discuss it with you."

"What plan?"

"The task force assigned to this case would like to use you to bring Mirga out of hiding."

Her eyes flew wide. "You mean, as bait?" She hadn't seen that one coming. "How would that work?"

"You would need to return to Paris, start asking questions on the streets as you did before. If Mirga tries to come for you again, we will be watching and waiting to arrest him before he can get near you."

She chewed on her lip. The plan seemed simple enough as long as the police did their job. And she had Nathan, although she could already picture his reaction. It wouldn't be a positive one.

However, her gut told her it wouldn't be as easy as the inspector had just made it sound. She waited for the other shoe to drop.

Pierron continued. "You would wear a tracker in the event Mirga or his men manage to abduct you." Another weary sigh gusted in her ear across the line. "It is risky, Mademoiselle. We cannot guarantee your safety. It might be best if you had extra protection."

And there it was.

The police were offering her the opportunity she'd been waiting for—bring down Mirga, avenge Catalina, and get her life back.

But it was dangerous. Almost foolhardy.

A fine tremor ran through her body. She needed to reign in her impulsiveness and look at this objectively. If she went off half-cocked, she'd not only put her life in danger, she'd endanger Nathan as well.

That, she wouldn't do, not even to avenge Catalina.

"Do you remember Nathan Long, the man who rescued me? He'll return to Paris with me." She hesitated, then said what she knew in her heart she needed to say. "He'd have to approve this plan."

She'd just made Nathan her bodyguard. Her dad would laugh at the irony.

After he got done having a fit that she'd even consider allowing herself to be used as bait.

"Yes, you should tell him. I'm sure he will agree that this approach is too dangerous." Pierron tsked. "I will tell the task force to find another way. We can use an undercover female officer. It will take time, of course, for her to establish a cover and gain the trust of the trafficked girls, but after what happened to the Giurescu girl, and now with the other girl missing—"

"Wait, what other girl?" Emily's heart hammered in her throat. *Please, God, no.*

Silence met her question.

"Inspector Pierron? What other girl?"

"Madame Légère has not contacted you? The younger girl, Maya, went missing this morning."

The news hit Emily like a stun grenade. A sharp pain lanced her chest, and the roaring in her ears messed with her equilibrium. "No."

"We will find her and protect her, Emily."

She dimly registered the inspector's use of her first name, an informality he'd never permitted himself. "Like you did Catalina?"

Grief and bitterness choked her. *This is all my fault.*

"We will do our best to ensure Maya has a different outcome." Pierron's voice was grim and tinged with guilt.

Or maybe she just imagined he felt guilty because she sure as hell did.

She ran the angles in her head. Mirga wanted revenge, and there was still the Syrian who would pay well to get her. But she had Nathan. Surely that would balance it out.

"I'll do it. I'll be the bait."

Nathan was slogging through administrative work for Dìleas when Emily tapped on his door and stuck her head in. "Got a minute?"

"Please. Save me from this mind-numbing busywork." He drank in her appearance like a man desperately in need of water. It had only been a couple of hours since their fun in the shower, and he was ready for a repeat.

Hell, he'd always be ready to make love to Emily.

"Inspector Pierron called me."

"News on Mirga?"

She didn't respond right away, her teeth worrying her bottom lip.

He tensed, knowing he wouldn't like whatever she said.

"The police are ramping up their efforts to lure Mirga out of hiding, and they want me to help them."

"Oh?" *Fuck no.* "How do they propose to do that?"

She fidgeted under his stare. "They want me to return to Paris, start asking questions on the street—like we'd already discussed—" she threw out before he could object. "They think Mirga will be motivated to come after me again, but this time they'll put a tracker on me and have people watching me the entire time, and I'll have you."

Nathan exploded from his chair, fury fueling his movements. "They can't find the bastard on their own, so they want to use you as bait? Please tell me you were smart enough to say no."

Emily's face reddened. She squared her shoulders. "Maya, the young girl I rescued with Catalina, disappeared this morning." Her eyes pleaded with him. "We need to lure Mirga out of hiding. This is the best way."

All he could think about was that bastard's cousin pinning a shackled Emily to the bed, his hand around her neck as he delivered a blow to her stomach. "You know what he has planned for you. Why the hell would you put yourself in danger like that again?"

She reached up to stroke his jaw, her gaze pleading. "You promised me we'd work together to bring him down."

The need to protect her swamped him and drowned both the rational and emotional parts of his brain. "I also told you we'd do it my way, or we wouldn't do it at all." He knew he sounded unreasonable, but the thought of losing her filled him with an emotion he hadn't felt since Afghanistan.

Fear. He was afraid.

She'd become his everything.

He trapped her hand, holding her to him. "My job is to protect you."

"No." She yanked her hand back, her eyes sparking with temper. "That's not your job. We agreed to work together as a team. We'll decide together. I want to do this, so let's find a way to do this. I'll be wearing a tracker. Even if Mirga's men managed to kidnap me, the police would be able to find me."

"Do you hear yourself?" A vicious pounding took up residence near his temple. "Even if Mirga's men managed to kidnap you? What if they also manage to hustle you out of France and into Syria before the police find you? What if Mirga decides to shoot you in the street instead?"

"You'll be with me," she whispered.

"I'll be dead," he snarled, "because that is the only way Mirga or any of his men will ever get any-fucking-where near you."

She reared back. "Why are you behaving this way?"

"Maybe because I care about you? Maybe I've decided your life isn't worth risking? For anyone." He searched for something to say that might sound rational. "What makes you think you can trust this Pierron? Mirga has to have people on the take in the police, and Victor Pierron is the one person in the department who knows everything about you. He also signed off on the official report on Catalina's death."

"He's a sweet old man on the verge of retirement," she shot back, her eyes narrowing. "What proof do you have that I can't trust him?"

"None. Yet." He spat out the words "But I have a bad feeling about this entire thing."

"Inspector Pierron is not an informant for Jules Mirga." He could see her struggle for calm. "He didn't want me to do this."

Then he never should have asked.

"What about your buddy, Bruce? You told me you first encountered Constantin Mirga at the train station when you returned to Paris after the wedding, and surprise, surprise, Fleming shows up in the nick of time to escort you safely to work. Maybe he isn't the boy scout you think he is."

Her jaw dropped as a look of stunned surprise settled on her face. "Now you think Bruce betrayed me? Nathan, you've lost your mind."

She rubbed her temples as if the headache pounding him had jumped to her. "Bruce had a nephew he helped get into recovery from drug addiction. He's not going to help a man like Mirga, who peddles drugs as well as sex."

"It's the people you least expect to betray you that put the knife in your back." He knew from bitter experience. He, Lachlan, and Ryder had all trusted Nadia Haider, their translator in Afghanistan. She'd set them up to die. Joe Logan's wife had trusted him to make sure Joe came home alive. He'd betrayed that trust when his teammate went home in a body bag.

She gave him another pleading look. "If I don't help the police capture Mirga, Maya will die. I can't live with that."

"I won't risk you." Of that, he was dead certain.

He loved Emily. She'd come to mean everything, and neanderthal or not, he wasn't willing to let her offer herself up as a sacrifice.

She reared back, tears forming in her eyes. "I'm not yours to risk."

Her words were a dagger to his heart.

Nathan's shoulders slumped as all the fight leaked out of him. "No, you've made that clear often enough. I thought things had changed." Emily was never going to love him because she wouldn't let herself. Her damned independence meant too much to her and, in her mind, he threatened that.

Hurt ignited his temper. He didn't think about his next words. "You don't trust me, do you? Well, you may not think I'm good enough for you, but your daddy does. He hired Dìleas—me specifically—to keep your pretty little ass safe."

"What?" She gasped, her face blanching as betrayal bloomed across her expression. "You've been working for my father this entire time? I'm a job?"

"Yes. No. *Dammit.*" He whirled, spearing his hands into his hair. He'd fucked this up big time. "You're more than a job."

"You don't care about those girls any more than Jules Mirga does." He could hear the unshed tears thickening her voice.

Dropping his hands to his hips, he stared at the ceiling, half hoping the right thing to say to her would be written in black ink on the white paint. "Maybe I'm too close to the situation. If you're so damned determined to run to Paris and serve yourself up to Mirga, maybe Ryder and his team need to take over your protection." He turned back only to find out he was talking to Emily's back as she marched down the hall to the guest room. He stomped after her.

Emily pulled her suitcase from the closet and threw it on the bed.

"Emily, wait. Listen to me."

"I've heard enough."

His heart sank at the hurt in her glistening eyes.

"I'm going to Sophia and Lachlan's; there's still time for me to get on a flight back to Paris tonight. Jules Mirga needs to be stopped before he murders Maya like he did Catalina." She brushed past him to the hall bath to gather her toiletries.

Nathan stood there like a dumbass, not knowing what to say. Maybe he should let her cool off at the Mackays' and try to reason with her again later.

When she finished packing, she zipped her suitcase.

He stood to one side and let her pass, staring at her ramrod stiff back as she wheeled it down the hall toward the door leading to the garage.

"Emily. We'll talk later, okay? After we've both calmed down." He didn't try to hide the pleading note in his voice.

Her shoulders sagged. "I'm not sure what there is left to say." She opened the door and left without looking at him.

Her car engine revved, then grew distant as she sped down his driveway.

Nathan slammed his palm against the wall. What now? His temper and his fear had both gotten the better of him.

This from the guy his teammates had nicknamed "Ice," and not just because of the color of his eyes. He'd had a reputation for being calm and cool under pressure, a no-drama guy. If his men could see him now, they'd be rolling on the floor laughing their asses off. Emily had ticked him off, scared the bejeezus out of him, and hurt his feelings all in one breath.

He punched Ryder's number into his phone. "I'm a fucking idiot."

It took Ryder a moment to respond. "What did you do?"

"The police want to use Emily as bait to lure Mirga out of hiding. Victor Pierron pitched the plan to her this morning over the phone. I told her what I thought of the idea, and it went downhill from there." Nathan drew a long breath and pinched the bridge of his nose. The woman was going to give him a migraine or a heart attack. Or both.

"What do you need?" Ryder asked.

Relief loosened Nathan's shoulders. He'd missed having battle buddies who had his six. Being part of Dìleas had given him that back, at least. "As soon as I know her flight, I'll send it to you. Don't let her out of your sight. And do some digging for me on Victor Pierron. The guy seems harmless enough, but I'm not convinced Mirga doesn't have someone in the police leaking information to him so he can stay one step ahead. I won't let Emily jeopardize her life if Mirga knows what's going on and sets a trap."

"Take a deep breath, mate. I'm on it," Ryder assured him before hanging up.

Nathan walked outside and stared up at the bright summer sky.

Emily had to be crazy if she thought this was a good idea.

He couldn't think straight where she was concerned. They might catch fire in the bedroom, but she'd erected a wall around her heart he couldn't seem to breach.

He rubbed his hand over his chest. The damn thing kept twinging on him. He might need to see a doctor.

CHAPTER TWENTY-SIX

THE DRIVE FROM NATHAN'S home to Sophia and Lachlan's condo passed in a blur of tears and recriminations.

Emily had thought she and Nathan would be a team.

She'd thought he cared about her, maybe even loved her.

But she'd been an assignment for her father.

And when it came down to finally taking action against Mirga, Nathan had gone all overprotective SEAL on her, just as she'd feared. Another helpless female to be guarded.

Not a teammate.

Pulling into the building entrance, she parked her car in one of the outside visitor spaces. Sal, the security guard stationed in the lobby, greeted her as she wheeled her suitcase to the elevator and pressed the button for the fifth floor. She'd stay here until she booked her flight.

Once inside, her bags hit the light oak floor with a resounding thud. She sagged against the door and blew out a harsh breath laced with more tears. For God's sake, she was tougher than this.

"Get it together." She stomped the floor for emphasis.

Sophia and Lachlan's bedroom door opened. "Emily?"

Her best friend stood at the end of the hall, hair mussed and eyes wide, wearing a short silk robe.

Crap. Emily's hand flew to her mouth. They were back?

Sophia took one look at Emily's tear-stained face, raced over, and threw her arms around her.

"I'm sorry," Emily stammered, "I thought you and Lachlan were still on your honeymoon."

Lachlan appeared from the bedroom in sweats and a t-shirt, his hair mussed as if he'd been sleeping or—Emily's gaze darted between the couple—he and Sophia had been doing what newlyweds do.

"We got back early this morning." Sophia's mouth turned down at the corners. "Lachlan finally told me what happened, and I wanted to come back and make sure you were okay."

Emily's lips firmed as a fresh surge of emotion threatened to make her humiliate herself. "I'm sorry."

It was one thing to cry in front of her best friend. She refused to break down in front of Lachlan.

"Where's Nathan?" Lachlan asked.

A fresh surge of anger sharpened her reply. "You mean the body-guard my father hired behind my back? He's at his house, where I left him."

Sophia's brows furrowed. "I thought you knew the admiral hired Dìleas?" The look she shot Lachlan had his shoulders heaving on a weary sigh. He dug a phone out of his sweats and held it to his ear before disappearing into the bedroom.

"I didn't realize you were home. I just, I needed—" Emily's throat swelled.

Sophia grabbed her hand and dragged her to the couch. "Let me get coffee; then you're going to tell me what's going on." A few minutes later, she returned with mugs and handed Emily one with cream and sugar. "I'll be right back." She disappeared down the hall.

Emily sipped the hot liquid and forced herself to breathe. The adrenaline flooding her system subsided, replaced by a nervous stomach and a face so hot she could serve as a landing beacon for Reagan National.

Sophia returned to sit beside her on the couch. "Lachlan is going to give us privacy." Her husband emerged, dressed in gray trousers and a white button-down. He cast a wary glance at Emily before bending to kiss his wife.

Emily looked away from the tenderness on his face as he brushed his lips over Sophia's. She pictured Nathan's expression when he wouldn't let her close her eyes and block him out as they came in each other's arms. Her heart gave a painful squeeze.

"I'm meeting Nathan at the office," Lachlan spoke to Sophia, but his eyes slanted in Emily's direction.

Emily's lips thinned. "Tell Nathan and my father I don't need Dìleas's services. I'm returning to Paris to work with the French police. They'll protect me."

Lachlan didn't say anything.

Smart man. Her nerves were strung so tight she might say something she'd have to apologize for later.

As soon as the door closed behind him, Sophia grabbed her hand. "Tell me everything."

Emily tilted her face to the ceiling. "The Cliffs Notes version? I tried to be proactive and help bring down the largest sex trafficker in Paris, and for my efforts, I got abducted, forced into a leave of absence from my job, and sent back to the States as punishment." Her lips trembled. "I thought I was doing the right thing. But now one of the girls I rescued is dead—murdered, Sophia!—and the other is missing."

"Oh my God." Sophia squeezed Emily's hands, her eyes huge. "No wonder your father wanted Nathan to watch out for you."

Emily shot her a baleful look. "Don't defend him. Or Nathan."

Sophia gave her fingers another squeeze. "What else is wrong."

"You know me," Emily met her friend's knowing gaze, "I tend to charge into situations on my own." She gave a sad laugh. "Nathan told me we'd be a team, and I believed him. I thought we'd bring down Jules Mirga together. But the police want me to return to Paris and help lure Mirga out of hiding, and Nathan freaked out. That's when he told me my father hired him as my bodyguard and I was a job." A tear slipped down her cheek. She sniffed and brushed it away. "Remember my vow to never fall for a Navy SEAL?"

Sophia grabbed a tissue box from the kitchen, set it on the coffee table, and handed one to Emily. "You are more than a job to Nathan. If he got upset, it's because he cares for you." She offered Emily a sympathetic smile. "Those bossy alpha types can be a handful, but they're worth it."

Emily gave a weak laugh and held up her hand. "Okay, Mrs. New-lywed, I don't need gory details. I'm returning to Paris." Sophia's disapproving expression had Emily's shoulders hunching. "I have to try and save Maya, the other girl, and bring down Mirga's sex trafficking empire once and for all. He needs to be stopped."

Sophia's lips pursed. Emily knew she wouldn't like what her friend had to say but made an encouraging motion with her hand anyway.

"I know you're angry at Nathan, but as your friend, I'm telling you what you plan to do is dangerous. Please don't do this alone."

"Maybe. I can't think straight around him." She pleaded with Sophia for understanding. "I have to go."

Nathan strode down the hall to Dìleas's offices and yanked open the glass doors, his gut still roiling from his earlier confrontation with Emily. He'd sent an email to the admiral, letting him know that he would need to come up with a new plan for Emily's protection, and then Lachlan called to say he and Sophia were back in town, Emily had shown up at their doorstep and he wanted Nathan to meet him at the office, pronto.

He'd screwed up big time, both his job as Emily's protection and, more importantly, getting Emily to trust him enough to let down her emotional guard.

"Hey." He brushed past Penny's desk and spat out the greeting like it offended his tastebuds.

"Everything all right, dear?" Penny called after him, concern evident in her tone.

He ground to a halt, raised his gaze to the ceiling, and turned back. Penny reminded him of his mother, and his mother would never tolerate him greeting her in such a rude manner. "Sorry, it's been a rough morning. Lachlan's back. He should be in shortly."

She favored him with an understanding smile that only made him feel like a bigger ass. "Can I get you anything?"

"No, ma'am. Thank you, though." He escaped to his office and went to stand in front of the windows as another sweltering summer day turned the air on the other side of the thick plane of glass into a muggy swamp.

Sucking in a deep lungful of air, he closed his eyes to shut out the world. Emily's betrayed expression danced across the inside of his lids.

Dammit. They'd been so close to a real relationship, and he'd fucking blown it. He shouldn't have gone all caveman on her when she told him about the plan to use her as bait. He should have told her earlier about her father's assignment.

Hell, he should have turned it down. He hadn't needed the admiral's money as incentive to keep Emily safe.

Now she didn't trust him. She believed his promise to work together was a lie.

His back teeth ground together. He should have picked up the bartender the night of Lachlan and Sophia's wedding. She would have been a one-and-done. It would have saved him a lot of heartache. But Emily had wrapped her hand around his shoulder and accepted his offer—a temptation he couldn't resist.

He'd been a goner ever since. There was no escaping the truth.

He loved Emily Rose Dane.

His forehead hit the glass with a thud. It was his own damn fault for thinking he wanted more after watching Lachlan and Sophia together.

A hard rap vibrated his door before it opened, and Lachlan stepped inside.

Nathan turned from the window to face his friend. "Assign Ryder to watch her. I'm compromised."

Lachlan shrugged. "Emily told me she doesn't want Dìleas's protection. We can't protect someone who refuses to work with us."

Nathan had to pick his jaw off the floor before he could respond. "That bastard Mirga's still out there. There is no way she should be without protection, especially since she's determined to return to Paris."

"Let her father hire a French bodyguard."

"What the fuck, Lach?" Nathan's blood pounded behind his eyes. "Nobody can protect her like I can."

Lachlan's lips twitched. "Like you can?"

"Like we can—Dìleas."

Hell.

Nathan scrubbed his hands through his hair and turned back to stare out the window.

Lachlan moved to stand next to him. "If it were Sophia, I wouldn't let anyone else be responsible for her safety, not even you—and I trust you with my life."

Nathan cocked his head to meet Lachlan's gaze. "I don't think Emily will let me anywhere near her now."

A hint of amusement lurked in Lachlan's eyes. "And you're going to let a little thing like that stop you?"

Nathan's reply was interrupted by his office phone buzzing. He strode to the desk and hit the intercom button. "Hey, Penny, now's not a good time."

"Admiral Dane is here to see you and Lachlan." Penny's modulated voice held an undercurrent of tension that had both Nathan and Lachlan stiffening.

Nathan muted the phone. "Fuck." He sent Lachlan an apologetic glance. "I sent the old man a message this morning. I didn't know he was in town."

Lachlan's mouth thinned into a grim line as he gestured for Nathan to unmute the call. "Send him to my office, Penny." He jerked his chin toward the door. "Let's go deal with the admiral."

Porter Dane was already waiting when Nathan and Lachlan entered Lachlan's office. He speared Nathan with a wintry gaze before he favored Lachlan with the same.

"Admiral, won't you please sit down?" Lachlan waved the older man to a nearby chair.

"I don't need to sit down," the admiral snapped. "I need one of you to explain why my daughter is flying to Paris this evening." His finger speared in Nathan's direction. "You, Lieutenant, were assigned to protect her. Why aren't you stopping her?"

The man might be an admiral, but Nathan didn't have to stand for his tone or finger-pointing. "It was a mistake to hide our agreement from her. Now she doesn't trust me. I can't protect someone who won't trust me."

The admiral's eyes narrowed, his gaze coldly assessing. "How did she find out?"

"I told her after she insisted on agreeing to this cockamamie scheme the French police have to use her as bait to lure Mirga out of hiding."

Lachlan spoke up. "Emily fired Dìleas Security Agency this morning."

"She can't fire you—she never hired you. I did, and I expect you to do your job, especially now that she insists on putting herself in even more danger." The admiral turned to Nathan. "I'm disappointed, son. I thought you could handle her. I expected you to keep her in the States until Mirga is behind bars."

Nathan's fingers curled into fists. The slow burn simmering in his veins ignited into a conflagration. It had already been a shitty morning. He didn't need Emily's father questioning his abilities. He stepped into the admiral, using his size and muscle to intimidate.

"Nathan." Lachlan's voice held a clear note of warning.

Ignoring his friend, Nathan locked glares with the admiral, nose-to-nose. He had to give it to the older man, he didn't back down an inch. "Emily is a grown woman who can make up her own mind." He enunciated his next words. "If I go to Paris, it won't be for you, but because I told her we were a team, and we'd bring Mirga down together."

Wait.

What the fuck did he just say?

Nathan stepped back, putting space between himself and the other man before he did something profoundly stupid. Despite his anger and frustration with Emily, his words felt right. "Go ahead, fire Dìleas. It'll make my job easier. I intend to safeguard Emily my way, and I don't give a damn what you want or think." Now it was his turn to finger point. "But I'm warning you, don't send someone to get in my way." He braced for the shit to hit the fan. He'd told off one of the most respected former senior officers in the United States Navy and a client of Dìleas. Their company was still building its reputation and needed to be on the good side of DC movers and shakers.

Lachlan was going to let him have it after the admiral left.

The corners of Admiral Dane's mouth quirked up.

Nathan's eyes narrowed. Was that a pleased look on the old man's face? What game was he playing?

Lachlan, the bastard, also appeared to be fighting a smile.

Son of a bitch. "I'm going home to pack." Nathan stormed out. He was a glutton for punishment. Emily was not going to be pleased to see him.

Too bad. She could fight all she wanted.

At least she'd be alive to do it.

"Ladies and gentlemen, please stow your luggage and take your seats as quickly as possible." The female flight attendant's voice echoed throughout the Boeing 777. "We are preparing to close the cabin door."

Outside Emily's window seat, figures in reflective uniforms scurried around the aircraft in the waning light. The aisle seat next to her remained empty, which was just as well; she wasn't decent company.

She swallowed at the dull sheen in her eyes, reflected in the window. *Suck it up, buttercup.* She'd made her decision and had to make it work. Maya needed her, and if Nathan refused to help, well, they were never meant to be.

Better to know now before she made the mistake of telling him she loved him.

A large body appeared in the glass. The man was too tall for her to see his face in the reflection. He tossed a laptop on the seat beside her and stowed his carry-on overhead.

She kept her head turned to hide her grimace. So much for curling up alone. Hopefully, her new seatmate wasn't a talker. He settled into his seat, his broad shoulders taking up his space and part of hers. His jean-clad leg pressed into hers.

Oh, this would not do. She shifted to face the man and froze. Her pulse took off running. "What are you doing here?"

Nathan grinned. A lazy, sexy grin that made her want to grab his face and suck on his tongue. "Taking a vacation. Paris is lovely this time of year, or so I'm told."

Her secret happiness dimmed as reality hit. "My father sent you, didn't he?" She'd called her parents to tell them she was returning to Paris. Their response had been less than favorable, to put it mildly.

Nathan leaned in close, backing her against the window. The resolve in his steady gaze set butterflies loose in her stomach. "I'm not here for your daddy, Emily. I'm here for you. Argue all you want, but if you intend to go ahead with this plan, I will make sure Mirga never gets the chance to touch you again."

Relief struck her hard, watering her eyes. In a corner of her soul, she'd been afraid to go back to France. Her kidnapping had shaken her sense of safety and belief in her ability to protect herself. And, if she was brutally honest, she already missed Nathan. "Thank you."

He studied her for a moment in silence. "The only thing I did for your daddy was find a way to get you to stay with me. Everything else between you and me? That's real. It's ours." The intensity of his stare lifted her bruised heart and sent it soaring.

She gave him a watery smile and slid her hand into his.

They didn't speak while the flight attendants prepared the cabin for departure and played the pre-departure video. The plane taxied to the runway.

"So, now what?" Her gaze fixed on the runway as the plane lined up to take off.

"Set up a meeting with Pierron. I want input on how this operation will go down, and he needs to know in no uncertain terms that I will be with you every step of the way."

The plane lifted into the air and the earth fell away, her spirits lifting with it.

Nathan had her six.

Everything would be okay.

CHAPTER
TWENTY-SEVEN

THEY LANDED IN PARIS early the following morning. Nathan's back and legs were stiff from sitting in a coach seat for eight hours, but it was an acceptable sacrifice for being able to sit next to Emily.

Emily arranged to meet Victor Pierron in a café not far from her apartment then emailed Minister Woodward, letting her know she was back in the country at the request of the French police.

They stopped by her apartment to freshen up and change clothes before heading to the café. Emily showered and changed into work clothes in anticipation of a meeting with Minister Woodward at the embassy. Nathan couldn't help but admire the shapely curve of her calves beneath her short black skirt, her pumps carrying just enough heel to elongate her already-long legs. The short-sleeved cranberry red silk blouse she wore made her eyes green today.

He glanced down at the tailored gray trousers, black belt, and light pink button-down he'd donned in anticipation of his meeting with Special Agent Goodwin later in the morning.

For once, they didn't look so mismatched together, with her all classy and him looking like a roadie for a metal band.

A light rain pattered the sidewalks in an unexpected gift from Mother Nature to tamp down the Parisian summer heat. They ordered coffee and croissants inside at the counter before finding a small table in the back corner of the brightly lit, cozy shop, forgoing the outdoor tables on the sidewalk with their bright blue umbrellas. Nathan sat facing the door, monitoring everyone who came in or even peered in through the front windows.

Several minutes later, Victor Pierron appeared at the wood-framed glass door dressed in a brown trench coat. He shook his black umbrella and closed it before entering. His eyes scanned the room, coming to rest on Nathan. Nathan could read the relief in both the man's face and his posture from across the room.

Pierron stopped at the counter to speak with the barista before shuffling in their direction.

"Inspector." Emily kissed the Frenchman's cheeks. Shadows darkened the inspector's features, and dark circles made his eyes appear sunken. The guy looked sick. Apparently, Emily noticed as well. She frowned. "Are you well?"

Nathan offered up a chair to the older man. The detective lowered himself to the seat with a groan. "I'm tired. Like all of us." His weary gaze connected with Nathan's. "It is good that you are here."

Nathan crossed his arms and glared down at the inspector. "I don't like this plan."

"Nathan, sit." Emily shot him a warning glare.

His jaw tightened. He pulled up another chair.

The inspector nodded. "I do not like it either, but the task force feels it is the best option to bring Mirga out of hiding." His lips tightened. "He is a man who holds grudges that he likes to address personally."

"That doesn't make me feel any better," Nathan replied to Pierron. His gaze stayed on Emily.

"Don't worry." She reached across the table to squeeze his fingers. "Between you and the police, I'll be safe."

He resisted the urge to snort at that. The only one he trusted to keep Emily safe was himself.

Emily touched the inspector's coat sleeve to bring his attention to her. "Have you any news about Maya?"

Pierron gave a brief shake of his head. "*Non*, I'm sorry."

"What do you need me to do?" Emily's fingers drummed on the table, a nervous habit that told Nathan she wasn't as confident about this operation as she claimed.

"Do what you were doing before. Go to work, go to the streets, ask questions." Pierron's temple glistened. He wiped his forehead with a napkin. "Mirga must believe you do not consider him a threat. It would be best if Monsieur Long maintained enough distance to convince Mirga you are unescorted, or he may not act."

Nathan noticed the man's fingers trembled as he reached into his suit coat and pulled out a small metallic disc and some flesh-colored tape. "Attach this to your skin. Place it under your clothing where it will not be visible. This is how we will find you if we lose visual surveillance."

Emily opened her hand. The inspector dropped the tracker tag onto her palm. "Go to the toilet before you leave this café and put it on. From this moment, always assume Jules's people are watching."

Emily shivered. "I'll do it now." She stood. "Be right back."

Nathan's gaze followed her to the restroom. "I'll have my tracker on her as well. That's non-negotiable."

"*Bien sûr,* of course," Pierron nodded. "I expected nothing less." He looked toward the restroom. "She is very passionate, *non*? But her bravery comes with a cost." His eyes darkened with an emotion Nathan couldn't decipher. "Mirga is not a man to be taken lightly. I had a relative who became, how shall we say, entangled with him once."

Nathan narrowed his eyes at the older man. "How?"

"Drugs." Pierron shrugged. "That was years ago, but it was a difficult experience."

"If that's the case, then why brush Catalina Giurescu's death under the carpet as a drug overdose when it was clear she was kidnapped, beaten, and raped before receiving a lethal injection of heroin?"

The inspector's skin turned to ash. "How do you know about the police report? It has not been made public."

Nathan leaned in, invading the older man's space. "It doesn't matter," he growled. "Why?"

"She was a girl from the streets." Pierron sputtered. "Many of them are drug addicts. We have no proof she did not take the drug on her own. Our witnesses told us she returned to her pimp of her own free will. I have nothing that ties her death directly to Jules Mirga." The detective's lip lifted in disgust. "That *connard* is too careful. He puts layers between himself and his crimes."

Nathan didn't like that answer, but Emily returned to the table before he could ask more questions.

The inspector stood. "I must go. I will be in touch soon with additional information from the task force." He gave a brief wave of his hand and shuffled out of the café.

"Yeah," Nathan muttered, even though the detective was gone, "we'll be in touch soon."

"Minister Woodward called while I was in the bathroom," Emily told him. "She wants to see me in her office after lunch today." Her eyes gave away her worry.

"It's all good, babe," he tried to reassure her. "She can't get mad at you for returning to Paris when the police asked you to."

He finished the rest of his coffee and gathered his and Emily's cups. "I'll escort you there. I'm going to check in with Agent Goodwin. Then I've got to meet with Ryder and pick up some supplies."

He needed one of Dìleas's new high-tech trackers for Emily and a weapon.

His man at the US Embassy had been arrested.

Jules Mirga paced the front salon of his cottage, his fury a living, breathing dragon that threatened to consume everyone around him. He couldn't get in touch with his other contact in DC. Someone had been careless and drawn the attention of the American authorities, and now his trans-Atlantic operation was threatened.

Ever since the Dane woman stuck her nose into his affairs, his business had suffered significant setbacks.

"Your lunch," Sami announced quietly behind him.

Jules headed to the dining table, eyed the salad and *jambon beurre* sandwich with disdain. He was tired of simple meals. He should have brought Anca, his cook and housekeeper, with him, but the fewer people who knew of his whereabouts, the better.

His phone rang in the salon. He snapped his fingers to get Sami's attention. "My *portable*."

Sami hustled to bring it to him.

His informant. He had better be calling with good news. "*Allô*."

"Emily Dane has returned to Paris and brought Nathan Long with her."

Finally, something was going his way. "Is the plan in place?"

"Yes, but I am pleading with you, do not harm Emily. If you kill the SEAL, you will have your revenge."

"I have no plans to kill her, *mon ami*." He had no need to. Where Emily Dane was going, she'd likely never be seen or heard from again.

Once the SEAL was dead and he'd made his deal with his client in Syria, this *crétin* was next. He'd become weak, untrustworthy.

"And the other girl. She is a child. Let her go."

Jules turned in his chair and glanced toward the stairs leading to the cellar. "As a gesture of goodwill, I will return the girl to her hometown in Romania, *d'accord*?" he lied. "Now stop fussing like an old woman and let us finish this."

He hung up, not giving the fool a chance to reply, and attacked his sandwich with renewed vigor. He might have to leave France for a while, but before he did, everyone who could bring him down would be dead.

Or wish they were.

Chapter
Twenty-Eight

EMILY AND NATHAN PASSED through the black, wrought iron gates surrounding the US Embassy. The rain had given way to blue skies and sunshine and the temperature was climbing fast into the upper seventies with a mid-afternoon forecast of eighty-three degrees Fahrenheit. They strolled into the main atrium and climbed the flight of stairs to Agent Goodwin's office on the second floor.

Nathan glanced down at her. "Call me when you're ready to leave. I'll be with Ryder."

On impulse, she stood on tiptoe, pressed a kiss to his lips, and was rewarded with a flare of surprise that warmed his icy eyes. "I will. You boys behave."

His answering grin was slow, sexy, and melted her insides.

She gave him a wave and took the elevator to the fourth floor. Several of her coworkers stopped her to say hello. Everyone politely skirted around the reason for her trip back to the States. By the time she reached her cubicle, her face was stiff from all the fake smiles. She plopped into her chair and stared at the stack of file folders on her desk. It was as if she'd never left and, at the same time, like she'd been away for months. Collect data. Issue reports. The job she'd been so eager to have suddenly felt meaningless.

"I heard you were back." Bruce's voice came from behind her shoulder. "Why didn't you tell me?"

She stood and hugged him. "I'm not officially out of the doghouse yet. I have a meeting in thirty minutes with Minister Woodward."

"So, have the police dealt with Mirga? I haven't heard anything."

"Not exactly." She motioned toward the hall. "Let's take a walk." She didn't need to share this conversation with the room, and her cubicle afforded scant privacy.

"Okay." Bruce's brows furrowed. "How about the gardens? The rain has cleared up."

Emily hesitated before agreeing. She wasn't sure if Nathan was still in the embassy, but it would be awkward if she ran into him while with Bruce.

Although Nathan had nothing to worry about where Bruce was concerned.

She'd made her choice.

They took the elevator to the main floor and wandered out to the embassy's interior gardens. The lush manicured lawn and meticulously landscaped flower beds glistened with the residue from the morning rain. Emily admired the neatly trimmed verdant hedges bordering the rainbow mix of annual and perennial blossoms. The scent of freshly mowed grass reminded her of childhood summers in Connecticut and Virginia. The pebbled path crunched beneath her black pumps.

"Inspector Pierron came to see me. The police have a plan to lure Mirga out of hiding." She chanced a look at Bruce.

"Please tell me this plan doesn't involve you." His eyes darkened. Impatience threaded his words.

"I'll wear a tracker, and the police will monitor me the entire time. Mirga will want to face me again if for nothing more than to gloat, and when he does, the police will arrest him." Saying the words aloud, the danger she was putting herself in hit home.

But Jules Mirga needed to be stopped. This was the best way. "Catalina is dead, and Maya is missing. I have to do something."

Bruce rubbed his forehead with a sigh. "I'm sorry about Catalina and Maya, but this is a terrible idea and dangerous. What if Mirga or his men kidnap you again?"

She shifted on her feet. Bruce probably wouldn't react well to what she said next, but he deserved to know. "Nathan Long returned to France with me. He's acting as my bodyguard."

Bruce snorted. "If he has any brains, he will nip this ridiculous notion in the bud."

"He wasn't thrilled," she admitted, "but we worked through it."

He stopped walking and faced her. "He's more than a bodyguard, isn't he?"

Her shoulders tightened at the resignation shadowing Bruce's face. "I'm sorry. You're a good friend. I know you wanted more."

Those simple words weren't enough. Bruce deserved better. She tried to convey with her eyes appreciation for his friendship and regret she couldn't offer him what he wanted. "I tried to fight my feelings for him, but..." she trailed off with a shrug.

"How are you going to make this work? Doesn't he live in the States?"

"We haven't gotten that far."

Bruce gave her a small, sad smile that made her feel two feet tall. "I hope he feels the same because you deserve the best." Worry replaced the melancholy in his brown eyes. "Mirga is dangerous, with tentacles everywhere in this city. Go back to DC with Nathan and stay safe."

"I can't." Her arrogant belief that she could single-handedly take down the crime lord had already cost Catalina her life. Maya was running out of time. If it wasn't already too late.

They turned around and walked back into the embassy, stopping in the elevator foyer beneath the framed copy of the 1783 Franco-Anglo-American Treaty.

Bruce gave her a hesitant smile, his eyes still tinged with disappointment. "Good luck with your meeting with Woodward. Once this business with Mirga is over, if you decide to stay in Paris, I hope we can still go out occasionally—as friends, of course," he hastened to add.

"Sure," she agreed. He was a friend, after all. But she wasn't going to lead him on. Even if things didn't work out with Nathan, she wouldn't stoop to using Bruce as a rebound. "I'll see you around."

The elevator doors opened, and he stepped in. She waited for the doors to close, her stomach twinging at having let him down. "Shake it off, Em," she lectured herself as she climbed the stairs to the second floor.

Minister Woodward was waiting.

When she reached the minister's offices, she gave a nervous nod to her administrative assistant, who indicated she was expected and to go in.

"Have a seat." Jacqueline Woodward directed Emily to one of the chairs in front of her mahogany executive desk.

Emily took the seat and waited, her heart a nervous thrumming in her throat.

"It seems Inspector Pierron has thwarted my efforts to keep you out of trouble." The minister steepled her hands in front of her as she looked at Emily. "Are you sure this is something you want to do?"

"I need to see this through. One of the girls I rescued is dead, and the other is missing."

The minister watched her for a moment, then sighed. "You can't shoulder the blame for that man's evil, Emily. You're bright, passionate, and a great asset to the foreign service."

Emily sat back in her chair and tried to stifle her surprise at the minister's words. After their last meeting, she'd never have expected her boss would sing her praises.

"Ending human trafficking seems to have become a passion of yours." Minister Woodward pulled out a folder from her desktop drawer and placed it between them.

"It's hard not to be passionate when you meet the people who're suffering from being exploited in such a horrible manner," Emily told her. Serving was in the Dane family DNA, it just took different forms, and she was starting to realize she hadn't given enough credit to her mother and grandmother for the roles they played raising families after they got married and left their careers.

She couldn't take her eyes off the folder. Was she being reassigned to another position? Another embassy?

"There's an opening in DC in the Trafficking in Persons Office," the minister said. "They're looking for someone passionate about the global impact of human trafficking who can coordinate assistance to governments and non-profits worldwide." She pushed the folder toward Emily. "I'm willing to recommend you for the position if you're interested."

Stunned, Emily hesitated before reaching for the folder. Was she ready to give up Paris? The job sounded promising and was more global in its outreach. And it was based in DC.

Which meant she could be near Nathan, and they wouldn't have to carry on a long-distance relationship.

"There's more information on the posting and application information." Minister Woodward nodded toward the file now in Emily's hand. "Think about it."

"I will. Thank you." Still reeling from the minister's unexpected support, she let herself out of her boss's office and headed back to the fourth floor and her cubicle, her mind racing.

A job in the TIP Office at State. The idea was intriguing.

Nathan answered her call on the second ring. "Hey, babe."

The endearment caused her heart to flutter. "Hey yourself. I'm done for the day."

"Give me twenty minutes and pick a place for dinner. Someplace that serves beef."

She snorted her disgust. "You should stop hunting for the perfect steak and start trying some of the cuisines the French are renowned for, like Boeuf Bourguignon or Coq au Vin."

"They sound fancy." The disdain in his voice made her bite her lip to keep from laughing.

"That's because they have French names—one's a beef stew, the other is chicken. Geez, you can take the man out of Texas, but you can't take Texas out of the man."

"Hooyah to that, darlin'. See you in twenty."

CHAPTER
TWENTY-NINE

NATHAN WAS WAITING JUST inside the fence when Emily emerged from the embassy. He'd changed out of his button-down and gray trousers back into his standard attire of jeans and black t-shirt, this one sporting the name of a well-known French heavy metal band, Gojira.

When she got close enough, he pulled her into his arms for a very public kiss. She felt his fingers slide through her hair to the back of her neck and press against her skull.

She pulled away and gave him a questioning look. "Did you just tag me?"

"I told you, I'm not leaving your safety in the hands of the police. If Mirga does manage to grab you, he may find Pierron's tracker, but it's doubtful he'll find mine." Nathan's arm wrapped her as they exited onto the street. "Where are we eating?"

"A restaurant near Mirga's most exclusive club in the Quartier Pigalle." She slanted an amused look in his direction. "Don't worry. It has an excellent reputation as a steak house. It's time to get on the streets and make my presence known." Her gaze traveled over his shirt. "I didn't know you were into the French metal scene."

The corners of his mouth quirked. "You told me to expand my palate."

She laughed. "I meant food."

Before she forgot, she texted Inspector Pierron and informed him of her plans and the route they would take so her police shadows could follow.

He texted back immediately. *Monsieur Long should not be seen with you.*

She made a face and held her phone up to Nathan so he could read the inspector's comment. "I didn't even think about that when I made our dinner plans."

"Damn. I really wanted that steak."

"Which means we shouldn't be seen together in the Metro either." Her shoulders hunched with the knowledge that even now, someone could be watching. "Or on the streets."

Nathan visibly tensed. She waited for him to change his mind about going along with the task force's plan and try to keep her from going.

"What trains are we taking?"

He was still on board. Her body sagged in relief. "We'll head to the Concorde Metro station, take the number 12 green line toward Mairie d'Aubervilliers, get off at Pigalle, then the number two blue line toward Porte Dauphine. The first stop is Blanche. That's where we'll get off."

He nodded. "When we get to Concorde, head straight to the platform. When the train pulls in, scan the cars before getting in. If you see anyone that looks familiar, or just gives you a bad vibe, text me." His hand cupped her face, his gaze searing her with its intensity, making her want to melt into him. "I'll be with you every step of the way, even if you can't see me."

She smiled. "You're hard to miss."

"You'd be surprised at what people don't see when they're not looking. I'm counting on Mirga to be focused on you." He dropped his hand and stepped back. "Go ahead. I'll be right behind you."

She immediately missed his warmth. Emily turned and headed for the Metro station without looking back, Nathan's presence an invisible cloak around her shoulders.

Her protector.

It didn't bother her to think of him that way now. They were a team. She knew that with him, she didn't have to sacrifice her freedom and sense of self to be in a relationship.

Maybe tonight, over that steak, she'd work up the courage to tell him she loved him.

Once inside, she followed the signs through the white tile and concrete tunnels to the platform for the green line. Cylindrical bars of light embedded in beams suspended from the ceiling lit each side of the platform. She loved the walls and ceiling at this station, covered in letters that appeared random to the eye unless you knew they spelled out the Déclaration des droits de l'homme et du citoyen de 1789, a document that outlined the values of the French Revolution and was conceived by none other than the Marquis de Lafayette and Thomas Jefferson.

The green and white train entered the station in a rush of noise and air. Emily scanned the cars in front of her and chose the one that was half full and had a good mix of people on board. It was unlikely Mirga would try anything on a Metro car surrounded by other passengers.

At least, she hoped he wouldn't.

The train's doors had just closed when her phone rang with a French number she didn't recognize. Maybe one of her police shadows? "Hello?"

"Mademoiselle Dane, you will listen and do exactly what I say, or Nathan Long dies." The voice was male and French.

She knew instantly who it was. "Mirga."

"You will exit the train at Madeleine. Take the *Église* exit. Do what is necessary to make sure your bodyguard does not follow, or he won't make it out of the station alive. I will be waiting. Hurry. You don't have much time."

Her heart thundered in her chest. The train was already slowing down to enter Madeleine station. How had Mirga found her so quickly? And he knew about Nathan. He must have had people watching the embassy.

"And in case you doubt me, I will have my man dot the "I" on his Gojira t-shirt with a bullet and you can watch Monsieur Long die on the dirty floor of the Metro platform."

Spots swam in her vision. Emily tried to suck in a calming breath. It didn't work.

Damn him. Mirga was always one step ahead.

She tried to think logically but panic short-circuited her brain. All she could think about was Nathan dying because of her. He would be furious if she ditched him.

But she wouldn't risk his life.

Her hand shook like a leaf in a windstorm as it crept to the back of her head, her fingernail scraping at the small tag Nathan had placed there.

The doors to the train opened.

She waited until passengers disembarked and new passengers entered.

The chimes sounded, a melodic voice warning in French that the doors were closing.

Emily bolted through the doors before she could change her mind, brushing the tracker from her fingers as she darted for the escalators that led up to the exit across from the Church of the Madeleine.

I'm so sorry, Nathan. She still had her phone and Inspector Pier-ron's tracker. Hopefully, the police were monitoring her and would arrest Mirga before Nathan again charged in as her white knight.

This time, Mirga and his henchmen were expecting him.

This time, he might not make it out alive.

"What the hell?" Nathan's hand slammed against the subway window as he watched Emily jump from her car and race toward the exit. The train accelerated away from Madeleine station, leaving him trapped inside. "Son of a bitch!"

A couple with two young children got up and moved to the other end of the car. He grimaced and threw them an apologetic glance.

The Metro map above the window showed the next stop as Saint-Lazare. He'd get off there and hoof it back toward Place de la Madeleine. It'd be faster than crossing platforms and waiting for a westbound train.

He rang Emily's phone. It went to voicemail. "Come on, pick up." He redialed, then did it again with the same result. What the hell had she been thinking, ditching him like that? This op had just turned into a goat fuck. His heart pounded furiously in his chest, remembering the last time he'd thought everything was under control and the world had burned down around him.

Hands shaking, he tried Pierron's number. The detective didn't answer. Nathan's inner voice was shouting obscenities at him now. Something was way off. He left a voicemail. "Why the fuck aren't you answering your phone? Emily bolted from the train at Madeleine. Get your people there, now."

Once the train reached the next station, Nathan sprinted from the car. People waiting to board parted like the Red Sea in front of him. He fast-walked his way toward the exit to the surface. If he ran like he wanted to, he'd be sure to have Metro police all over him.

His phone navigation app said it was a nine-minute walk. He'd make it in five.

Emily peered around frantically to see if anyone was watching before calling Victor Pierron. "Mirga contacted me, I got off at Madeleine. He's here somewhere. I had to ditch Nathan and the tracker he gave me." Her voice cracked. "Mirga knew what Nathan was wearing and threatened to shoot him if he followed."

She was almost to the top of the stairs that led to the street. Her phone kept beeping with incoming calls from Nathan, which she ignored. "Please tell me you are tracking me."

"Be careful," Pierron's voice reeked of tension, "I have officers on the way. If Jules is there, we will arrest him."

"And if he's not here but his goons are?" She reached the street exit and spotted a familiar black BMW SUV waiting at the curb.

Silence greeted her. "Hello? Inspector?" *Crap.* Had they gotten disconnected? The timing couldn't have been worse. If Nathan had managed to get off the train, he'd be here any second. She dropped her cell in her purse. It wouldn't be good for Mirga to see her on the phone. Not until she knew Nathan was safe.

The SUV's front passenger door opened, and Sami jumped out. He opened the back passenger door and indicated with a jerk of his head that she should get in.

Emily's gaze darted frantically, searching for her police saviors.

"*Allez.*" Sami beckoned with an impatient gesture.

Emily stepped cautiously to the SUV and peered in. Hulk was at the wheel. The back seat sat empty. "Where's Mirga?"

The barrel of a gun jabbed her ribs. Sami pushed her into the back seat and followed her in. "You'll see him soon enough." He raked her with a hostile sneer. "Where is your bodyguard, eh?"

She beat back a shiver of fear with a burst of bravado. "Obviously not here. Otherwise, you'd be dead." Not the smartest thing to say, but she'd bet money if Mirga wanted her killed, he'd take great pleasure in doing it himself.

Hulk pulled into traffic. Emily stared out the window and tried to block out her captors as they rode south on Rue Royale. Mirga had made his move. She still had the police tracker and her phone. It wouldn't take Inspector Pierron long to find her. Squeezing her eyes shut, she fought panic. She wanted justice for Catalina and to save Maya.

More than anything, she wanted to see Nathan again.

Sami rifled through her purse and extracted her phone. He thrust it toward her. "Open it." His eyes promised retribution if she didn't do as told.

She placed her thumb over the home button. The screen lit up, littered with missed call notifications.

Sami grabbed the device. He looked at the screen and grinned, holding it up to her. "The bodyguard, *non*?" He sent Nathan's contact information to a number he typed into Emily's phone.

Her pulse took off like a rocket. Why was he so interested in Nathan? It was her they were after.

When he finished, Sami lowered the window and tossed out her cell.

Emily whipped her head around to follow its trajectory, gasping as her lifeline ricocheted off the street and was crushed by a delivery truck.

Nathan's long legs ate up the distance as he maneuvered around pedestrians strolling down the tree-lined street, his guidepost the towering Grecian columns of the Church of La Madeleine.

He called Ryder. "I've lost Emily. She took off at the Madeleine subway stop before I knew what the hell she was doing. I got off at Saint-Lazare and am doubling back. She's not answering her phone."

Something happened to make Emily ditch him. Someone had gotten to her.

Her tracker still showed her at the Madeleine Metro station, but her phone showed her moving south, away from the station, at a rate of speed that indicated she was in a moving vehicle.

Why the hell hadn't she answered his calls or texted him?

Why hadn't she trusted him to have her six?

"I think she took off the tracker I gave her." He nearly choked on the words. "Her phone's moving south, but the tracker isn't."

Ryder cursed. "I'll track down Victor Pierron and find out if the police have her under surveillance."

"If they do, I haven't seen any sign of it. Pierron didn't answer my fucking call. Mirga is no fool." Nathan dodged a woman coming out of one of the boutiques lining the sidewalk barely in time to keep from mowing her down. "The first thing he and his men will do is dump her phone and look for a tracking device. They'd better locate her and fast."

"I'm on it, mate," Ryder assured him.

Nathan's shoulders loosened a fraction as he hung up. He'd focus on Emily and let Ryder handle the police.

He called her number again. "Emily, babe, I need you to call me as soon as you get this message. Please." The words "I love you" stuck in his throat. When he finally told Emily how he felt, it wouldn't be over voicemail.

Please, God, let me get the chance.

A gnawing whisper of fear formed in his gut and migrated up to his chest with every unanswered message he left on Emily's phone.

He'd sworn he would keep her safe.

He'd failed her.

Like he'd failed Joe.

The ride to their destination was only thirty-five minutes, but it felt like a lifetime. Emily spent every second of it wondering why the police hadn't made an appearance and could only conclude they were waiting for her captors to lead them to Jules Mirga.

The two men had remained eerily silent on the drive, ignoring any attempts on her part to extract information. She peered out the window as their vehicle slipped through a gap in a white aluminum border fence, about six feet tall and plastered with warning signs to keep out.

They drove into a dirt-packed courtyard and parked in front of the remains of a two-story hotel that looked to be undergoing demolition.

Tucked into a grove of trees in the southeast corner of Noisy-le-Grand, the lot was a secluded spot of blight amidst the more modern manufacturing facilities they had passed. The exterior walls facing the courtyard had been gutted, construction debris piled in front of the building's carcass. The floors and interior sidewalls were intact, reminding her of the dollhouse her grandmother had given her when she was a child, the front façade a beautiful two-story yellow stately home, the back open to each room so Emily could decorate with tiny furnishings.

"Get out." Sami waved his gun at her.

She stepped from the vehicle.

He shoved her toward one of the open ground-floor rooms. A thick layer of concrete dust coated the floor, along with pieces of sheetrock and stripped electrical wiring. She stared at the exposed beams over their heads, praying they were more stable than they looked.

"Take off your clothes," Sami ordered. Hulk stood behind Sami. The big man's greasy smile made her stomach churn.

Fear beat its wings inside her skull, desperate to break out. "I thought you were taking me to Mirga." Now would be an excellent time for the police to make an appearance.

"As soon as we make sure you're clean." Sami's eyes glittered in the shadowed interior. He pointed his gun at her. "Strip."

She set her purse on the filthy concrete and stepped out of her pumps. Her brother had told her about his Navy SERE training—Survival, Evasion, Resistance, and Escape. He'd been proud that no matter what they did to him, he didn't break.

She wouldn't either.

Moving slowly to hide trembling knees, she fumbled with the buttons on her blouse. She removed it and laid it next to her bag. Reaching behind her, she unzipped her skirt and let it drop to her ankles along with her gaze.

"Keep going."

Her lashes lifted enough to see Sami gesture with his pistol at her underwear.

Refusing to let them see her cringe, she retreated deeper into her mind, unhooked her bra, and let the straps slide down her arms. She dropped it to the floor and slid her panties down to join her skirt, stepping out of both.

Against her will, a tremor shook her. She closed her eyes and prayed that the police were on their way. If Sami and Hulk intended to rape her, should she put up a fight, even if it meant she died? Or should she focus on staying alive and buy herself time to escape if she could?

Maya. Emily would endure whatever she had to if it meant she had a chance to save the girl.

Where were the damn police? She didn't have her phone, but she was still wearing the tracker Victor Pierron had given to her.

What if she was out of range? Or it wasn't working?

Footsteps drew near. Her eyes flew open at Sami's approach. He shoved his gun in the back of his pants, then ran his hands roughly over her skin, leaving nothing untouched. Hulk leered, his wandering gaze almost as invasive as Sami's dirty fingers.

She gritted her teeth and fought back bile at the intimate invasion.

Sami pulled the tracker tag off her hip. "Take off your jewelry."

She unhooked the gold hoops in her ears. Her watch was next, then her bracelet. She handed them to Sami. Her fingers lingered on the clasp of the gold chain holding her grandmother's broach. Nathan had scooped the necklace off the bed when he'd rescued her from

Constantin Mirga's house in Seine-Saint-Denis and had repaired the broken link. Somehow, in all that chaos, he'd known how important it was to her. She dropped it into Sami's waiting palm.

He threw her jewelry into her purse. "Get dressed."

Relief held her motionless for a split second, then she fumbled into her clothes, brushing off the dirt, her thoughts chaotic. Now that she wasn't in immediate fear for her life, other questions arose. Why had they wanted Nathan's number earlier? Where was Maya? It was no use trying to question these two. She'd have to get in front of Jules and hope she could use his arrogance and narcissism against him.

She bent to retrieve her purse.

"Leave it." Sami grabbed her arm. "Let's go."

Nathan glanced at his watch. Emily had been out of his sight for almost an hour. In another hour and a half, it would be dark.

Time was not on their side.

He refused to think about what she might be going through. *Focus on the mission—find Emily.*

The restless energy twitching his muscles needed a release. He bounded up the four flights to her apartment rather than wait for the elevator. He let himself in with the spare key she'd given him, flipped on the overhead light, and fell back against the door he'd just closed.

Emily's essence was everywhere. Even though they'd only returned this morning, he could smell her—vanilla and spice.

"Fuck!" He bellowed into the apartment, not caring who heard. The back of his head hit the door with a resounding thud, the pain not sharp enough to dull the one shredding his guts with anxiety like a chainsaw.

Pierron wasn't returning calls. He'd gone radio silent, and no one at the Judicial Police would tell Ryder where he was other than he was "on assignment."

Nathan crossed the tiny apartment in long angry strides. Emily needed him. He'd been cut out of the loop after she'd taken off his tracker. Her phone had stopped transmitting signals somewhere on Rue Royal shortly after. As he'd expected, Mirga and his men ditched or destroyed it so Emily couldn't be tracked using it.

Don't do this to me. Tension sat heavily on his shoulders. Something was off. Someone had answers, and if Pierron was ghosting him and Ryder, he'd find someone else who knew what the hell was going on.

He punched in Agent Goodwin's cell number. The other man answered promptly despite it being after work hours. "Glad you called. We've nabbed two individuals in the passport forgery scheme thanks to your information."

"Mirga has Emily. She ditched the tracker I gave her, and her phone isn't transmitting. Pierron won't return my phone calls. Can you use your contacts and track down the other police task force members? I need to know what they know."

"Jesus," Goodwin swore. "I'll get back to you."

Nathan tucked his phone in his back pocket and opened the door to Emily's bedroom. He wanted to lay down on her bed, close his eyes, and pretend she was next to him, her sweet and spicy scent soaking into his skin.

Ryder was on his way to pick him up and bring him back to his house. "You need food and rest. Let's work the problem together, mate," Ryder had told him. "We'll get Emily back."

There was one more call he needed to make, and this one would be akin to pulling the fire alarm in a high rise.

"What's wrong?" Lachlan asked.

"Emily's missing. I can't reach her. The police won't tell me or Ryder anything." Nathan paused when his voice cracked. "I need you, brother. Contact the admiral and get him to pull strings and get you here as fast as possible. If I can locate Emily, I'm going after her, screw the police. And if I go in, Jules Mirga isn't coming out alive."

Chapter Thirty

Hulk turned onto a dirt road that wound through a forest on the southern outskirts of Noisy-le-Grand. Fifteen minutes later, the vehicle rounded a curve, past the vestiges of an old farm to a small two-story stone cottage. A high, vine-covered stone wall surrounded the cottage, enshrouding the home in a verdant privacy screen. The A-frame roof had curved brown tiles, worn from age. The main entrance was varnished wood, as were the shutters framing the casement windows and a set of French doors to the right of the front door. A colorful array of summer flowers and bushes in various shades of green, yellow, and purple surrounded the home.

Any other time, she would have found the place quite charming.

A young man in his late teens stepped outside, his soulless eyes locked on Emily.

She drew back into her seat at his stare. This one might be young, but he had the aura of a killer. He made no attempt to hide the pistol in his grip.

Sami gestured for Emily to open her door and step out. The waiting teen grabbed her arm, dragging her toward the cottage.

Her heels wobbled on loose gravel as she struggled to keep pace. "Slow down."

Sami yelled, and the boy slowed. He pulled her up the short stone steps into the cottage and released her with a shove.

She stumbled, then steadied herself and straightened. The entry hall opened to a small parlor on her right and a kitchen with an oval table surrounded by chairs to her left. The dining set was similar to what Nathan had in his home and if she survived this, she might have to convince Nathan to update his.

In the sitting room, a man with short, wavy black hair sat in an upholstered chair by the unlit wood fireplace. He turned his head, his dark eyes meeting hers, and her blood chilled.

"Welcome, Mademoiselle Dane, to my quaint little country home." Jules Mirga perused her with cold disdain. "It isn't much, but my other properties seem to have come under police scrutiny."

Her sympathetic tut dripped with sarcasm. "Bummer. I guess that's what happens when you commit crimes and kill children."

Sami placed a chair behind her and roughly shoved her onto it. She winced as he zip-tied her wrists to one of the wooden slats at her back. The kid with the soulless eyes zip-tied her ankles to the chair legs.

"Where's Maya?" *Please let her still be alive.*

Mirga's lip curled. "Your concern over an insignificant girl made you careless." He reached for the pack of cigarettes on the round pedestal table next to his chair, pulled one out, and lit it. The tip glowed bright red as he inhaled. When he exhaled, Emily caught a whiff of cloves. "You'll see her soon enough."

Maya was still alive. She closed her eyes and sagged into the chair. The crime lord was right. She'd made a mistake giving away her concern, but she didn't care.

Lifting her lids, she glared at her captor. "Why bother with me? The police know you kidnapped me and murdered Catalina. You should be more worried about spending the rest of your life in jail than petty revenge."

Jules tilted his head to the ceiling as if contemplating his answer and blew out a column of smoke. "You've cost me. Time, money, girls. A valuable informant." His focus returned to Emily and his expression hardened. "And possibly a very lucrative transatlantic business. I cannot allow that to go unpunished."

"You mean the one where you ferried drugs and money to the US using trafficked women and girls?" He was such a pig. She couldn't wait to see him carted away in handcuffs. The police were probably putting a plan in place right now to storm the cottage and rescue her and Maya.

Something Navy SEALs were proficient at. Nathan would know what to do.

Jules leaned forward with a sadistic smile. "My client will tame that insolent mouth of yours and put it to better use. He was most disappointed I could not deliver you to him."

Emily stifled a shudder at the mention of the Syrian so Mirga wouldn't see how much his words frightened her. If he or his client moved her out of France, the chances of anyone finding her were almost nonexistent.

"Why did you murder Catalina?" Let's see if the jerk was arrogant enough to confess all of his sins. If she survived this, she'd be the star witness for the prosecution.

Mirga took the bait. "She was a stupid girl, impulsive and headstrong, but she was a favorite of my clients. And she knew things. I needed to send a message to my other girls that I will not tolerate this kind of behavior." He stubbed out his cigarette. "It's your fault she's dead. If you hadn't interfered, Catalina would be alive, and you and Maya would not be here with me."

His accusation stung. She'd been naïve about the danger involved in crossing this psycho, and Catalina and Maya had paid the price, but she would not allow him to deflect responsibility for his actions. "No one is to blame but you. You're the one who preys on innocent women and girls and exploits them for your own greed and power. You're a rapist," she spat, anger edging out her fear, "a drug dealer, a sex trafficker, and a murderer. And God knows what else."

Jules stood abruptly, moved to Emily, and held her chin in a bruising grip, forcing her to look at him. "Enough of this. You know nothing of my life or the circumstances in which I had to survive." His gaze narrowed, the speculation in his eyes setting her on edge. "Your bodyguard, he's the one who killed Constantin, *non*? He was a professional soldier, yet my cousin's death was personal, done with passion. I think you mean something to this man."

Emily's insides iced.

This was why Sami had wanted Nathan's information. Somehow, Mirga found out Nathan had been the one to rescue her and kill Constantin.

"Nathan's not the one you want. He's just a bodyguard my father hired after I was rescued."

The crime lord's smile reminded her of a shark—cold-blooded, unfeeling. "Don't worry. I will let him know where he can find you."

No! Emily tugged against her restraints, panic overriding her need to appear unfazed. "You don't need to involve him. It's me you want. Nathan didn't do anything."

The Frenchman's brows rose in a show of mockery. "Really? He arrived in France shortly after Constantin and Sami tried to pick you up at Gare du Nord until your embassy friend interfered, and he left France the same time you did." Mirga's features twisted into an ugly mask of rage. "Your bodyguard killed my cousin. You will watch him die before I turn you over to your new master." He ran his finger down her face before placing his lips next to her ear. His breath smelled of cigarettes and wine. "I will enjoy giving him a slow, agonizing death. While he is dying, I will tell him in great detail what is in store for you."

Why was it taking the police so long to act? She'd ditched the tracker, thinking she was protecting Nathan, but it had all been for nothing. He was going to walk into an ambush.

Emily's chin slumped to her chest. Her throat closed, making it hard to breathe. She'd been so stupid, impulsive. So sure she could handle this on her own. What would it cost her?

Everything, if Mirga managed to kill Nathan.

She hadn't even told him she loved him.

Sami pulled a switchblade from his jeans pockets and cut the plastic ties binding Emily's ankles and wrists to the chair. He yanked her to her feet.

Pins and needles stabbed her limbs, and she stumbled on stiff legs.

If the police didn't arrive soon, her only option would be to try and make a run for it with Maya. She'd rather die trying to get free than wish she was dead as the sex slave of some terrorist.

The sun had disappeared behind the horizon. Table lamps gave off a soft glow inside the cottage, creating a false impression of coziness. Off to one side of the small kitchen, a white wooden door led to the cellar. Sami dragged her down rough-hewn stone steps to the metal door at the bottom.

Emily noted the electronic keypad lock. Either Mirga had invested in several cases of premium Grand Cru or wine wasn't the only thing stored beneath the house.

Sami punched in a code and opened the door. Light spilled into the pitch-black interior.

A whimper came from the darkness, sending Emily's heart into her throat.

He shoved her forward and she tripped, hands and knees slamming onto hard-packed dirt. The door closed, the deadbolt sliding into place with the finality of a cell door clanging shut in a movie.

The hairs on her neck rose with a shiver that hunched her shoulders. "Hello?" Maybe she'd only imagined the sound. She pushed to her feet. Something brushed her face and she yelped, heart pounding, clawing at air until her fingers found string.

A light? Did she want to see who or what else was in the room with her?

You can't defend against what you can't see.

She squared her shoulders, breathed deep, and yanked on the string. Light flared from a naked bulb. Dropping into a crouch, she blinked rapidly to acclimate her eyes as quickly as possible.

Dirt floor, stone walls. Wine racks as tall as her chin stretched out in rows, resembling library stacks. The ceiling was low, the top of her head brushing the light bulb when she straightened.

She rubbed her arms briskly against the chill, breathing in humid air from the afternoon rain.

"Emily?" A timid voice came from over her right shoulder.

She whirled. "Maya?"

The girl huddled, shivering, on a thin mat between two wine racks.

Emily dropped to her knees and wrapped Maya in her arms. The girl's skin was clammy, her lips tinged a faint blue.

"I'm sorry, so sorry. Are you okay? Did they hurt you?" A stupid question. Emily wanted to snatch it back the minute it left her lips. Purple and yellow mottled Maya's face. Bruises in the shape of fingertips banded her upper arms. She needed food, water, and medical attention.

Maya's gaze darted away, an unspoken answer to the real question Emily was afraid to voice.

Bile worked its way to the back of Emily's throat. She swallowed it but couldn't keep the fury down. Abusing a thirteen-year-old? Mirga and his henchmen didn't need to go to jail—they needed to die. "It's going to be okay—the police will be here any time now." Was she trying to convince Maya or herself?

Stay positive for Maya. For all she knew, the police really were getting into position to storm the cottage, arrest Mirga and his men, and free them. One good thing about being held below ground, they were safer if bullets started flying. Nathan might be outside even now, surveilling the cottage, determining the number of enemies and the best way to proceed. If he found them first, Mirga wouldn't be able to spring a trap on him. The thought buoyed her spirits.

For about two seconds.

They should have raided the cottage by now.

The pieces of a puzzle she'd ignored too long started to fall into place, twisting her stomach into knots of dread. Someone with the police was on Jules Mirga's payroll. Mirga always seemed one step ahead of the law. He'd known when she returned to Paris, and that she'd arrived on the train from London. He'd known where Fondation Espoir's safe house was located, sent Daniel to lure Catalina out of hiding, kidnapped Maya.

Leaving Maya where she found her, Emily inspected every nook and cranny of the windowless space, running her fingers under and along each section of stone, searching for an opening or weakness in the mortar, finding none.

Nerves strung tight, her gaze kept returning to the locked door. She wasn't sure when Sami would return and what would happen when he did. Her mind shied away from the answer. She shivered from the chill. Her stomach growled, reminding her she hadn't eaten in forever.

Her mouth felt like a desert, and the beginning of a headache warned of dehydration.

Dusty bottles of expensive reds from Bordeaux and Burgundy lined the walls, taunting her. A room filled with liquid and no corkscrew.

Emily stifled a semi-hysterical laugh. If she couldn't drink it, she might be able to use it as a weapon.

Grabbing two bottles, she turned out the light. When her eyes adapted to the darkness, she returned to Maya. The girl needed rest, and it might come easier without the harsh glare of the bare bulb keeping her awake. Emily shuddered. Or spotlighting any nocturnal creatures that might be in residence.

And if their captors returned, she wanted the advantage of seeing them before they saw her. Maybe she'd be able to get the drop on one, stun him with an expensive Bordeaux to the head, and grab his gun.

The night wore on with painful slowness, the temperature continued to drop, and blackness deepened to obsidian. Emily leaned her head against the wall and huddled with Maya for warmth. Shivers racked the girl's body, too weak to fight the chill. Emily tried to distract her as best she could with light-hearted stories pulled from her childhood.

The stone at her back was cold. So was the dirt floor beneath her. If only she'd thought to wear slacks this morning instead of a skirt. Maya's fevered body curled in her lap. Emily brushed the girl's hair from her face gently, trying to avoid swollen, bruised skin. Exhausted, she shivered and let her tears fall. Right now, being brave and optimistic was too hard.

Doubt crept in, and fear. She could end up disappearing into a hellhole at the mercy of a sadistic man. Maya would end up like Catalina, her death not even a blip on society's radar.

And Nathan...

Nathan could end up in Mirga's hands. Tortured before the crime lord granted him the mercy of a bullet. All because he'd been her savior. Because he was still trying to protect her.

Because she'd been so damn determined to be the hero who acted alone.

Emily's breath caught on a sob. She dug her teeth hard into her bottom lip to stifle it so as not to wake Maya. It wouldn't do any good for the girl to see her this way. Nathan had been a SEAL. She had to have faith that he'd be able to take care of himself and not get killed trying to save her.

If he died...

It's not fair. The silent scream echoed in her head. They deserved more time.

They deserved to have what Lachlan and Sophia had.

People were right when they said your life flashed before you when you think you're about to die. Only it wasn't in an instant. It was a spinning Merry-Go-Round of memories from when she was a child to the present. Holidays with her family, when her father walked through the door after each deployment, the family dogs they'd loved and lost, fights with her brother, and the many times they'd been co-conspirators. Quiet talks with her mom. Drop-off day at college. Passing the Foreign Service exam and getting her first assignment. The memories dried her tears and saw her through the night until the pitch-black gave way to murky shadows, chased away by daylight Emily could only sense.

An electronic beep and the sound of the locks retracting gave her scant warning before the door flew open, and the silhouette of a man filled the entrance. *Sami.*

Her body jerked to attention, fingers curling around the long necks of the wine bottles she'd hoarded the night before.

Maya whimpered. She lifted her head from Emily's lap and pressed against the stone at her back, knees to chest.

The teenage boy from yesterday strolled in behind Sami. His gaze landed on her hands, wrapped around the bottles. The pistol in his grip lifted, the barrel pointed straight at her. There was no anger or amusement at her expense. His expression remained blank, and that scared her more than anything.

Emily slowly unwrapped her fingers from the bottles.

He probably wouldn't shoot her. She was too valuable to Mirga. But she couldn't take the chance he'd shoot Maya.

"Jules wants to see you." Sami hauled her to her feet, steadying her as she swayed against him, stiff from the cold and a full night in one position.

"Maya needs to come." No way was she leaving the girl in this hole alone.

Or worse, with that young psychopath.

"He didn't ask for her." Sami yanked her toward the exit.

She dug her heels into the packed earth as best she could but couldn't match his strength. "I'll be back, Maya. Don't worry," she called over her shoulder as Sami forced her up the steps. She prayed that was true.

Mirga sat in the kitchen, sipping coffee and smoking. He spread butter on a croissant before setting the knife down and taking a large bite of the pastry.

Emily's mouth watered, and her stomach rumbled. She stared at the blade and envisioned driving it into his throat. Her momentary revenge fantasy drowned in ice-cold reality. Even if, by some miracle, she caught all three men unawares, two had guns.

She'd be dead, and then who would save Maya?

Mirga trained his shark's smile on her. "I hope your accommodations were suitable."

She glared daggers. "Maya needs food, water, and to use the toilet. As do I."

He took another bite and chewed slowly, his cold eyes assessing. "Such demands, Mademoiselle. I do not want to be accused of being a poor host." He gestured with the hand holding his pastry. "Omar, see to the girl. Sami, escort Emily to *les toilettes*."

The bathroom door didn't lock. Emily willed it to stay shut as she used the toilet, washed her hands, then cupped them and gulped water from the sink. Cool liquid trickled into her stomach and woke her parched cells. Leaving the water running to mask sound, she carefully opened the cabinet doors, looking for razor blades, tweezers, anything she could hide in her pocket or bra to use as a weapon.

No such luck.

A loud pounding on the door startled her. "Hurry up."

She closed the cabinets and turned off the water just as Sami opened the door.

"Do you mind?" She gave him her haughtiest glare as he yanked her back down the hall to Mirga and shoved her into a kitchen chair. A glass of water and a croissant sat on the table in front of her. She glanced longingly at Mirga's coffee.

Beggars can't be choosers. She gulped the water greedily, then tore into the pastry.

"I wanted you here when I telephoned your bodyguard."

The buttery bread turned to dust in her mouth.

Mirga's predatory grin widened. He tapped his cell phone and put it to his ear, his gaze never leaving Emily's.

"Nathan Long? It's Jules Mirga." He barked out a short laugh. "Such language, Monsieur Long." His voice lowered, simmering with an undercurrent of cold rage. "You killed my cousin. I have something you want. I propose an exchange."

Emily shook her head, denial in every cell of her body. Mirga wasn't letting her go. Nathan should call his bluff.

"Proof?" Jules placed the phone close to her lips. "Say hello, Emily."

A flash of black in her peripheral vision confirmed Sami had trained his weapon on her. "Don't come, Nathan, it's—" Sami's hand slapped over her mouth, his pistol digging into her temple.

Jules put the phone back to his ear. "She's alive and, so far, unharmed. I will text you the address. From central Paris, it will take thirty minutes. In thirty-five minutes, Emily will be on her way to Syria unless you take her place. Come alone, or she dies." The crime lord's fingers tapped on the screen before he powered down the phone. He dropped it on the floor and brought his boot down until the device was mangled shards.

With a final sip of coffee, Mirga wiped his mouth and stood. "Let's not keep your bodyguard waiting." He signaled his men with a nod. "Bring the girl. We have no more use for her."

Sami bound Emily's wrists with a plastic flex cuff—in front of her this time instead of behind her back—before hustling her to the SUV from yesterday.

The boy, Omar, appeared with Maya. The girl stumbled, too weak to walk. Omar boosted her into the rear cargo hold like baggage and climbed into the back seat next to Emily.

Emily's brain spun in frantic circles. She was running out of time.

They all were.

CHAPTER
THIRTY-ONE

Thirty minutes. Nathan input the address into his navigation app as he hurried from Ryder's kitchen, where he'd been mainlining caffeine, to the small room off the main floor study Ryder had retrofitted into a tactical closet vault with a biometric lock.

Pressing his thumb to the fingerprint sensor, he unlocked the vault. He grabbed the shoulder holster containing a Glock, pocketed an extra magazine clip in the mission pants he'd changed into, then strapped a fixed blade to one ankle and a compact Sig 365 to the other. A lightweight armor vest went over his black t-shirt. He concealed it with a blue-gray plaid button-down despite the warm weather.

If these assholes were out to kill him, he didn't intend to make it easy.

His gaze fell on the small flesh-colored skin tags, one of which he'd placed beneath Emily's hair at the base of her skull. Using GPS and cellular technology, these babies weren't even on the market yet, but as Dìleas's resident technology expert, he'd managed to get his hands on some. He placed one of the small tags behind his ear.

The night had been pure hell.

No Emily.

No way to locate her.

No word from anyone.

It was a good thing Ryder had kept him from hunting down Victor Pierron and breaking him in half when the man finally called back and confessed the police didn't know Emily's location but were putting all available resources on the case.

Assaulting a detective and spending the night in jail wouldn't have helped him find her.

He hadn't known if she was dead or alive until Mirga's call. His eyes were gritty from lack of sleep, and acid churned his gut. His usual pre-mission calm was missing in action.

Emily isn't a mission.

She was his life.

He grabbed keys off the hook in Ryder's kitchen, raced outside, and ripped off the canvas cover from his friend's Porsche. *Better to ask for forgiveness than permission.* Ryder had driven the Range Rover to pick up Lachlan and the admiral at the airport, and Nathan had no time to waste.

Emily's desperate voice rang in his ears. *Don't come.* She knew Mirga intended to kill him.

His cell rang. He glanced at the screen. *Agent Goodwin.*

Nathan tucked the phone between his ear and shoulder as he started the Porsche and backed it out of the courtyard, one hand on the wheel, the other on the gear shift. "Tell me you got the coordinates to Emily's location from the task force."

"There is no task force." Goodwin's voice was grim. "Pierron lied to us."

"Son of a bitch." Nathan hung up and focused on his driving. He didn't have time to deal with the DSS right now, not when every second depended upon him reaching Emily on time.

Pierron had set Emily up.

It all made sense now. Pierron had Emily's research on Mirga and could keep Mirga one step ahead of the law. He'd known the location of the safe house where Fondation Espoir had taken Catalina and Maya. He knew Nathan had been the one to rescue Emily. He'd been the one to sweep Catalina's death under the rug.

Pierron had been the one to lure Emily back to Paris.

Heading east on the interstate, Nathan pinpointed the target location on the southeast side of Noisy-le-Grand.

Hang on, baby.

Emily was alive, and she was strong. It didn't matter what happened to him as long as she was safe.

He gripped the steering wheel, his knuckles white. Jules Mirga had signed his death warrant.

The situation couldn't be any worse—an unfamiliar location where the enemy held all the advantages. He had no plan other than to improvise and rely on his training.

He dialed Ryder and let out a curse when the call went to voicemail. "Ryder, Mirga contacted me." He rattled off the coordinates the crime lord had given him. "I'm wearing a tag, amigo, in case this isn't the final destination. Agent Goodwin called. Victor Pierron is dirty. He's Mirga's mole in the police department."

He tried Lachlan's number next. It also went to voicemail. Lachlan and the admiral must still be in the air. "Hey Lach, Jules Mirga wants to trade Emily for me. He knows I'm the one that took out his cousin. I gave Ryder the address in Noisy-le-Grand. If..." Nathan hesitated. *If I don't make it.* "I'll take out as many of them as I can. Promise me you won't stop until you've got Emily."

Eight minutes down. He pressed the accelerator and prayed.

He arrived with two minutes to spare, almost driving past the gap in the white fencing. Someone had removed a section near the tree line, just wide enough to get a car through. Inside, the two-story skeleton of a half-demolished hotel greeted him. The low-slung Porsche scraped over potholes in the dirt-packed courtyard.

If he didn't die saving Emily, Ryder would probably kill him for trashing his expensive toy.

Central casting couldn't have picked a better location for this to end badly. Solid fence, six feet high. Surrounded by trees. Closed off from the street. Nobody passing by in a vehicle would see a thing, and it wasn't a pedestrian-friendly area.

He parked in front of a large mound of construction debris and killed the motor. Twisting in his seat, he scrutinized the trees surrounding the building and courtyard.

Was Emily somewhere inside, or did the bastards plan to ambush him out here? He craned his neck up to the wide-open second story, searching for the telltale glint of light off a scope or the muzzle of a gun. Chances were good Mirga's boys weren't military trained. If they were, he'd be dead before he knew the direction of the bullet.

A black beamer with tinted windows appeared in his rearview mirror and rolled up to the building. Two men stepped out, weapons pointed in Nathan's direction.

Nathan palmed the Glock and stepped from the Porsche, keeping it between him and the new arrivals.

The driver was as tall and muscular as he was, with a short beard and shoulder-length dark hair.

The other guy looked like a teenage serial killer.

Nathan's stomach dropped. He didn't want to kill a kid, but it wouldn't be the first time he'd defended himself against someone so young, twisted by life or ideology.

He squinted, trying to peer through the SUV's tinted windows. "Where's Emily?" He couldn't open fire on these assholes if Emily were in the vehicle. And if she wasn't, he needed one of them alive long enough to tell him where Mirga was holding her.

"*Venez.*" The big guy beckoned him. "We take you."

Nathan cocked a brow at the asshole. "Do I look like a fucking idiot? Not until I know Emily is alive, unharmed, and on her way to Paris." His finger tapped the Porsche's roof. "In this car."

The driver shrugged his massive shoulders. "You do not come; she and the girl die."

Emily wasn't alone. The girl must be Maya. Now he had to worry about liberating both. Nathan grimaced. He'd been dealt a lousy hand in this round of poker. "I need proof Emily is still unharmed."

The boy spit out rapid-fire words at the big guy gesturing to Nathan and the Porsche. He probably wanted to know why they didn't just shoot him here and take the sports car.

The driver shook his head, dismissing the kid, and pulled out his phone. He spoke in French, keeping Nathan in his sight. "*Écoutez,*" the big man held out the phone, "listen."

"Monsieur Long, we had an agreement. My patience is wearing thin." Jules Mirga's voice sounded tinny on the speakerphone, and Nathan had to strain to hear across the distance.

He raised his voice to be heard. "I need to know Emily is with you and unharmed."

"Nathan don—" Emily's words ended in a wail of pain.

Nathan's body jerked against the side of the car, his palm squeezing the butt of the pistol. His finger hovered over the trigger. "Hurt her again, and I will kill you."

"If my men do not arrive with you in ten minutes, I will call back and let you listen to Emily scream."

The big man returned the phone to his back pocket.

Shit. Nathan was out of time and options. Lachlan and Ryder wouldn't know where he and Emily were unless they were able to locate his tag.

He made a show of putting his weapon in the glove box before locking the car and slipping the key under the left rear wheel well. Hopefully, Ryder would find it before anyone else did.

Raising his hands, he moved around the Porsche toward the men.

"Omar." The driver spoke to the boy and gestured toward Nathan. It didn't take the kid long to divest him of his phone, backup handgun, and knife. Omar ran his fingers along the blade's spine, his dark eyes gleaming.

"Be careful with that," Nathan drawled. "It's my favorite, and I'm gonna want it back."

Omar grinned and slipped the knife into his boot. He patted Nathan's chest and rattled off more words to the other man.

"The *gilet*," the driver patted his chest and pointed at Nathan. "Off."

Nathan tensed. What were his chances of using the kid as a human shield and taking out the other man with his backup handgun, currently tucked into Omar's waistband?

He dismissed the idea. If it all went sideways, he couldn't help Emily.

Stripping off his long-sleeved shirt, he unstrapped the tactical vest and placed it on the ground.

He'd be walking naked into the lion's den.

Omar scooped up the vest and threw it in the back of the SUV. He tossed Nathan's phone on the ground and opened the rear passenger door, gesturing with his weapon for Nathan to get in. Nathan shrugged back into his plaid shirt. He didn't need it anymore, but

Emily might if her clothes had been...his throat swelled on a surge of anger and fear. He forced calmed back into his body.

Once Nathan was seated, the big guy got behind the wheel, executed a three-point turn, and squeezed through the gap in the fence onto the main road.

A memory of Chief Petty Officer Ray, one of his instructors at BUD/S, flashed into Nathan's head. The Chief bent over him as he made himself into what SEALs called a "sugar cookie" for the hundredth time, dousing himself in the frigid Pacific waves off Coronado and rolling in the sand until gritty misery invaded every inch of his body.

"Do you have what it takes to be an elite warrior, Mr. Long?" the SEAL had screamed in his ear.

"Hooyah, Instructor Ray," he'd yelled back, exhausted and shivering.

He stared out the window from the back seat as Noisy-le-Grand's industrial landscape turned into forest.

No weapons, no backup.

The only easy day was yesterday.

He'd made it through training and some pretty hairy missions. The chances of him coming out of this alive weren't looking good.

An evil grin tilted his lips. He'd been a goddamned United States Navy SEAL, and not just any SEAL, he'd made it through selection to be assigned to DEVGRU, Tier One.

If he were going to Hell, he'd take all the motherfuckers trying to hurt Emily with him.

CHAPTER
THIRTY-TWO

THE VEHICLE NATHAN RODE in stopped between an old stone farm-house that appeared to be vacant and a two-story barn that had seen better days. The driver hit the horn in a short, sharp blast. Weathered reddish-brown doors on the barn opened partway with a creak of rusty hinges.

Omar gestured toward him with his weapon. "*Allez.*"

Showtime.

Nathan stepped out of the SUV and into the barn, muscles tensed, fingers flexing with the need to act. Until he assessed the situation, he would play the docile prisoner. He blinked as his eyes adjusted from bright sunlight to shadowed interior.

Emily stood handcuffed with a plastic tie in the center of the building, a dark-haired man directly behind her.

He drank in the sight of her. Relief loosened his shoulders even as cold rage iced his veins at the gun pointed at her head. Her clothing was dirty but intact, her skin—what he could see of it—unmarked by violence. The unnamed fear lurking beneath his skin ebbed away, allowing his brain to switch to combat mode.

"Nathan." The fear in Emily's voice gut-punched him.

He took an instinctive step toward her. A big hand clamped onto his shoulder and cold steel pressed into the back of his neck.

He unclenched his fists and forced his body to relax beneath the driver's punishing grip.

Movement along the back wall drew his attention. A young girl huddled in the corner. Ugly patches of red and purple marred her face and arms, her clothes soiled and torn. *Maya*. Her dark brown eyes, dull and lifeless, met his.

His cold rage heated, caught fire. *I'll fucking kill them all.*

The hand on his shoulder slid to his back and shoved, forcing him further into the barn.

"Monsieur Long." Jules Mirga stood next to Emily and the asshole holding her at gunpoint. "As you can see, we have honored our end of the agreement. Mademoiselle Dane is alive and unharmed."

Nathan eyeballed the man he'd seen only in photographs. Mirga was a short little bastard who likely suffered from a Napoleonic complex and had made up for his lack of stature by becoming the most violent and cunning gangbanger on his block.

He'd enjoy offing the prick.

The driver brushed past him, his handgun replaced by a rifle. He climbed a rickety-looking wooden ladder to the hayloft over the main barn doors and sat on the edge, peering down on the group.

Four hostiles. Nathan mapped out a plan in his head. The driver would be first. Judging from how he held his long gun, he wouldn't have time to swing it into position before Nathan took him out, using Omar as a shield. Omar was next. That left the asshole with Emily.

And Mirga.

Nathan had to bank on the fact they wanted Emily alive and would fire in his direction instead of at Emily or the girl. It was a calculated risk.

What if he was wrong?

Fear stole his breath.

He hadn't seen the hostiles on the ridgeline in Afghanistan. He hadn't been able to call off the Apache helicopter in time. He hadn't stopped Joe from charging toward the insurgents and getting caught in the exchange of missile fire.

If Emily died?

He wouldn't survive it.

"On your knees," Mirga ordered.

"No!" Emily's voice rang out, pitched high and filled with terror.

Nathan needed to buy time in case Lachlan and Ryder were searching for them. He sent Emily a reassuring look as he sank to the dirt floor. *It's gonna be okay.*

His focus turned to the crime lord. "You want to know why your cousin is dead? His security was shit. And he was too busy smacking a woman around to see the threat coming at him."

Mirga's face mottled in anger. "Look at you. The Navy SEAL," he sneered. "One of your country's finest warriors. On your knees because of a woman." He pointed to where a rope, battery, wires, and an assortment of tools sat in a pile. "How long will it take before you plead for the sweet release of death?"

A cold sweat trickled down the small of Nathan's back. Elite military training had honed his pain tolerance, but Emily and Maya didn't need to witness what was about to happen. "Let Emily and the girl go now. I'll be dead before she can get help. You'll have your revenge."

Emily lunged. "No, Nathan—"

The man behind her grabbed her around the waist and jammed his gun into her temple. "*Putain!*"

Nathan threw up his hand. "Stop, babe." He gentled his tone. "Don't worry about me."

"How touching." Mirga lit a cigarette, his hand cupping the flame. In a fucking barn with hay, no less. Maybe he planned to turn the place into Nathan's funeral pyre after he killed him. The Frenchman took a deep inhale and gave a hoarse laugh. "I have a client who has waited long enough to meet Emily. And for all the trouble she's caused, I think she should see the consequences of her actions."

Nathan bit back a string of expletives. His gaze shot to Emily. Her eyes blazed with fury in a face gone ashen.

His woman still had fight in her.

Good. She was going to need it.

He'd give her the best chance he could, but she would need to play an active role in saving herself and Maya. He smiled, trying to keep any hint of regret out of his eyes and the tilt of his lips. If only they'd had more time.

"Em." He willed Emily to focus on him, then let his gaze shift to touch on each man in the room in the order he planned to take them out. Returning to meet her stare, he gave a faint nod.

Her eyes widened. She tilted her head slightly in acknowledgment.

Nathan blew her a kiss.

She lifted bound hands to give him one in return. A tear formed on her lashes, breaking free to trickle down her cheek.

The emotion on her face made his heart trip. Words of love hovered between his lips.

He clamped them tight. Chances were high he wasn't coming out of this alive, and he wouldn't put that burden on her.

"Omar," Mirga said, "let's make our guest compliant."

Nathan's head whipped in the kid's direction as Omar lifted his pistol and pulled the trigger.

The punch to Nathan's thigh dropped him on his ass. The report of the weapon firing cracked through the barn.

Emily screamed.

Son of a bitch. Blood oozed from a small round hole mid-thigh. Nathan cranked his neck around and spared a brief glance at the larger, jagged exit wound on the back of his leg. At least the bullet had missed bone and his femoral artery, or he'd be done before he got started.

It didn't hurt. Yet. The burning, hot poker sensation would come after the adrenaline wore off.

Gritting his teeth, he pushed back up onto his knees and leveled a feral grin at Omar. *Nice try, motherfucker. Come closer.*

"Tie him to the post." Mirga pointed to a nearby support column.

Now or never. Nathan readied himself. If they tied him up, his one shot was gone.

Omar slung the rope over his shoulder and stepped closer, grabbing Nathan's bicep.

Nathan's left hand whipped out and latched onto Omar's pistol. He grabbed the kid in a headlock, aimed high and fired. The driver perched in the loft slumped, his long gun falling from useless arms.

Nathan powered to his feet using his good leg and Omar as a crutch. His nerve endings woke up, sending daggers of fire through his thigh. He shoved the pain into a mental compartment and slammed the lid. With a violent twist, he broke Omar's neck and used one arm to hold the kid's limp form as a shield.

Gunshots rang out. Omar's body jerked. Heat seared Nathan's left flank, then his bicep. He retreated to the only cover available, an abandoned stall, before dropping the corpse.

Two down, two to go.

Mirga had disappeared behind a giant bale of straw. The other hostile used Emily as a shield.

Nathan didn't have the shot.

"Stop, or she dies," Mirga shouted from his hiding place.

"You won't kill her. She's too valuable." *Please, God.* Nathan prayed that was true. A chill racked him, and he blinked away dizziness. He was leaking from a few different spots now, and if he didn't end this soon, he'd be unable to protect Emily and Maya.

"Are you willing to take the chance? Drop the weapon," Mirga demanded, "and come out before your woman's brains are splattered across this barn."

At Mirga's words, the guy holding the gun to Emily's temple curled his finger around the trigger.

Fuck. He had to give Emily a fighting chance, and if that meant his time was up...

So be it. He limped into the open on unsteady feet.

A muzzle flashed. Nathan's collarbone snapped. His arm dropped, his weapon slipping from useless fingers.

"Nathan!"

He heard Emily's scream as he staggered, then dropped like a bag of concrete, his head bouncing off the hard-packed dirt. The barn rafters overhead taunted him. A metallic scent filled his nostrils and coated his tongue with iron.

Get up, sir! Or are you planning to ring out today?

"No, Instructor Ray," he mumbled. He shifted onto his side to face his enemy. Pain lanced his shoulder. His left arm wouldn't work. His thigh was on fire, as was his side.

Mirga was walking toward him with a sadistic smile, weapon raised.

Nathan felt around for a gun. There weren't any within reach. His vision grayed, enveloping Mirga in a monochrome patina. A sharp pain stabbed his chest. He fought for each breath.

His gaze sought out Emily's. "I'm sorry, babe." He tried to put everything he was feeling, regret, love, in his eyes so she'd know.

She'd know what he hadn't said out loud.

I love you.

Emily's scream of rage reverberated through the barn. She threw her head back and caught her captor in the nose.

He jerked with a curse, his pistol dropping from her temple.

She whirled, clawed at his face like she was trying to scoop out his eyeballs.

The man howled, dropping his gun.

With a violent twist of her hips, she slammed her elbows in a powerful arc into his temple.

He fell, motionless.

Nathan laughed. Or at least tried to. It came out more like a weak hack.

Miss Emily Rose Dane was a force to be reckoned with. She'd save herself.

Her hands still manacled, Emily snatched the pistol, pivoted, and squared off against Mirga, whose weapon pointed at Nathan's head.

"Do you think you can shoot me before I put a bullet in your lover's brain?" Mirga's voice reeked of arrogance and disdain. His finger curled around the trigger.

Nathan's eyes drifted shut. He pictured Emily.

"Drop the—"

A loud crack sounded, cutting off the crime lord's words. Mirga's weight collapsed on top of Nathan.

Nathan grunted and shoved the bastard to the side, the movement sending shards of agony through his body.

A neat round hole decorated Mirga's temple, his eyes open and unseeing.

Damn, never bet against the daughter of a Navy SEAL.

"Nathan." Emily was next to him, her voice frantic.

He raised bloody fingers to her pale, tear-stained face. "That's my girl."

Darkness sucked him into oblivion.

CHAPTER
THIRTY-THREE

Blood. Too much blood.

Soaking into the dirt floor in the barn. The smell of copper and death threatened to upend her stomach.

"Stay with me, Nathan." Emily's voice broke.

He'd passed out and now lay deathly still, his face leaching of color.

How many times had he been shot?

She looked around frantically for something to use to staunch the bleeding. Her gaze skittered away from Jules Mirga. She'd done what her father had trained her to do. Shoot to kill. She'd worry about the consequences to her psyche later.

A rustling over her shoulder jerked her head around. Sami had regained consciousness.

He struggled to his feet, snatched the gun she had dropped in her desperation to reach Nathan, and aimed it at her, his face full of hate. "*Putain!* I'm going to kill you."

Her body refused to move. Every last molecule of air left her lungs.

She wouldn't reach Mirga's weapon before Sami pulled the trigger.

And she refused to beg for mercy, knowing she'd get none.

Her hand crept to Nathan's chest. "I love you, Nathan." He couldn't hear her, but she needed to say it. "I love you."

A strange calm settled over her. She closed her eyes and waited for death.

A crack filled the air. Emily flinched.

No pain. *Strange.*

She reached out with her senses. Her knees still rested on the dirt floor. Heat from Nathan's body still warmed her palm.

Had Sami missed?

She cracked one eye open.

Mirga's enforcer lay crumpled on the ground. Victor Pierron stood at the barn doors, a pistol between his palms.

Her body sagged as relief flooded her. "Thank God." The police were here. Finally.

"Nathan needs help. *Hurry.*" Her voice cracked on the plea.

Pierron walked over to Sami and stooped to examine him.

"Inspector, where are the others?" Surely he hadn't come alone. "Call an ambulance."

The inspector spared a glance at Maya, still huddled in the corner. The sight of the girl seemed to make the man's shoulders droop even more than usual.

He shuffled to where Emily crouched over Nathan, his gaze lingering on Jules Mirga's lifeless body. He bent to pick up Mirga's gun.

Panic tightened Emily's throat. "They're dead. You need to call for help. Nathan still has a chance." She caressed his clammy skin. *God,* she hoped that was true.

He'd survive. He had to.

Victor's heavy sigh jerked her head back up. He was staring at Nathan, a look of regret in his faded blue eyes. "He killed Jules?"

Her neck prickled with foreboding. "No, I did." Something wasn't right.

Pierron nodded in approval. "*Bien fait*, Emily. He needed to die."

"Where are the other officers? Why aren't you calling an ambulance?" Her heart thundered as a hard knot of dread formed in her stomach. "What did you do, Victor?"

Victor's head dropped to his chest. He stepped away from where Emily crouched over Nathan. Out of her reach, his gun still in his grip.

"I thought your SEAL would be the hero. Kill Mirga, save you." He shrugged. "Free me to live my retirement in peace."

Emily got to her feet, betrayal and a sense of hopelessness filling her. "Why?" she whispered. All this time, she thought the detective had been helping her bring down Jules Mirga, and he'd been working with Mirga instead.

"Hmmm?" He seemed lost in reverie for a moment. Tears glistened in his eyes. "My son. He fell into drugs many years ago and made the mistake of crossing Jules." The inspector gave Emily a sad smile. "He made—what is the famous saying? An offer I could not refuse."

"He wouldn't hurt your son if you became his informant," she guessed.

Pierron shook his finger almost as if he were lecturing her. "Not hurt, Mademoiselle—kill. When I agreed to keep him informed of police activities involving his business, he paid for my son to get off drugs and found him a legitimate job in the south of France. Pierre is clean. He has a good job. He's happy. He's safe."

The inspector glanced over her shoulder at Nathan. She was afraid to follow his gaze. Afraid Nathan might already be gone.

She had to find a way out.

Her gaze fell to the pistol in Victor's grip. Would he have the guts to shoot her if she rushed him?

He continued speaking, the need to confess an urge he couldn't defeat. "I was so close to retirement when you took up your crusade, Emily. Jules was so angry, determined to punish you. You may not believe me, but I tried to warn you. And I begged Jules to leave you alone. I offered him Nathan if he would not kill you. I knew your SEAL could take care of himself." Pierron shook his head and glanced again at Maya in the corner. "It got out of control. So many deaths, so many lives ruined."

He took another step away from Emily. His hand holding the gun lifted.

"Don't do this, Victor. It's not too late to end this the right way. Too many people have died already." Her throat clogged. "Please."

Sirens wailed in the distance.

"It is too late," he whispered. "There is no escaping what I've done."

Emily dropped to her knees and draped herself over Nathan.

His breaths were so shallow she could barely feel the rise and fall of his chest.

She gave Victor a defiant glare. "If you are going to kill me, you'll have to look me in the eyes when you pull the trigger."

This time, she wouldn't close her eyes like she did with Sami.

If she, Nathan, and Maya—oh God, poor Maya—were going to die, she'd make sure Victor Pierron could never close his eyes without seeing her face.

Because he wasn't a sociopath like Mirga had been. He was a desperate man trying to dig himself out of a hole that had grown deeper and deeper until he couldn't escape.

The sirens were close now, coming in their direction. Maybe Victor hadn't noticed.

She needed to try and stall some more.

It was as if he'd read her mind. "I hear them, Emily. Time is up."

The gun in his hand was pointing at her. Then it wasn't.

Victor put it under his chin.

Pulled the trigger.

Emily screamed and turned her head. She heard his body hit the ground with a soft thud.

"Emily!" Lachlan stood in the barn's doorway, Ryder behind him.

"Lachlan." His name tore from her on a sob. She'd never been so happy to see a familiar face in her life.

Lachlan turned to Ryder. "Deal with the police when they get here and get us a bloody ambulance."

Ryder wheeled around and disappeared back outside.

Lachlan ran to Emily. Ignoring the bodies around him, he dropped to his knees on the other side of Nathan and ran his hands over his friend's body. "*Mo bhràthair,* don't you fucking die on us." He yanked off his belt and wrapped it around Nathan's upper thigh, then pulled a knife from his boot and used the tip to create a new hole in the leather to cinch it tight. "Help me get his shirt off."

She held out her zip-tied wrists. Lachlan sliced through the plastic tie with a quick flick of his blade.

Together, they tugged off the plaid button-down Nathan wore over his t-shirt.

His face was too pale, too still.

Lachlan tore the fabric into strips, handing Emily several scraps. "Wad up a piece and then tie it in place over the entry and exit wounds on his leg."

She thrust her hands under Nathan's thigh. *There.* Blood seeped from a ragged hole the size of a golf ball. The back of Nathan's jeans was soaked, the dirt floor beneath him caked with blood. Sweat broke out on her forehead, her stomach flip-flopped, and her vision swam.

Blood-stained fingers snapped in front of her face. Lachlan's stare lasered in on her. "I need you to stay with me. Nathan needs you."

Swallowing back bile, she nodded and took several deep breaths.

Police in black helmets and body armor with jackets that said "BRI Police" swarmed into the barn. They stopped short at the site of Lachlan and Emily working over Nathan. The unit commander began to bark orders in French.

She ignored them as she pressed a wad of cloth into the wound on the back of Nathan's thigh, then held it in place with another strip of material and tied it as tightly as she could, cursing inside at her clumsy fingers. She did the same to the smaller entrance wound on the front of his leg.

Ryder appeared next to her. The Brit's unflappable demeanor faltered as he looked at Nathan. "Five hostiles, all dead, including the one up there." He pointed to the loft. A drop of crimson fell through a crack in the boards to the barn floor as if on cue. "The girl needs a doctor."

"Get the first aid kit from yer car and a blanket." Lachlan's accent had thickened, broadcasting his emotions. "And tell the police we need a medevac. Now."

Ryder gave a tight nod and raced out of the barn.

Emily glanced to the far wall, where Maya huddled silently, watching them through deadened eyes. She hadn't given much thought to the poor girl through all of this.

"Everything will be okay, Maya." *Please let that be true.* It felt like a pathetically inadequate assurance, given everything the girl had witnessed and been through herself.

She turned her attention to Lachlan. "How did you find us?"

"Nathan. He left us a message before he came for you and gave us the coordinates of his meeting location. He wore a tag so we were able to track him here."

Lachlan had sliced Nathan's black t-shirt down the middle, exposing his chest. He palpated Nathan's abdomen, then pressed his knee against the wound in Nathan's side and held scraps of cloth against the entry and exit wounds on Nathan's shoulder. "We need to get him on his side, make sure his airway stays clear."

"I took off my tag." Emily felt sick at the confession. "Mirga told me if I didn't find a way to give Nathan the slip, they'd kill him. Jules found out Nathan killed his cousin and was planning to lure him into a trap, using me as bait."

Lachlan's hand, covered in Nathan's blood, gripped hers briefly before letting go to continue rendering aid to Nathan. "It's not your fault. None of this is your fault. The inspector was Mirga's mole in the police."

Her stomach heaved, and she battled to keep nausea at bay. She couldn't look at Victor's body, what he'd done to himself. "I thought Victor was going to kill us. Instead, he took his own life."

"Good," Lachlan snarled. "Saved me the trouble."

She didn't respond to that. A part of her felt sorry for Victor. His love for his son led him into a deal with the devil. But too many people had suffered and died because of his actions.

The commander of the elite French unit approached. "A helicopter is on its way."

Emily ran her palm down Nathan's stubbled jaw. His lips had a bluish tinge, his skin cool to the touch and clammy.

"Don't you leave me, Nathan Long—you hear me?" She placed her ear on the trident tattoo over his heart. It barely rose with each shallow, rapid breath. Her tears mingled with his blood.

"Please, don't leave me."

CHAPTER
THIRTY-FOUR

CRIMSON SMEARS COATED HER hands, stained her clothing, and mingled with the dried tears on her cheeks.

Emily leaned in to study her vacant expression in the hospital bathroom mirror. White walls surrounded her. Her feet stood on large squares of light gray tile. Disinfectant cleaner and copper melded in her nose and coated the back of her throat, cramping her stomach. Water flowed from the faucet into the stainless-steel basin, the mini-waterfall white noise to her numbed mind. The clinical starkness of her surroundings only served to emphasize the splashes of red painting her body like a gruesome work of art.

If she cleaned up, washed Nathan's lifeblood down the drain, it might be the last piece of him she ever had.

The face in the reflection paled.

The door creaked partway open. Red hair spilled through the gap, followed by wide, hazel eyes.

"Emily?" Sophia Mackay's hand swept to her mouth before dropping to her side. She stepped the rest of the way into the small room. "Let me help."

Emily let her friend guide her hands to the warm water, lather them with soap, and rub them clean. Rosy-tinted bubbles gathered at the drain before disappearing in the rush of water. "How are you here?"

"I flew over with Lachlan and your parents. Your dad used his connections to get us a private jet flight right after Nathan's call to Lachlan that you'd been taken. I couldn't stay in the States, not knowing..." Sophia reached for a paper towel, wet it, and then dabbed gently at streaks on Emily's face. "Nathan's still in surgery. Don't give up hope."

"It's my fault."

"No, it's not. You can't think like that." Sophia's delicate features hardened. "This was Jules Mirga's fault. You were trying to save lives."

"I was arrogant. I didn't think about the danger. I kept pushing Nathan away. Now, he might"—She couldn't breathe, she couldn't—"He'll never know I—"

Sophia squeezed her hands. Hard. "Nathan's not going to die. You'll have the chance to tell him how you feel."

Emily clung to her friend's calm, sure words like a life raft.

"By the way." Sophia dug into her pants pocket, then took Emily's hand and placed an object in it.

"Nana's pendant." Emily's fingers curled around the gold sunburst.

"Lachlan and Ryder found your purse at the site where Nathan left Ryder's Porsche." Sophia took hold of Emily's arm. "Come on. Your parents are waiting."

Emily let Sophia guide her down the hall to the surgical waiting room. Large windows let in natural light. The walls were covered with a faux wood veneer and soft lighting emanated from the white ceiling. A woman in blue scrubs sat behind a small reception desk.

Her parents, Ryder, and Lachlan waited in the open seating area. Emily hurried forward and crumpled into the shelter of her mother's arms.

Her father hovered next to them. "Thank God you're okay." A suspicious hint of wetness gleamed in his eyes. He kissed her forehead, his stern features softening.

She searched his face. "Any word?"

"No, but no news means he's still fighting."

Lachlan joined them from the corner of the room, stuffing his cell phone into his pocket as he reached them. "I've spoken to Nathan's family and promised I'd touch base as soon as we know anything." He lifted his chin at Ryder. "Any update from the police?"

"They've raided Victor Pierron's home and interviewed his wife." Ryder's tone was grim. "She knew about Pierron's deal with Jules Mirga. At first, Mirga simply wanted information in return for overlooking their son's drug debts and getting the boy into rehab and a job in the south of France. When the police raided Mirga's businesses, he threatened to expose Pierron. The inspector felt trapped. Things escalated out of control when Mirga abducted Emily the first time, then murdered Catalina and kidnapped Maya."

Emily spoke up. "Victor saw Nathan as his way out, both to save me and himself. If Mirga set his sights on Nathan, Victor figured Mirga would be the one that wouldn't come out alive. I'd be safe, as would his secret. He'd be free." She was sorry Victor had decided to end his life, but she would have a hard time forgiving him for the part he played in destroying so many lives.

A female voice emanated from an overhead speaker, summoning a doctor to the ER. Emily started at the stark reminder of where she was, and that Nathan hadn't been the only victim transported from the gruesome scene at the barn in Noisy-le-Grand.

"Where's Maya?" she asked Ryder. Guilt wrapped its bony fingers around her and squeezed. She'd left the girl in the care of strangers to be with Nathan.

"Maya's in good hands," he assured her. "She's with a nurse specialized in treating sexual trauma, and Madame Légère from Fondation Espoir is on her way. She said she'd started to build a rapport with

Maya before Mirga abducted the girl from the safe house. Everyone assumed that Catalina left voluntarily, so Madame Légère didn't recognize the potential threat to Maya until it was too late."

"I need to see her." Emily took the tissue her mother offered and wiped her eyes. "But first, I think I'll stop at the chapel down the hall."

"I'll go with you." Her mother stepped forward.

Emily gave her a gentle but determined smile. "Thanks, Mom, but if you don't mind, I'll only be a few minutes." She included Sophia in her gaze. Her best friend would want to be with her, too, and she needed to be alone.

Promising them she'd be back soon, she went to the chapel.

The room was small, peaceful, and—Emily was grateful to see—empty. Four rows of ruby-colored glass votives filled a table to the left of the altar.

Emily took a wooden taper stick from its holder, held it to the flame of a lighted votive, then to the unlit wick of another candle.

A prayer for Nathan.

She lit two more for Catalina and Maya.

Her fingers hovered over a fourth, then dipped the flame to the unblemished wax—one for Victor Pierron.

She took a seat on the first pew, near the wooden crucifix, and made the sign of the cross. Back to her childhood roots. The sharp, golden points of Nana's pendant dug into her palm. She fastened it around her neck, its familiar weight soothing.

"It's been a while." She directed her words at the crucifix. "I need you to let Nathan live. It's selfish, I know, but he doesn't deserve this."

She blotted her face with the tissue and huffed out a forlorn laugh. "He's probably had enough of me—I haven't exactly made his life easy. I've pushed him away so many times."

The flame from Nathan's candle reached higher, the tip playing peek-a-boo over the rim of the red glass. She watched it dance. Let her mind blank and just be still.

The chapel door opened behind her with a quiet woosh.

Emily turned. Her father stood at the entrance.

She clutched the back of the pew, her heart racing. "Nathan?"

"There's still no word from the OR." Porter Dane strolled down the aisle and lit a candle before taking a seat next to Emily.

She leaned her head on his shoulder, soaking in his strength. "You were right."

"About what?"

"Me being headstrong, rushing into dangerous situations without considering the consequences." Her throat tightened. "And now Nathan's paying the price."

Her father said nothing, his gaze fixed on the flickering votives. She waited for the "I told you so" to start.

"I know you think I was over-protective. You chafed at every attempt I made to keep you safe," he finally said.

Her jaw tightened. "Especially when you didn't treat Alex the same way because he was a boy."

Her father's shoulder tensed beneath her cheek. "You are my baby girl, Emily. My only daughter. Forgive an old man for wanting nothing more than to wrap you up and keep you safe from the evil I've witnessed too many times in this world." He angled his body toward her and cupped her chin. "And the harder I tried, the more you rebelled. Why do you think I taught you how to shoot? Why I had you take self-defense courses? I knew how much you valued your independence, even as a teenager, and I wanted you to be prepared." His expression turned grave. "And you were. You saved your own life and Nathan's too. And that girl."

The sheen in his eyes, coupled with the pride written across his face, almost undid her.

"I'm proud of you, Rosebud. You scare the hell out of me with your big heart and stubborn will. I did the best I could to keep you safe."

She gave a teary laugh. "Like siccing a Navy SEAL bodyguard on me?"

"You can thank me later for that."

Her jaw dropped, eyes flying wide before narrowing at the satisfied gleam in her father's eyes. "Were you scheming to have Nathan and me end up together?"

The admiral shrugged. "I knew there was a spark, one you'd never admit to because of Nathan's background. I took advantage of the situation when the opportunity presented itself."

Of course you did. Emily shook her head. She should be angry with him for interfering in her life.

Again.

But he hadn't created the connection between her and Nathan—he'd simply put them together long enough to see if it would flourish.

"You are a meddling old man," she told him with grudging amusement.

"Father knows best."

Emily's laugh hiccupped into a mournful whimper. "Daddy, what if Nathan doesn't survive?"

Her father pulled her into his arms, his hand brushing over her hair. "He will, baby. He's got something to live for."

"What's that?"

"You, Emily. He'll live for you."

The chapel door swished open to show Ryder in the doorway. "The surgeon is on his way to the waiting room."

Emily jumped to her feet. "Is Nathan out of surgery?"

"The nurse had no information other than to say the doctor would answer our questions." Ryder held the door open for her and her father, then followed them down the corridor, a silent sentinel in their wake.

They'd just returned when a man in green scrubs entered. His posture radiated relaxed confidence and Emily immediately pegged him as the surgeon. She gripped her mother's hand.

He peeled off his surgical scrub cap, revealing short, golden-brown hair giving way to white. "I'm Dr. Bouchet." His accent was slight and judging from the way he spoke English, he'd spent some time in the States. "Nathan made it through surgery."

Emily swayed from the release of tension. Her father gripped her upper arm, steadying her.

The surgeon continued. "He was in shock from blood loss, and his blood pressure bottomed out. He had entry and exit wounds from three separate projectiles, a collapsed lung, and internal damage, although not as bad as expected. We stopped the bleeding, gave him a blood transfusion, inserted a chest tube, and removed his damaged spleen. His clavicle is fractured, but fortunately, bullet fragments missed major organs other than the spleen, which he can live without. The next twenty-four hours will be critical to his recovery."

"Can I see him?" Emily asked.

Dr. Bouchet shook his head. "Not yet. He'll be in Post Op for a couple of hours. Once he's stable, he'll be transferred to the ICU. After he's settled, you'll be able to see him briefly. He's been intubated and will be kept sedated for the next twenty-four hours." The surgeon's tobacco-colored gaze gentled as it touched on Emily before encompassing everyone in the group. "My advice would be to get something to eat, freshen up, get some sleep. There's nothing you can do at this point. We'll monitor Nathan and keep you apprised of his status."

He acknowledged the chorus of thanks with a brief nod and left.

Emily tilted her face to the sterile white ceiling. *Thank you.*

"Rosebud," Admiral Dane spoke up, "you need sleep. Come with your mother and me to a hotel."

"No, Dad, I'm not leaving until Nathan regains consciousness, and I know he's okay."

Her father's face tightened. "Emily—"

"I'll stay with her." Sophia intervened. "You and Mrs. Dane find a hotel. It's been a long day for all of us. I'll have Lachlan take me to Emily's apartment to get fresh clothing and toiletries. We'll be back soon."

Emily nodded before motioning to her parents. "Go. Get some rest."

"Ryder will stay with you until Sophia and I return." Lachlan's expression signaled she'd be wasting her time if she argued.

She kissed her parents and hugged Sophia before waving the Danes and Mackays off.

Ryder had taken up vigil nearby. Emily collapsed into the chair beside him, her body a boneless sack of exhaustion.

"Why didn't he wait, Ryder? Why didn't he wait for his teammates before he came for me?"

"Because you're more than a job to him. Nothing would have stopped him from coming for you the second he knew you were in danger." Ryder regarded her with a tilt of his head, his gaze assessing. "The question is, what is he to you?"

Emily licked her suddenly dry lips and forced herself to admit the truth aloud.

"He's everything."

CHAPTER
THIRTY-FIVE

NATHAN FLOATED IN A vast expanse of midnight blue.

Compressed air flowed through his regulator, inflating his lungs. His throat closed around a foreign object, and he gagged.

Can't breathe. Panic wasn't an option at this depth. He tried to clear his regulator, but his hand dawdled through heavy water to his face.

The high-pitched shriek of an alarm pierced the abyss.

Cool, dry fingers wrapped around his hand. The soothing voice of a mermaid echoed in his head in French-accented English. "Welcome back, Nathan. You need to stay calm—you have a breathing tube. We'll remove it as soon as we can." The mermaid switched to French. "*On demands Doctor LeMonde.*"

Midnight melded into the murky green of shallow waters behind his eyes. Nathan focused on the sounds of dry land—a rhythmic wheeze, a steady beep, the hushed tap of soft-soled shoes, the rustle of clothing.

He bench-pressed open heavy lids.

Fuzzy images of light and shadow appeared.

A figure moved over him.

He kept blinking until the world focused and revealed a brunette with a pixie cut dressed in green scrubs, her attention on a monitor near his head.

Something grabbed his bicep and squeezed, then gradually loosened with a hiss.

The same thing with both of his legs.

Squeeze. Release.

His lashes drifted shut. He felt like he had battled a Mack truck and lost, and now he was at the mercy of a giant python, slowly squeezing him to death.

What the hell had he been doing?

A mission?

No, he'd resigned his commission, that much he remembered.

He forced his sluggish brain to work.

A barn. A man with a pistol aimed at his head.

He didn't appear to be dead. That was a plus. Emily had—

Emily!

He lifted his head, tried to make his legs move, gagged again on the hose down his throat. Wires and tubes held him captive. Knives stabbed his midsection and shoulder.

"Nathan, we need you to stay calm."

The woman in green was back, and she had brought a friend, an older woman with blonde hair pulled back into a low ponytail.

The unmistakable scratch of Velcro and then fabric caressed his wrists. He fisted his hands and tugged.

Trapped.

His lips peeled back as a harsh grunt rattled his chest.

Emily.

A man in green scrubs and white overcoat moved into his line of vision. "Nathan, I'm Dr. LeMonde. I cannot remove your breathing tube until you calm down." He spoke in heavily accented English.

Nathan willed his body to still if that was what it would take to get free.

"Are you ready?"

He nodded.

"Breathe deeply and cough."

The doctor withdrew the tube in a slow glide. The nurses removed the wrist restraints.

Nathan swallowed and winced, his throat tenderized meat. "Emily." Her name came out as a feeble croak.

The brunette placed her hand behind his neck and held a straw to his lips. He sucked down precious drops of cold water before she took it away.

"Your fiancée is right outside. Give us a few minutes to check your vitals."

Fiancée?

"Tall...blonde?" He coughed again, and the nurse brought the straw back to his mouth.

The other nurse, the one with the ponytail, laughed. "That is the one. Do you have another we should know about?"

He tried fiancée out in his head.

It felt right.

"She's okay?"

"She is fine." The nurse patted his arm. "She has not left the hospital since you arrived. I know she will be happy to see you are awake."

"How long?" *Jesus,* it hurt to talk.

"Almost two days." She smiled. "Your fiancée was right—you do have beautiful eyes." She lifted his gown to one side, examining the white bandages across his thigh, waist, and chest.

His left shoulder hurt like hell. He shifted and groaned. Shards of pain stabbed him from every angle. "Emily."

The nurse injected something into the IV bag hanging on the pole next to him. "I will let her in to see you, but only for a few minutes.

I have added something to your IV for the pain so you can rest, and I will let Dr. Bouchet know you are awake."

The two women exited with a swish through the glass doors of his semi-private fishbowl. Machines surrounded him that chirped, hissed, clicked, and whirred.

Now that he was awake, that would get annoying pretty damn quick.

A few minutes later, the doors slid open again.

Emily.

She tiptoed to the foot of his bed, dressed in jeans and white cotton shirt beneath a navy-blue cardigan, her hair pulled back from her face with a headband.

The all-American girl.

He drank in the sight of her, alive and unharmed.

"Hi." Dark circles shadowed her eyes and her face appeared drawn. She looked like she hadn't slept in a week.

He'd never seen a more beautiful woman.

"Come here." His voice still sounded like it had been sandpapered. He beckoned with his fingers.

She remained where she was, out of reach. Her gaze darted around the room, refusing to land on his face.

Dread sat on his chest, clogging his throat like that breathing tube had. "What's the matter? Maya?"

Emily jerked, her eyes finding his. "What? Oh, no, Maya's fine. Well, not fine, but in good hands. She's recovering physically. I'm praying she'll heal emotionally. The hospital discharged her this morning." Her reassuring smile departed as quickly as she'd offered it up.

The pressure on his chest deepened.

Silence filled the space between them, the air thick with unspoken emotion.

He plastered a smirk on his face. "So, fiancée?"

Emily blushed a pretty shade of pink, and his smile widened, turned genuine. She stared at her hands, clutching the rail next to his sheet-draped toes. "I wanted to make sure they would let me see you."

More silence ate up precious moments.

She was killing him here. Was she summoning up the courage to cut him loose? Had he imagined her declaration of love when he lay on the floor of that barn, falling into a deep, dark hole?

I love you, Nathan.

The drugs the nurse injected into the IV were starting to blur his edges.

He needed to know. She wasn't going to walk away from him again and pretend it wouldn't rip out his soul.

"Emily—"

"Nathan—"

They spoke in unison.

Emily's face crumpled. Her tears came out of nowhere, overflowed, weaving sorrowful trails down her cheeks. "Please, let me say something first."

The monitor on his left let out a high-pitched screech.

The doors slid open. The nurse with the pixie cut entered the room, her expression a question mark. She glanced at Emily, then him, before turning off the alarm. "Your heart rate accelerated suddenly. How do you feel?"

Like I've been dropped into a hot zone in the middle of a firefight.

"I'm okay."

"Don't overdo it." The nurse patted his arm, but her stare fixed on Emily.

The doors slid together behind her as she exited.

Nathan steeled himself. "What did you want to say?"

"I love you."

His mouth opened and shut, then did it again, a fish drowning in air.

Emily moved closer and peered at him. "Are you still with me?" She waved a hand in front of his face. "Did you hear what I said?"

He grinned—a big sloppy, high-as-a-kite grin. "Go on."

She looked at him like he was two cards shy of a full deck, but she'd stopped crying. She leaned down and brushed her lips against his.

He inhaled her scent and tried to trap it in his lungs. Golden strands of hair caught on the stubble along his jaw.

Her eyes, luminescent in the harsh hospital lighting, met his and held firm. "I was so afraid I'd lose you. I'm sorry I kept pushing you away. I was scared to love you, scared I'd have to give up my independence to be with you." She brushed a hand over his hair, then caressed his cheek. "Please tell me you'll forgive me."

Always.

"Love you. Team." His tongue was thick and clumsy; the words slurred out. He had more to say but whatever that nurse pumped into his IV had caught up to him. "Fiancée…"

Emily laughed. Her slender fingers wrapped around his hand and squeezed. "Sleep, baby. I'll be here when you wake up."

He could only manage a weak flex of his fingers in response as the medication pulled him under.

CHAPTER THIRTY-SIX

THE SUN SHONE BRIGHTLY through the window of Nathan's hospital room as he finished packing his duffel. He took one last look around the space that had served as his accommodations for the past week.

Ryder lounged in the recliner next to the bed, dressed in a pair of designer jeans and a white t-shirt that looked like silk. "Look at this, mate." Ryder held up the electronic tablet he'd brought with him. "This is what we should buy you for Christmas."

Nathan squinted at the photo of a Level IIIA bulletproof jean jacket, then gave Ryder the stink eye accompanied by an eloquent finger. "I don't plan to make getting shot a habit, amigo."

Ryder grinned. "Ready?"

Nathan nodded. Dr. Bouchet had agreed to release him only after he assured the French surgeon he was taking a private jet back to the States and would check in with a physician after he arrived.

His skin itched, and not just from stitches.

Emily had some last-minute thing come up at the embassy. She'd called Ryder and asked him to take Nathan to the airport.

To say Nathan was disappointed would be a vast understatement.

Despite the fact she'd been to see him every night after work until the nurses kicked her out, he missed her already. He was headed home to Virginia. Admiral Dane had told him to get the hell out of Dodge while the US and French authorities wrangled over the fact he'd killed a few people during his stay.

Emily was staying in Paris, her job and diplomatic immunity firmly in place. That, and she'd done the French government a favor by offing Mirga and exposing Victor Pierron.

He shoved a hand into the pocket of his jeans, his insides tightening. They'd find a way to make this Transatlantic thing work.

Ryder grabbed hold of his duffel and they stepped out into the corridor.

The day shift nurses hurried over to say their goodbyes. Nathan embraced Geneviève, the brunette with the pixie cut. "I'll miss you." He winked at Patricia, the blonde. "You, too. Tell my night shift ladies I'll miss them as well."

"Perhaps you will return and visit, *oui*?" Geneviève wagged her finger. "But as a visitor, not as a patient."

Patricia pointed to the wheelchair parked next to his door that he'd been doing his best to ignore. "Sit. I know you are a big, tough man, but you have to use it."

"I'm perfectly capable of walking." He leaned down to whisper in her ear. "I won't tell if you won't tell."

Patricia continued to point, her expression no-nonsense.

He gave a disgusted sigh, "Yes, ma'am," and lowered himself into the chair.

Ryder wheeled him, still grumbling, out to his car.

Nathan eased into the front passenger seat of Ryder's SUV with a groan. It would take a few weeks before he was back in fighting shape, but with Emily staying in France, what else did he have to do?

Work, rehab, dream about making love to a woman an ocean away.

Ryder turned right onto Quai du Maréchal Joffre/D7 and headed for Paris-Le Bourget rather than Charles De Gaulle. Le-Bourget handled business aviation. Admiral Dane had pulled another of his many strings and gotten Nathan a ride back to DC in a sleek corporate jet, complete with a nurse who'd monitor him en route.

"Your face is a wet weekend, mate."

Nathan grunted at Ryder's comment. He stared out the window at the passing traffic. "Maybe I should move to Paris. I could do most of my work for Dìleas anywhere there's a good internet connection, fly back to visit clients when needed."

Ryder's silence made Nathan's neck tighten. "You know, most of the time, I like that you don't talk much." His chest rose on a deep inhale. He winced at the stabs to his shoulder and below his rib cage. "Now isn't one of those times."

The Brit glanced at him. "Are you afraid Emily will stop loving you if you're not in the same city?"

Well, he'd thought it, but it did sound a bit silly when Ryder said it out loud.

"Not stop loving me." Nathan grimaced. "At least, not right away. Maybe carry on her life and career without me and get used to that, and one day, realize she doesn't need me on her team anymore to be happy."

"You were in the military. Couples are apart quite often when one spouse deploys."

"Yeah," Nathan nodded, "and I've seen plenty of those relationships fail. I had to pick up the pieces with more than one of my guys when they came home and their wives had taken the kids and served them with divorce papers."

Oh Hell. He was depressing himself—he needed to lighten the mood.

He eyeballed Ryder. "What about you, amigo? With those movie-star looks, I'm sure you've had your share of ladies. Didn't any of them hold your interest for longer than a night or two?"

Ryder didn't answer. Nathan's gaze shot to the other man's knuckles, whitening around the steering wheel.

Hmmm. Looked like he'd hit a nerve instead of poking fun.

"One." The word rasped out, low and curt, from between Ryder's lips.

"Only one? High school sweetheart?"

"University."

Nathan waited for Ryder to say more. When the silence stretched into minutes, he gave a mental shrug. Some things were buried deep for a reason, and it wasn't his place to pull out the shovel and start digging.

Muffled strains of ZZ Top's "Strut" escaped from his hip. He answered his phone with a smile. "Hey, darlin', I was just thinking naughty things that involved you, me, and various food items that melt at body temperature."

Emily's giggle was music in his ear. "You're a pig. I miss you already, and even if you weren't leaving, I'm pretty sure the doctor hasn't cleared you for that kind of fun."

"Screw the doctor."

Emily's voice sobered. "Listen, I know I told you I'd meet you at the airport and see you off, but Minister Woodward just called a meeting of my division, and there is no way I can leave."

Nathan stiffened.

Chill. Emily had a job to do. She had already missed a lot of work. He brushed aside the sudden ache in his chest. "Yeah, sure. I understand. Ryder will have to be the one to kiss me goodbye."

A disgusted grumble came from Ryder and an outright laugh from his woman.

Emily's voice roughened. "You'd better rest and get healthy."

"I will. Stay out of trouble, you hear? I love you." *Jesus.* He sounded like a lovesick teenager.

"I love you too, and I miss you already." She made a kissing sound and hung up.

Nathan continued to stare at his phone. After growing up with an overprotective father and brother, she valued her freedom. He wouldn't be the one to clip her wings even though he wanted nothing more than to have her sleeping next to him every night at his home in Virginia.

She'd been through hell the past few weeks. This time apart would be good, give her a chance to settle back into her life and decide for herself how he fit into it.

He wanted desperately to make her his fiancée for real. But he didn't want to ask her when she still felt guilty about him getting shot.

If Emily said yes, it needed to be because she'd made a place for him in her life.

Because she wanted him to watch her six. Forever.

CHAPTER
THIRTY-SEVEN

"ARE YOU SURE THIS is what you want?" Minister Woodward sat at her desk in her office, her pen poised over the paper Emily handed her.

Emily sat on the other side of the desk. She glanced around at the ornate, neoclassical moldings on the walls, the heavy silk drapes that framed the tall French windows, and the crystal chandelier hanging from the high ceiling.

"I'm sure." She'd miss a lot about Paris and her work at the embassy.

But her new job would allow her to address human trafficking on a more global scale. And it was closer to home. To her heart.

She reached up and touched the pendant around her neck with a smile.

The minister nodded. The pen made soft scraping noises as she added her signature and slid the paper across the desk.

"I think it's a good move for you. And after everything you've been through lately, a change of scenery might not hurt." Her lips tilted into a slight smile. "How is Nathan?"

"Grumpy. Complaining about restrictions the doctor put on him while he heals."

Missing her as desperately as she missed him. Phone sex couldn't replace his touch, his scent, the warmth of his big body next to hers.

"Men. Such babies when they're sick or hurt. They should try childbirth."

Emily choked on a laugh. Minister Woodward had always been a bit formal, so her comment caught Emily off guard. "True."

"Good luck. With the new job and the man." The minister stood and reached her hand across the desk.

Emily stood as well and shook it. "Thank you, Minister Woodward, for everything."

Now that she'd been formally accepted to her new position in the Office of Trafficking in Persons, and Minister Woodward had signed off on her transfer, she only had two weeks to hand over her work duties, pack up her apartment and get herself settled in DC. She hadn't told anyone about her plans, not even Nathan. It had been hard to keep it a secret, but she hadn't wanted to get his hopes up and then not get the job.

Bruce was waiting for her when she returned to her cubicle. "Is it done?"

Her breath left her on a deep exhale. "It's done."

"I hope your boyfriend appreciates what you're doing for him."

"It's not just for him. It's for me too." The soul-deep reality of that statement hit her.

She wasn't giving up anything. She was gaining something. Her life was richer, more fulfilling, with Nathan in it.

Bruce cocked his head and narrowed his eyes at her. They'd managed to slip back into an easy friendship for which she was grateful. "Remember what I told you before you left for your friend's wedding?"

"What?" With all that had happened, Sophia and Lachlan's wedding felt like forever ago.

"I said make sure you don't spend so much time focusing on the job that you miss out on everything else. Looks like you took my advice."

He snorted. "Although you could have been a bit less dramatic about it."

Emily laughed. "Bruce?"

"Yeah?"

"Shut up and help me pack."

Two weeks later, Emily pulled her Lexus up to the steel gate blocking Nathan's driveway. Fall had begun to color the leaves in Virginia, and summer's intense heat and humidity had given way to more tolerable temperatures.

It had been six weeks since Nathan returned to the States. She'd had to bite her tongue hard every evening when they video-chatted to keep from telling him the news about her new job and impending move back to DC.

Now she wondered if her idea to surprise him wouldn't turn out to be a colossal mistake.

By now, the cameras mounted on his gate pillars would have picked up her car.

Her stomach cramped. She gave herself a mental shake. *Too late to 'what-if' now.* She dialed Nathan's number.

"Emily?" His baritone timbre sent a familiar tingle through her.

"Permission to come aboard, Lieutenant?" She disconnected before he could respond.

The steel gate slid open with a clang. She lowered her window and saluted the cameras, then navigated past the No Trespassing signs along the driveway and around the bend to Nathan's home.

He waited at the bottom of the front porch steps barefoot in a pair of gray athletic shorts and a black Disturbed concert t-shirt.

Emily parked and peeled sweaty palms from the steering wheel. Nathan looked good, healthy—not like a man who'd been shot multiple times. His t-shirt hugged a chest as muscular and fit as before. His hair was longer and tousled like he'd been running his hands through it. Stubble shadowed his face.

A jolt of need squeezed her heart before heading south. She stepped from the car, her feet rooted next to the driver's door. "Hi."

He reacted to her greeting like it was a starter's pistol, reaching her in two long strides before he yanked her into his arms, his mouth finding hers.

The scents of ocean breezes and home surrounded her.

She ran her hands over his shoulders and back, mindful of his injuries, feeling his strength. Love, longing, need—she poured it into him through her lips and fingertips.

They broke apart, panting for air.

"Why didn't you tell me you were coming?" Nathan punctuated his question with a sweep of lips over her face and neck.

She shivered, trying to think straight under his sensual assault. "I wanted to surprise you."

"Mmmm," he murmured, still nibbling. "Happy birthday to me. How long can you stay?"

Bird wings flapped in her chest and throat. She linked her hands behind his neck and gazed into ice-blue eyes she'd never get tired of admiring. "For as long as you want me. I accepted a position in DC. My new job starts Monday."

Nathan stepped back, forcing her hands back to her sides. Cool air blanketed her where his warm body had been.

"You took a job in DC?" His brows lowered. "Why didn't you tell me?"

Her throat suddenly a desert, Emily swallowed. "I didn't want to disappoint you if it fell through."

His fingers brushed through his hair before gripping the back of his neck. "I know how important your career is to you, Emily. I don't want to be the reason you step off the fast track. You may not resent me now, but eventually, you will." His expression turned sheepish. "I, ah, I've been talking to Lachlan about moving to Paris. I can do my job anywhere there's a good Internet connection and—"

She threw herself at him, cutting off his words. "I couldn't possibly love you more than I do right now."

Nathan's arms surrounded her, cocooning her with gentle, comforting strength.

Her heart lightened and expanded to her rib cage. "This was my choice, Nathan. I belong here. With you. It was time to leave Paris, and I'm eager to start my new position." She traced his jaw with her fingers. "Who knows? I may apply for another overseas posting in a couple of years, and we can go together."

His smile flooded her with warmth. The desire backlighting his eyes electrified every nerve ending in her body.

"You've got a deal." He bent and lifted her into his arms.

She caught the wince before he could mask it. "Put me down. You're still healing."

"Almost better. You can kiss my boo-boos."

Refusing to release her, he carried her through the front door and down the hall to his master suite, laying her in the middle of his bed.

His big hands trembled as he fumbled with the buttons on her blouse. "Screw this." He yanked, sending buttons flying. He tugged down her bra, his mouth finding her nipple with the urgency of a heat-seeking missile.

A hot current of need shot from her breast to her womb.

Climbing between her legs, he spread her thighs and rubbed his hard length against her center with a wicked twist of his hips.

"Nathan." Her back arched. She almost came on the spot from the suction of his mouth and the sensation of him grinding against her. She couldn't think, could only give herself up to his impatient ministrations and let herself feel.

He tugged off her slacks and panties. "I've missed you." His voice rumbled, deep and sexy, as he tasted his way down her body.

She squirmed, panting at the sensory overload.

He didn't give her time to breathe before he scooted down, his broad shoulders keeping her spread wide. His mouth found her center, and he sucked hard, using his tongue to drive her straight to the peak.

He plunged two fingers deep.

Emily screamed, every organ in her body spasming in a freefall of pleasure. Fireworks exploded in her brain. Her nails dug into his fabric-clad shoulders.

When she could breathe again, she opened her eyes.

Nathan placed a soft kiss on her stomach. "I've missed this."

She tried to form a coherent sentence about how much she loved him and had missed him too and failed.

He sat up, ripping his t-shirt over his head.

She couldn't help her sharp inhale at the bright pink gashes at his collarbone, bicep, and waist. Reminders that he was still healing.

"Maybe we shouldn't—"

He cut her off with a kiss. "We should. I'll be fine."

"Now who's being stubborn?" She urged him to his back with a gentle push.

He complied with a sexy grin that lit up his face and melted her heart. "I'm a guy. And you're hot. And I love you."

Her eyes misted. "I don't deserve you." She cupped his jaw, reveling in the scrape of stubble beneath her palm.

"Yeah, you do, and I deserve you." Tilting his hips, he shimmied out of his shorts and threw them across his bedroom.

She looked down at herself and laughed. Her shirt still hung from her shoulders, her breasts spilled over her bra, and she was naked from the waist down. She shrugged off her shirt and unhooked her bra, dropping them over the side of the bed. Her grandmother's pendant dangled from her neck.

Nathan rubbed his fingers over the gold starburst. "No matter what you get into, that necklace always finds its way back to you."

She grinned. "That's probably my Nana's doing—running the show from the other side. She is, after all, my father's mother."

A small, misshapen, dark pink crater decorated Nathan's thigh. She paid reverence to it with her tongue and to all the other fresh scars that branded his body.

His hands roamed her body as she explored him. Their breaths grew increasingly ragged until he flipped her onto her back and slid into her with a gentle thrust.

He filled her, every inch. Body and soul. They made love in a slow, careful rhythm.

"I love you, Nathan."

"I love you, too, babe."

Emily soaked in the emotion in Nathan's eyes as he moved over her, tension coiling in her body. It didn't take long for another release to overtake her, and Nathan followed.

They lay curled in each other's arms, her head on his chest, his heart pounding a steady, strong rhythm.

"Well, that was a helluva lot better than what I'd originally planned for this afternoon." His deep drawl vibrated beneath her ear.

She laughed, filled to the brim with contentment.

Jules Mirga, Victor Pierron, and her own stubborn need to do everything on her own had almost taken Nathan from her. She wouldn't let anything or anyone get between them again, not even herself.

She was home.

Eight Weeks Later

Emily stepped onto the blue-line train toward Franconia-Springfield at the Foggy Bottom Metro and checked the time on her phone. She was meeting Nathan and the Mackays at six-thirty for dinner in Old Town.

The train lurched forward. Her grip tightened on the pole before she navigated to an open seat. The twenty-minute ride gave her plenty of time to reflect. In only two months, her life had changed dramatically. She was settling in, both with Nathan and her position in the international programs division of the Office of Trafficking in Persons.

Life was good. Amazing in fact. She'd never been happier.

But how would Nathan react to her latest news?

When the train pulled into Braddock Road station, she exited.

Nathan waited on the island platform next to the escalators leading down to street level. He wore clean, unripped jeans and a pale blue button-down beneath a navy sport coat instead of a heavy metal t-shirt.

People still gave him a wide berth.

Her body shook on a silent huff of laughter. She'd probably avoid him, too, if she didn't know a teddy bear existed beneath that resting badass face.

Their gazes connected across the open platform. Nathan grinned, the expression transforming his features from scary to arresting.

Her breath caught. Sexy, dangerous, and all hers.

He met her halfway, pulling her into him with a kiss that made her toes curl. "Missed you." He held her hand as they stepped onto the escalator.

"You saw me this morning."

"That was ten hours ago, babe." His whisper caressed her ear. "All I could think about was ice cream."

Heat crept from her womb to her breasts and spread across her face as she remembered exactly how he'd eaten his ice cream last night. "You're a perv."

He rewarded her with another kiss.

She thought back to the restlessness that had plagued her at Sophia and Lachlan's wedding. She realized she'd been jealous of the happiness and contentment in Sophia's eyes.

When she looked in the mirror now, those same feelings reflected back at her.

She squeezed Nathan's hand, then tugged him to a stop out of the path of the other pedestrians on the sidewalk. Sucking in a breath to steady herself, she met his gaze and dove in. "I have exciting news. I wanted to tell you before we meet with Sophia and Lachlan. My boss has offered me a position on the team that monitors our anti-slavery funding projects in Africa."

Nathan hugged her. "Congratulations."

She bit her lip.

"But?" He eyed her knowingly.

"It involves a fair amount of travel."

His gaze narrowed. "You thought I'd be upset?" He cupped her face in his hands. "Em, I know how much your work means to you. I would never want you to turn down an opportunity you're passionate about. We'll make it work."

"I love you." She gripped fistfuls of his blazer and yanked him down for a lingering kiss.

"Get a room," a middle-aged man in a Philadelphia Eagles t-shirt muttered as he passed by them.

She and Nathan broke apart with a laugh.

"I love you too," Nathan said. "We're a team. Always remember that."

Emily looped her arm through his as they strolled along the street. She'd run from Nathan, afraid of his need to protect her, of losing herself in loving him.

Nathan had pushed past her fears like the kind of dominant, protective man she had vowed to avoid and shown her that love was a strength, not a threat to her independence.

They were a team.

Let the adventures begin.

THE END

If you loved Nathan and Emily's story, please consider leaving a review on Amazon and/or Goodreads.

Excerpt from Missed Opportunity

Dileas Security Agency, Book Three

THE APPOINTMENT AT WILLIAMS Advanced Avionics wasn't until fourteen hundred on Monday. Ryder arrived early.

The company occupied the entire top floor of a six-story red-brick building in Fairfax, Virginia. He parked his rental Chevy Suburban in one of the open spaces. The weather was sunny and warm. He slid back into his suit coat, fastened the top button, and straightened his tie, then took the lift to the sixth floor.

His heart thudded faster with every passing number on the panel.

The doors opened to reveal a dark wood reception desk that dwarfed the black-haired, twenty-something woman in a maroon knit top seated behind it. The name Williams Advanced Avionics hung on the soft gray wall in a bold splash of metallic blue and silver. To the right of the reception desk was a small seating area with a dark blue couch and two solid gray armchairs surrounding a dark wood coffee table.

Ryder stepped to the desk, ignoring the receptionist's widening brown eyes. "Good afternoon. I have an appointment with Ms. Williams." His gaze dropped to the hardcover textbook in front of her. *Managing Risk Through Catastrophe Modeling*.

Impressive.

"Um," the woman stammered. "May I ask your name?" Copper stained her dusky cheeks.

It's not what you think.

In his opinion, he didn't resemble the British actor everyone mentioned when they met him *that* closely, but he knew the effect his appearance had on people. They paused. Assessed. Having a similar accent as the other man didn't help.

"I'm from Dìleas Security Agency." He left out his name.

The receptionist picked up her phone. "Ms. Williams? A man from Dìleas Security Agency is here to see you." She nodded at Ryder as she hung up and pointed to the seating area. "She'll be with you in a moment. You can wait over there."

"Thank you." Ryder could feel her gaze linger on him as he walked over to the couch and picked up the magazine on the coffee table, *Aviation Week*. A restless energy plagued him, making sitting impossible. He dropped the magazine back onto the table and instead stared out the window overlooking the car park and landscaped natural areas.

In the distance, the cluster of high-rise buildings in nearby Tysons Corner dominated a skyline of mostly low and mid-rise buildings in the region. The canopy of trees showed faint signs of autumn with patchy spots of pale yellow, but the full display of vibrant gold, orange and red wouldn't take place for another few weeks.

He'd dreamed of Nathalie last night—the way she looked when they were together, lying on a blanket in the Oxford Botanic Garden on a crisp spring day, a faint mist coating her skin as they traded kisses while pretending to study. He'd pretended, at least. She'd been the better student all around.

He'd try to distract her by running his lips along the back of her neck, sliding his fingers beneath the hem of her jumper to stroke the satiny skin of her back. She'd shiver in the cool, damp air and swat at him with a mock frown, even as her eyes promised hot, sweaty nights.

Not even an ice-cold shower had tamed the hard-on he'd woken up with this morning in his hotel room. Taking matters into his own hands, he'd cursed Nathalie for the power she still held over his memories.

And that's all she was. A memory.

One he would put into proper perspective once he met the current version of Nathalie—as far removed from the girl she'd once been as he was from the boy who'd loved her.

The reality of standing in her father's company—her company now—waiting for her to receive him brought him back to the task at hand. Lucas Caldwell wanted Nathalie safe. His job was to perform a threat assessment and convince her that Dìleas could be of service.

He texted Penny that he'd be meeting with Williams's president in place of Caleb and asked her to email a copy of his credentials to Nathalie.

Next, he performed a quick scan of his surroundings. The lift opened directly into the reception area and only required an access key after six p.m. What about the stairs? Someone knowledgeable could access the sixth floor via the emergency stairwells, even with the doors locked on the stairwell side. No security cameras were evident.

He made some notes on his phone to send to Nathan so the former SEAL could do a sweep of company spaces and recommend security upgrades. These offices were a soft target that needed to be hardened as much as was reasonably possible.

"Sorry to keep you waiting." A sultry alto he remembered all too well came from the hallway to his left.

He shoved his memories, along with any residual emotion, into the far recesses of his brain and slammed the door before pivoting to face the woman who'd walked away from him without a backward glance.

His heart jolted like it had been defibrillated back to life.

Eight years.

The photograph hadn't lied. She'd grown from a pretty girl into a stunning, self-assured woman. She wore a tailored black jacket over a copper-colored blouse with a matching slim black skirt that ended just above her knees. On her feet were black shoes with modest two-inch heels. She'd pulled her hair back into a low bun and conservative gold hoops adorned her ears.

The college girl with curly hair and oversized sweaters had transformed into a sophisticated corporate executive.

Nathalie froze, her outstretched hand halting midway. Shock and recognition paled her face. She rocked back slightly on her heels as if buffeted by a strong breeze. "Ryder?"

He tensed, ready to leap forward and catch her if she crumpled even as part of him took grim satisfaction in her response.

She shot the receptionist a questioning look before returning her gaze to meet his. "Someone from Dìleas Security Agency is supposed to be meeting with me."

"Hello, Nathalie. That would be me." He kept his voice level, ruthlessly tamping down his own reaction from the shock of seeing her again. "Penny Turner should have emailed you my credentials."

Five minutes ago.

She regained her composure quickly, impressing him. "Let's go to my office. Angie, I don't want to be interrupted." Her last comment she directed to the receptionist before twisting on her heels and marching back down the hall, leaving him to follow or get left behind.

Her back to him, he allowed his lips to twist into a bitter smile.

That, at least, hadn't changed.

Missed Opportunity *(Dileas Security Agency, Book Three), Available*
on Amazon

Bonus Freebie

Want to know how it all began for the men of Dìleas Security Agency?

Sign up for my newsletter at cssmithauthor.com and I'll send you the prequel novella, The Mission, for free!

ALSO BY C.S. SMITH

ACKNOWLEDGMENTS

Writing *Missing in Action* was so much fun! Nathan and Emily's chemistry was special from the first time they met in *Near Miss,* and I knew they needed their own story. I love all my characters but I have to admit that Nathan has an extra special place in my heart as a book boyfriend.

I have so many people to thank:

My family for putting up with my craziness (during the editing process in particular), and for being my biggest cheerleaders.

My awesome Killer Writers: Nancy, Vicki, and Tina, and my CWC Womens Fiction critique group for chapter-by-chapter critiques, beta reads, and all-around moral support.

Drs. Matt and Jenn made sure I could make Nathan suffer without killing him or causing irreparable damage.

My editor, Liana forced me to flesh out my lack of descriptions and scene setting and asked picky questions that resulted in a much better story. My copyeditor, April ran a fine-tooth comb over the results and surprised me—the detail freak—with some amazing fact-checking.

Any and all mistakes are mine alone.

About the Author

Heat, Heart, and Heroes -- Steamy Romantic Suspense

C.S. Smith parlayed her degrees in government and national security studies into various careers as a policy analyst, export manager, and director of a city government committee on global connectivity. Her love of spine-tingling romantic suspense can be traced to her formative years in Washington, DC, surrounded by intrigue and good-looking men in uniform—including the one she married.

A native New Englander who has spent over half her life in North Carolina, she has joined the ranks of empty nesters, leaving only her husband and "faux" Golden Retriever at her mercy.

For more information, please visit cssmithauthor.com or connect with her on social media:

a   amazon.com/author/c.s.smith

f   facebook.com/

◉   instagram.com/c.s.smithauthor/

Made in United States
North Haven, CT
26 September 2023

42004833R00219